IRON WHEELS AND BROKEN MEN

Iron Wheels

THE RAILROAD BARONS

and Broken Men

AND THE PLUNDER OF THE WEST

by Richard O'Connor

G. P. Putnam's Sons: New York

Copyright © 1973 by Richard O'Connor

SBN: 399-11120-4

Library of Congress Catalog Card Number: 72-97304

PRINTED IN THE UNITED STATES OF AMERICA

Contents

Introduction 7

1. The Template of Corruption 17
2. The Union Pacific Arrows West 37
3. Crazy Judah's Dream 67
4. A Frenzy of Expectation 93
5. Along the Sod House Frontier 115
6. Gold from the Russian Steppes 143
7. The Invasion of the Indian Territory 165
8. Railroad War in the Rockies 187
9. A Vision of What Might Have Been 211
10. California's Octopus (I) 235
11. California's Octopus (II) 259
12. A Brandishing of Pitchforks 281
13. "All Montana Needs Is Rain" 309

14. The Coming of Amtrak   337
     Notes on Sources   351
     Selected Bibliography   365
     Acknowledgments   367
     Index   369

Introduction

I N less than two generations Americans conquered the West, or possibly savaged it beyond redemption. The disillusionment that resulted from our Western experience is one of the traumas afflicting the American psyche. It began almost the day, more than a hundred years ago, they drove the famous golden spike to symbolize the linking of the first railroad to the Pacific coast. In heedless pursuit of everything the American spirit hungered for, we were enabled to overrun a virgin wilderness with the utmost dispatch, but we are just now receiving an accounting of its actual and accrued cost. For several generations, however, those of us born west of the Allegheny Mountains were conscious of some part of the misery entailed in that headlong and ruthless subjugation. We know, at least, that the term "pioneer" meant something a lot less glamorous than a man in a bear coat with a long rifle over his shoulder and keen blue eyes studying the horizon for an Indian to drop in his moccasined tracks.

This is neither an overview of the now-crumbling railroad industry nor an alarm-ringing exercise on behalf of the currently fashionable concern for a trampled environment. In the days of Amtrak, why flog a dead (iron) horse or hang a dead tycoon? Yet any consideration of how the railroads facilitated the "conquest" of the American West inevitably constitutes a cautionary bulletin from the past. The Western railroads in the last century, like oil and aviation and several other industries today, occupied a special position with the government. They were handed grants, subsidies, and legislation which favored them to the detriment of the public interest. In addition, they were permitted to make hundreds of millions through fraudulent contracts, stock and bond manipulations; to organize private armies and wipe out buffalo herds and Indian tribes; to brutalize immigrant labor; to bring out and then abandon thousands of settlers in a territory utterly and naturally hostile to such settlement. As always, it was done on grounds of national necessity. Humanity of course does not learn from such cautionaries. In recent years Soviet Russia attempted the same headlong, "conquering" methods in colonizing the steppes of Central Asia.

This work will focus on the panoramic unfolding of Western settlement as seen, not from the boardrooms of Broad Street which the old robber-baron studies assumed as a vantage point, but from the underview of the victimized. I am not interested in exposing the skulduggery and thimbleriggery of the wizards of nineteenth-century finance, except briefly in passing, but in the effects on millions of human beings of their methods of colonizing the West. The angle of vision is from west to east, from the standpoint of the losers in that monumental process which Jack London bespoke through one of his fictional characters, "We're the white folks and the children of white folks, that was too busy being good to be smart. We're the white folks that lost out."

Not that it is my intention to glamorize the losers. They high-tailed it west largely for their own selfish reasons rather than the attainment of any Jeffersonian ideals of extending the blessings of democracy. They were close to rabid on the subject of manifest destiny, of the God-given right of the Anglo-Saxon race and their allies (meaning northwestern Europeans) to subjugate and rule the lesser breeds. Or as Jack London's character put it, "We are pre-eminently a religious race, which is another way of saying we are a right-seeking race."

By the thousands and hundreds of thousands they had journeyed west in the wagon trains to seek the Promised Land west of

8

the hundredth meridian, only to find themselves stripped of illusion, trapped on sterile prairies or crammed into the slums of Oakland or Seattle. They had fought and struggled their way west to claim fertile lands, tap mineral riches, build up cattle herds, or engage in profitable commerce. Instead, they found the good claims staked, the opportunities monopolized (often by Eastern capitalists), the land often infertile and parched. Inevitably they felt that they had been swindled by those who had used them as pawns in a game played by men as cool and calculating as the grand masters of chess. And naturally they blamed sinister and amorphous forces generically labeled "Wall Street" or "Eastern capitalists" for luring them out into the wilderness with such garish but unfulfilled promises.

But there was more to it than swiveled-tongued promoters and scheming financiers. It took more than a slickly worded prospectus for a man to abandon his share of a family farm in Ohio, pack up his family and all his portable possessions, and head west in a canvas-covered wagon. Almost from the foundation of the Republic, a golden aura had surrounded the public's conception of the West. Gold was the thematic note sounded endlessly, with land and open space and freedom tinkling in counterpoint. This was at the bottom of the great illusion that sent men westering, the undying vision of the new Edens, the promise of a second chance. America has always been the land of the second chance. If not Ohio, then Montana; if not Montana, then Alaska . . . until the last geographic possibility has been exhausted.

In the romantic view, the West had always been a paradise awaiting development, with the frontier farmer an idealized figure, the plow a sacred symbol, the railroad a harbinger of progress. A nation of yeomen, independent and politically responsible, was envisioned. As one publicist wrote in 1815, the "inhabitants of this region are obviously destined to an unrivalled excellence in agriculture, manufactures and internal commerce; in literature and the arts; in public virtue, and in national strength."

Social reformers like Horace Greeley speculated that settling the West would operate as a "safety valve" and prevent social and political pressures from building up to the revolutionary stage in the Eastern cities. Regarding the "landless millions," he wrote:

"When employment fails or wages are inadequate, they may pack up and strike westward to enter upon the possession and culture of their own lands. . . . Strikes will be glaringly absurd when every citizen is offered the alternative to work for himself or others." Frederick Jackson Turner sounded the same safety valve theme forty years later when it was no longer valid—the frustrations of the luckless pioneers, who were in the vast majority, had simply built up more pressure—and insisted as late as the mid-1890's that the West was "a magic fountain of youth in which America continually bathed and was rejuvenated."

All this was intellectual speculation, the cozy theorizing of Easterners, but it attracted more attention than the warnings against the garden-of-the-world concept. Lieutenant (later General) Gouverneur K. Warren was sent west on an exploratory mission in the 1850's and came back warning that Nebraska was "near the western limit of the fertile portion of the prairie lands," that beyond the ninety-seventh meridian was land suitable in the long run only for grazing.

Against such warnings was posed the slogan of the pseudo-scientists that "Rain follows the plow"—just *how* not being explained. There were other serious misconceptions. Many thinkers believed the urban proletariat would head out west to seek a new life, but on the whole it preferred more familiar surroundings, squalid though they might be. The settlers were mostly farmers looking for wider and more fertile lands.

Nor would the actual pattern be that of numerous small holdings, supporting millions of hardworking families. As early as 1871 Henry George was deploring that landownership was being concentrated, with factory farming prefigured by the invention of the steam plow and other agricultural equipment. "We are not only putting large bodies of our new lands into the hands of the few, but we are doing our best to keep them there, and to cause the absorption of small farms into large estates." A few years later in an obscure work titled *Clarel* Herman Melville was viewing the conquest of the western spaces as the spark of "the class-war, the rich-and-poor-man-fray," with the result that the American West would become an "Anglo-Saxon China."

What made it all possible, for good and ill, was the extraordinarily rapid extension of the railroad system beyond the Mis-

10

sissippi. The settlers themselves could move out in wagon trains, as their vanguard did, but it took massive transport to supply them and to haul their products to the Eastern markets and the ports for Europe. And there was an equally important military aspect to the railroads, one which has always accounted for the government's tenderness toward that industry. The military value of the railroad became acutely apparent during the Civil War. The largely conscripted Union Army was often outfought by the Confederate forces, but the Confederacy could not prevail against the industrial might of the North, not least its network of railroads east of the Mississippi. Time after time, Union armies were reinforced swiftly and to the point of great superiority through rail transport. One man who observed the military adaptability of the railroads with the keenest interest was General Granville M. Dodge, who became chief engineer of the Union Pacific's construction. By happy coincidence, before assuming that role, he had also directed the operations which cleared the Indians away from the projected railroad's right-of-way. It was no coincidence at all, subsequently, that the Western railroads were heavily employed in subjugating the dissident and hard-fighting tribes of the Great Plains and elsewhere: cavalry leaping off trains and going into action before the redskins could escape and regroup.

America shot its iron arrows into the western spaces and transfixed an aboriginal race in captivity. Not the artificial boundaries of the reservations into which the Indians were eventually herded, with instructions from Washington bureaucrats to learn how to plow a straight furrow and stop bothering the white men who were stealing their ancestral lands, but the railroad lines served as the walls of their prison.

Not only did they physically imprison the Indians, but economically they also trapped the white settlers in a freight-rate structure designed to squeeze the last dollar of tribute out of those who were forced to use the railroads to ship their produce. A brand of grass-roots radicalism called Populism swept the plains states like a prairie fire, the one American credo that owed nothing to European political theory but that sprang out of the ravaged earth. Its echoes are still heard in the speculations of New York intellectuals and, conversely, in the speeches of Governor

George Wallace, whom they regard as a Neanderthal. Many contemporary politicians are proud to claim populist tendencies, perhaps because it springs directly from native soil and uniquely regional grievances, because it is a direct response to concrete problems.

In 1890 there was a convergence of Indian and white despair and resentment little noted by historians. That was the year when the Sioux, the paramount tribe of the northern plains, made their desperate attempt to break out of the white man's cage, with the so-called Battle of Wounded Knee as its tragic culmination. It was also the year that Populism began gathering so much support that it polled more than 1,000,000 votes in the national election two years hence. Summoning visions of a pitchfork-waving army descending on Washington and Wall Street, it was an indication that the second generation of white settlers was little more satisfied with their lot than the Indians they forcibly displaced.

There were few real winners in the "winning of the West," about as many proportionately as in a lottery or sweepstakes. The art of exploitation was well developed by the time the stampede westward began. It took capital, more than luck, brawn, or brains, to share in the rewards. The Rockefellers and their associates, for instance, were adding to their enormous holdings by working coal mines in Colorado, buying into Montana copper, and taking over Kansas oilfields, without ever journeying west of the Mississippi. It was a process of colonization, complete with frockcoated viceroys, mercenary armies, and restless natives. In order to make the West safe for investment, you had to plant colonies of yeomanry, capable of supporting themselves on the land and picking up a rifle when necessary, who could be persuaded that they were acting as the vanguard of civilization, the torchbearers of progress, and, above all, the sharers in the promised abundance. It would take the passing of a generation before they realized that they had been bilked, that they were serving the purposes of cleverer men, and by then it was too late for anything but futile protest.

We never learned. Alaska would be plundered as thoroughly as Montana. We were so entranced by the illusion of the West as an endless bonanza, so hesitant to interfere with what appeared to be a natural process of individual enterprise, so enchanted with the idea that any determined man could share in all the good things if he worked hard enough that no real effort was made to control the exploitation and share out its rewards more evenly.

There were alternatives to the savage irresponsibility with which we fell upon "the new Eden." We could have preserved not only the land but the aboriginal culture; we could have heeded warnings that the possibilities of even a guaranteed paradise are finite. As early as 1877 the director of the United States Geological Survey went out to Montana to investigate how much exploitation the high plains could stand. What he saw and envisioned for the future impelled him to undertake a wider study. John Wesley Powell, a year after the traumatic wound of the Little Bighorn was inflicted upon American self-esteem, then drew up a suggested constitution to govern the new society he hoped would arise in the West, one that would take into account both needs and the inevitable limits to satisfying those needs. It would be a cooperative society in which individuals, otherwise free to pursue their own ambitions, acknowledged their responsibility toward each other in a harsh and inhospitable environment. The northern plains, as Powell and his associates determined, could take only limited development; therefore, settlement must be strictly controlled. They also urged the preservation of what was left of the Indian way of life and envisioned a society in which the Indians would have their rightful place but with as many of the hardships and hazards of a primitive life eliminated as was practicable. The Indians would be allowed to evolve gradually and as naturally as possible and become an independent part of the larger Western society.

Despite his prestige, despite or because of the sensibility and humanity of his proposals, Powell's report was allowed to molder away in the archives of the Library of Congress, eventually to become merely a reminder of what might have been, of the measureless suffering that might have been spared. A choice was made: immense profitability for the few instead of decent habitation for the many. It could satisfy only the bitterest misanthrope that one of those profiteers, Jay Gould, with $100,000,000 to his name, died of tuberculosis, known to the nineteenth century as the "poor man's disease."

The Western "sea of grass," the seemingly endless high plains

13

were overrun. The arid steppe was overpopulated. The fragility of the prairies' ecology was ignored—who knew or cared that the Sahara had once been fertile? Once the virgin sod was broken, gale-force winds whipped up dust storms and whirled whole farms into the big blue noncommittal sky.

Settlers by the thousands, displacing Indians by the thousands, were needed to provide a market for the railroads. The corporate balance sheets would not wait upon humane process or orderly planning or even history. Corporate expense had to be justified by immediate profits. So the railroads promoted a hasty and heedless settlement on the lands along their rights-of-way, simultaneously profiting by the sale of lands given them by an overly generous government and by creating a captive market for their enterprises.

Their endeavors were governed entirely by the profit motive but were cloaked in the bright and fast-dyed colors of legend. The construction and operation of the Western railroads was part of the great American myth, as essential a chapter in the saga of the West as gunfighters and pony express riders. One railroad alone, the Union Pacific, has been endlessly glorified in print and on film. For all time, no doubt, that dwindling part of the American imagination which dwells upon the past will retain images of Indians being confronted by the iron horse, of coolie gangs and brawling Irishmen laboring over mountain grades, of wood-burning locomotives pierced with arrows and heroic engineers yanking down on the Johnson bar to outdistance bands of pursuing Indians . . . and always of that golden spike being driven at the meeting of the rails in Utah. This is an underside of that myth which needs to be examined.

RICHARD O'CONNOR

Iron Wheels and Broken Men

1.

The Template of Corruption

Society, as created, was for the purpose of one man
getting what the other fellow has, if he can, and
keep out of the penitentiary.
—MILTON H. SMITH, president of
the Louisville & Nashville

I N the 1960's American railroads started collapsing, with
seeming suddenness, like buildings with foundations
hollowed out by termites. Actually the process had begun a
hundred years and more before. Almost from the years before the
Civil War when the first Western railroads were organized, they
were so thoroughly and recklessly looted that financially they
have been an uncertain investment ever since. The construction
of the Western railroads was presented to the public as a
glamorous saga of venture capital—even Abraham Lincoln was
taken in by their propaganda and served their purposes—and
under cover of all that hectic romanticizing the government was
persuaded to hand over subsidies and grants of public land totaling hundreds of millions of acres to encourage the enterprise.
Thus heartened, the railroad pioneers, mostly from comfortable
offices far removed from the hardships of their corporate endeavors, speedily enriched themselves at the public expense. One
noble adventurer in this field, according to his admiring
biographer, with "the exercise of his rare judgment and untiring
energy" was connected "with not less than twenty-five different
lines." His reward as a public benefactor was a fortune estimated
at between $60,000,000 and $90,000,000.

17

Never were the opportunities for a talented and venturesome entrepreneur so quickly and richly rewarded, provided that he was not burdened by a sensitive conscience and that he understood the several complexities of railroad promotion. The key word was "promotion," not operation, which was profitless drudgery. The main idea was to grab all you could and make off with the proceeds before investigating committees, grand juries, and bilked electorates discovered what you had been doing under the guise of forwarding white civilization through the wilderness.

First you selected a grandiose title for your operations, the Oshkosh & Pacific, for instance, even though you had barely enough capital to buy stationery and print a bond issue. Then from various state legislatures you received a charter for construction of your lines; a map showing projected construction was usually enough in those optimistic days. In return for passing out part of the bond issue to legislators and other influential citizens, you obtained land grants of alternating sections (640 acres) along your proposed right-of-way. You were rich before the first yard of ballast was tamped down. A separate land company would be established, with insiders participating. You began construction only after selling off part of the land grant and after obtaining cash subsidies from the grateful state legislatures and peddling mortgage bonds in Europe, where investors were eager to believe prospectuses promising a bonanza in Western railroads and to haul out their gold coins hoarded in mattresses against just such a fortuitous possibility. The construction, too, would be undertaken by a separate company, also composed of insiders, and the rails for the Oshkosh & Pacific would be laid at an enormously inflated cost to holders of the railroad's securities. Many railroads were built without their promoters putting in a single dollar of their own money.

With the line nearing completion, you advertised in European newspapers and in Western Europe for people to come out and colonize your right-of-way. They would come out on your railway and buy your land and provide eventually the business your successors needed to keep operating. If they had little cash left to start farming, if they were unable to cope with the harsh climate, endemic diseases, Indian raids, locust swarms, and other indigenous hazards, if they starved or froze to death during their first winter out on the snow-drifted prairies, that was none of your concern. If you were cagey enough to have conceived the scheme in the first place, you were nimble enough to have sold your interests in the Oshkosh & Pacific by then and gone on to more profitable enterprises in another state.

The template for railroad promotion was fabricated in the 1850's by two Eastern gentlemen little remembered now except by financial historians, who can only marvel at their ingenuity while deploring their methods.

One was John I. Blair of New Jersey, whose name in later years was haloed by philanthropic efforts, the other was Russell Sage, whose widow funneled the ill-gotten proceeds of his career into the Sage Foundation and created a postmortem aura of charity and humanity around a name more than adequately cursed when its bearer was alive. Both came of the generation following the first John Jacob Astor and Commodore Vanderbilt, who set the style and created the methods of American capitalism. And both, almost simultaneously, Blair in Iowa and Sage in Wisconsin and Minnesota, adapted that style and demonstrated a mastery of those methods in promoting the first Western railroads. Both, too, not so coincidentally, were involved in the Union Pacific's carnival of greed and corruption—the very paradigm of railroad promotion. Experimenting with several railroads with names as obscure now as those of the lives they ruined, Blair and Sage showed the way for those who joined in the exploitation of the West.

Bribery was only one of their tools in prying open the public and private vaults which financed their activities. Years after their activities had become malodorous, even though they were lesser figures among the robber barons of the Gilded Age, Governor William Larrabee of Iowa concluded that they had made use of more subtle methods than simple payment of cash to suborn their accomplices. They determined the "weakness and wants of every man whose services they were likely to need," Larrabee noted:

> Men with political ambition are encouraged to aspire to preferment, and are assured of corporate support to bring it about. Briefless lawyers are promised corporate business or salaried at-

torneyships. Those in financial straits are accommodated with loans. Vain men are flattered and given newspaper notoriety. Others are given passes for their families and their friends. Shippers are given advantage in rates over their competitors. The idea is that every legislator shall receive for his vote and influence some compensation which combines the maximum of desirability to him with the minimum of violence to his self-respect.

The railroads also managed to keep the legislators on their side through diligent lobbying:

> In extreme cases influential constituents of doubtful members are sent for at the last moment to labor with their representatives and to assure them that the sentiment of their districts is in favor of the measure advocated by the railroads. Telegrams pour in upon the unsuspecting members. Petitions in favor of the proposed measure are also hastily circulated among the more unsophisticated constituents of members sensitive to public opinion and are then represented to them as an unmistakable indication of the popular will. Another powerful reinforcement of the railroad lobby is not infrequently a subsidized press and its correspondents.

Larrabee's conclusions, arrived at some forty years after Blair and Sage operated with such audacity on his territory, were borne out by the thousands of pages of testimony taken before investigating committees long after the swag was divided and the damage done. Not so visible on the public record was the human suffering, among Indians as well as white settlers, caused by the railroads in their headlong methods of populating the wilderness they intended to exploit. There was no one to investigate or care much about the thirty settlers massacred at Spirit Lake, Iowa, or the hundreds more killed by enraged Indians in the "Sioux War of 1862." Each of the victims—men, women, and children—had been lured westward by the promises of the railroad promoters. Their lives were sacrificed to the haste and greed with which those entrepreneurs populated the prairies and ignored the justifiable resentment of the bronze men who were being so ruthlessly shoved aside. Worse yet, the methods of Blair and Sage were to be adopted and expanded upon when vaster territories were opened to the west, sufferings on a larger scale resulted, and massacres far bloodier took place.

Sage was an upstate New Yorker who early in a career which might, in part, have served to inspire Horatio Alger, grasped the loving relationship between politics and finance. As a boy he clerked in his brother's grocery store, then branched out on his own as a small trader and accumulated the seed money for a wholesale grocery business he established when he was only twenty-three years old. In the next dozen years he shouldered his way to a position of some prominence in Troy and won a seat on the City Council. From that vantage point he watched with sly interest the construction of the Troy & Schenectady Railroad with $750,000 in public funds. As a council member and a member of the railroad's board of directors, he and his fellow insiders mismanaged the railroad's affairs to the point where it appeared ready to sink into bankruptcy. All the time he was aware of the fact that the New York Central was eager to acquire the Troy & Schenectady as well as other small upstate lines. By then Sage had formed a company with himself as president to take the municipal railroad off the city's hands, a gesture which the ill-informed citizenry viewed as a demonstration of his civic devotion.

With a grand air of performing his duty, Sage and his company acquired the Troy & Schenectady for a down payment of $50,000, with another $150,000 to be paid the city in fourteen years. He and his fellow boodlers then sold the railroad to Vanderbilt's New York Central for $900,000. Not only that, but he and his friends shared in an $8,000,000 bond issue distributed as a bonus to the owners of various short-haul lines the New York Central was linking together. His share in the venture came to well over $1,000,000. And the Troy electorate was so grateful to him for bilking them that in the early 1850's they twice elected him to Congress.

By then the possibilities of western railroading had already attracted Sage's attention. His first foray in that direction came in the summer of 1851, when he journeyed out to Milwaukee at the request of Wisconsin businessmen who were trying to raise construction funds for the Milwaukee & Mississippi Railroad. A glimpse of the black earth of the Wisconsin farmlands and the

21

industrious German immigrants they had attracted convinced Sage that this could prove to be a magnificent opportunity for a railroad promoter. Sage's vision proved to be a strikingly accurate one: A railroad through those rich farmlands could and would make millions. The eventual result of his ponderings was the Chicago, Milwaukee & St. Paul, a carrier which, according to one railroad historian, absorbed more component lines than any other American road (the Milwaukee & Mississippi, the Milwaukee & Watertown, the Racine, Janesville & Mississippi, the Milwaukee & Northern, the Ontonagon & Brule River, the Chicago & Pacific, and about fifteen other Midwestern companies).

For the moment, however, Sage's schemes were balked. Instead of raising money for the Milwaukee & Mississippi, he made a takeover bid and failed. Undeterred, he settled back and waited for a few years until the backers of the Milwaukee & Mississippi threw in their hand for lack of funds. He then organized the La Crosse & Milwaukee and obtained a charter to build a railroad straight across the state from Lake Michigan to the Mississippi. In addition, he acquired at bargain prices the Milwaukee & Fond du Lac and the Milwaukee & Green Bay, whose trackage existed only on paper, as did the La Crosse & Milwaukee's. So far Sage's railroad system was only a spider web of lines drawn on a state map. As an influential member of Congress, however, Sage pushed through enactment of a measure which granted Wisconsin 2,388,000 acres of public land to be distributed to railroad builders.

With various distinguished collaborators in the New York financial district, Sage was now ready to begin operating in bold style. The offices of the La Crosse & Milwaukee and of its bewildering array of successor companies were not in Milwaukee but at 23 William Street, New York City. This served as headquarters not only for Sage but several other silk-hatted gentlemen who shared his vision of railroads stretching through the upper Middle Western farmlands and all the way to the Pacific coast. Part of a cast of characters which popped up time after time in various reprehensible scenes of railroad history, they included John A. Dix, a future Civil War general and president of the Union Pacific, and Samuel J. Tilden, an enormously resourceful lawyer

22

who became the Democratic Presidential candidate in 1876. Other Wall Street figures, assured that Sage's tenacity and craftiness would make it a success, joined the venture.

In 1856 Sage opened the throttle on his venture by issuing $1,000,000 in what were later termed "corruption bonds" by a select committee of the Wisconsin legislature. The La Crosse & Milwaukee bonds were shared out to thirteen state senators, seventy assemblymen, a number of state officers, plus $246,000 worth to newspaper editors and other influential citizens who could have blown the whistle. Governor Coles Bashford was awarded $50,000 in bonds for his benign influence. To demonstrate their gratitude for the share-out of corporate sweeteners, the legislators loyally pushed through land grants, the value of which was later estimated to be $17,000,000. Thus Sage had distributed a million in fancily engraved paper in return for land worth seventeen times that much. He then proceeded to organize a construction company which would build the railroad at a vastly inflated cost to be borne by the ordinary stockholders while Sage and his clique shared in the separate company's equally inflated profits.

Two years after the land grants were awarded, the ferment of civic wrath blew the lid off the "corruption bonds"; a legislative investigating committee rooted out the scandal and damaged a lot of hitherto impeccable reputations. Former Governor Bashford hastily decamped for Arizona after selling his $50,000 worth of bonds at the panic price of $15,000.

At the same time, with the title La Crosse & Milwaukee so stained by scandal, Sage and his colleagues in William Street adroitly organized the Minnesota & Milwaukee Railroad and placed their assets in the new company. A short time later the Milwaukee & Minnesota was transformed into the Milwaukee & St. Paul, with ordinary stockholders duped and trimmed at each stage of the corporate apotheosis. In later years Sage connected the line from Milwaukee to La Crosse with another from Chicago to Milwaukee and still another from La Crosse to St. Paul. He clung to this system until selling his interests in 1880, all the while extorting money from Wisconsin and Minnesota farmers through the sort of freight rates to be expected of a ruthless monopoly. He

23

further profited by building spur lines and selling them at grossly inflated prices to the Chicago, Milwaukee & St. Paul.

Despite the distressing aspects of his operations in Wisconsin, Sage jumped the state line into Minnesota with even greater facility and more considerable success. He and his New York associates organized the Minnesota & Pacific and promised to "open up the primitive Northwest." The Chicago, Milwaukee & St. Paul was only the "first division," as they proclaimed, in a road which would extend to the Pacific coast. Naturally, in return, they expected certain favors of the state of Minnesota. Among them was a grant of 14,000,000 acres of prime timber- and farmland, bestowed them on the supposition that they would build a line from St. Paul to Winona. They also received subsidies and tax exemptions. A bewildering sequence of events ensued. With all those assets, the Minnesota & Pacific was suddenly plunged into bankruptcy. Sage and company organized a new company, the St. Paul & Pacific, into which the assets of the Minnesota & Pacific had been diverted, to the dismay of the ordinary stockholders of the latter. The maneuvering by which Sage and his fellow insiders profited so exorbitantly was plotted by Attorney Samuel J. Tilden, who in 1876 would be presented to American voters as the "great reformer" and the "evangel of pure and uncorrupted Democracy," but it was Sage who manipulated the levers. And it was Sage who "severed" 30,000 acres of the richest farmland in Stearns County from the grant to the Minnesota & Pacific and placed them among his personal holdings. It wasn't until 1905, almost a half century later, that the state retrieved those 30,000 acres, and then only after Sage had forced the farmers settled on them to pay him a "fair market price" or get off the land.

Whenever creditors or cheated stockholders tried to recover their losses, Sage and his clique knew they could rely on a sympathetic friend in court. Stockholders' and creditors' suits came up regularly before Judge John F. Dillon in the U.S. circuit court in St. Paul. Judge Dillon was a far-seeing man who realized that empire building required a certain latitude for the builders, and he consistently ruled in their favor. His sympathy was particularly valuable when Sage and his friends, having completed part of the new trackage they had promised, mortgaged their venture for $13,380,000 to a number of banking houses in Holland. The mortgage money quickly evaporated after being funneled through the railroad conglomerate headquartered in William Street. Involved suits were brought on behalf of the Dutch investors, but they came up before Judge Dillon, who maintained his protective attitude toward Sage and his colleagues. Not too surprisingly, given the prevailing moral climate, Judge Dillon retired from the federal bench to become counsel for Sage and Jay Gould when they assumed control of the Union Pacific.

Perhaps one of the most disastrous effects of Sage's empire building, aside from the financial ruin of those unwary enough to invest in his companies, was the hope raised, only to be betrayed, in the thousands of people who began filling up the open spaces for which the railroads acted as a suction pump. A decade before the passage of the Homestead Act thousands of people uprooted themselves and came to settle on the land grants of Minnesota and Wisconsin. Most came to the forests believing every word of the expert publicity concocted by the railroads, knowing little of the problems of clearing lands thickly wooded for centuries, understanding even less the problems of reaching an accommodation with the Indians, and totally ignorant of the lengthy process of building a civilization from the ground up.

Among these hopeful innocents was a young Irish-American from Philadelphia named Ignatius Donnelly, whose career as a radical prophet and literary eccentric was ignited by the betrayals he experienced and the injustices he encountered as one of the railroads' early victims. In time he became one of the most vigorous and effective opponents of the railroads and Eastern financiers whose iron arrows had impaled so many of his fellow pioneers.

In 1856, dazzled by the promotional efforts of the Minnesota railroad builders, Donnelly bought 800 acres of uncleared land on the west bank of the Mississippi just below the territorial capital of St. Paul, intending not merely to farm his acreage but to establish a flourishing city there—and not merely a city but a cultural capital of the Northwest. Undoubtedly he was one of those wildly imaginative and furiously energetic men the nineteenth century produced in much greater quantity than our own.

25

On founding Nininger City, which he named for a boyhood friend, he decided that it would be a model community where art and the intellect would flourish beside industry and agriculture. If Russell Sage's vision tended to encompass a West webbed by rail trackage, Donnelly, along with several other, more pragmatic idealists, saw the trans-Mississippi provinces as a chance for new beginnings for the nation: the railroads, so soon to be unmasked as capitalism gone rogue wild, might even propel those utopian schemes toward fruition.

Donnelly had hardly staked out his town lots before he established a monthly journal, *The Emigrant Aid Journal*, which broadcast his message and cast its net for future citizens of Nininger City. The periodical's logotype was a splendid affair which depicted Nininger City as the capital of the Northwest, if not, possibly, the universe. It took up about half the front page and showed steamboats racing upriver to Donnelly's projected cosmopolis, trains steaming across the prairies in the same direction, covered-wagon trains also converging on Nininger City. Studying the logotype took almost as long as to read the journal's contents, for it also showed fruits and vegetables growing in bumper quantity, men plowing, others engaged in scholarly debate, and bore the quotation "Dost thou know how to play the fiddle? No, replied Themistocles, but I understand the art of raising a little village into a great city."

An Athenian idealism, in fact, governed Donnelly as a city builder. He sold his town lots for $6 apiece, at cost, and stipulated there could be no turnover in their ownership to encourage speculation. He wanted the sort of citizenry which would devote itself to work and, equally, to intellectual pursuits. Within a year his dream of a New Athens in the Minnesota forests began to take on substance. *The Emigrant Aid Journal* was being circulated by the thousands in the East and was placed in the reading rooms of transatlantic steamers to catch prospective settlers on the wing.

Nininger City was bustling with construction activity, and was becoming a boom town. The Atheneum Company, a literary group, had been organized under Donnelly's leadership. An inn called the Handyside House had been constructed; its menu offered nine kinds of meat and fowl, with charlotte russe and ice cream for dessert, and its wine list included champagne and other imported vintages. Donnelly not only saw to the citizenry's physical nourishment but also instructed his followers on the evils of slavery, the care of farm equipment, the virtues of raising lavender for the sachet market, and the villainies of the Eastern bankers.

By early 1857 the population had grown to about 1,000 and was still growing when a financial panic occurred, banks closed, and factories shut down. Donnelly may have thought that he had isolated Nininger City from the petty alarms and trivial crises of the outside world, but the panic of '57 showed him his error. The final blow to his hopes fell early in the spring when Sage's railroad announced that it would not pass through Nininger City but chose the nearby town of Hastings instead. On receiving that news, regardless of the Athenian ideals with which it had been inculcated, the whole population packed up and moved elsewhere. By the end of the year the town was deserted and grass was waist-high in the main street. Only Ignatius Donnelly and his wife stayed on, in the big frame house they had built. They continued to live in the ghost town, in fact, for another half century.

A lesser man might have been crushed, but Donnelly was as resilient as a sideshow's India rubber man. The collapse of Nininger City had made him a heated foe of the railroads and banks, which, he believed, were exerting a malign influence on the national destiny. It was up to him to find a way to save the country. Thus began a career in hell raising, in inflaming demands for social and economic reform, that was to provide sleepless nights for many of those whom Donnelly designated as the enemies of American democracy. If only Sage had run his tracks through Nininger City, Donnelly might have contented himself with overseeing the development of his community of yeomen and scholars, and many capitalists would have slept better in the future. Instead, his bitterness over the way Nininger City had been dumped into the discard propelled him onto a wider stage. Politics was the first arena into which he flung himself; he ran for lieutenant governor and was elected, then was sent to Congress and made an impressive record. But the Republican bosses found that Donnelly was inclined to be a maverick, and eventually they arranged his comeuppance.

27

Back in ghostly Nininger City with a second career in ruins the spirited Donnelly then took up the pen and began the third stage of his life as a prophet and polemicist. The lost continent of Atlantis had always fascinated him—wasn't it one of his Athenians who passed down the word of its rumored existence? —and he began work on a book titled *Atlantis: The Antediluvian World*. He made such a persuasive case for his theories that it sold a million copies and is still in print. In *The Great Cryptogram* he aroused an uproar with his claim that Francis Bacon was the real author of the works attributed to William Shakespeare. The success of those ventures financed a weekly paper called *The Anti-Monopolist* in which Donnelly summoned before his assizes and promptly convicted a long list of "enemies of the people," including land speculators, railroad magnates, bankers, and advocates of high tariffs and hard money. At the same time he welcomed the foundation of the Grange, with a million and a half rural members organized to defend themselves from the railroads and banks.

He was an international figure, known as the Sage of Nininger, which at least put his ghost town on the world's intellectual map, when the inspiration struck him to write one of those cautionary novels (Jack London's *The Iron Heel* was one, George Orwell's *1984* another) which arouse a more than merely literary apprehension in the world. As Donnelly saw it, the United States would become a savage dictatorship if present trends continued. In *Caesar's Column*, he pictured a nation ruled by a plutocracy with the farmers turned into serfs and the factory workers into a sullen urban proletariat. The plutocrats, governing through a police force called the Demons, have managed to crush any attempts at opposition by the employment of such weapons as radio, television, and fleets of dirigibles dropping poison-gas bombs, all of which Donnelly invented in his imagination decades before the prototypes reached the drawing board. The masses revolt and are slaughtered, and the United States collapses in total destruction. A ray of hope was allowed to penetrate this morbid view of the American future. A few decent and intelligent Americans escape by dirigible to Africa, where they found a new nation designed along the lines Donnelly advocated, with an equal distribution of land and no railroads or banks to befoul what he envisioned as a sort of Christian Socialist democracy.

Caesar's Column was published in the early 1890's, just when many people were beginning to suspect that there were more unsolved problems around than the Founding Fathers had provided against. Its impact was considerable; Donnelly's despair for the American future was echoed, though less eloquently, in millions of minds. It heightened fears that the growth of industrialism, paralleling the decline in Western agriculture as it staggered under the burden of mortgages and exorbitant freight rates, would combine with the concentration of economic power to create just such a plutocracy as Donnelly's imagination conceived, followed by the apocalypse he projected a century hence. If anyone deprecated Donnelly's warnings, it was to doubt that America could carry on for another hundred years.

The novel undoubtedly gave strong impulse to the rises of Populism and the foundation of the National People's Party in which, as will be seen, Donnelly became a leading figure. He felt quite at home with Populism's grab bag of splinter parties: the Greenbackers, the Single Taxers, the Knights of Labor, the Grangers, the Socialists, and even a few stray Prohibitionists. With Populism, Donnelly finally found the platform from which to deliver his jeremiads against the railroads, which had not only ruined his dream of a utopian Nininger City but were also guilty of wholesale thefts from the public domain. The public lands appropriated by the railroads through bribery and corruption, he endlessly preached, must be recovered by direct political action; otherwise "we will be making a gun that will do everything but shoot."

Obviously Russell Sage and his colleagues, in their high-handed fashion, had raised up a formidable enemy in Donnelly. Some of this enmity was inevitable, because a railroad could not serve every community that yearned for its services without zigzagging all over the map. It did not help the cause of the railroads that their headquarters were often in New York and that their ownership lived and plotted in the Eastern cities.

The old bugaboo of absentee landlordism seemed to many who settled the Western prairies to have followed them from their

European origins: princelings in Monte Carlo gambling away the money squeezed from their tenants. "The roads," Dr. Frank H. Dixon, the Iowa railroad historian, wrote, "had it in their power to make and unmake cities, to destroy the businesses of individuals, or to force their removal to favored points. The people were quickly up in arms against this policy. The flame of opposition was fanned by the bitter feelings aroused through absentee ownership, so prevalent in the Western states at this time. A well-settled conviction possessed the people that the owners of capital, directing their operations in absentia and through intermediaries, limited their interest in Western affairs to the amount of dividends which they could squeeze from the shippers."

Nowhere was this more apparent than in Iowa, where John I. Blair was operating about the same time Sage and his friends were monopolizing transportation in Wisconsin and Minnesota. Using the same methods of suborning state and national legislatures, Blair and his fellow entrepreneurs obtained $50,000,000 in subsidies and land grants totaling almost 5,000,000 acres of the rich rolling farmlands of Iowa. His chosen instrument was the Sioux City & Pacific, a line of much more modest trackage than the title indicated. It was no mere coincidence that many members of Congress who voted for Blair's subsidies and land grants were also directors and stockholders of the Sioux City & Pacific. Few of their fellow citizens believed them when they later claimed to have bought the stock.

Certainly the Sioux City was lavishly and lovingly treated by the legislators. It received not only a land grant of 100 sections but $16,000 in government bonds for every mile of track it laid. The track laying was done by a separate construction company at greatly inflated prices, with Blair and his sons and friends as chief participants. In extending the railroads through the Iowa flatlands practically no grading was necessary, and expert testimony before the Pacific Railroad Commission indicated the cost of building the railroad should have totaled no more than $2,600,000. Yet Blair's construction company bled the railroad for more than $5,000,000, or an excess profit of almost 100 percent.

Blair was understandably pleased by the balance sheets on those transactions and proceeded to build the Dubuque & Sioux

City line under the same cozy arrangements. Like so many other Western railroads, Blair's were financially crippled by the artificially high construction costs imposed on them. They were so burdened by mortgage bonds and other forms of indebtedness that they were virtually insolvent by the time the first train highballed it over their rails. Yet there was more money to be squeezed out of the venture, and Blair further enriched himself by selling his Iowa lines to the Chicago & Northwestern.

It wasn't until years later that the public learned just how badly it had been swindled in its feverish desire for rail service or understood just how much of the public domain had been turned over to the railroad builders in exchange for promises the latter never fulfilled. Long after his state's railroads had been built under the charter granted by an act of Congress in 1856, Governor J. G. Newbold of Iowa mourned:

> The first land grants made by Congress were turned over to the companies absolutely, although the act of Congress contemplated the sale of the lands by the State as earned, and the devotion of the proceeds to the construction of the railroads; the companies were permitted to select the lands regardless of their line of road; and they were allowed, virtually, their own time to complete the work, notwithstanding that one main object of the grants was to secure this completion at an early day. Townships, towns and cities have been permitted to tax property within their limits to help build the roads, and the revenue thus derived was turned over absolutely to the companies constructing them, while much of the property of these companies practically escapes municipal taxation.

But the most disastrous effect of uncontrolled and often unnecessary expansion of the Western railroads was seldom considered, except when news came from outlying settlements that Indians, outraged by the way their tribal preserves were being compressed by the incursion of settlers, were on the rampage. Had the railroads not advertised far and wide for warm bodies to colonize their rights-of-way, had they made the smallest effort to arrive at an accommodation with the Indians before flooding their hunting lands with pale-faced farmers, trouble might have been avoided. The Indian, however, was merely a Stone Age barbarian who had unaccountably survived in the modern world,

31

and it was up to the Indian Bureau to keep him quiet with rations or the U.S. Army to quell him if handouts failed.

Uncontrolled migration in both Iowa and Minnesota resulted in the death of hundreds of settlers and more hundreds of Indians, thanks to the business policies of Russell Sage and John I. Blair and their associates. The Indians were never mentioned, of course, in their railroads' advertising and promotional copy. Many of the settlers, coming from Europe, had only the faintest idea of how much their incursion might affront the aboriginal inhabitants. Nor had they any conception of the fierce pride of the Yankton and Santee branches of the Sioux, among whom they were settling, or their reputation as warriors.

Indian displeasure was not long in displaying itself. The first outbreak occurred in Iowa in 1857, just a year after the land-grant legislation was passed by Congress. Thirty settlers at Spirit Lake were massacred. The Sioux war party then moved across the Minnesota line to the town of Jackson and killed two storekeepers and ambushed a group of white men rushing to their assistance. The whites immediately organized for retaliation, and as often occurred, it was misdirected. A party of settlers, mostly armed with scythes lashed to long poles, descended on a Sioux village innocent of any participation in the Spirit Lake massacre and chased the survivors of their attack across the prairie.

That was a warning of Indian restiveness over the thousands of settlers being brought to their country by the railroads. It went unheeded. Instead, the construction of Sage's railroads in Minnesota and their spur lines greatly speeded the white colonization. All through the decade of the fifties the settlers flooded in, particularly to the fertile Minnesota Valley. There had been settlements of Welsh and Germans in the valley previous to that, but not in sufficient number to alarm the Santee Sioux. Then came 18,000 Germans and 12,000 Scandinavians to increase the population of the valley tenfold during the decade. They built not merely villages but a sizable town called New Ulm, which its planners predicted would become a city of 100,000.

Upriver the Sioux watched anxiously as they saw their hunting ranges turned into farmland. So far they had been kept under control by government rations, to replace the game formerly available, and by the Regular Army unit garrisoning Fort Ridgley. Military control slackened with the coming of the Civil War and the draining of Army posts all along the frontier.

An eloquent, intelligent, and ambitious young chief named Little Crow meanwhile had assumed the leadership of the Sioux tribes in Minnesota. He attended an Episcopal church every Sunday, having been converted to Christianity in childhood (his son became a YMCA leader, his grandson a Protestant minister). The whites were confident that Little Crow, as a fellow Christian, would keep his people in line. They apparently were unaware of the fact that Little Crow had attained supremacy among his people by promising that he would drive the whites out of the Minnesota Valley. Yet Henry Thoreau, who traveled out to Minnesota for his health in 1861 and visited the Sioux reservation at Redwood, observed in a letter to Horace Mann, Jr., that the Indians were growing increasingly restive and "probably have reason to be so."

Little Crow and his followers saw their opportunity in the summer of 1862 when news came of the Union Army's defeat at Second Bull Run. Five thousand Minnesotans had marched off to join the Union forces; there was only a cadre of regular soldiers at Fort Ridgley and an ill-trained militia to back them up.

The Sioux launched a coordinated and well-planned attack on August 18, 1862, throughout the valley—the bloodiest day for whites in the history of the frontier.

By the score, by the hundreds, white settlers were slaughtered without warning, without a chance of defending themselves. Their names may be recovered now only in crumbling newspaper clippings and memoirs long out of print, but they fell as victims of the greedy and reckless colonization policies of Russell Sage, who, like Chief Little Crow, went to church every Sunday and reckoned himself a sturdy Christian.

The blood sacrifice for the railroad builders' disregard of how the Indians might resent wholesale incursions of their territory was, by all contemporary accounts, a ghastly affair. A dozen government employees were killed at the Indian Agency compound at Redwood. Almost simultaneously the Sioux attacked a German settlement at Sacred Heart Creek, near New Ulm, and fourteen-year-old Mary Schwandt watched while her mother and

33

father, her two brothers, her pregnant sister, and her brother-in-law were tomahawked to death. Mary herself was taken captive but later rescued. Down the road another family was slaughtered, and their bodies were thrown on a funeral pyre of broken furniture. Closer to New Ulm, family after family was wiped out. Almost every farm and settlement in the valley were attacked that hot summer's day as hundreds of Little Crow's warriors struck repeatedly and without mercy in what they saw as a last chance to recover their lands. That night thirteen families of settlers, crowded into eleven wagons and whipping up their horses in a dash for safety in New Ulm, were halted by a Sioux war party, which opened fire and killed most of them.

Two days later Little Crow concentrated his scattered bands for an all-or-nothing attack on Fort Ridgley, which he hoped to capture for its stock of muskets and ammunition. The tiny garrison managed to hold out, and Little Crow then turned his attention to New Ulm, which, with its neat rows of brick houses, its churches and stores and breweries, represented all that was hideous about white civilization. Hundreds of Sioux warriors massed on the bluffs overlooking the Minnesota River and the town and on August 23 launched themselves against the barricades behind which most of the male population of New Ulm was waiting with every weapon they could lay hands on. Once again Little Crow was repulsed, but only after twenty-six of the townsmen were killed and all but ten of the town's houses were destroyed.

With the Eastern newspapers reporting that almost 500 settlers in the Minnesota Valley had been killed, a militia force of 1,400 men was organized to deal with Little Crow. It suffered a disastrous ambush but finally managed to outmaneuver the Sioux. Surrounded by superior forces, Little Crow was finally persuaded to surrender and allow the militia to recover 269 white captives taken during his lightning assaults on the settlements in the valley. Retribution was stern: Thirty-eight of the Sioux leaders were hanged on a huge scaffold, the largest execution in American history. Little Crow himself, having opted against surrender, was finally tracked down and shot to death in a farmer's berry patch.

The fact that it had caused the death of hundreds of people, white and Indian, was no reason for the builders of a rail-borne empire in the West to discard their policies. As the railroads extended westward after the Civil War, as the thousands of settlers swelled to hundreds of thousands seeking the new lands promised them, the railroads enlarged upon their program of heedless expansion and bore without flinching the tragedies and suffering and hardships of the hordes they transported to a hostile wilderness.

2.

The Union Pacific
Arrows West

When the greatest railroad in the world, binding
together the continent and uniting two great seas
which wash our shores, was finished, I have seen
our national triumph and exaltation turned to
bitterness and shame. . . .
—SENATOR GEORGE HOAR of Massachusetts

I T took an act of civil courage to oppose the building of the
Western railroads. The concept of a train steaming over
plains and mountains from the Mississippi to the Pacific coast
had fevered the national mind, had captured the popular
imagination to the extent that any opponent of a transcontinental railroad appeared in the light of an enemy of progress.
President Lincoln was a fervent exponent of rail construction
westward. General William T. Sherman proclaimed that "it
would be a work of giants" to build a railroad to the Pacific coast,
and "Uncle Sam is the only giant I know who can grapple the
subject." Even Thaddeus Stevens, one of the more querulous
members of Congress, was moved to enthusiasm for the project
and declaimed, "The Western soil is but a platform on which to
lay the rails to transport the wealth of the furthest Indies to
Philadelphia, Boston, and Portland, scattering its benefits on its
way to St. Louis, Chicago, Cincinnati, Buffalo, and Albany. Then
our Atlantic seaports will be but a resting place between China,
Japan, and Europe." And to Joaquin Miller, the California poet,
a coarser member of the Walt Whitman school, "there is more
poetry in the rush of a single railroad train across the continent

37

than in all the gory story of burning Troy." To oppose the transcontinental railroad in the early 1860's was almost as unthinkable as it was, one century later, to raise doubts about the worth of space exploration.

One result of all that ululation was the Pacific Railroad Act of 1862. Another was the organization of the Union Pacific, which under the terms of its charter was to build westward from the hundredth meridian in the territory of Nebraska to join in Utah with the Central Pacific, which was to build eastward from California. The progress of that construction was watched with national pride bordering on hubris, its completion an occasion for the utmost jubilation.

Yet in less than a decade that triumph of engineering, of human muscle over natural obstacles was being viewed with rue and more than a tinge of jaundice by the American people and some of their leaders. That was a characteristic of railroad history: billowy hopes punctured by the reality of human greed and fecklessness. Disillusion followed the first express down the new tracks; promises were never fulfilled, and it generally turned out that thieves had been operating under cover of the noise of construction.

The honest and forthright Senator from Massachusetts George Hoar summed it up when he said, "When the greatest railroad in the world, binding together the continent and uniting two great seas which wash our shores, was finished, I have seen our national triumph and exaltation turned to bitterness and shame by the unanimous reports of three committees of Congress that every step of that mighty enterprise had been taken in fraud."

Under government sponsorship, the Union Pacific was created during the months when the Union Army was reeling back from successive defeats by the Confederates. Perhaps the distraction of war accounted for the intricate and cumbersome structure which Congress erected to govern the construction of the transcontinental railroad. The Pacific Railroad Act provided a charter for the Union Pacific Railway Company, which was to build westward from the one hundredth meridian and would be joined by four branches built from four different points along the Missouri River. One hundred and fifty-eight commissioners from twenty-five states and territories, plus five more representing the government's interest, were to be selected as a sort of governing body. They would elect the railroad's officers and open subscription books for the $100,000,000 in capital stock to be offered the public.

Soon enough the commissioners were brushed aside and financial and promotional genius took over. Less than a year after the enabling legislation was passed, a group of large stockholders met and briskly proceeded to vote the Union Pacific into an independent company without any direct supervision from the government's commissioners. Some of the country's more prehensile financiers, bankers, and company promoters—meeting in New York City, naturally—took over the railroad for their own purposes, having already secured Congressional backing for the seizure of corporate power. They included August Belmont, the American agent of the Rothschilds and enormously wealthy in his own right; Erastus Corning, president of the New York Central; Thomas A. Scott, the leading developer of the Pennsylvania Railroad; Leonard W. Jerome, millionaire stockbroker and future grandfather of Winston Churchill; William E. Dodge, the copper magnate; Samuel Sloan, president of the Hudson River Railroad; Moses E. Grinnell, wealthy shopowner; Samuel J. Tilden, preeminent among the railroad lawyers; Moses Taylor, a banker with a majority interest in the Lackawanna Railroad; Ben Holladay, stage-line operator; and Thurlow Weed, the New York Republican boss. One of the largest stockholders, and soon to be the moving spirit of the enterprise, was Thomas C. Durant, a former physician who had turned to railroad promotion and was blamed for having bungled the affairs of the Michigan Southern, the Rock Island, and the Mississippi & Missouri in the recent past. Their first move was to elect to the UP presidency John A. Dix, now a major general on active duty but formerly an associate of Russell Sage; a general's twin stars made a nice camouflage. Durant was named vice-president and general manager.

The scent of boodle was in the air and reaching sensitive nostrils in Washington. A melon was about to be sliced and was awaited by palates knowledgeable about the possibilities which developed immediately after the company's affairs were disengaged from the government commissioners.

Deserving though he may have been of the "Honest Abe"

sobriquet, President Lincoln, the insiders believed, would present no problem. He was busy with the war, and railroad men had been foremost among those who secured his nomination for the Presidency. Among those who worked most diligently on behalf of his candidacy were John A. Dix, Thomas C. Durant, John I. Blair, and other railroad promoters. A railroad attorney had written the railroad plank in Lincoln's platform. And as the biographer of the chief construction engineer of the Union Pacific would write, those men "played a powerful role" in securing passage of the enabling legislation, "nor is it undue emphasis to assert that these combined groups finally moved Mr. Lincoln to throw the weight of his influence" behind further measures to enrich the Union Pacific's promoters.

By way of showing their gratitude for the Presidential favor, the Union Pacific's directors ordered a sumptuous private car, furnished in black walnut and upholstered in dark-green plush, before a mile of track had been laid. Some intuition, perhaps, caused President Lincoln to refuse to ride in the car. After his assassination, however, the private car draped in black crepe bore his body back to Illinois.

Another and more fervent friend in the Lincoln administration was John P. Usher, who was Assistant Secretary of the Interior in 1862, when the Pacific Railroad Act was signed. His career was an interesting study in converging interests. He arranged the appointment of Samuel J. Tilden as a federal commissioner of the railroad, although Tilden was also a heavy stockholder in the Union Pacific. The day following that curious appointment Usher wrote Tilden instructing him to place money in Usher's account at a brokerage specializing in railroad securities. In January, 1863, Usher was promoted to Secretary of the Interior and thus was enabled to appoint the government's directors on the Union Pacific board. He resigned from the Cabinet in May, 1865, and immediately was named general counsel of the railroad, a post which he held to the end of his life.

Before anything could be done about lining individual pockets among the Union Pacific insiders, an atmosphere of delirious enthusiasm for the railroad had to be created, one which would persuade the public to forgive almost anything connected with the enterprise (a similar enthusiasm generated on behalf of the various space programs would induce forgiveness for the contractors a century later when various components were found faulty).

Propaganda, though an infant science in those days, was well esteemed by the railroad promoters. A fog of goodwill had to be manufactured as a screen for operations which honest folk might abhor. For this purpose Thomas C. Durant was able to turn to an old friend and associate, George Francis Train, whose strange and spectacular genius was difficult to define. By eloquent mouth, facile hand, and agile brain, he at the very least created the legend of the Union Pacific, even if he did not "organize" it as he later claimed. His career is beyond brief description. Calling himself the "champion crank of the universe," once running for the office of "dictator of the United States," he was an international promoter who often made—and lost—a great deal of money; he made a trip around the world in eighty days that inspired Jules Verne's famous novel; he was an eloquent orator and a skilled publicist. Most of his contemporaries considered him a half-mad genius of the written and spoken word; as one journalist of his time wrote, he was a man who "might have built the Pyramids, or been confined in a straitjacket for eccentricities."

Train's peculiar genius stamped its benchmark on every aspect of the Union Pacific's development. Durant enlisted his help as a professional drumbeater, but he was much more than that. For several years he all but personified the Union Pacific while those who would benefit in much greater measure were content to operate in a beneficial obscurity. A tall, dark man with a Mephistophelean manner and a mass of curly hair, who somehow looked like a professional magician, he addressed public meetings, appeared before Congressional committees, charmed cow-country legislatures, buttonholed and persuaded moneyed people to invest in the railroad's stock. In a time which appreciated extravagant personalities, he was the perfect front man.

Something of his florid style may be recaptured in the speech he gave at the groundbreaking ceremonies for the eastern terminus in what was then the prairie village of Omaha on December 2, 1863. It contained not only his exuberance, which he had the ability to transmit to people who should have known better, but his genuine sense of the American potential.

41

"Before the first century of the nation's birth," he bellowed against the wintry wind, "we may see in the New York depot some strange Pacific railway notice: 'European passengers for Japan will please take the night train. Passengers for China this way.'"

This may have been stretching hyperbole to the breaking point, but he roared on:

> Down with England and up with America! When they spoke of our national debt I asked them what right England had to monopolize the entire national debt of the world! I told them *Deo volente* that one of these days we would roll up a national debt that would make them ashamed of themselves.
>
> The Pacific Railroad is the nation, and the nation is the Pacific Railroad. Labor and capital shake hands today. The two united make the era of progress. Congress gives something toward building this great national thoroughfare—not much, but something; say a loan of government credit for thirty years, for $16,000 a mile and 20,000,000 acres of land. But what is that in these times?

Then he made the most astounding prophecy of the afternoon on that bleak prairie which, so thinly populated at present, stretched to the Rocky Mountains: "Ten millions of immigrants will settle in this golden land in twenty years."

With promises and prophecies like that, uttered in tones ringing with confidence, Train inspired the country and made it amenable to the demands placed before it by the Union Pacific. His grandiose visions helped encourage Congress to be wildly generous in subsidizing and encouraging what was now a venture of private capital aided by public funds and grants. The Union Pacific thus was given a federal subsidy varying from $16,000 to $48,000 a mile, depending on the topography, toward construction costs. In addition, the railroad was awarded a land grant of alternate sections totaling 12,000,000 acres. State legislatures were equally generous. After listening to George Francis Train's orisons to the future of a rail-webbed West, the territorial legislature of Nebraska, as one observer wryly commented, gave the Union Pacific "nearly every power imaginable, save that of reconstructing the late rebel states."

Train's more or less original genius was also employed in

creating the Crédit Mobilier, two words which would stink for a generation and which still convey a whiff of the crassest sort of political corruption. (Train himself, however, was not responsible for the more villainous uses which the top dogs found for the device.) Some sort of holding company had to be organized to siphon off excess profits from construction and to disburse *douceurs* to influential politicians, indirectly, not through the Union Pacific. The game had become more sophisticated, the Wisconsin experience having shown how indiscretions could be punished by investigating committees, and the specter of ex-Governor Bashford, a fugitive baking away in the Arizona wilderness, was always before them.

It was Train who found the proper vehicle for the Union Pacific's more covert operations. Rooting around the Pennsylvania archives, he found the charter for a company called the Pennsylvania Fiscal Agency, which was awarded by the state's General Assembly in 1859 and permitted it to engage in practically any commercial enterprise except banking. It would be a wonderful portmanteau for the varied activities the UP's insiders had in mind. The company was moribund, and Train was able to buy its charter for a mere $25,000. His next task was to persuade the General Assembly to allow a change in the Pennsylvania Fiscal Agency's name; a few strategically placed bribes took care of that problem.

The new designation was the Crédit Mobilier of America. While living, wheeling, and dealing in the France of the Second Empire, Train had studied the amazing success of the Pereire brothers, Emile and Isaac, in operating the Société Générale de Crédit Mobilier. Originally it had been organized to make loans on personal (or mobile) property—as its name indicated—but the brothers had branched out into brokerage and banking, and before Napoleon III's regime collapsed they came close to dominating the French financial world. Another creation of the Pereire brothers, which Train would also adapt, was the Crédit Foncier, which was a mortgage-loan bank.

Under the elastic charter acquired secondhand, the Crédit Mobilier could do practically anything it pleased; in a sense it was the disreputable seedling of the trusts, Standard Oil and the rest, that followed. The uses which Thomas C. Durant, who

43

quickly made himself president of the new company, found for it were as scandalous as they were diverse. Durant was so pleased with Train's concoction that he awarded him $25,000 in cash and $25,000 in Crédit Mobilier stock as a bonus. And soon that stock was finding its way into far more distinguished and much more prehensile hands than those of George Francis Train.

Train then devoted himself to a furious bout of lobbying in Washington and in the spring of 1864 managed to push through Congress an amended Pacific Railroad Act, which doubled the Union Pacific's land grant and reinforced the government's guarantee of its securities. Train prevailed despite the opposition of Representative Elihu B. Washburne of Illinois, Lincoln's close associate and General U. S. Grant's sponsor, who protested what he called "the greatest legislative crime in history."

This new and massive handout from Congress naturally began attracting more investors to the Union Pacific, and with the Civil War winding down, actual construction could start. And the gravy train could start rolling long before the first UP train was marshaled in the yards at Omaha. Very lucrative contracts were awarded via the Crédit Mobilier, even while Representative Washburne was crying out that the U.S. Treasury was going to be tapped for $95,000,000 before the government's patronage of the project was finished.

Train, having done so much of the donkey work, having whipped up so much enthusiasm and created the atmosphere necessary to obtaining the massive governmental support, was elbowed aside. Train then flung himself into the role of town boomer. Acquiring 80 acres of land around Omaha, he organized the Crédit Foncier to sell town lots and promote other enterprises. One little project he undertook was to build a seventy-room hotel, the Cozzens House, in sixty days. He was determined to build Omaha village into a prairie metropolis and advertised its future glories all over the country: "Prosperity, Independence, Freedom, Manhood in its highest sense. . . . Throw down the yardstick and come out here if you would be men. How many regret the non-purchase of that lot in Buffalo, that acre in Chicago, that quarter-section in Omaha? A $50 lot may prove a $5,000 investment. Paris to Pekin in Thirty Days!" Train could have made an enormous fortune if his enthusiasm had not evaporated, but soon he went on to more spectacular, if less profitable, endeavors. To a large extent, the Union Pacific was his brainchild, but he was content to let other men bring it up.

His old friend Durant was more than willing to assume that responsibility. Getting construction under way was proving a problem, however, because of the balkiness of the road's first chief engineer, Peter Dey, and his awkward sense of honor. Dey could see no virtue in padded contracts, just because they would enlarge the girth of the fat cats participating in the Crédit Mobilier, and besides, he didn't get along with the high-handed Durant. "Mr. Durant has got the whole thing in his hands," Dey wrote a friend, "but he is managing it [Union Pacific] as he does everything else—a good deal spread and a good deal do nothing. He considers it a big thing—the big thing of the age—and himself the father of it."

What outraged him even more than Durant's bumptiousness was the matter of the contracts let for the construction of the first hundred miles of track. His estimate was for $30,000 a mile. Durant awarded contracts boosting the cost to $60,000 a mile. Dey smelled graft and wrote out his letter of resignation. "I do not approve of the contract for building the first hundred miles from Omaha west, and I do not care to have my name so connected with the railroad that I shall appear to endorse the contract."

With that starchy citizen out of the way, Durant had to find himself another able construction engineer. The man he had in mind was Grenville M. Dodge, a hardheaded and hard-driving engineer, but unfortunately the Army had first call on Dodge's services. In 1861, at the age of thirty, Dodge had taken command of an Iowa regiment. Since then, largely for his skill in rebuilding railroads behind the Union armies of the West as they advanced on Atlanta, Dodge had been promoted to major general of volunteers. Close to the end of the war he was placed in command of the Department of Missouri, with all Kansas, Nebraska, Colorado, and Utah as his military responsibility. Very fortunate, that assignment. Dodge had already agreed to take over as chief engineer of the Union Pacific. His new command would be the area which had to be cleared of hostile Indians before construction could proceed.

It soon appeared that the toughest problem confronting the

railroad builders was that posed by the Indians, who were swarming angrily over the Great Plains and trying to prevent the invasion of their hunting lands by the thousands of whites determined to settle west of the Mississippi at the end of the Civil War. Dodge estimated that his undermanned regiments were facing battle with 25,000 hostiles.

His superior, General John Pope, outlined the situation in terms more compassionate than those generally used by soldiers —or railroadmen:

> There is not a tribe of Indians on the great plains or in the mountain regions east of Nevada and Idaho but which is warring on the whites. The first demand of the Indian is that the white man shall not come into his country; shall not kill or drive off the game upon which his subsistence depends; and shall not dispossess him of his lands. How can we promise this, with any hope or purpose of fulfilling the obligation, unless we prohibit immigration and settlement west of the Missouri river? So far from being prepared to make such engagement with the Indians the government every day is stimulating the immigration. Where under such circumstances is the Indian to go? It is useless for the government to think of undertaking to subsist large bodies of Indians in remote and inaccessible districts. Whatever may be the right or wrong of the question our past experiences in America reveal that the Indian must for the most part be dispossessed. The practical question to be considered is how the inevitable can be accomplished with the least inhumanity to the Indian.

General Dodge campaigned as vigorously as his limited resources permitted to drive all the dissident tribesmen away from the proposed right-of-way of the Union Pacific. A later generation might have judged him as harboring a conflict of interests. He could never build his railway until the Indians had been driven north of the Platte; more than that, he wanted them swept north of the Black Hills of Dakota Territory to keep them well out of the path of railroad progress, but the Johnson administration restrained him from wholesale measures of "pacification."

Ethical questions like conflict of interest did not greatly trouble most men of Dodge's generation because they felt that they had a tremendous job to do, in a limited time, and they could not afford to be inhibited by too frequently consulting their consciences. Further, he and his fellow generals of the Union Army had destroyed the Confederacy, fellow Caucasians, with a ruthless use of military power; why should they hesitate to employ what remained of that power on men of another race? General Dodge, with the UP contract in his pocket, undertook a tour of inspection of the western section of his vast command; it turned into a Union Pacific survey party. In the Wyoming Black Hills, General Dodge, an old surveyor, located Lone Tree Pass, through which the railroad would build on its route over that spur of the Rockies.

On May 6, 1866, he quit the Army and took up his duties with the Union Pacific. Urged on by Durant, who was under heavy criticism for the delays in construction and the outlays of cash for padded contracts, Dodge got cracking immediately. Within a month he had organized the whole operation along military lines, with a chain of command leading straight to his office in Omaha; scattered engineering parties were concentrated and provided with armed escorts, and materials for construction were stocked. There had been lengthy squabbles over what route the Union Pacific should take, but Dodge decided the matter, later remarking:

> There was never any great question, from an engineering point of view, where the line, crossing Iowa and going west from the Missouri river, should be placed. The Lord so constructed the country that any engineer who failed to take advantage of the great open road out of the Platte valley, and then on to Salt Lake, would not have been fit to belong to the profession.

Within three months, the energetic young Dodge (then in his middle thirties) got the project moving. Only 40 miles of track had been laid from 1863 to May, 1866. Under his direction six times that much was accomplished during the balance of 1866.

At rail's end, 40 miles out on the prairie from Omaha, under the scorching sun of the Great Plains, his construction crews started pushing westward. The bosses of the tracklaying gangs were two brothers from Ohio, Jack and Dan Casement, both tiny men, "a pair of the biggest little men you ever saw," but as tough

47

and hard-driving as Dodge himself. Jack Casement had been a brigadier general in the Union Army. Out on the Nebraska steppe he took command of a force of 1,000 men and 100 teams of horses. This hardcased crew included ex-soldiers from both the Union and Confederate armies, mule skinners, failed farmers, runaway youths from Eastern families, bushwhackers from the border wars, newly arrived immigrants, busted gamblers, problem drinkers, and a heavy sprinkling of ex-convicts. Most of them were Irish, with a sprinkling of German immigrants, Mexicans and Anglos. At the moment it was the closest thing to the Foreign Legion you could find north of the Rio Grande.

When Dodge came out to inspect the work force, he must have felt much like Wellington looking over his levies and shuddering. They looked like a convention of desperadoes. "Boys," Dodge told them in a brief speech, "I want you to do just what Jack Casement tells you to do. We've got to beat that Central Pacific crowd!" Shrewdly enough, he had invented another enemy for them. The Central Pacific was building east from California and had got the jump on the Union Pacific. Dodge was making it a point of honor for his work force to outdo the other gang, hoping no one would notice they were slaving all the harder for the greater profit and glory of a distant corporation.

All the workmen were armed with rifles and revolvers and told they might often have to defend themselves from Indian attack. A boarding train, virtually a mobile arsenal, followed the construction crews up their newly laid track. There were racks for a thousand rifles in the train's four cars, as well as offices for the Casement brothers and their chief assistants, bunks for the bosses (while most of the tracklayers, graders, teamsters, and herdsmen slept in tents), and a rolling kitchen, which provided the unvarying diet of bread, beef, beans, pie, and coffee.

The military would provide protection to the extent it could, but the frontier regiments were thin on the ground. Mostly the work force would have to defend itself. General Sherman, a Union Pacific enthusiast like most generals, because a railroad network in the West would allow them to bring that vast territory under control all the quicker, was airily certain that there wouldn't be much trouble with the Indians. From his comfortable headquarters in St. Louis, he observed, "No particular danger need be apprehended from the Indians. So large a number of workmen distributed along the line will introduce enough whiskey to kill all the Indians within 300 miles of the road." Sherman prided himself on his tart humor, but his talent for prophecy had often been found wanting. True enough, the country was flooded with cheap, raw whiskey. It could almost be said that the UP was built on whiskey, but there were a lot more angry Indians swarming around the countryside than there were whiskey peddlers. General George Crook, who was much closer to the situation than the military division headquarters in St. Louis, embroidered on Sherman's statement by remarking that it was tactically impossible to surround three Indians with one cavalry trooper.

The man who signed on the payroll of the Casement brothers, in fact, was committing a desperate deed. He not only had to toil with pick and shovel, haul timbers and iron rails, or handle a team of horses on the grading crews, but had to risk his life against raiding Indians and, equally likely, against his brawling, often drunken comrades. And morally he was exposed to more dangers and temptations than the New York Tenderloin could offer.

As construction pushed westward, it was accompanied by a mobile Gomorrah, sometimes called Moving Town or more accurately Hell on Wheels—a tent city which provided the workers with the sort of amusements considered suitable for red-blooded men. This was a tent city operated by and for whiskey sellers, prostitutes, and gamblers. Every payday Hell on Wheels, first located at Fort Kearney on the Platte, then at North Platte, then at Julesburg, Colorado, took the earnings of the labor force and gave them in return a splitting headache, possibly a broken nose or lumpy jaw, and quite probably a venereal disease. There is no evidence that Hell on Wheels was a direct subsidiary of the Crédit Mobilier, but certainly its officers smiled complacently on that lively enterprise. It was only when a group of gamblers began running Hell on Wheels along the lines of a Barbary Coast deadfall that General Dodge finally ordered Jack Casement to "clean up." Three weeks later Dodge asked Casement if the gamblers had been taught a lesson. Sure, replied Casement, "they're all out in the graveyard." Casement had organized a storm troop of a hundred ex-soldiers, descended on the tent city,

49

and, without so much as a drumhead court, wiped out the tougher characters. Nobody mentioned anyone's constitutional rights because such niceties were declared nonexistent west of Omaha.

Regarding one of those mobile Gomorrahs, the one at North Platte, Henry M. Stanley, then a roving correspondent in training for his quest of Dr. Livingstone, wrote with awe and fascination:

> Every gambler in the Union seems to have steered his course for North Platte, and every known game under the sun is played here. The days of Pike's Peak and California are revived. Every house is a saloon, and every saloon is a gambling den. Revolvers are in great requisition. Beardless youths imitate to the life the peculiar swagger of the devil-may-care bullwhacker and black leg, and here, for the first time, they try their hands at the Mexican monte, high-low-jack, rouge-et-noir, three-card monte and that satanic game, chuck-a-luck, and lose their all. On account of the immense freighting done ... hundreds of bullwhackers walk about, and turn one street into a perfect Babel. Old gamblers who revelled in the glorious days of "flush times" in the gold districts declare that this town outstrips them all. . . .

Aside from the moral dangers of Hell on Wheels, the backbreaking labor, and the constant threat of Indian attack, the Union Pacific's workmen lived and labored under the crudest conditions. E. C. Lockwood, who joined that force as a boy in his late teens, would always remember the lice and bedbugs, generically known as cooties, which infested the encampment. Many of the men preferred to take their bedrolls out on the prairie and sleep out in the open to get away from the parasites. They risked being caught in one of those sudden raging attacks of rain and wind called Platte storms, which seemed determined to devastate the countryside.

William Henry Jackson, who became a noted Western photographer after surviving his experiences as a UP construction worker, had signed on with the Casements after being jilted by a girl in Vermont and choosing between the Union Pacific and the French Foreign Legion, which was then fighting for Maximilian and Carlotta in Mexico. Those Platte storms were the most

50

frightening of the experiences he would recall. One day in July, 1866, he wrote in his diary:

> It came down raging and howling like a madman, tearing and pulling away at the wagon sheets as though it meant to vent its fury on us personally. It rocked and shook us and started some of the wagons on their wheels. Ours was broadside to the storm and we had serious apprehensions that we should be capsized. After a short spat of hail, the rain came down steady torrents—the roaring thunder and the flashing lightning were incessant, reverberating through the heavens with an awful majesty of sound and lighting up everything with the brilliancy of day. The storm did not last long, but its force and fury were indescribable. The rain came right through the wagon sheets, but we hauled a buffalo robe over our heads and so slept dry all night.

Even more hazardous was the life of the surveying parties which worked ahead of the tracklaying force, often hundreds of miles from rail's end and almost as far from the nearest garrison. Civil engineers, rodmen, flagmen, chainmen, axmen, and teamsters were included in the surveying parties. Hunters accompanied them to shoot game while the projected right-of-way was surveyed. Generally they were escorted by a squad of cavalry, sometimes a company when they ventured into particularly hostile country. Every morning the troopers fanned out and occupied the knolls overlooking the survey to stand off any surprise attack. At night they stood sentinel duty. "Their campfires burn brightly after nightfall," a surveyor recorded in his diary, "and the solemn tread of the sentinel, with bright gleaming carbine, assures one if, in the still hours of the night, we are attacked, the enemy will receive a warm reception." Despite such precautions, the surveying parties were often attacked and their members killed or wounded.

As the summer progressed and the UP tracks steadily advanced westward over the Nebraska plain, with an average of four iron rails laid per minute, the work force swelled to several thousand men and work trains with a total of 250 freight cars kept bringing the materials forward. The locomotives burned cottonwood cut into six-foot lengths, which the firemen swore was so green it sprouted when it was heaved into the firebox. Despite the prairie

51

sun, the sudden storms, and other perils, construction was more than keeping pace with the terms of the Casement brothers' contract. The tracklayers labored like demons under the broiling sun, spurred on by work incentives offered by Jack Casement. First he offered the tracklayers a pound of tobacco apiece if they could lay a mile of track in one day. They easily exceeded that. Then he offered an extra half day's pay if they would lay a mile and a half of track. Finally, stepping up the pace to a pre-Stakhanovite level, he was paying double time to his crews for laying two miles of track daily. By August that first summer track's end was in the vicinity of Grand Island, 150 miles west of Omaha.

And then came the Indians, first in peaceful curiosity, then swarming like wasps from a broken hive.

A fairly tame Sioux chief named Spotted Tail came calling with a number of his braves and a half-breed interpreter when the tracklayers reached Grand Island. Spotted Tail was reputed to be a moderate, therefore an anomaly among his fiercely independent people, and was greeted like a visiting foreign dignitary by one of Casement's foremen. He and his braves watched the tracklaying operation with great interest, then were shown through the cars of the boarding train, with a somewhat significant halt in the arsenal with its hundreds of rifles racked to the ceiling. E. C. Lockwood was a member of the escorting party and recalled that he "noticed one Indian put his hand out of a window and measure the thickness of the wall of the car. As he looked to another Indian, I could imagine hearing him say, 'I wonder if a bullet could go through.' " The Casement foreman invited the chief and his followers to sit down to the noon meal of bread and beef with the tracklayers. They accepted, but having come in contact with whites before, they sensibly refused to eat until the white men had fallen to and they were assured that the food wasn't poisoned. Until the last moment, it was a friendly and sociable meeting with red men and white. Just before departing, however, Spotted Tail announced that he believed the railroad should provide him with all the flour and beef he and his braves could carry away. Angry words were exchanged. As Spotted Tail rode off, according to Lockwood, he "threatened to come over some night with three thousand warriors and clean us out." The night patrol around the camp was doubled for the next few weeks, but Spotted Tail did not carry out his threat.

Other Sioux were less alarmed by reports that the construction workers were well prepared to defend themselves. Late in August the new trackage was snaking its way into the sandhill country, the undulations of which offered a better chance of surprise attack than the flatter country it had been traversing. At Plum Creek, about 200 miles west of Omaha, came the first of a series of Indian attacks. The raid occurred just as General Dodge was inspecting the work at the end of the tracks. About 10 miles to the east the locomotive of a freight train lost its steam and was stalled on the tracks. From the sandhills to the south a large band of Sioux suddenly appeared. They swarmed over the train and captured the crew. The attack was witnessed from a telegraph station, the operator of which immediately alerted the main camp at Plum Creek. Dodge went into action at top speed, gathered up twenty volunteers, hooked his private car onto the nearest locomotive, and steamed down the tracks to the rescue. A show of force was all that was needed. The Indians jumped off the captured train and onto their ponies and galloped away. No harm done, except to a freight car they had set afire. But that little skirmish was the beginning of twenty months of determined campaigning by the Plains Indians against the coming of the iron horse.

The temper of the Indians, hardly improved by a series of broken treaties or by the columns of migrants coursing over their prairies in numbers they could hardly comprehend, kept worsening that summer. It reached the explosive point the last month of that year. The western Sioux tribes had been driven north of the Platte into the Powder River country, and now the Army was proposing to build forts along the Bozeman Trail, which led north from Fort Laramie through that country, to open up Montana Territory. Ignoring the Sioux's objections, the Army had proceeded to build Fort Phil Kearney on a branch of the Powder River, and this was the focal point of Indian resentment. A worried General Sherman was touring his Western outposts and writing the Chief of Staff in Washington:

> We are in no condition to punish the Indians this year. Our troops are barely able to hold the long thin lines that are traveled

53

by daily stages and smart parties of emigrants. By next year this railroad [Union Pacific] will enable us to put a regiment of cavalry at Fort Laramie, which can punish the Indians, who are evidently disposed to contest our right to make roads leading to Montana.

By now the Plains Indians, principally the Sioux and Cheyenne, were entirely aware of the situation confronting them. They could see that the iron horse was not merely a white man's toy but a monstrous thing capable of bringing in settlers by the hundreds of thousands; their own living space was being compressed with every mile of track laid; the buffalo herds on which they depended for subsistence were being driven farther and farther away from the Platte hunting grounds, while regiments of cavalry could be transported in a matter of hours, with their mounts and supplies, to any trouble spot. The Indians would resist with desperate courage, but as General Sherman put it, "the poor devil," meaning the Indian, "naturally wriggles against his doom." The railroads were making white settlement an inexorable and irresistible force.

When the blue northers roared down and the first snows came, the Union Pacific's tracklaying army had to settle into winter quarters. It was the worst winter in the Western territories in many years. The ice was thick enough on the Missouri to allow the UP's engineers to build rails over it to link Council Bluffs and Omaha. North Platte was now the advance base, to which freight trains hauled mountains of supplies in preparation for the heavy work schedule planned for the summer of 1867, during which Dodge hoped to extend his trackage as far as Fort Sanders in Wyoming Territory, almost 300 miles west of North Platte. Meanwhile, as Dodge was assured by General Sherman, the Army would be campaigning vigorously to keep the Indians well north of the railroad. Military activities and railroad construction, it is evident from the many letters exchanged by Dodge and Sherman that winter, were tightly coordinated. The military was well aware of the fact that it could subjugate the dissident tribes and protect the white settlements only with the help of the speeded-up communications afforded by the railroads and telegraph. And Dodge was equally aware of how much his success depended on military protection. He understood that Sherman

54

would have to withdraw cavalry patrols along the railroad in order to beef up the forces taking the field that spring, but "what you and I know," as he wrote Sherman, "is going to be hard to make a lot of Irishmen believe," referring to his construction force. "They want to see occasionally a soldier to give them confidence, and that is all we need to get labor on the line." Therefore he urged Sherman to allot 5,000 troopers to protect the Union Pacific's line of communications. Sherman could only promise "every man I can get and spare."

Early in that harsh winter it became apparent that the Army would have few troops to spare from field operations. On December 21, 1866, came the "Fetterman massacre," named for an overeager officer who led eighty-one of his troopers into a Sioux ambush near Fort Phil Kearney. Captain William J. Fetterman and his command were wiped out to the last man, and the fort was placed under siege by thousands of warriors gathered under Chief Red Cloud. It was evident that the Army's main efforts that spring would be directed at clearing the Powder River country, and the Union Pacific's work gangs would have to rely on themselves.

While Dodge and the frontier generals were ·worrying over what the spring would bring, the army of construction workers was devoting itself to gambling, boozing, and consorting with the dance hall girls in its winter quarters at North Platte, which had suddenly become a riproaring town of 5,000 population. Cheap whiskey was the chief staple of local commerce. Nightly there were shootouts, and barrelhouse music jingled and jangled till dawn while coyotes howled on the outskirts of the jerry-built town in counterpoint to the revelry. Occasionally the winner of some homicidal contest would be hanged from one of the telegraph poles as a suggestion that North Platte was not entirely beyond the rule of law, no matter how crudely administered. North Platte was isolated from the world for weeks at a time as blizzards stopped all railroad traffic.

It was a hard winter all around, and the spring brought no great amount of relief. The toughest year of the Union Pacific's existence was just beginning. The letters Jack Casement wrote home to his wife told the story of one disaster after another. "Miles of Road is washed away in the Platte Valley so that we cannot get over the Road for a few days even if it stops raining," wrote Casement, whose syntax was inferior to his qualities of leadership. "We are all in a heap generally." They were "in a heap" because the spring thaws, melting a record snowfall, brought the Platte well above the flood stage. The Platte and its tributaries washed out miles of track, bridges, embankments, and telegraph line. All western Nebraska seemed to be under several feet of water. And just at that time Dodge was being harassed by conflicting orders resulting from a power struggle between rival groups of investors, the "New York crowd" headed by Durant and a Boston faction which would soon gain the upper hand.

Just after the flooded rivers subsided and Dodge was able to resume construction westward, the Indians began resisting his encroachments with more and determined attacks on his personnel. Early in May the plains tribes were swooping down on stage lines and isolated ranches and tearing down telegraph lines, and on May 20 a worried General Dodge was writing a harassed General Sherman:

> I am beginning to have serious doubts of General [Augur's] ability to make a campaign into the Powder River country and at the same time give ample protection to the railroad, the mail routes and the telegraph. His forces are too limited. When we went into the Powder River country in 1868 we had more mounted troops to hold the stage routes alone than Augur has in his entire department.

Five days later his forebodings were confirmed in full and bloody measure. At Overton, Nebraska, 70 miles from North Platte, a Sioux war party jumped out of a weed patch, fell upon a section gang of six men, and killed and scalped all but one, who managed to escape and hide in the prairie grass. Later the same day a larger war party swooped down on the camp at rail's end 100 miles to the west just when three government commissioners were visiting the advance headquarters on the Casements' boarding train. Four graders working on the track nearby were killed. The workmen dropped their shovels and picked up their rifles to drive off the attackers. Dodge, who had accompanied the commissioners, hauled out his revolver, jumped off the train and ran up and down the tracks trying to organize resistance and urging a hot pursuit of the raiders. No one offered to join him in the chase as the Indians retreated up a ravine, and Dodge returned to the train in an evil temper. "We've got to clean the damn Indians out," he raged at the commissioners, "or give up building the Union Pacific Railroad. The government may take its choice."

That same vexed and tragic day the sorely beset General Dodge received a letter from Oakes Ames, the Congressman from Massachusetts whose clique had just seized control of the Union Pacific, that various disasters in the field were to be compounded by guerrilla fighting among his superiors. Durant, Ames wrote Dodge, was full of spite over his ejection from the presidency and replacement by Sidney Dillon:

> I cannot understand such a change as has come over the Doctor [Durant]—the man of all others who had from the beginning stolen whenever he had the chance, and who is today, we think, holding stock, and a large portion of his stock, on fictitious claims and trumped-up accounts. He is now in open hostility to the road and any orders he may give you, or any parties under you, should be entirely disregarded.

And while corporate infighting was occupying the company's headquarters in New York, Dodge was confronted by increasing troubles on his own front. Time after time, Army protection was proving inadequate, and the self-protective measures of his own men were tragically insufficient. On June 14, L. L. Hills, who had been in charge of surveying the line from North Platte to Cheyenne, was working with ten surveyors near the crossing of Cow Creek, not far from that newly established advance base of the railroad. Hills and another man had wandered away from the main party, which was guarded by six troopers from the Second Cavalry, when a band of Indians rode down on them from a ravine. Hills' body was found with nineteen arrows and five bullet wounds in it, while his companion, though gravely wounded, managed to escape.

A short time later Percy Browne, one of the most trusted members of Dodge's engineering staff, was leading a survey party near Rock Creek, Wyoming, trying to locate a feasible route for the railroad in the rough country between Fort Sanders and

57

Green River. Browne and four assistants, guarded by eight cavalrymen, were surprised by a war party of 300 Sioux. They defended themselves on the crest of a knoll, fighting off successive attacks from noon until sundown. Just before the Indians withdrew into the twilight, Browne was fatally wounded in the abdomen.

Dodge groaned aloud when he heard the news. It was obvious that the Indians were swarming all over the country west of Cheyenne and would present possibly insuperable problems when the tracklaying gang moved over the Wyoming plains and into the mountains. Dodge complained in a letter to his new boss, Sidney Dillon, that the "best and most promising" of his men were being picked off in advance parties far beyond the range of reliable cavalry protection, yet it was only the most skilled and resourceful men who could be trusted with the work of surveying the route ahead.

The growing boldness of the Indian forays against the railroad and its builders was evidenced on, of all days, the Fourth of July, 1867, in the tent town of Cheyenne. Thousands of boomers had rushed to the new town, which was even wilder than North Platte and had to be subjected to an iron-broom sweep of the disorderly elements. Cheyenne was now orderly enough for a Fourth of July celebration at which General John A. Rawlins, the Army Chief of Staff then touring the Western outposts, delivered the oration. After the speechmaking, most of the population got drunk. A band of Cheyenne descended on the outskirts of the town and killed several Union Pacific workers who were sleeping off the effects of celebration, then rode around the town whooping and frightening the wits out of the hung-over citizenry. General Rawlins was so impressed by the demonstration of Cheyenne insouciance that he told Dodge, "I'm going to tell Grant that this road can't be built without double the strength you have."

Ten times the present military strength, as Dodge probably informed the visitor from Washington, would barely have been sufficient to guard the hundreds of miles of Union Pacific track, its depots and telegraph stations, its exposed survey parties. Dodge was worried to the point of breaking down, and wrote UP president Dillon an almost incoherent letter on July 27: "How long I can stand it God only knows. . . . Indians on the plains have been very bad for two weeks. . . . They have been attacking everything and everybody. . . . Sick as I am, I believe I shall get through to Salt Lake if the Indians do not kill off all my party. It takes the nerve out of them losing so many. . . ."

The morale of Dodge's organization, so admirably equipped for miraculous feats of engineering but incapable of fighting an Indian war at the same time, was further endangered a month later. A bloody incident at Plum Creek station, 59 miles *east* of North Platte, demonstrated one untoward and unexpected result of the military's current campaigns. The bulk of the frontier cavalry was sweeping the Cheyenne out of western Kansas. Unable to confront the cavalry on equal terms, the Cheyenne, having been driven into Nebraska, seized the opportunity of attacking the Union Pacific.

The Indians were becoming more sophisticated in their methods of attack. The iron horse, they came to realize, could be crippled by other means than killing or terrorizing its operators. Near Plum Creek station they discovered the joys of derailment. This was at the crossing, symbolically, of an old north-south trail the Indians had been using for centuries.

On August 6 a band of Cheyenne watched a train go by, about four miles east of Plum Creek station, and decided to demonstrate what the Stone Age could do to nineteenth-century technology. Finding some loose ties beside the tracks, they lashed them to the rails with telegraph wire, which they ripped from nearby poles. Then they waited in concealment. Along toward dusk a handcar came up the tracks with six section hands aboard. It struck the rail block and flung the men off the car. Five were killed immediately, but a hardy young Englishman named William Thompson broke away from the Cheyenne braves intent on braining him. One warrior rode him down and knocked him out with his rifle butt. When Thompson came to, he made the horrified discovery that he was being scalped and became one of the few men who lived to tell about it. He watched the Indian ride away. Blood-dimmed though his vision, Thompson saw his scalp, with its long blond hair so highly prized by scalpers, slip from the Indian's belt. Thompson retrieved it.

Half-unconscious from pain and loss of blood, he hid himself in the tall grass and watched helplessly as two trains, both freights, came up the tracks and the Indians deployed for another ambush.

The first freight was derailed when it struck the barrier erected by the Indians. The locomotive jumped the tracks, pulling with it the tender and five following cars. Both the engineer and the firemen had been injured in the derailment and were immediately killed by the Indians, who then set about looting the freight cars, opening packing cases, and setting fire to whatever they had no use for. Meanwhile, the conductor and three other trainmen, who had been riding in the caboose at the rear of the train, slipped away and ran down the tracks to warn the following train.

The second train came to a screeching stop, took the survivors aboard and then backed as speedily as possible to the Plum Creek station, where the engineer paused only long enough to sound the alarm and then continued his backing eastward.

William Thompson's ordeal had not ended. He watched from his hiding place as the Cheyenne tapped a whiskey barrel plundered from the derailed freight. When he judged that the braves were drunk enough, still clutching his scalp, he came out of hiding and staggered four miles to the Plum Creek station. He arrived there just before a rescue train pulled in. Placed on the floor of a boxcar, with his scalp in a pail of water beside him, Thompson somehow survived the jolting journey back to Omaha. His hopes that a doctor would be able to sew his scalp back on were dashed, and that grisly sourvenir eventually was presented to the Omaha Public Library for display under a glass dome.

Though there was a divot on the top of his head, about seven by nine inches, young Thompson could count himself lucky. Seven other men had been killed in that ambush.

Worse yet, from the executive point of view, the Indians had learned the technique of train wrecking, and Dodge had no doubts that word of the Plum Creek experiment would spread by drum and runner and smoke signal to all the tribes. It was suggested by a government commissioner that he halt construction for six months until the military could get a better grip on the situation. Dodge wouldn't hear of it. "If we stop now we may never get started again," he protested in a letter to Oakes Ames. "I'll push this road to Salt Lake in another year or surrender my own scalp to the Indians."

He kept ranging up and down the line of construction, urging on his supervisors and foremen, and himself making the 700-mile trip from Fort Sanders to Salt Lake City on horseback. (Brigham Young, a railroad enthusiast who was determined that the Union Pacific should pass through his city, was his host in Salt Lake City.) Despite Indian raids, the construction force, now beefed up to include 3,500 graders working on the rough terrain of southern Wyoming, had pushed on from Julesburg, in the northeast corner of Colorado, up the 100-odd-mile stretch along Lodge Pole Creek.

Julesburg had replaced North Platte as the advanced headquarters, and its state of morality had not improved with the elevation in status. As the new Hell on Wheels, which served only to separate the laborers from their hard-earned pay, it was gaudier and noisier than any of its predecessors, whole battalions of whores and gamblers having arrived to reinforce the original contingent. As one rather prim UP workman wrote back to his wife in the East, "Vice and crime stalk unblushingly in the mid-day sun." H. M. Stanley, on a roving mission for the New York *Herald*, dropped in at a dance hall called the King of the Hills and professed to be taken aback by the "debauchery and dissipation" he witnessed:

> The women appeared to be most reckless, and the men seemed nothing loth to enter a whirlpool of sin. These women are expensive articles, and come in for a large share of the money wasted. In broad daylight they may be seen gliding through the sandy streets in *Black Crook* dresses [a style initiated by the brash musical comedy which had been titillating NewYork, the *Oh! Calcutta!* of its time], carrying fancy derringers slung to their waists, with which tools they are dangerously expert. Should they get into a fuss, western chivalry will not allow them to be abused by any man whom they may have robbed.
>
> At night, new aspects are presented in this city of premature growth. Watchfires gleam over the sealike expanse of ground outside the city, while inside soldiers, herdsmen, teamsters, women, railroad men, are dancing, singing or gambling. I verily believe there are men here who would murder a fellow-creature for five dollars. Nay, there are men who have already done it, and who stalk abroad in daylight unwhipped of justice. Not a day passes but a dead body is found somewhere in the vicinity with pockets rifled of their contents. But the people generally are strangely indifferent to what is going on. . . .

The Union Pacific continued to be amazingly tolerant of conditions in the tent cities of its camp followers which dogged its progress westward. Not only did the company regard its work force as a mob of bogtrotters from the more impoverished sections of Ireland who could be amused and distracted only by such brute pleasures as boozing, brawling, and fornicating, but North Platte and now Julesburg served another purpose: They stripped the men of their pay and forced them to keep working for the railroad no matter how desperate conditions became.

The only thing that counted with the builders was getting the tracks laid and especially completing construction in time to satisfy the government contracts.

By the end of the year, through slave-driving methods, the trackage had nearly reached Evans Pass. The hellion population of Julesburg moved up the line to Cheyenne. Everyone was proud that 245 miles of track had been laid in 1867 despite the spring floods and Indian attacks. On November 14 there was a hoedown in Cheyenne to celebrate the year's triumphs. Most of those attending soon forgot the speeches made by president Sidney Dillon and Jack Casement, but a banner boasting "The Iron Horse Snorts Defiance at the Rocky Mountains" was long remembered. Thereupon General Dodge, having been a successful, though absentee, candidate for Congress from Iowa, left to take his seat in Washington.

Eighteen sixty-eight looked like a promising year for construction, and the head office in New York was clamoring for 400 miles of track to be laid during the new year. The work force had been enlarged and now included 3,000 men cutting wood for ties, despite three feet of snow, in the Medicine Bow Mountains. There was a surge of hope that the Indians would be easier to get along with, another peace commission having been sent out from Washington to meet with the dissident chiefs and pacify them with a new slate of promises (which would, as always, be unkept). Just in case the palavering failed, the Army was standing by with 5,000 troops deployed along the railroad between Omaha and the Salt Lake Valley, with a 1,000-man garrison posted at Fort D. A. Russell on the outskirts of Cheyenne. There was an optimistic atmosphere over operations in the West, but also a lengthening shadow cast by Congressional suspicions that there was something malodorous about the financing of the Union Pacific. Meanwhile, the struggle for power in New York continued with first Ames, then Durant issuing pronouncements and having them contradicted by the other party. And there was the Central Pacific, driving steadily eastward and gobbling up territory the Union Pacific had staked out for itself.

Ahead of the construction workers, laying track with metronomic efficiency on the heels of the hundreds of grading teams, stretched the broad and level Laramie Plains, with the Rockies rising to the south and west. The UP route crossed the Continental Divide on the western side of the Laramie Plains, and beyond lay the desolate Bitter Creek country, the Wasatch Mountains, and finally the Salt Lake Valley.

Construction began earlier that year, in March, favored by an unusually early and mild spring. General Dodge, meanwhile, was trying to hold down his seat in Congress, where his influence was invaluable to the railroad, and was directing operations west of Cheyenne from a desk in the Interior Department. He soon learned that a chief engineer could not operate from Washington, no matter how loyal and intelligent his subordinates in the field.

Thomas C. Durant had made an end run around the "Boston crowd" and persuaded the Union Pacific's executive committee to empower him to go out west and take charge of construction. As soon as he heard of it, in mid-June, Dodge took leave of Congress and hastened westward. Nobody was going to ruin *his* railroad. On arriving in Cheyenne, he found that Durant was making engineering decisions right and left, changing the route through Wyoming, moving the repair shops from Cheyenne to Laramie, and predicting the tracklayers would reach Salt Lake City before winterset. Racing on to Laramie on a special train, Dodge found Hell on Wheels set up there and doing a roaring business. The hellions were informed they might as well pack up and go back to Cheyenne. "The repair shops will remain in Cheyenne," he firmly announced. Then he sought out Durant for an immediate showdown. "Durant," he declared in deliberate tones, "you are now going to learn that the men working for the Union Pacific will take orders from me and not from you. If you interfere there will be trouble—trouble from the government, from the army, and from the men themselves." Durant turned away without replying.

There was a more decisive confrontation a month later when Dodge, Durant, and UP president Sidney Dillon met with Generals Sherman and Grant, the latter then running for President of the United States, and a whole constellation of frontier generals, including Philip H. Sheridan, who would replace Sherman in command of western operations as soon as Sherman took Grant's place as general in chief. On July 26, the group met at Fort Sanders, its dominating figure, naturally, being the dour little General Grant, who was a shoo-in for the White House. Durant opened the proceedings by charging Dodge with selecting the wrong routes and wasting the investors' money.

"What about it, Dodge?" General Grant asked.

"Just this," Dodge replied, verbally frugal as always. "If Durant, or anybody connected with the Union Pacific, or anybody connected with the government changes my lines, I'll quit the road."

Grant quickly ended the dispute by saying that the government expected the Union Pacific to be finished on schedule and wanted Dodge to continue as chief engineer. Durant, knowing what they meant when embittered veterans spoke of the generals' trade union, which of course included Dodge, threw in his hand as gracefully as possible.

Dodge was driving his construction crews as hard as possible through the summer of 1868. He ranged up and down the line and exhorted his engineers and foremen to keep the pressure up. Before the end of July the forward base was pushed on to Benton, where the Red Desert began, 700 miles west of Omaha. The line between Benton and Green River was being graded by the first week in August, despite a succession of excursion trains bearing Easterners curious about the great railroad-building project, including "all the professors of Yale College," as Jack Casement complained. Before autumn yielded to winter, the grading crews had advanced well beyond Salt Lake City. The Indians had been far less active that season, though late in September they wrecked their last Union Pacific train between Alkali and Ogallala, Nebraska. The fireman was killed, but the attackers were driven off by the passengers firing from the windows of their car, which, unlike the freight cars ahead, was not derailed. Passenger cars were then equipped with overhead racks containing loaded rifles. The pioneer customers of the Union Pacific obviously were a hardy lot.

The Union Pacific's epic of construction was just about ending. The Wild West would soon be safe for tourism. Yet the UP's struggle for existence was still going on. The Central Pacific, as will be seen, boasted powerful political connections and was determined to build farther east than had been agreed upon. It was aiming for Salt Lake City. Dodge, on the other hand, had decided that the most feasible route for his road was to skirt the northern shores of Salt Lake and continue on to Ogden. A spur line could be built south from Ogden to Salt Lake City. The Mormon leader was outraged because he wanted the main line to go through his own heavenly city. Dodge finally brought him around, but only after Brigham Young, as he told his followers, had experienced a vision in which God commanded the Mormons to "help the Union Pacific."

It often seemed that divine intervention, whether or not inspired by the Mormons, was necessary to keep the Union Pacific rolling. Early in 1869 Dodge met head on with the Central Pacific's chief engineer, Samuel S. Montague, and a collision between those two strong-minded men was something like two locomotives battering each other. Without preamble Dodge told Montague, "I intend to build the Union Pacific to the north of Salt Lake. Our tracks will reach Ogden the first of March. Yours cannot possibly be within two hundred miles of this point by then. What we should do is to get together and decide upon a meeting-point somewhere west of Salt Lake. How about it?" Montague could only reply that he didn't have such dictatorial powers as the Union Pacific's chief engineer possessed and couldn't say how far east the Central Pacific would build, but at least he could inform Dodge that the Central Pacific also would run north of Salt Lake City because that was the most feasible main-line route.

For a time it looked as though the Union and Central Pacific would not join but would build parallel lines through Utah, which would have been economic nonsense. But that wasn't the worst of the UP's troubles. For one thing the corporate treasury was exhausted. At Durant's urging, construction had continued through the winter of 1868–69 despite the snowstorms swirling through the Wasatch Mountains; Dodge later estimated that it cost four times as much to build a railroad in high altitudes during the winter as in more clement months. At the same time the vast hinterland which the Union Pacific was designed to serve and which was rapidly filling up with settlers ill equipped to cope with the hazards of their new environment was besieged by armies of grasshoppers. The insect plague ruined the first crops, and the price of flour jumped to $8 a hundred pounds. Deeper in the background, but coming to the fore, were the scandals to be revealed by the investigation of the Crédit Mobilier and the corruption it had engendered.

For the moment, however, it was the tracklaying competition with the Central Pacific, with the possibility that instead of meeting and joining the two railroads would pass each other with an unfriendly nod, that was uppermost in the builders' concerns. A great prize in empire building was at stake, and it would take all the available powers of the government to settle the matter. Settlers and Indians alike were considered mere disinterested bystanders in the contest which directly affected their lives and fortunes.

3.

Crazy Judah's Dream

THE conception of a transcontinental railroad with a terminus on the California coast and proceeding eastward over what conventional wisdom regarded as the impassable barrier of the Sierra Nevada took place in the mind of a man generally believed to have a few shingles loose in his upper story. There was nothing unusual about this: Most of the railroad pioneers were considered to be crazed enthusiasts, single-minded fanatics, or mad visionaries. The very idea of building rails capable of carrying long trains of freight and passengers over terrain regarded as the impenetrable domain of mountain goats seemed to partake of madness. Even those who had participated in the general lunacy known as the California gold rush believed Theodore Judah, whose current obsession was building the Central Pacific, to be unhinged. He was known as Crazy Judah.

Californians, if they had taken the trouble to investigate, would have learned that Judah was as sane as any monomaniac could be. His obsession was building railroads where other men said it couldn't be done. A humorless and opinionated Yankee, he had learned his profession both in theory, at a technical institute, and in practice as a construction engineer for Connecticut railroads.

67

While still in his middle twenties he had accomlished the first of his impossible projects by building a railroad over the Niagara Gorge. For most of his short career he would listen to people saying, "It can't be done," and would reply with an impassioned and detailed demonstration that it damn well could be done. In 1854, when he was twenty-eight years old, he began his long campaign to convince Californians that they could and should be connected by rail with the Eastern markets.

Like George Francis Train when he was beating the drum for the Union Pacific, but without Train's magnetic personality, Judah ranged California trying to rally enthusiasm and raise funds for his project. During his first year he did manage to build a railway between Sacramento and the placer mines in the Sierra foothills as a demonstration of his ability. For the next several years he implored the moneymen of the state to supply him with sufficient funds to start construction on a line which would end their dependence on shipping and the long sea route around Cape Horn. To those exhortations, the California bankers posed their sensible topographical objections: the Sierra Nevadas, which would have to be surmounted, were 150 miles wide; crossing that barrier would require an ascent from Sacramento of almost 7,000 feet in a distance of 105 miles; building would be hampered by the fact that from November to January the mountain trails were made impassable by the heavy snows. Judah brushed aside those objections with the impatience of a man who understood the art of engineering. He staged a Pacific Railroad Convention in San Francisco in 1859, and he went to Washington and lobbied in Congress for the Pacific Railroad Act.

On returning to California, he conducted a survey of the Sierras so that he could tell prospective investors, as he said, "Here are the actual maps, the profiles, the estimates on my routes." Immediately after locating a pass through the mountains near the mining town of Dutch Flat, he drew up his plans for construction. Spreading his papers on the counter of a Dutch Flat drugstore, he wrote out "The Articles of Association of the Central Pacific Railroad of California"—the seedling from which eventually grew the Central Pacific-Southern Pacific system and sprouted a number of immense fortunes.

The turning point was reached one June night in 1861, when

68

Judah, having failed to arouse enthusiasm among the financiers of San Francisco, held a small public meeting in Sacramento to obtain pledges of assistance. Among those attending the meeting were four merchants, cautious, longheaded and tightfisted men, who somehow caught the virus of Judah's obsession. Later they would be known as the Big Four and acclaimed as men of imperial vision, but it was a borrowed vision, and they rode to eminence on the shoulders of a man whom they would discard.

The four men who drank in Judah's words that evening were a wholesale grocer named Leland Stanford, who had a taste for politics; Charles Crocker, a dry goods merchant; and Mark Hopkins and Collis P. Huntington, who were partners in the hardware store in which Judah held his meeting. At first glance they must have seemed to Judah a typical grouping of cheese-paring small-town merchants, but their personalities were strikingly diverse. Crocker was a born slavedriver, a bull-like man with the energy and determination to oversee the construction when Judah was disposed of. Stanford, future governor of and Senator from California and founder of the university bearing his name, fancied himself as a manipulator and schemer; a Central Pacific lawyer once characterized him as having "the ambition of an emperor and the spite of a peanut vendor." Huntington was a solidly built young man, supremely hardheaded and ruthless, "scrupulously dishonest," as a journalist once described him. "He is not altogether bad," Ambrose Bierce would write of him. "Though severe, he is merciful. He says ugly things of the enemy, but he has the tenderness to be careful that they are mostly lies." Hopkins was a thin, bent, prematurely aging man who, it was observed, drank a half cup of tea while his partners would plow through a six-course dinner; a bloodless creature who regarded himself as the balance wheel of the quartet, who could wheedle them into agreement when their personalities clashed or their aims diverged in separate orbits.

Judah sized them up as storekeepers of limited imagination who would be frightened off if he talked about building the western section of a transcontinental railroad. So he confined his outline to the purely local features which they could comprehend. A link over the Sierras would enable them to control trade with the Nevada mines. They would be able to stifle their competition

69

and become the merchant princes of northern California. Crazy Judah was convincing enough that June evening to persuade the quartet to advance the cash to incorporate, with Stanford as president, Huntington vice-president, Hopkins secretary-treasurer, Judah chief engineer, and to push survey parties into the Sierras that spring.

Judah's dream began to take on substance slowly because Californians were reluctant to invest in a railroad while eager enough to sink money into wildcat mining ventures, but it was given impetus when Congress passed the Pacific Railroad Act and designated the Central Pacific to build the section to the Nevada line. It wasn't until January 8, 1863, that ground was broken on the Sacramento levee to signal the start of construction, upon which Stanford delivered a windy speech and Crocker called for "nine cheers for the Central Pacific." Nine, instead of the usual three, cheers indicated that at least one member of the quadrumvirate was beginning to think big.

It was the venturesome Crocker who quit the board of directors to avoid tiresome legal complications, substituting his brother on the board, and formed a separate construction company to build the first 18 miles of track. Judah didn't care much for that maneuver. He also differed with the Big Four over how to proceed with the construction. The Big Four wanted to build the first 40 miles as quickly as possible because they could then obtain the federal 5 percent bond issue. Judah, on the other hand, wanted those tracks built as solidly as possible. He saw that he would be unable to work with men who viewed a railroad, to him the supreme human accomplishment, as something merely to be wrung for the last dollar of profit. Quarrels arose, but it was four against one, and Judah was constantly overruled. His engineering genius was regarded by his partners as a paltry thing compared to that bond-issue prize glittering atop the government's money tree, and they bought him out for $100,000. Judah was still obsessed with building the Central Pacific along sound engineering principles. He headed east by ship from San Francisco, on the long voyage his efforts were designed to eliminate, to try to persuade Commodore Vanderbilt to buy out the Big Four. En route he caught yellow fever, and he died a week after landing in New York. His role in conceiving, planning, and starting work on the

Central Pacific was always ignored by the Big Four. Later, as their joint biographer Oscar Lewis observed, they "accepted easily the roles of men of vision, who had perceived a matchless opportunity and grasped it with courage. It was a role none of them deserved." Sixty years after his death a monument to Theodore Judah was erected in Sacramento, but it was the rairoad's employees who subscribed the funds, while the four men who rose to wealth and power by adopting and expanding on his conception in ways he could not have foreseen always studiously ignored their debt to his memory.

On the slenderest margins of financing, the Central Pacific began creeping its way eastward from Sacramento. With Crocker as general contractor, a competent and forceful engineer named Samuel Montague had taken Theodore Judah's place. It took months to drive pilings across the American River outside Sacramento and build the first section into the foothills. The Big Four may have caught the railroad fever by then, but they were determined to operate on the principles they had absorbed as small businessmen. "We will pay as we go and never run a dollar in debt," as Huntington expounded in one of their deliberations. "If we can't pay a hundred workmen, we will pay fifty; if not fifty, then ten; if not ten, one. We will employ no more than we can pay." They held to that rule as long as possible, until the costs of labor and materials began to snowball, but by then the government bonds and Eastern capital were helping finance the construction.

The Sacramento quartet quickly learned that successful railroading depended to a large extent on access to the state and national treasuries, an access which could be facilitated not only by diligent lobbying in Sacramento and Washington but by soliciting the goodwill of the electorate. The Big Four did not hesitate to present themselves as public benefactors of towering stature and were so artful in their public relations, at first, that Leland Stanford was swept to the governorship. One method of currying public and legislative favor was the excursions and outings they began running as soon as a respectable amount of track had been laid.

On March 19, 1864, they played host to two-thirds of the

71

legislature, their families and friends on an excursion to the end of track, then 22 miles from the California capital. The editor of the Sacramento *Union*, a fervent supporter of the project, supplied a lyrical account of the occasion on which the Big Four wore their beaming public masks:

> The locomotive Governor Stanford led the van, gay with star-spangled banners and other devices, and on the platform car next behind rode the Union Brass Band, with ten melodious and harmonious instruments of sound. . . . Twenty-two miles were soon accomplished, bringing the train to the new granite quarries, where a halt was called and the cars in a twinkling were emptied. . . . Soon after the evacuation of the cars, it was discovered that a large stock of baskets had been piled upon the turf, each of which contained a dozen bottles with something in them. Also, there was a bountiful bread and cheese accompaniment. . . . President Stanford and Contractor Crocker did the honors of the occasion with all that urbanity for which they are distinguished. The return trip was particularly jolly, and the expedition reached the city without accident, and with colors flying, about five o'clock. . . .

Down in San Francisco, however, the Big Four had made enemies in numbers commensurate with the lengthening of their railroad. San Francisco investors were warned against the project by an anonymously written and published pamphlet titled *The Great Dutch Flat Swindle*, which asserted that the Central Pacific had no intention of building beyond that foothill mining camp and that it was simply a scheme to attract investors' money. This was untrue. Stanford, Hopkins, Huntington, and Crocker, in varying degrees, had been infected by Judah's determination to build a railroad over the Sierras. They had even committed their own money, scraped together during years of bargaining over the counters of their mercantile establishments, to meet the payroll and buy supplies.

Private investment and government subsidies, in any case, kept the project afloat, and the toughest problem confronting them as they faced the challenge of the high snow-crusted Sierras was recruiting a labor force. The thousands who had joined the forty-niners' stampede to the goldfields could not be induced to join the Central Pacific's pick-and-shovel brigade; most had found other occupations, or had joined the Union Army, or were still looking for another bonanza. Hundreds were sent to the end-of-track camps by labor agents, but only two in five, as Crocker reported, actually reported to the foremen on the job, and most of those quit as soon as they earned enough to pay the stage fare to Virginia City and its booming mines. Crocker did not scruple to hire child labor for the man-killing work on the mountain grades. At least one twelve-year-old boy, named Robert Gifford, was hired by Crocker personally to lead a team of horses hauling a dump cart, for which he was paid 75 cents a day and board during his three months of employment.

The hard-driving Crocker was so desperate he turned to various outlandish schemes to find men so hard pressed by circumstance that they could be forced to work twelve hours a day, six days a week on his construction gang. Unfortunately for Crocker there was no influx of Irish immigrants to the California ports such as benefited the rival Union Pacific. One plan he pushed vigorously but unsuccessfully was to persuade the War Department to send him 5,000 Confederate prisoners of war, with a few companies of Union infantry as a guard detail, but the war ended before that scheme could mature. Casting about wildly for an alternative, he and his partners decided to tap the nearest source of cheap labor, the peon masses of northern Mexico, but even they were not so impoverished that they could be lured north to work for the Big Four.

There was only one other possibility, abhorrent though it was to all concerned: the thousands of Chinese immigrants who had come over during and after the gold rush and were now working as house servants, operating laundries or restaurants, reworking abandoned mines, or otherwise eking out marginal existences. But, the partners fretted, would it be politically wise to enlist such a despised minority on what was proclaimed to be the noble mission of building a transcontinental railroad? At his inauguration as governor in 1862 Leland Stanford had termed the Chinese a "degraded" race, "the dregs of Asia," and announced that he would support the state legislature in any measures it proposed to halt Chinese immigration. It would be difficult for him, as president of the Central Pacific and governor of California—there were no piddling concerns over "conflict of interest" in those days—to backtrack on statements such as that.

The Central Pacific was in a bind. The only available labor was Chinese, but who could stomach the possibility that the railroad's detractors would start calling it the Chinese Pacific? Among the Big Four only Crocker, who was the most directly concerned with the problem, favored hiring droves of Chinese. To objections that the frail Orientals, weighing an average 110 pounds, could not stand up to the hard labor in the high Sierras, he pointed out that their ancestors had built the Great Wall of China, and besides, he had observed that his houseboy, Ah Ling, worked harder and longer hours than any white man he knew.

The strongest objections were voiced by James H. Strobridge, a hot-tempered Vermont Irishman, who was the head foreman of the Central Pacific's labor force. "I will not boss Chinese," he told Crocker. "I will not be responsible for work done on the road by Chinese labor. From what I've seen of them, they're not fit laborers anyway. I don't think they could build a railroad."

Strobridge's attitude was only a reflection of most Californians at a time when racism was openly and unabashedly expressed. Most of the Indians had been eliminated, and there were few blacks around to irk anyone, so the Chinese were the largest and handiest minority to kick around. They were regarded as subhuman, as heathen, as utterly alien to the American way of life; they preferred rice to potatoes, opium to whiskey, and they wore their hair in pigtails. It was all right for them to do the laundry, but the thought of their doing a man's work—even that which white men rejected—was thoroughly repugnant. And it was ridiculous to believe that a horde of rice-eating barbarians could undertake a job that white men couldn't do on a decent diet of meat, potatoes, and whiskey.

Even Strobridge saw the light, however, when a crew of white tracklayers threatened to strike for more pay. He agreed to Crocker's proposal that fifty Chinese be employed and given a tryout. The first lot was hauled in flatcars to the end of track, and their quiet efficiency was astounding. Without supervision, they set up their own camp, boiled their rice, had supper, and went to sleep; at sunup they were hard at work with pick and shovels. And it was incredible how much work they could do on a diet of rice

74

and dried cuttlefish. Before the day ended Crocker wired Sacramento to send up another contingent of fifty Chinese. Soon the Central Pacific's agents were rounding up all the available Chinese and forwarding them to the Sierra camps, where the horde swarmed like blue ants over the right-of-way and worked like demons for $40 a month and all the rice they could eat.

Soon nine-tenths of the Central Pacific's work force was Chinese. They kept to themselves and well away from the remaining tenth, mostly Irish, when the latter brooded over their whiskey bottles on the inequities of a life in which a scrawny heathen Chinese was paid as much as a brawny God-fearing white man. As the utterly practical Charles Crocker said of the Chinese, "Wherever we put them, we found them good, and they worked themselves into our favor to such an extent that if we found we were in a hurry for a job of work, it was better to put the Chinese on at once." He hoped to scrape up 15,000 in California and in China itself, and even Governor Stanford allowed that "without them it would be impossible to complete the line in time."

Within six months the Central Pacific had rounded up 2,000 Chinese, and white labor organizations, though they had turned down the work themselves, were raising a clamor of protest. In reply, the Central Pacific propagandists began referring to "the Asiatic Contingent of the Grand Army of Civilization." It was amazing how sheer necessity converted even such sturdy racists as Leland Stanford to a more tolerant attitude. By the end of 1865 the company was contracting with a San Francisco firm which had connections in Canton to import whole boatloads of Chinese recruits. Six months later there were 6,000 at work on the Central Pacific right-of-way, many of them engaged in the effort to bore the quarter-mile Summit Tunnel through the granite backbone of the Sierras. Even the white men laboring at their side were becoming more tolerant, especially since the influx of Chinese resulted in their being promoted to foremen or powdermen. White dignity was thus preserved.

By late in the autumn of 1866 the end of tracks was at Cisco, 94 miles east of Sacramento, above the 6,000-foot level. Snowstorms began swirling through the mountains in early October, but the work continued through the winter, many times at a snaillike pace. Often 15 feet of snow covered the right-of-way. It took five locomotives to push one snowplow through the Sierra drifts, and there were frequent avalanches. One whole camp—men, buildings, and equipment—was swept into a canyon and was buried until spring. At times the snow was so heavy that the work was confined to boring out the Summit Tunnel, where Chinese, shoulder to shoulder, chipped away at the granite and progressed at an average rate of eight inches a day. The granite spine of the summit was so impenetrable that it flattened the tips of chisels and picks. A Swedish chemist named Swanson, who was working at the scene, produced the new explosive called nitroglycerin, so volatile and eccentric that it caused frequent accidents, one of them costing chief foreman Strobridge the sight in one eye. It took a whole year to complete the quarter-mile Summit Tunnel.

In the tunnels [one observer of the winter scene reported] the men worked securely; otherwise they toiled on in the canyons where there was less of snowfall, and great fires constantly burning to keep them from freezing. . . . Men froze or slipped down the steep canyon to their death, other men took their places, and the work went on.

More than one squad a foreman saw as they clung to the hillside, above them the white mountain heads, below them the canyon down 300 feet, perhaps more, deep snow at the bottom, snow above and about them, while they dug and blasted at the frozen earth. Then there would be a shout, a rumbling sound that the watchers knew too well, the impending field of snow would rush down the mountain, a great cloud of snow dust would arise with a sullen roar, and when the air was clear, peering down the canyon they would see a wide spreading of tumbled snow on the white expanse and maybe a man's arm sinking, or a pickax, and the squad was gone. In the spring when the snow melted they might find the bodies; or the freshet might carry them off to beat them to pieces on the boulders. It was but fifteen or twenty Chinamen gone. What mattered?

The Big Four at that point had little time to fret about the welfare or safety of its Chinese work force. They were worrying over reports that the Union Pacific had finally got under way and was hitting its stride across the Nebraska steppe. At the present rate of construction the Big Four might find themselves with a line built only to the Nevada border. The Central Pacific's share of the transcontinental railroad, as ordained by the Pacific Railroad Act, would include only the unprofitable haul over the Sierras unless it could push its way across the Nevada deserts and into Utah.

To gain a larger share of the transcontinental trackage, the Central Pacific's directors would have to arrange more financing, drive its work gangs harder, and lobby in Washington for approval of plans to build as far east as possible. The lobbying effort was placed in the capable hands of Collis P. Huntington, that humorless fellow with the face of a Holbein portrait, who packed a suitcase with a Bible, a set of spare collars, and sheaves of U. S. currency and made himself a familiar in the Congressional cloakroom. A $600,000 bond issue for the Central Pacific was voted by the hitherto reluctant and skeptical citizens of San Francisco.

The human energy required to keep the construction moving over the backbone of the Sierras and down the eastern slopes continued to be supplied by fresh contingents of Chinese immigrants. Without the reinforcements from mainland China, Crocker and his colleagues confessed, the railroad would have been stymied. Ships of the Pacific Mail Steamship Line were pressed into the ferrying service across the Pacific, with the voyage taking from thirty-five to forty days. Most of the recruits were farm boys from the Sinong and Sinwai districts outside the city of Canton. They were rounded up by agents of the San Francisco labor contractors, who advanced their passage money and took it out of their wages with an interest rate as high as 60 percent a year. When they arrived in San Francisco, they were met by representatives of the Chinatown tongs, but even that sponsorship did not spare them their first ordeal in Chinese-hating San Francisco. First they were pawed over by customs agents who were convinced that every Chinese immigrant was an opium smuggler. Once they reached the Embarcadero and the streets around the docks they had to run the gauntlet of white hoodlums constituting themselves as a reception committee charged with demonstrating the glories of a free society. Some members of the San Francisco clergy tried to protect them from such assaults.

77

One of those protectors, the Reverend O. Gibson, described with forthright indignation how the Chinese were first received on American soil, despite the fact they would work on a railroad which would become essential to the California economy:

These Chinamen, with their shaven crown and braided queue, their flowing sleeves, their peculiar trousers, their discordant language, and their utter helplessness, seem to offer special attractions for the practice of those peculiar amenities of life for which the San Francisco hoodlum is notorious. They follow the Chinaman through the streets, howling and screaming after him to frighten him. They catch hold of his queue, and pull him from the wagon. They throw brickbats and missiles at him, and so often these poor heathen reach their quarter of this Christian city covered with wounds and bruises and blood, received at the hands of parties whom Chinamen suppose to be fair representatives of this boasted Christian civilization. Sometimes the police have made a show of protecting the Chinamen, but too frequently the effort had been a heartless one, and the hoodlums have well understood their liberties under our sacred guardians of law and order.

Through the efforts of the Reverend Mr. Gibson and likeminded citizens, the Chinese Protective Society was organized and sent its representatives to meet each immigrant ship with armed guards to convoy the new arrivals to Chinatown.

Fueled by a menu that seemed by Western standards to be exotic and outlandish, including abalone, Oriental fruits and vegetables, salted cabbage, vermicelli, seaweed, bamboo sprouts, and mushrooms, as well as the staples of dried cuttlefish and rice, the swelling army of Chinese laborers toiled through the winter in the cold, thin air of the high Sierras. The new thousands made it possible to work day and night shifts. Many of them lived like moles, boring tunnels below 40-foot drifts. During 1867 there were 12,000 workmen slaving away on the 40-mile stretch from the summit to the eastern base of the mountains.

A group of distinguished Easterners, including Speaker of the House Schuyler Colfax, soon to be Vice President in the first Grant administration, came out to inspect a marvel which was being heralded in the Eastern newspapers. Albert Richardson, who accompanied the party as the New York *Tribune*'s star correspondent, was fascinated by the spectacle of the blue-uniformed Chinese flailing away at the natural obstacles confronting the railroad:

> They were a great army laying siege to Nature in her strongest citadel. The rugged mountains looked like stupendous ant-hills. They swarmed with Celestials, shoveling, wheeling, carting, drilling and blasting rocks and earth, while their dull, moony eyes stared out from under immense basket-hats, like umbrellas. At several dining camps we saw hundreds sitting on the ground, eating soft boiled rice with chop-sticks as fast as terrestrials could with soup-ladles.

In June, 1868, the tracks finally reached the Nevada line. So far the Central Pacific, as the company's auditors claimed twenty years later, had cost $23,000,000; the actual outlay, in gold, was about $14,000,000. Building the railroad, Stanford, Huntington, Crocker, and Hopkins learned, was an exceedingly profitable venture. To forestall any future complaints about the way profits were siphoned through Crocker & Company, the general contractors, a new construction company called Contract & Finance was formed, with the Big Four, naturally, as partners; its books were kept in such an obscure, deliberately entangled condition that tracing the financing of the Central Pacific would have been all but impossible. Even so, the books of the Contract & Finance Company were destroyed by a mysterious but opportune fire in 1873, just after the Crédit Mobilier scandal broke.

There was no doubt that the Big Four was learning the cardinal principle of railroad management even as the first trains began trundling over the California mountains. They saw to it that freight rates on the railroad were substantially higher than those of the old wagon roads, and already the newspaper in a foothill town was groaning: "Enormous prices are charged for freight and it is slow in coming. The only benefits so far experienced from this road are higher freights, not only in Winter but in Summer, than our merchants have ever paid before. The embankments are so miserably built that they give way under the soaking rains of this climate, and long delays are occasioned." Even the friendly Sacramento *Union* was outraged by some of the Central Pacific's practices, especially when it was learned that three large boxes of nitroglycerin were left unguarded in a Sacramento freight shed for ten hours, during which the new superexplosive could have devastated a large part of the town. "The quantity contained in these boxes was enough, of course—had they been roughly handled—to have produced terrible destruction of life and property." The apprehensions of the citizenry at the Central Pacific's rear base were only increased a few weeks later when newspaper dispatches told of how a ship carrying nitro had blown up in Panama, killed fifty persons and destroyed 400 feet of pier. The CP was forced to stop importing the explosive.

An even greater amount of controversy arose over the railroad's determination to push through Congress a bill removing from the Pacific Railroad Act the clauses forbidding the Central Pacific to extend its trackage beyond the California-Nevada line. The Big Four were now determined to build as far as Salt Lake Valley and its richness of resources. In Congress those ambitions clashed with the aims of the Union Pacific when Senator Henry Wilson of Massachusetts, a firm and financially interested supporter of the UP, presented a letter from the eastern railroad protesting that the Central Pacific's determination to press eastward from Nevada would jeopardize negotiations the UP was conducting for a $20,000,000 loan from English, German, and French bankers. Largely because of the lobbying efforts of Collis P. Huntington, the CP's measure was passed, and the restrictions on its construction were lifted.

A UP supporter in the House remarked bitterly to Huntington that there must have been "great corruption and much money used in passing that bill." To which Huntington, who believed that money talked louder than charm or diplomacy, sarcastically replied, "I'm surprised to hear you speak in that way of your associates here. But I will be frank with you, and tell you that I brought over half a million dollars with the intention of using every dollar of it. . . ." Actually, Huntington didn't have a half million available for such purposes, but legislators from Sacramento to Washington, in the golden future, rarely found him unwilling to listen to their pleas that public service was a costly sacrifice.

In the blistering summer of 1868, laboring in clouds of alkali dust, the Central Pacific's Chinese horde was working over the waterless Nevada plain. By then the Union Pacific's construction gangs had passed over the summit of the Rockies at Sherman, Wyoming, and Crocker cracked the whip over his workmen with the slogan "a mile of track for every working day." There was a speedup which could only have been recaptured, perhaps, in a Charlie Chaplin film: picks swinging in a merciless tempo, horse-drawn scrapers and graders working on the double, ties and tracks laid at a frantic pace, other crews building culverts behind them as though driven by fiends. The only reason for that man-killing pace was that for every mile of track eastward, the gentlemen in San Francisco and Sacramento who were heavily interested in the CP's financial destiny were further enriched by hundreds of thousands of dollars. Every time you gaze upon a painting or sculpture in one of the California art galleries endowed by one of the Big Four you may reflect that it was paid for in the sunstrokes, heat exhaustion, ruptured muscles, and broken bones of nameless, faceless men laboring under a desert sun for a little more than $1 a day—and wonder whether the utmost artistic perfection was worth the price paid for it.

Two hazards which cost the lives of so many of the Union Pacific's work force did not confront the Central Pacific's. There was no Hell on Wheels following the CP construction because the largely Chinese workers had no use for red whiskey or white women; they were saving their money, once the barracudalike labor contractors were paid off, to go back to China and buy their own small farms. And there was no Indian menace. The tribesmen along the Central Pacific's right-of-way were a docile lot, Diggers and Snakes in northern California, Piute and Shoshone farther along. Furthermore, the Central Pacific's builders were more cautious about invading Indian territory than the Union Pacific's. They even arranged a treaty with the Piute and Shoshone. As Huntington explained the principal clause, "We gave the old chiefs a pass each, good on the passenger cars, and we told our men to let the common Indians ride on the freight cars whenever they saw fit."

Charles Crocker, known to his Chinese workmen as "Cholly Clocker," drove his construction gangs so hard during 1868 that by the end of the year they had completed 362 miles of track, only

3 short of what Crocker had demanded of them. The mobile army, which Crocker boasted was the largest ever assembled for "the work of civilization," traveled in long strings of boxcars which weekly moved to a new siding.

And the slave-driving pace continued through the early months of 1869. On April 10, Congress was to designate Promontory Point, six miles west of Ogden, Utah, as the juncture with the Union Pacific, but meanwhile, the Central Pacific was determined to drive as far eastward as possible, what with hundreds of thousands of government subsidy dollars to be gained with every mile of track laid. Crocker sent his grading crew far in advance of the track laid so far, 300 miles to the east, in fact, and his surveyors were sighting through their instruments in the Salt Lake Valley. Meanwhile, General Dodge's surveyors were working almost as far west as the California line. It was all a bluff, of course; the two roads would have to meet somewhere or court economic disaster because two transcontinental lines paralleling each other a few miles apart would have been ridiculous. For considerable distances, in fact, the construction crews of the rival roads in Utah were laboring within sight of each other.

During the several weeks before Congress finally stepped in and ordered them to join at Promontory Point, a guerrilla war broke out between the Union Pacific and Central Pacific forces. It became a quasi-racial confrontation between the UP's Irishmen and the CP's Chinese (though about a tenth of the CP's crews, mostly foremen now, were also Irish). The Chinese, though considered a docile species, gave as good as they got.

The two lines came closest together on the eastern slope of the Promontory Range, where at one point the rival, 1,000-man grading crews were only a hundred feet apart. The CP's Chinese were working on higher ground and at first ignored the UP's Irishmen swinging their picks below them. The Irish started the hostilities by bombarding the Chinese with rocks and frozen clods of earth. The Chinese promptly escalated by rolling boulders down on the Union Pacific right-of-way. At night there were occasional gunshots.

With all the dynamite lying around, it was inevitable that the rivalry would become more explosive; no one knew exactly what caused the conflict, certainly not company loyalty, and the top men on both sides, Crocker for the Central Pacific and General Dodge for the Union Pacific, made every effort to halt the hostilities, which could only damage company property. Apparently it was a case of maintaining racial superiority, the UP's Irish resenting the fact that pigtailed coolies were accorded the dignity of doing "white man's work."

As one historian described the short-lived war on the Promontory Range:

> By accident or design, boulders occasionally rolled down from the Central's line, higher on the hillside, while startled Irishmen dropped their picks and scurried out of their paths. The Union's powdermen sometimes laid blasts rather far to the right of their own line, and a thousand graders looked on in innocent wonderment as the earth parted and Chinese and scrapers, horses and wheelbarrows and picks fountained upward. The Orientals regathered their forces, buried the dead, and continued placidly about their business until another blast brought another temporary pause. But the sport ended when a section of the Union's line mysteriously shot skyward and it became the Irishmen's turn to take time out for grave-digging.

In the final incident, in fact, several Irishmen were buried alive.

The great task was ended by the time the first balmy spring breezes blew down from the snow peaks of the Rockies. On May 10, 1869, at Promontory Point, the Central Pacific and the Union Pacific were ceremonially joined, and it became possible—though indubitably hazardous, given the safety records of the various railroads—for a man to board a train in New York City and travel all the way to San Francisco on the dusty plush of the passenger cars.

It was a day of jubilation throughout the United States, the biggest celebration since Lee had surrendered to Grant at Appomattox. Most people could barely grasp the fact that a double strand of iron rails now stretched from coast to coast; the first step toward conquering the continent, all that bleak and hostile space as mysterious and romantic as the interior of Africa, had been taken. But everyone knew that, somehow, it was an accomplishment to be celebrated. More cannon were fired on that May 10, though they were not shotted, than at the Battle of Gettysburg.

83

No city celebrated with greater fervor than Chicago, which now became the railroad capital of the United States; a seven-mile cavalcade of almost every vehicle in the city paraded through the streets of the Loop and was paralleled by fifty tugboats steaming along the lakefront.

The focal point, of course, was Promontory Point, where the symbolic golden spike—actually there were several—was driven to join the rails of the Union Pacific and the Central Pacific. Considering the splendor and the significance of the occasion, the arrangements were somewhat mismanaged and lacked the coordination which had marked the actual construction. It was delayed for hours while the whole nation waited for word to be telegraphed from the shantytown in Utah that the rails had been joined.

The Central Pacific's party, headed by Leland Stanford and Mark Hopkins, with the two supremely practical men of the quadrumvirate, Huntington and Crocker, absenting themselves from what was really only a ritual, arrived on the scene first. Its flag-decked special rolled in early in the morning to find about 500 people, mostly construction workers from the two railroads and the raffish citizens of Promontory Point, waiting for the ceremony to begin. The occasion was to be drenched in alcohol, in the best American tradition, with fourteen tent saloons set up to slake the assembled thirsts and dispense Red Cloud, Red Jacket, Blue Run, and other brands of rotgut for the commoners; the nabobs in the special trains would, of course, bring their own champagne.

Noon passed, and the UP special bearing Thomas C. Durant, General Dodge, the Casement brothers, and other magnificoes was still nowhere in sight. Parties of excursionists from Salt Lake City rolled in and joined the mob in the tent saloons. The telegraph instruments chattered with impatient inquiries up and down the line: When was that damned spike going to be driven? It wasn't until about midafternoon that the UP special finally appeared and disgorged not only the dignitaries, but several companies of the Twenty-first Infantry and the regimental band.

Three photographers set up their cumbersome, wet-plate cameras to record the historic scene, the saloons were emptied of their patrons, and everyone waited for the ceremony to begin.

There was a last-minute hitch caused by a final dispute between the brass hats of the two railroads, a contretemps more worthy of rival tenors claiming center stage. Darius O. Mills, a San Francisco financier, as spokesman for the enormously self-important president Leland Stanford, declared that the final spike should be driven by the Central Pacific president. At length he pointed out that Stanford was the highest official present, Durant being merely the *vice*-president of the Union Pacific, that the Central Pacific had begun its construction earlier and was the first to be incorporated. On behalf of Durant, who was huddled in a black velvet coat against the chill wind, General Dodge asserted that the Union Pacific was much the longer road and more important to the national destiny. "At one time," wrote a correspondent from the San Francisco *News-Letter*, "the Union Pacific positively refused connection, and told the Central Pacific people they could do as they liked, and there would be no joint celebration."

While the nation held its breath, the matter was finally adjudicated. Stanford and Durant would each drive in a golden spike. First, however, a clergyman present to sanctify the occasion—his presence was as inevitable as that of the tent saloons—delivered an invocation so lengthy and comprehensive that his listeners were certain he had recited most of American history since the Pilgrims landed, all of it demonstrating that God smiled more enthusiastically on American endeavors than those of other nations. "We have got the praying done," one telegrapher flashed the word up and down the line. "The spike is about to be presented."

Finally, with the slightly infirm strokes of men unaccustomed to the sledgehammers which had built their railroads, Stanford and Durant drove home the golden spikes, which were quickly removed and replaced by iron ones the moment the ceremony was ended. Otherwise, it would have taken a company of infantry to guard the sacred symbols. One UP locomotive and another CP engine slowly steamed toward each other and gently bumped each other's cowcatcher, a moment more or less immortalized by a scrap of verse written by Bret Harte for his *Overland Monthly* in San Francisco:

What was it the engines said,
Pilots touching—head to head?

Nobody really cared what the engines said, but all present were required to listen to lengthy speechifying, without which the occasion would hardly have been legitimate, certainly not typical.

Stanford, being a politician, was by far the most garrulous of the orators present. After expanding on the glories of that triumph of construction, he launched into an attack on the federal government for having "interfered" with the building operations. Millions in the taxpayers' money had been dumped into the CP and UP treasuries, and many private fortunes had been made through the diverse methods of siphoning off that money, but Leland Stanford was not in a grateful mood. In a final burst of arrogance, he declared that the subsidies given the Central Pacific by the government were more of a hindrance than a help.

That was too much for the Casement brothers, who had bossed the Union Pacific's construction and knew as well as anyone that neither railroad would or could have laid a mile of track without the government dole. Dan Casement climbed on the shoulders of his brother Jack, rearing above the throng, and shouted at Stanford: "Mister President, if this here subsidy has been such a big detriment to the building of your road, I move you, sir, that it be returned to the Government with your compliments."

Stanford turned puce with outrage and dismounted from the platform. (For years he would maintain that both the government and the American people were not sufficiently grateful to him and his fellow moguls for having built the Central Pacific. Once at a dinner party in his San Francisco home he expanded on this theme and detailed the countless sacrifices he and his partners had made to provide California with a rail link to the East. He was particularly indignant about the government's insistence on being repaid money it had lent the railroad, and one could almost picture him and other members of the Big Four as waifs threatened with mortgage foreclosure by Uncle Sam. It did not pass unnoticed by his listeners that the old crocodile was

snuffling into his beard while surrounded by the lavish appoint-
ments of his dining room, including a vase on the sideboard
valued at $100,000. One of his guests, Justice Stephen J. Field,
whispered to his neighbor, "You need only look around the room
to see how shamefully these gentlemen have been treated by an
ungenerous and ungrateful government.")

The principals in the ceremony retired to Stanford's private
Pullman car for a late but elaborate lunch washed down by
vintage wines. Meanwhile, the hoi polloi were treated to coarser
food and more ardent spirits, with the Central Pacific picking up
the bills totaling $2,200, which brought an awesome amount of
buffalo humps and cheap whiskey in the year 1869.

Along toward dusk, with Stanford and Durant each clutching
his golden spike, the two special trains backed away from each
other and headed back to New York and San Francisco, leaving
Promontory Point to the most glorious blowout in its otherwise
drab history. That night, with the dignitaries and praying parsons out of the way, there was a torchlight parade followed by a
banquet and a grand ball—and so much free booze it threatened
to wash away the newly laid railroad tracks. There were other
celebrations, complete with fireworks, in cities and towns
throughout the United States that night, but Promontory Point
could claim the highest alcoholic content of any of them. Quite
unnoticed in all the jubilation was the widow of Theodore Judah,
who locked her door against any callers that day in her hometown
of Greenfield, Massachusetts. "It seemed to me," she wrote, "as
though the spirit of my brave husband descended upon me, and
together we were there [at Promontory Point] unseen, unheard of
men."

The hangover would afflict more than the grubby citizens who
picked themselves off the board floors of Promontory Point on the
grim morning of May 11. Its symptoms, approaching the stage of
delirium tremens, were national in scope and severely afflicted
what orators gravely called the "body politic." Skeletons were
about to come clattering out of a dozen Washington closets, and
some promising political careers were soon to be tarred by scandal. Bribe takers, of course, have always suffered more than bribe
givers.

The nation would gradually learn the cost of building railroads at the frantic pace dictated by the compulsion of builders to grab all they could before the official guardians of the public treasury were prodded into wakefulness. So hasty had been the construction, so shaky the roadbeds in many places, so unshored the embankments against the possibility of washouts, so ramshackle the bridges thrown over the mountain streams that there was a long and tragic succession of accidents on both railroads. It was almost as risky traveling out west a century ago as it is today on one of the freeways radiating from Los Angeles.

For the railroad magnates, however, their creations continued to prove immensely profitable. Not to ordinary investors, who were cleaned out time after time, but to the insiders and manipulators who controlled the financial workings of the railroads. The companies were simply hollowed out by corporate looters using methods then just close enough to being legal to keep the railroad presidents and their associates out of prison. Glenn Chesney Quiett analyzed the technique some years ago:

> Lawyers, business geniuses, and financiers combined their talents to create a complex financial structure for the railroads of the country which permitted the insiders to reap enormous profits and often to squeeze out other investors for large losses. The owners of the larger railroads controlled smaller roads which they leased to the larger at exorbitant rentals, turning surplus earnings into deficits. The directors also often made it a point to own the companies that made repairs on the railroads, built and owned the bridges, operated the connecting ferries, sold the coal and supplies; and every operation was apt to turn profits into their pockets. New issues of stocks and bonds flowed forth from the printing presses in bewildering variety, part being sold to investors, part being freely bestowed on the insiders, with the result that the capital structures, upon which interest and dividends had to be paid, were highly inflated. To meet the charges on these watered securities, freight-rates had to be raised to inordinate heights, farmers and producers suffered, and the consumer had to pay the bill. When the bill grew so staggeringly heavy that it could no longer be borne, one after another of the railroads went through bankruptcy, receivership and reorganization. . . .

In the popular mind, however, this deliberate mismanagement of the railroads was a much smaller crime than that perpetrated under the code name of Crédit Mobilier. Rapacity was expected of entrepreneurs and businessmen, but the country had not yet grown completely cynical about the motives of politicians, nor was it willing to view complacently the spectacle of politicians making off with their boodle.

By later standards the Crédit Mobilier was not the grossest case of venality in American political history. Because of the incredibly muddled state of the Union Pacific's financial records, it was impossible to say just how much the insiders siphoned off in inflated construction costs through contracts awarded the Crédit Mobilier. For many years it was generally believed that the actual cost of the UP from Omaha to Promontory Point was approximately $50,000,000 but that $94,000,000 had been charged through corruptly arranged contracts. Painstaking investigation in later years has whittled down the $44,000,000 in "juice" to between $13,000,000 and $16,500,000. In any case, a great deal of money went into the wrong hands.

Even the public, innocent as it was of such matters a century ago, when high finance, like tiger hunting, was a preserve of the wealthy, began to suspect there might be something offbeat about the financing of the Union Pacific when Crédit Mobilier declared its first dividend—100 percent!—in December, 1867.

Just a month later the public would have been even more scandalized if any of its representatives had been allowed to attend a very private meeting of the chief stockholders of the Crédit Mobilier in a guarded parlor of the Fifth Avenue Hotel in New York. This was a select group. Anyone could buy Union Pacific stock, but Crédit Mobilier was a juicy proposition reserved for the manipulators and those members of Congress who could be expected to use their influence on behalf of the company in which they had more than a rooting interest.

That early January day in 1868 the bigwigs who owned Crédit Mobilier were sorely perplexed. They had only 650 shares of stock left to distribute, and three interested parties—Thomas Durant, Oakes Ames, and Henry S. McComb, of Wilmington, Delaware—all were putting forth vociferous claims. Both Ames and Durant asserted that they had made promises to members of

Congress which had to be satisfied. McComb, a vindictive man with an unsavory reputation stemming from Civil War contract scandals, insisted that 375 shares had been promised to him three years earlier. No one could remember any such promise made to McComb, and president Sidney Dillon remarked that his claim was "so base and fraudulent that, in presenting it, he had shown himself to be a scoundrel unworthy to associate with gentlemen." The stockholders agreed with that indictment, turned down McComb's demand, and split the remaining stock between Ames and Durant. McComb went away muttering threats which everyone—mistakenly—laughed off. They would all remember and rue the name of Henry S. McComb.

Crédit Mobilier became more odoriferous with each passing year. One year after that fateful stockholders' meeting, Charles Francis Adams, Jr., the grandson and great-grandson of two American Presidents and himself a member of the Massachusetts Board of Railroad Commissioners (and, ironically enough, a future president of the Union Pacific), published an article titled "The Pacific Railroad Ring" in a periodical of small but influential circulation. It blew the whistle, but it was largely ignored because the nation just then was enthralled by the approaching juncture of the rails in Utah. Crédit Mobilier, Adams wrote, was only:

> another name for the Pacific Railroad ring. The members of it are in Congress; they are trustees for the bondholders; they are directors; they are stockholders; they are contractors; in Washington they vote the subsidies, in New York they receive them, upon the plains they expend them, and in the "Crédit Mobilier" they divide them. . . . Ever-shifting characters, they are ubiquitous; they receive money into one hand and pay it into the other as a contractor. Humanly speaking, the whole thing seems to be a species of thimble-rig, with difference from the ordinary arrangement, that whereas "the little joker" is never found under the thimble which may be turned up, in this case he is sure to be found, turn up which thimble you may. Under one name or another, a ring of a few persons is struck at whatever point the Union Pacific is approached.

For three more years the scandal quietly simmered, with the Democrats, riven by Civil War issues and long to be powerless in

90

the national sense, occasionally and gingerly trying to lift the lid on the brew.

The lid, finally, was blown off. Henry S. McComb began litigation in Pennsylvania, where Crédit Mobilier was incorporated, against the insiders' company over those shares he claimed to have been promised. His attorneys introduced letters from Oakes Ames, not the most discreet of men, in which the latter discussed placing the Crédit Mobilier shares among members of Congress, "where they will do us the most good." That phrase was to be used time after time in belaboring those involved in the conspiracy. McComb also included in his suit a list of Congressmen whom, he claimed, Ames had mentioned as prospective subscribers to the Crédit Mobilier stock.

Early in September, just when Grant was campaigning for his second term in the White House, the New York *Sun*, by no coincidence a Democratic organ, picked up the story and emblazoned it under the headline: THE KING OF FRAUDS: HOW THE CREDIT MOBILIER BOUGHT ITS WAY INTO CONGRESS. It included the list McComb mentioned in his suit, every name of which represented a man running for reelection. All, of course, denied any connection with the Crédit Mobilier, but many later were forced to recant their denials.

The new Congress, under the pressure of public opinion, was forced to investigate the charges. A select committee in the House and another in the Senate began taking months of testimony on which of their members had bought Crédit Mobilier stock (at $100 par, when it was worth much more). The men who suffered the most from that double-pronged inquiry were Oakes Ames and Representative James Brooks of New York, who was one of the government's directors on the UP board. The House committee at first recommended that both men be expelled, then opted for a vote of censure, in which the whole House concurred. Brooks died of a heart attack a few days later. Ames went home to Massachusetts a broken man and died of a stroke. They were by no means the chief malefactors, but they were made to suffer the most, first because the Republicans needed scapegoats to protect more eminent figures, and second because Ames, in effect, had testified for the prosecution against those colleagues who had bought Crédit Mobilier stock. Most heinous of political crimes, he had named names when, by the ethos of practical politicians, he should have uttered vague generalities. As Claude Bowers (*The Tragic Era*) would write, the Congressional censures were voted to warn "corrupt politicians against turning state's evidence."

That mordant view would seem to have been justified by the results of the investigations. No one else was censured, as might be expected of a political body sitting in judgment on itself, but some hitherto hallowed reputations were severely damaged. Speaker of the House James G. Blaine was cleared, but the taint would contribute to the failure of his future candidacy for the Presidency. Three Vice Presidents were more indelibly stained by their participation in the Crédit Mobilier shareout. The political career of Schuyler Colfax of Ohio, Vice President in the first Grant administration, was ruined. Henry Wilson, Vice President in the second Grant administration, retained his place as presiding officer of the Senate. Levi Morton, despite Ames' testimony, was to serve as Vice President under Benjamin Harrison. The reputation of Representative James A. Garfield of Ohio suffered from Ames' testimony, too, particularly since the House investigating committee accepted Ames' word over his, yet he would be elected the twentieth President of the United States in 1881. Since he was assassinated within months after taking office, it might have been better if the electorate had demonstrated a longer memory of the Crédit Mobilier scandals. Scores of lesser political figures were involved, and perhaps the career of a possible future President was blighted. The financial and industrial magnates equally guilty of corrupting or being corrupted not only escaped any sort of censure for their actions but were regarded with a sneaking admiration for their "smartness," an attribute much valued in what had become known as the Flash Age.

Neither the amount nor the method of stealage involved in the railroad-building operations was sensational by modern standards, perhaps, but the whole affair, in its total effect, would contribute heavily toward the decline in public morality. Nothing would equal it until the Teapot Dome scandal a half century later. Just four years after the first transcontinental railroad was completed, its public image was damaged beyond repair; it had become a synonym for the collaboration between conscienceless businessmen and corruptible politicians.

4.

A Frenzy of Expectation

The iron key has been found to unlock our golden treasures, and hopeful anticipation of better days are prevalent among the people. With railroads come population, industry and capital, and with them come the elements of prosperity and greatness to Montana.

—Montana newspaper in 1875.

E VEN in the soberest and most calculating of men, the expansion of the Western railroads, with other transcontinental lines soon paralleling the Union Pacific-Central Pacific, aroused fever dreams of anticipation. In the seventies the prosperity of the country depended as much on the railroads and their continued growth as it would later on the automobile industry. Urban growth was directly related to rail service; likewise the development of industrial and agricultural enterprises. That close affinity between the railroads and national prosperity seemed dangerous to only a few of the most cautious types, though it would become strikingly apparent in 1873, just two years after the Crédit Mobilier scandals indicated the railroads were equally menacing to public morality.

The possibilities of opening up virtually two-thirds of the continent aroused hallucinations and created that most dangerous of psychological climates, overexpectation. It seemed to the promoters of that vision that nothing they hoped for could be regarded as too grandiose. Their viewpoint, in a sense, was European. They looked on the American West as something that could be converted into a western Europe, which it never could

93

and never can be; climate and geography, not to mention topography, were against them. America and Europe share the temperate zone, but the American weather is harsher and more violent, and much of the West more closely resembles the steppes of Central Asia than the gentle conformation of Europe (though interrupted by the Alpine ranges) from the North Sea to the Carpathians. It was simply not true, though it would take many decades for the truth to be recognized, that a state like Montana could become another France. The "wide open spaces" so often hymned were also parched and sterile and afflicted by the most violent extremes of searing summers and sub-Arctic winters. Men looked west and fancied they saw the baroque skyline of a Dresden limned against the horizon, but what they got was the smelter stacks of Butte; imagined a Paris rising from the grasslands and got an Omaha. For an America intent on industrializing itself within a quarter century, it may not have seemed such a bad bargain.

None was more deliriously optimistic, more afflicted by the prophecy syndrome than Jay Cooke, head of the great Philadelphia banking house bearing his name. One might have expected the most longheaded calculation from a Philadelphia banker, particularly one who had become so preeminent in American finance that he handled the government bonds which paid for the North's share of the Civil War. Strangely enough for a banker, he was cursed by an ebullience which seemed out of place in the gray precincts of a countinghouse. Ten years after his unguarded optimism about the prospects of Western railroading had brought about the panic and severe depression of 1873, the historian Eugene V. Smalley wrote:

> . . . his great defect was a want of caution and foresight. He failed to understand that alternate expansion and contraction is the law of finance, and that the business of the world progresses like the frog in the well of the old arithmetic problem, which leaped up three feet and fell back two. Mr. Cooke's schemes were based on the delusive idea that the pendulum of trade and finance always swings upward. He did not make provision for the inevitable downward swing.

Cooke in 1869 became fascinated by the prospects of the projected Northern Pacific Railroad, which would run from St. Paul to Puget Sound, about as bleak and unpeopled a slice of territory as could have been selected. That year he agreed to sell $100,000,000 worth of bonds to finance the Northern Pacific, a gigantic effort for those times, based mainly on his belief that he could unload the issue in Europe. A Cooke partner was dispatched to sell the Paris branch of the Rothschilds in the venture, but was turned away emptyhanded. Cooke himself met two German bankers in Washington who agreed to form a European syndicate to handle $50,000,000 worth of the issue, but that possibility collapsed when the Franco-Prussian War broke out.

That left the American market which, given its size at the time, was already overstocked with railroad issues. Cooke, however, utilized the nascent arts of advertising and publicity to boom his Northern Pacific bonds. In daily and weekly newspapers, magazines and direct-mail circulars, with paid advertisements and editorials published on threats of withdrawing that advertising, he made the Northern Pacific a household name and the Pacific Northwest a paradise waiting to be claimed and exploited. "For many months," a contemporary historian wrote, "it was almost impossible to take up a newspaper in any part of the Northern States without finding something in it concerning the Northern Pacific. Prominent statesmen and army officers wrote letters describing the merits of the country the road was to traverse. Generals, members of Congress, Governors of States, and the Vice President of the United States gave the weight of their endorsement to the project." This barrage of publicity proclaimed that the Northwest, the territories of Washington and Oregon, would provide bumper crops of grain every year, that the forests of Washington alone would yield more timber than those of all the rest of the world, that the mountains were rich in all kinds of precious minerals, and that warm Pacific winds made the winters almost as balmy as Florida's. Cooke's publicity men may have gone a little too far, because soon the Northwest was being referred to as "Jay Cooke's banana belt."

From 1870 to 1872 his banking house managed to peddle enough of the bond issue to build about 600 miles of railroad. As always, construction costs had been greatly underestimated.

95

Those 600 miles cost $30,000,000, which took the railroad up to Bismarck, North Dakota, and left Montana, Idaho, and Washington still to be traversed. In other words, the Northern Pacific in 1873 ended up in the no-man's-land of Dakota Territory, and there was no more money in the Northern Pacific treasury to proceed with the construction, a situation which a saddened investor memorialized in verse parodying Tennyson:

> Broke, broke, broke,
> By railway loans, J. C.
> And I would that my heart could utter
> The thoughts that arise in me.

What resulted was one of the more horrendous crashes in American financial history. Money had become tight, and Cooke couldn't sell enough bonds to finance the completion of the railroad. The Northern Pacific was forced to go into receivership. In September, 1873, Jay Cooke was compelled to close the doors of his establishment, the mightiest until the rise of the House of Morgan. The panic spread overnight to New York, where prices plunged on the stock exchange, then to the rest of the country. Western emigration practically came to a halt as one of the landmark depressions gripped the country. Out on the sodhouse frontier of Kansas and Nebraska, settlers who had staked everything on the promises of the railroad builders suffered even more intensely than the hundreds of thousands of unemployed in the Eastern cities; they had just survived a plague of grasshoppers and army worms and had lived through a series of Indian uprisings, and now they died by the hundreds of their privations. It would be a long time before any glamor was attached to the designation of "pioneer."

Such headlong methods of railroad financing as that which ruined Jay Cooke were a common but not inevitable feature of the building of the Western roads. As evidence of more conservative methods there was the relatively stodgy history of the Chicago, Burlington & Quincy, which moved west at the ruminative pace of the inchworm. It took almost three decades, in fact, to expand from its beginnings as the Michigan Central, move across northern Illinois, and extend itself through Iowa and

Nebraska. It finally reached its Denver terminus in 1882, but only after each stage of its progress had been carefully plotted. The cautiousness with which the Burlington road was built into one of the major carriers, with little or no bilking of its investors, was largely due to the character of its guiding force, John Murray Forbes, a longheaded Boston financier, and his brother R. Bennet Forbes. The Forbes brothers had entered the China trade in their youth, had won the confidence of the mercantile mandarins of Canton, had been not too scrupulous to avoid profitable contact with the opium traffic (this was an essential for American and British traders who hoped to prosper in the treaty ports), and had come home with the seed money for great enterprises. Some of that slightly tainted profit from their Chinese ventures went into the Michigan Central, of which John Murray Forbes became the first president in 1846. During the next four decades Forbes and his equally cautious associates built the Burlington into a solid institution which belied the necessity for the more hectic methods of their rivals.

Not even the Crédit Mobilier scandals and the depression of '73 directly caused by reckless public support of the railroad promoters' fantasies could quench the enthusiasm or entirely deflate the enormous hopes of those who foresaw endless expansion in the Western territories. The town boomers moved right behind the railroad construction crews, and every man of ambition saw himself as the founding father of a future metropolis. Every buffalo wallow and trading post saw itself expanding into a city, if only a railroad could be lured in to its direction.

Long before the frenzy abated, its more grandiose aspects became the subject of satire. As early as 1871, with the town-building mania just rising toward its peak, it was satirized on, of all unlikely places, the floor of Congress. One January day the Honorary James Proctor Knott of Kentucky rose to offer a few remarks on a bill to bestow a large grant on a hopeful enterprise titled the St. Croix & Bayfield Railroad with its terminus in Duluth. The thrust of its proponents' arguments was that Duluth would thus become the Byzantium of the Great Lakes.

Off the cuff, with his Southern mellifluousness laced with gall and wormwood, Representative Knott delivered what has always been regarded as a masterpiece of Congressional humor as he mocked the pretensions of the railroad promoters and town boomers. In a mock-orotund sermon, he devastated one of the brightest sectors of the contemporary version of the American Dream and took less than ten minutes to do the demolition job:

Years ago, when I first heard that there was somewhere in the vast *terra incognita*, somewhere in the bleak regions of the great Northwest, a stream of water known to the nomadic inhabitants of the neighborhood as the River St. Croix, I became satisfied that the construction of a railroad from that raging torrent to some point in the civilized world was essential to the happiness and prosperity of the American people. I felt instinctively that the boundless resources of that prolific region of sand and shrubbery would never be fully developed without a railroad constructed at the expense of the government. . . .

Duluth! Duluth! The word fell on my ear with a peculiar and indescribable charm, like the gentle murmur of a low fountain stealing forth in the midst of roses, or the soft, sweet accents of an angel's whisper in the bright, joyous dream of sleeping innocence. . . . But where, sirs, was Duluth? Never in all my limited reading had my vision been gladdened by seeing the celestial word in print. I rushed to the library and examined all the maps I could find, but I could find Duluth nowhere. I knew it was bound to exist, in the very nature of things; that the symmetry and perfection of our planetary system would be incomplete without it. . . . I was convinced that the greatest calamity that ever befell the benighted nations of the ancient world was in their having passed away without a knowledge of the actual existence of Duluth; that their fabled Atlantis was, in fact, but another name for Duluth; that the golden orchard of the Hesperides was but a poetical synonym for the beer-gardens in the vicinity of Duluth. . . .

Then, sir, there is the climate of Duluth, unquestionably the most salubrious and delightful to be found anywhere on God's earth. Now, I have always been under the impression that in the region around Duluth it was cold enough for at least nine months of the year to freeze the smokestack off a locomotive. But I see it represented on this map [he displayed a map supplied by the Minnesota legislature] that Duluth is situated exactly halfway between the latitudes of Paris and Venice, so that the gentlemen who have inhaled the exhilarating air of the one or basked in the golden sunlight of the other may see at a glance that Duluth must be a place of untold delights, a terrestrial paradise. . . .

As to the commercial resources of Duluth, sir, they are simply illimitable and inexhaustible, as is shown on this map. . . . Look at it, sir, do you not see from these broad, brown lines drawn around this immense territory that the enterprising inhabitants of Duluth intend some day to inclose it all in one vast corral, so that its commerce will be bound to go there whether it would or not? And here, sir, I find on the map that within convenient distance are the Piegan Indians which, of all the many accessories to the glory of Duluth, I consider by far the most estimable. For, sir, I have been told that when the smallpox breaks out among the women and children of that famous tribe, as it sometimes does, they afford the finest subjects in the world for the strategical experiments of any enterprising military hero who desires to improve himself in the noble art of war. . . .

When Representative Knott of Kentucky sat down, with the House still echoing with the roars of laughter his speech had brought, not only had he won an intramural fame as one of that body's rare humorists, but he had punctured the grandiose claims of railroad promoters and town boomers. Petitions for land grants thereafter were considered in the mordant illumination of his speech. After 1871, in fact, Congress became increasingly wary of granting land and subsidies regardless of the pressure of railroad lobbyists. Congress was becoming aware, too, of how the railroads played one settlement against the other in raising funds for construction, a practice in some cases amounting to extortion. A delegate to the California Constitutional Convention disclosed just how the Central Pacific worked on the hopes of various towns which were competing for attention from the railroad:

They start out their railway track and survey their line near a thriving village. They go to the most prominent citizens of that village and say, "If you will give us so many thousand dollars we will run through here; if you do not we will run by," and in every instance where the subsidy was not granted, that course was taken, and the effect was just as they said, to kill off the little town. Here was the town of Paradise, in Stanislaus County; because they did not get what they wanted, they established another town four miles from there. In every instance where they were refused a subsidy, in money, unless their terms were acceded to, they have established a depot near to the place, and have always frozen them out.

In similar fashion the Union Pacific played off the aspirations of Omaha and Council Bluffs to become the eastern terminus. President Lincoln had designated Council Bluffs as the terminus, but the Union Pacific circumvented him, having developed large real estate interests in Omaha through George Francis Train's organization of the Crédit Mobilier's sister company, the Crédit Foncier. And for years Cheyenne was virtually a company town in the UP's fiefdom because it had been favored over other claimants for the repair shops.

Just how towns could blossom almost overnight through the railroads' patronage was strikingly recorded by William A. Bell, a young Englishman and a Cambridge graduate who accompanied the Kansas Pacific's survey parties as a photographer. Later he published a book on his observations which won him a fellowship in the Royal Geographical Society. He wrote:

> Wholesale town-making may not be a romantic theme or one capable of being made very attractive to the general reader; but it is the great characteristic of this part of our route, and is only to be seen to perfection along the line of these great railways. On the Platte, where the central line across the continent often advances at the rate of two miles a day, town-making is reduced to a system. The depot at the end of the line is only moved every two or three months; and as rich valleys are far scarcer in this section of country than in Kansas, the town usually moves also, while nothing remains to mark the spot where thousands lived, but in a station, a name and a few acres of bare earth. Last winter, Cheyenne was the terminal depot on this route, and increased in size to 5,000 inhabitants. A man I met at Denver, who had just come from Cheyenne, told me that while he was standing on the railway platform, a long freight train arrived, laden with frame houses, boards, furniture, palings, old tents, and all the rubbish that makes up one of these mushroom cities. The guard jumped off his van, and seeing some friends on the platform, called out with a flourish, "Gentlemen, here's Julesburg." The next train brought some other city, to lose for ever its identity in the great Cheyenne. . . .

100

Relocation and instant urban renewal obviously had been pioneered a century before it was the cause of much greater anguish. Whole towns were carted around in nervous anticipation of becoming a great commercial center, always at the whim of the railroad. A town builder could never be quite sure that his prospects would not be swept away overnight, especially since many of such hopeful ventures were based on the location of railroad repair shops and the employment they would provide. William F. Cody, later better known as Buffalo Bill, was the victim of the Kansas Pacific's caprice during his brief career as a town promoter. He had slaughtered a record number of buffalo under contract to a Kansas City firm which provided the meat for the Kansas Pacific's construction crews before deciding to establish the town of Rome, Kansas, on Big Creek, a mile from Fort Hays. Cody and his partner staked out town lots and watched while hundreds of settlers appeared with the contemporary version of prefabricated housing, "balloon-frame" buildings, which could be set up and hauled away with great rapidity—a necessary form of construction in the days when towns kept chasing after the railroads.

One day Cody returned from a hunt to find his town of Rome literally vanishing before his eyes: "The town was being torn down and carted away. The balloon-frame buildings were coming apart section by section. I could see at least a hundred teams and wagons carting lumber, furniture, and everything that made up the town over the prairies to the eastward." Rome moved just one mile and overnight metamorphosed into Hays City because, as Cody learned, a land agent for the Kansas Pacific had decided that that was where the railroad's repair shops would be located.

As William Bell learned, there was a lot of money being made by speculators selling town lots on the premise that the railroad would bring everlasting prosperity:

> Thousands of dollars, are daily won and lost all along the line by speculating in town lots. A spot is chosen in advance of the line, and is marked off into streets, blocks, and town lots, sometimes by the railway company, sometimes by an independent land company. As the rails approach it, the fun begins, and up goes the price

101

of the lots, higher and higher. At last it becomes the terminal depot—the starting-point for the western trade—where the goods are transferred from the freight vans to the ox trains, and sent off to Denver, to Santa Fe, Fort Union, and other points. It then represents a scene of great activity, and quickly rises to the zenith of its glory. Town lots are bought up on all sides to build accommodation for the traders, teamsters, camp-followers, and loafers, who seem to drop from the skies. This state of things, however, lasts for only a time. The terminal depot must be moved forward, and the little colony will be left to its own resources. If the district has good natural advantages, it will remain; if not, it will disappear, and the town lots will fall to nothing. . . .

One of the "mushroom" railroad towns which sprang up almost before his astonished eyes was Salina, Kansas, located on a grassy plain between the Smoky Hill River and the Saline Fork. The main street was a river of axle-deep mud, all but impassable:

On each side of this main street were wooden houses, of all sizes and in all shapes of embryonic existence. Not a garden fence or tree anywhere to be seen. Still paddling about in the mud, we came to the most advanced part of the city, and here with found three billiard saloons, each with two tables, and the everlasting bar. . . . Opposite was a row of substantial stores, having their fronts painted. The builder here was evidently a rash speculator. He did not look upon Salina as a Julesburg, but intended to tide over the stage of depression. . . . On each side was a hotel, at the door of which—it being just mid-day—the landlord was ringing furiously a great bell to announce to the inhabitants that dinner was ready. And what a dinner!—fried fish, fried mutton, fried eggs, fried mush (a great luxury), fried potatoes and fried pudding—all swimming in grease; bad coffee without milk, dough cakes without butter, and muddy water out of dirty glasses. . . .

From young Mr. Bell's queasy recollections, it is apparent that Western cooking, in which a skillet and a pail of grease were the essentials of any recipe, was one of the principal hazards faced by the pioneers.

Speculation in town lots had become feverish by the time the Union Pacific and Kansas Pacific had built their right of ways through Kansas. Land boomers were making small fortunes in

102

every likely spot along the way; the four-month-old town of Wyandotte was selling building lots for $1,800. Albert Richardson of the New York *Tribune* came upon the hamlet of Osawakee when 100,000 acres of public land were distributed with more haste than legality, and observed that "David's covetousness for the wife of Uriah was no stronger than the lust of the frontier Yankees for territory." Two thousand men had rushed in for the wholesale land grabbing. Theoretically the land was sold to the highest bidder, but actually it was parceled out at $1.50 to $4.50 an acre. "The 'settler,' who lived fifty or a hundred miles away, had built a cabin or driven a stake upon his claim, and could therefore swear that he was a bona fide resident! The constructive squatters respected each others' rights and protected their own. The first man who ventured to bid against one of them was instantly shot down; so there was no further competition. Many sold their newly-acquired lands to speculators at double the cost. . . ."

Richardson warned, however, that speculating in the jerry-built and highly mobile towns along the railroads was a high-risk venture, particularly for the sheltered easterner inclined to believe the eupeptic prose of the promoters' brochures:

On paper all these towns were magnificent. Their superbly lithographed maps adorned the walls of every place of resort. The stranger studying one of these fancied the New Babylon surpassed only by its namesake of old. Its great parks, opera houses, churches, universities, railroad depots and steamboat landings made New York and St. Louis insignificant in comparison. But if the newcomer had the unusual wisdom to visit the prophetic city before purchasing lots, he learned the difference between fact and fancy. The town might be composed of twenty buildings; or it might not contain a single human habitation. In most cases, however, he would find one or two rough cabins, with perhaps a tent and an Indian canoe on the river in front of the "levee." Anything was marketable. Shares in interior towns of one or two shanties sold readily for a hundred dollars. Wags proposed an Act of Congress reserving some land for farming purposes before the whole Territory should be divided into city lots. Towns enough were started for a State containing four millions of people.

103

The collapse of each projected city, hastened by the panic and depression of '73, meant the ruin of thousands of hopefuls out West and back East; nothing like the town-building craze would be seen until the Florida real estate boom of the 1920's, which ended in a disaster of equal proportions. "It was not a swindle," Richardson pointed out, confessing that he had been caught up in the lunacy himself and had borrowed $150 to buy a quarter section near Osawakee, "but a mania. The speculators were quite as insane as the rest. . . . When the collapse came, it was like the crushing of an egg-shell. The shares had no more market value than town lots on the moon. Cities died, inhabitants deserted, houses were torn down."

Even such a naturally endowed city as Denver, with its claims to being the commercial center of the Rockies, had a difficult time maintaining its supremacy when it appeared that building a main-line railroad through the city would present insurmountable difficulties. The citizens had enlisted Jim Bridger, the famous scout, to find a route directly over the mountains, and he came back proclaiming the feasibility of the Berthoud Pass, over which a wagon road was quickly built.

The question was whether a railroad could climb such steep mountain grades. Under pressure which Denver interests brought to bear on the Union Pacific's board of directors, General Dodge was persuaded to attempt finding a route to bring the UP's main line through Denver instead of Cheyenne. Dodge himself led the survey party late in 1866. He had ruled out the Berthoud Pass as too rugged for railroad engineering in its present state and led a party over the Hog Back. Dodge and his companions struggled into a snowstorm so bad the mules in the pack train foundered. They had to abandon their mule train in the mountains and finally found shelter in the Boulder Valley. This experience provided an excuse for the UP to rule out Denver. The route through Cheyenne was more than 100 miles longer, but the Crédit Mobilier was receiving a subsidy of $48,000 a mile from the government; the Cheyenne route enriched the company treasury by half a million, and Denver, despite its natural attributes, was abandoned to the fate of the railroadless town.

It just showed what could happen when a town was cut off from rail service. Early in 1867 many Denver businessmen were closing down their establishments and joining the rush to Cheyenne. It looked as though Denver, a few months earlier so certain it would expand as the trading center of the mountain states, was doomed to wither away. Business, it was observed, was rushing past 100 miles to the north and Denver's 7,000 citizens wondered whether they weren't living in a future ghost town. The *Rocky Mountain News* protested, a trifle too shrilly, that "this Cheyenne excitement is *not* going to kill off Denver."

The newspaper was moved to greater indignation a short time later when Cheyenne moved to carve Wyoming Territory out of Colorado and the Dakotas, and its Union Pacific sponsors, with all their clout in Washington, pushed an enabling act through Congress. "Colorado," the *News* roared, "objects to submitting to the slicing up of its territory for the mere convenience of a town on wheels [Cheyenne] which last fall was at North Platte, this spring at Julesburg, this fall at Cheyenne, and will be next fall at Rocky Mountain City or some other point on the Laramie Plains." Denver's next-best hope of a rail connection was the Kansas Pacific, which was building slowly westward to the south of the Union Pacific. That possibility exploded when a KP official appeared in Denver and demanded that the city contribute $2,000,000 toward the project, it would have meant a levy of almost $300 for every man, woman, and child then living in Denver.

Late in 1867 the more aggressive citizens of Denver formed the Board of Trade and pledged themselves to build their own rail link to the lowlands, if necessary. For inspirational purposes, George Francis Train, that spellbinding prophet, the exponent of power through positive thinking who had created Omaha with a wave of his cigar was imported to address a mass meeting and lead Denver into the promised land. Citizen Train was in good voice that night and vibrated with an optimism that electrified his audience. His voice pealing out like chords from a mighty pipe organ, he proclaimed, "Colorado is a great gold mine! Denver is a great fact! Make it a great railway center!"

But it takes more than hot air to create great enterprises, and Train was able to offer practical suggestions, as well as revival-meeting apostrophes. Denver should build its own railroad to

Cheyenne; it could follow the topographically easy route along the South Platte much of the way and thus could be done for an average cost of $20,000 a mile. A few days later, still dazzled by Train's oratory, some of the more prosperous citizens organized the Denver Pacific Railway Company with a stock issue of $2,000,000. There was enough affluence left from Denver's boom years, when it served as rear base for the Pikes Peak gold rush, and the mattress money only had to be coaxed out of its hiding places.

Colorado's territorial delegates to Congress obtained the usual land grants and subsidies, along with permission to bond the Denver Pacific (a misnomer, since the rails would run north to Cheyenne instead of west to the Pacific, but all self-respecting railroads included Pacific in their title during that era), at $32,000 a mile. Denver was linked to Cheyenne by rail and from there to the East and West coasts, and the city prospered accordingly. Civic pride had saved it from isolation, though sooner or later a railroad from the outside would have penetrated the mountain barriers. Soon travelers, perhaps a trifle giddy from the mile-high altitude, were proclaiming Denver "the American Paris."

A similar display of civic determination resulted eventually in the selection of Atchison, Kansas, as the eastern terminus of the Atchison, Topeka & Santa Fe. A small but dedicated group of educated young men from the Eastern states had converged on Atchison before the Civil War, foreseeing that it could become a transportation hub. It had been the headquarters of Ben Holladay's stage line and of wagon freighting to the West, and it was at the confluence of early trails from California, Colorado, Montana, and the Southwest. Geographically it was in a central location: a straight line from Chicago to Santa Fe and one from St. Louis to Fort Kearney would intersect very close to Atchison. Obviously Atchison should be the junction point of railroads running from Chicago to the southwest and from St. Louis to the northwest. Yet Kansas City, St. Joseph, and Leavenworth were also competing for the same prizes, and it was Kansas City that got the main-line bridge over the Missouri in 1869. Atchison's promoters would not give up; they had landed in a Missouri river town with little but their carpetbags, but they had managed to drive out the Southerners who had actually founded the place.

106

They were imbued with the go-getting spirit, and they formed a tight little clique: Colonel John A. Martin, editor of the *Daily Champion*; U.S. Senator J. J. Ingalls; Albert Horton of the State Supreme Court; James Brewer (a future Justice of the U.S. Supreme Court); Baily Waggoner; and several others.

Colonel Martin endlessly exhorted both the citizenry of Atchison and the railroad builders on the city's advantages in the *Daily Champion*:

> Nature, in fashioning this beautiful and fertile valley, in establishing the course of its streams, the altitude of its hills, and the windings of its valleys, destined Atchison to be the metropolis of the Missouri Valley and the "Great Railroad Centre of Kansas.". . . We have the opportunity. The gods are favorable. A vast productive area, penetrated by railroads and inhabited by an energetic and intelligent population, surrounds us in every direction. If Atchison is not without a rival on the Kansas frontier within the next ten years, it will be from a wanton and stupid disregard of the conditions which are requisite to the growth of cities.

Local and outside capital was enlisted to send several rail lines radiating from Atchison, including the Atchison & Pike's Peak, which its sponsors intended to push beyond Colorado to the Pacific. The Kickapoo Indians, perhaps the most amiable tribe on the plains, were diddled out of a large part of their broad and fertile reservation to clear the way for progress. A hopeful project called the Central Branch was launched to hook up with the Union Pacific. Much of the local energy went into pushing the Central Branch as a possible line to the Pacific, yet because of a lack of financing, the railroad straggled westward for a mere 100 miles and ended up in a cornfield in the valley of the Little Blue River. At one time there were half a dozen small railroads radiating from Atchison and aspiring, with Eastern capital, to become a transcontinental giant. Finally, however, the Atchison to Topeka segment of the Atchison, Topeka & Santa Fe was completed, and the town's vigorous promoters secured their outlet to the Southwest and eventually to the Pacific.

Equally vigorous but much less successful was the effort of

Montanans to rope in and corral the iron horse on which so much hope of prosperity seemed to depend. The whoosh of Union Pacific trains far to the south and the extension of the Utah Central from the UP junction at Ogden to Salt Lake City aroused an anguished desire among the people of Montana Territory, who felt that with freight wagons and stage lines their only link to modern transportation, they were isolated and ignored in their northern solitudes.

The plaintive quality of their attitude, the feeling that they were being deprived of their rights as American citizens to have at least a depot and a train pulling in regularly, was conveyed by the query of Colonel A. G. P. George: "Why is money scarce and hard to get?"

He supplied his own answer: "Because we have no railroad—no outer market. Because this Territory loses annually half of the whole tax, for the want of facilities which are enjoyed by almost every other portion of the United States."

That was what hurt, the feeling of unjust deprivation. The locomotive had become a secular god in the United States of the early seventies. Not to have one of his temples close by caused psychological wounds quite as penetrating as the financial and commercial handicaps burdening a section without railroad service.

The Helena *Independent* and most other Montana journals began a drumfire barrage of editorials demanding that the territory somehow shoulder its way into the railroad age. The railroad, the *Independent* pointed out, was an "iron wand" which when waved over the hidden wealth of the territory would cause the earth to open up and a "golden cornucopia" to empty itself on a deserving citizenry. "The iron key," the editorial continued, "has been found to unlock our golden treasures, and hopeful anticipation of better days are prevalent among the people. With railroads come population, industry and capital, and with them come the elements of prosperity and greatness to Montana."

Thanks to the propagandizing of the railroads when they were urging state and national legislatures to grant them land and cash subsidies, the most remote sections of the nation were convinced that all they needed was a wave of the "iron wand" to enter a millennium of prosperity. Once they had profited from con-

108

struction of their main lines, however, the railroads were not overeager to build feeder lines into a profitless hinterland; they had to backtrack, despite tremendous political pressure, on their initial selling job. A railroad was like a tree. If it sent out too many shoots and branches, its financial energy would be sapped. Corporate ears thus must be stopped up against the pleas of the importunate hinterlanders; let them develop their country and make it worthy of the railroads' attentions.

Montanans could not wait for that golden dawn, knowing like all Americans that opportunity must be seized rather than wooed. They formed a Committee of One Hundred to whip up the demand for rail service and created a "paper railroad" called the Montana, National Park & Utah with Samuel T. Hauser, a Helena banker, as president. Hauser, a former civil engineer and railroad builder in Missouri before the Civil War, thus became the standard-bearer of the cause. He tried to obtain backing from Salt Lake and San Francisco bankers and financiers, but money was tight in the wake of the '73 panic, and railroad financing was regarded as highly speculative in the light of Jay Cooke's collapse. The Northern Pacific was bogged down on the Dakota steppe, and no one knew if its tracks would ever continue westward toward Puget Sound. The Utah Northern seemed a better bet, though it had only reached up across the Utah-Idaho line to Franklin and was bogged down for two years. Furthermore, the Utah Northern was letting it be known that even a narrow-gauge extension into Montana would cost $5,000 a mile.

The last resort of the railroad boomers, led by Hauser and other enthusiasts, was to call on the territorial legislature to subsidize any road building into the territory. They campaigned tirelessly for public support of a program which included a $2,500,000 bond issue. Torchlight parades were held in the principal cities and towns. Mass rallies summoned the electorate to demand action by the legislature. A parade through the streets of Diamond City, near Helena, featured placards reading "Political death to opponents of railroads."

In Helena, the territorial capital, there were sound statistical reasons for the almost frenzied concern over obtaining rail service. In the decade before 1875 Helena's population had almost doubled, but local commerce was stagnant. Montana was rich in minerals, and the goldfields were still producing about $1,000,000 a year. Quartz and silver mining were bounding upward, and soon there would be a bonanza in the thick veins of copper underlying sections of the territory. Montana also boasted a cattle herd of 275,000 head and a total of 250,000 sheep. Forty sawmills were exploiting the timbered parts of the territory.

Yet it was mostly a one-way traffic, with the freight wagons coming back empty after hauling away the raw materials Montana provided. The territory found itself in the classic dilemma of an underdeveloped country. It was giving up its ore and cattle, paying total wagon-freight charges of $2,500,000 a year, and getting precious little in return. At the same time the mining industry was threatened with a slowdown in the near future. Importing the heavy machinery necessary to reduce low-grade ores was not only difficult via freight wagon but prohibitively expensive. Helena businessmen, who were beginning to shut up shop and move out of the territory, pointed out that it cost $30 a ton to transport ore from Helena to the Utah Northern's railhead in Idaho and double that to bring back merchandise. And if the freighter didn't have a load for his return trip, the mine operator was charged $90 a ton from Helena to the railhead. As always, the toughest part of developing a remote area was not in plowing the virgin land, finding and extracting minerals from the earth, or exploiting the forests, but in finding an inexpensive way of sending those products to the market. Such a means would never be found, of course, because when the railroads finally appeared, they only brought more refined techniques of squeezing the producers for all they were worth.

There was another reason for Montanans to yearn for railroads which had more to do with personal survival than the territorial economy. The railroads would help solve the "Indian problem." Montana had its share of cheated and embittered tribesmen, and a few years hence would be the site of the Battle of the Little Bighorn. It had not escaped Montanans' notice that in the last few years there had been large-scale colonization along the Union Pacific's line in Nebraska and that Indian troubles had faded away. The iron horse could bring up cavalry so quickly, and speed its deployment, that attacks on settlements near the railroad were unprofitable. If Montana had rail service, it also could lure in

110

settlers for its endless, empty plains. The Helena *Independent*, taking note of the railroads' protective aspect, urged that it would be more sensible to spend money on railroad construction than on maintaining a more extensive network of military installations.

Hauser and his collaborators, particularly those in the journalistic sector, created such a favorable atmosphere for railroad legislation that early in 1876 the territorial legislature wildly overreacted. The lawmakers seem to have been convinced that if they didn't act promptly, an enraged electorate would descend on Helena and string up their representatives to the lampposts. They overwhelmed the railroad promoters with three different bills, the total cost of which would have put the territory in hock for the rest of the century. One, which would have subsidized the floundering Northern Pacific to the extent of $3,000,000, was later rejected in a referendum. Another would have provided a $1,500,000 subsidy for the Utah Northern's narrow-gauge line. A third would have provided rail service, through feeder lines, for eastern and northern Montana.

The legislative response, of course, was self-defeating. Once dilatory, it had suddenly provided too much. The bond market would never sustain three different issues, all based on the presumed profits of railroading in an underdeveloped section of the country.

In the next year or two hope was revived when Jay Gould became the controlling influence over the Union Pacific, which then took an interest in pushing the feeder line north from its connection at Ogden, Utah, into Idaho and Montana. The Utah Northern was reorganized as the Utah & Northern, given transfusions of Gould money and began building north. Since Gould was popularly regarded as the shrewdest, as well as the trickiest, figure on the American financial scene, Montanans assured one another that trains would soon be streaking all over the territory. Construction on the Utah & Northern reached the Montana-Idaho line. Various Eastern capitalists or their scouts were reported nosing around Butte to determine the extent of its mining prospects.

Rail service from the south seemed so certain that Helena and Butte could start wrangling over which city should be the terminus of the Utah & Northern. The Helena newspaper main-

111

tained that the territorial capital should have the terminal as a natural right. Butte sneered at such pretensions and was confident that its mineral resources would attract the entirely pragmatic men who ran the railroads. "The trouble is that Helena thinks she is New York or Boston," the Butte journal commented, "whereas she is an unimportant village separated from the natural terminus of the road, which is Butte, by a distance of seventy miles and a range of mountains."

It was Butte's ores which decided the matter and brought the Utah & Northern terminus to the mining town, which was soon receiving the shipments of heavy milling machinery that presently caused a copper boom. Soon came the smelters and all the noisome aspects of "progress," of staggering wealth for a few men based comfortably in the East, that turned Butte into possibly the most miserable city in the Western world. Later it would become known through the correspondence of Union Pacific president Sidney Dillon that the Union Pacific had been propelled into taking over the Utah & Northern northward from Idaho only because the Northern Pacific had started building westward again, and the Union Pacific wanted to claim as much of the northern tier as possible. The clamoring needs of the Montanans had nothing to do with the sudden spurt of construction and the linking of Butte to Ogden. And eventually the railroads would bring in more problems than the state could handle without a disastrous strain on the social fabric.

All over the West there was an outcropping of overexpectation whenever the possibility of a railroad appeared on the horizons of towns that aspired to become trading centers, if not metropolises, overnight. Late in the century it would become positively delirious when the craze spread to Southern California. Railroad promoters egged on town boomers and real estate speculators until all were glassy-eyed with self-hypnosis; California in the nineties would not learn the lesson of Kansas in the seventies. The speculative frenzy reached such proportions that it was satirized in a fake handbill for the "new town of Balderdash," a put-on that could serve to limn, with only slight exaggeration, the whole history of the delirium. It read:

112

To meet the great demand for another new townsite, we have secured 10,000 acres of that beautiful land lying on the top of Old Baldy, and will lay out an elegant town. . . . The land is away up and has attracted more attention than any other spot in Southern California. Nine thousand acres will be at once divided into fine business lots 14 by 33 feet. All lots will front on grand avenues 17 feet wide and run back to 18 inch alleys. For the present one-tenth of the entire tract will be reserved for residences in case anyone should want to build, but judging from the success of other similar schemes none of it will be needed for this purpose. To accommodate the inquisitive who are afraid to invest without inspecting the property a fast balloon line will be started in the near future. Parties will be permitted to return on the superb toboggan slide to be built in the sweet bye and bye. . . .

5.

Along the Sod House Frontier

The winters are short, dry and invigorating.
—Union Pacific handbook.

I F you were considering a move west to buy land at $3 to $5 an
acre from grants the sellers had received free from the government, you might study your prospects either in the railroads'
promotional literature, which was highly polished and imaginative, poetic stuff that sang of the promise of a new and bountiful
land, or you might bone up on the subject by wading through
pamphlets and monographs of expert opinion, which made dull
reading and were often discouraging in their drearily realistic
approach.

"Rain follows the plow," one cheerily optimistic, pseudoscien-
tific sloganeer maintained. Just how that could be was not
explained.

Never mind that as early as the 1850's Lieutenant Gouverneur
K. Warren, who had scientific training and later commanded a
Union Army corps, was sent west on an exploratory mission and
came back warning that Nebraska was "near the Western limit of
the fertile portion of the prairie lands," that beyond the ninety-
seventh meridian was land suitable in the long run only for
grazing. One of the early explorers of the West, Major Stephen H.
Long, drew a map across which he inscribed in heavy block letters

THE GREAT AMERICAN DESERT over much of the lands which the railroads and land speculators were offering as prime agricultural country. Later experts warned that the Great Plains were an arid, treeless steppe which could support only a thinly spread population.

Then, too, there was the matter of technology catching up with the headlong rush of settlement. Not for several years after the completion of the first transcontinental road were there means of fencing off the farmlands from those devoted to grazing. "It would be a mistake," Walter Prescott Webb observed, "to assume that the railroads deserve all the credit for the settlement of the Great Plains. It would have been possible to build railroads in the Plains as early as 1850. But had the railroads been built, it would still have been impossible for the farmer to occupy the country. His coming, trying enough at best, had to await certain other factors and was almost wholly out of the question until after 1875. Not until then could the land of the Plains be fenced, and without fencing agriculture is impossible in a country occupied by cattle."

In 1871 a Department of Agriculture report warned that while a man could go west and buy a farm for the $20 in land-office fees, under the Homestead Act, it would cost him $1,000 "scantily" to fence in his newly acquired property. A thousand dollars now is merely the down payment on an automobile, but in the 1870's it was a small fortune. Such fencing, the Department of Agriculture explained, was necessary "mainly for mutual protection" of a whole group of settlers against "a single stock-owner, rich in cattle, and becoming richer by feeding them without cost on the unpurchased prairie. This little community of twenty families cannot see the justice of the requirement which compels the expenditure of $20,000 to protect their crops from injury by the nomadic cattle of their unsettled neighbor, which may not be worth $10,000 altogether." Wooden rail fences were difficult to build on the treeless plains, hedge fences such as were grown in Europe (the *bocage* country of France, for instance) proved impracticable for the vaster extent of Western farms, and technology caught up with the settlement process only with the development of barbed wire.

The northers that swept down the Great Plains from the Arctic Circle early in the winter, the blizzards which could rage for days, the hot summer winds were also taken in account by those who had studied the environment with scientific detachment rather than the hope of enriching themselves by persuading other people to go west for the sake of the marketplace. The winds alone, disregarding the bitter winters and summer droughts and insect plagues, should have been enough to give a knowledgeable man pause. "Very striking is the broad zone of the Great Plains," Professor Robert D. Ward wrote in his study of the subject, with "winds which are ocean-like in character, as vast stretches of the Plains are themselves ocean-like in their monotony and in their unbroken sweep to the faraway horizon. No more striking story of the wind velocities on the Great Plains has ever been given than Captain Lewis's description of the occasion, on the famous Lewis and Clark expedition, when one of his boats, which was being transported on wheels, was blown along by the wind, the boat's sails being set! . . . Over this great treeless open country, but little retarded by friction, blow winds of remarkable uniformity and of relatively high velocity. . . ."

The siroccolike summer winds, hot as the mouth of a blast furnace, were equally disastrous. "The chief characteristics of these winds," Professor Ward cautioned, "are their intense heat and their extreme dryness. They come in narrow bands of excessively hot winds, ranging from perhaps one hundred feet to half a mile or so in width, in a general hot spell, with intermediate belts varying from a few yards to a few miles in width of somewhat less terrific heat between them. . . ." In one season more than 10,000,000 bushels of corn withered under the summer wind. Professor Ward cited one summer in which the Southern Pacific had to suspend rail service because the rails were expanded out of alignment by the heat.

The aridity of the plains prevented the growth of trees, as the first settlers learned when they had to build their houses out of chunks of sod rather than timber, and instead promoted a carpeting of a wide variety of grasses. The tall grass of the low plains and prairies and the short grass of the high plains may have caused poets to ululate over the "sea of grass" which extended to the foothills of the Rockies, but they indicated stern ecological limits. "Grasslands," wrote two experts on the subject, "characterize areas in which trees have failed to develop, either

117

because of unfavorable soil conditions, poor drainage and aeration [that is, drying from the sun and wind], intense cold and wind, deficient moisture supply, or repeated fires." One of the most frightening aspects of living out on the prairies, in fact, was the fires which could explode over the horizon and approach with the speed of an express train, destroying everything in their path. The moment a farmer sighted a lick of flame on the horizon, his only hope was to pile his family into a spring wagon and try to outrace the leaping, bounding wall of fire.

From such a selective course of reading, which few undertook, it was apparent that only the hardiest, most determined sort of people could settle themselves on the Great Plains with little more than a spade, a plow, a team of horses, and perhaps a few hundred dollars, with any hope of survival.

Nonsense, declaimed the "handbooks" and other promotional material broadcast by the railroads and land promoters.

"The winters," a Union Pacific handbook sunnily asserted, "are short, dry and invigorating."

Inspired by such messages, thousands of innocents were brought to the plains, dumped out on the prairie with their few possessions, and left to fend for themselves. The fittest would survive and necessarily become good customers of the railroads. The rugged annals of those who settled Kansas and Nebraska are full of the tales of how they battled for survival by literally burrowing into the ground like prairie dogs to take shelter from all that salubrious climate they had been promised.

Even the youngest, hardiest, most intelligent and resourceful, even those unencumbered by family responsibilities, were hard pressed to survive. There was Peter Bryant, who came out from Illinois in his early twenties to buy land near Holton in northeastern Kansas; he was able-bodied and well educated and a bachelor, yet it took years for him merely to pay off a few hundred dollars' indebtedness incurred in equipping his farm. He had to write his family back in Illinois to send him a barrel or two of flour to see him through the winter and in his letter indicated how difficult it was to lay by even a few dollars:

> I have got $25 salted down that I calculated to go home with along towards spring, but that plan will be knocked on the head.

118

But what troubles me is where I am going to get the rest [to pay off his $50 indebtedness]. I have tried to sell a yoke of cattle, but I cannot do it for the money. Then I tried to borrow. One man offered to lend me $50 and take a mortgage on my place and 20 percent interest.

I tell you I am devilish sick of this buying land on tick [that is, on credit], and if ever I do it again, I want you to take your gun and shoot me. My place has cost me nearly $600 besides the work I have done on it, and if anybody should offer me $500 for it tonight, they would not have to offer but once. Here I am paying 10 percent for money to buy land that won't pay 2 percent. Almost as good a bank to put money in as Binghams Mill dam. But if I get out once, see if I get in again, and if I don't have better luck, tell father he may expect another begging letter in the course of a week. . . .

The ordeal of a family man was all the greater, and had little of the cozy sentimentality of the anonymous bard (possibly in the pay of the railroads) who wrote "The Little Old Sod Shanty," certainly without ever having lived in one:

> And we would make our fortunes on the prairies of the west,
> Just as happy as two lovers we'd remain;
> We'd forget the trials and troubles we endured at the first
> In the little old sod shanty on my claim.

One who would not have subscribed to those sentiments was Matt Hawkinson, husband and father of two, whose farmhouse in Spencer County, Indiana, burned down, and there seemed to be nothing to do but go homesteading out west. Hawkinson consulted a railroad handbook, presumably the Union Pacific's, which proclaimed: "The traveler beholds, stretching away to the distant horizon, a flowering meadow of great fertility, clothed in grass and watered by numerous streams, the margins of which are skirted by timber."

Early in March, 1871, Hawkinson packed himself, his wife, Mary, and their two children, Tom and Hildy, on a westbound train which took them to Grand Island in the middle of the Nebraska steppe. Snow still covered the prairie, and in every direction there was nothing but the flat bleak land and the big gray sky that seemed to encompass everything.

119

The Hawkinson chronicle, dramatic only in its testament to human durability, could stand for thousands of others who found themselves flung out in the empty spaces west of the ninety-sixth meridian. One notable thing was how little time those people devoted to feeling sorry for themselves. The Hawkinsons bought a bull team and a wagon and set out on the 60-mile journey across the prairie to Willow Creek, where Matt had acquired a homestead.

They started from absolute scratch. The first night the family spent around a fire of buffalo chips—the only available fuel out on the plains—with the howl of coyotes borne on the wind. The next morning Hawkinson allowed his oxen to graze along the banks of Willow Creek, while Matt, starting at the surveyor's mound, paced off the 160 acres which would be his land. Even as he paced along, it occurred to him how much simpler it was establishing a homestead out on the plains; under the thick springy grass was black soil, fine and powdery, ready for the plow. There were no trees to be felled and roots to be extracted through many hours of toil. The virgin sod was just waiting to be broken. Back home in Indiana it had taken his grandfather thirty years of backbreaking labor to clear forty acres.

Thus, in one late-winter morning, Matt Hawkinson became one of the thousands of sodbusters, imported by the railroads, given a quarter section of land, and told he had to develop his holding in six months or give it back to the government. If he failed, no one would weep for him. The railroad would be glad to take him back east, if he had the fare for himself and his family. There were no grants, subsidies or handouts of any kind from the government; no bank money available for loans to homesteaders. All he had was his muscles and the skills passed along by the peasant generations.

Matt Hawkinson's first task was to build a shelter for his family. He hitched his team of oxen to the plow and cut 18-inch furrows of sod formed by the wiry switch grass and bluestem. The chunks of sod would be used to line, build an entrance and a roof to a dugout clawed into the side of a low ridge. The earth would be his home for a long time; "a hole in the ground," his wife Mary mourned, thinking back to the wooden house in Indiana that had burned to the ground. Mary thought that living in a dugout,

120

casting themselves back to the ways of the cave dwellers would turn them all into troglodytes; that their children would grow up savages, and Matt himself would lose all his ambition. There was something degrading about burrowing into the earth like animals. On the way from Grand Island the Hawkinsons had come across a young Swede who was living in a dugout on Blue Creek. A blond giant with grass stems in his hair, the Swede told them that, sure, there was plenty of water around. Too much of it for the Swede at the moment. He had dug deep into the bank of Blue Creek and inadvertently acquired running water when the flow of a spring came through his back wall. The way he laughed at his predicament, accepted it as a joke on himself, somehow had infuriated Mary Hawkinson. She was determined that her family would not succumb to acceptance.

So she persuaded Matt to build a sod-walled house above the ground. He cut willows from the bank of the creek for roof poles. The roof was formed by a layer of grass placed across the poles, then topped with a layer of sod. It wasn't perfect; rainwater would drip for days through the sod roof, but at least the Hawkinsons escaped the stigma of being throwbacks to the cavemen. It was noticeable all over the Nebraska prairie, pioneer historians observed, that the bachelors lived more snugly in dugouts while married men were required to build houses.

That spring Matt plowed up his 160 acres while his son, Tom, followed him and dropped seed corn into the furrows. The first crop would be "sod corn," growing between the grass roots of the newly furrowed soil, but the next year, when the soil was loosened by wind and rain, there would be a real crop. The only cash crop that first year at Willow Creek would be the bleached buffalo bones left behind by the hide hunters. With the help of his son and daughter Matt gathered piles of the bones, loaded them into his wagon, took them to the nearest settlement with a general store (which collected the bones for a fertilizer plant in Omaha) and traded them for a door for his sod house, a window, stovepiping, and a barrel of provisions.

That summer other settlers came to the long ridge overlooking Willow Creek. More sod houses sprang up from the prairie, and more fields were broken by the plow. Soon, as Matt envisioned it, there would be vistas of wheat ripening in the sun, roads

121

stretching along the lines between sections, and settlements springing up where the roads crossed. Wheatridge, he thought, would be a nice name for the country. He could see its possibilities, although some decades before Major Stephen Long had dismissed the whole region as "the abode of perpetual desolation." A man with guts could prosper here if he and more particularly his wife could stand the loneliness and isolation and frequent setbacks. For years he would have to live much as those farmer-soldiers the Roman Empire had sent out to its frontiers 2,000 years before, but sooner or later a civilization would rise from the beginnings of Matt and his neighbors.

There was little to find in the way of recreation, little scope for the imagination caged by the empty horizons and the infinite sky. The monotony of their surroundings was so much more oppressive than their native Indiana woodlands and meadows; never did they match the splendor of the prose in the railroad's promotional literature. The Hawkinson family's only diversions were visits to the neighbors, a monthly trip to the settlement store, and walks out on the prairie. Every undulation of that windswept landscape was treasured, anything that broke the monotony of flatness and bleakness: A boulder with wild flowers growing around its base, the burrows of a prairie dog village, the grassy hollows where buffalo (killed to feed the men who built the railroad that brought the Hawkinsons to Nebraska Territory) had once wallowed but now were a flowering tangle of pea vines—such things became landmarks in the family's collective memory.

There were other and less pleasant landmarks they would recall for their grandchildren and great-grandchildren: the terrible three-day blizzard of early '73 when the Hawkinsons had barely established themselves; the sky-blackening grasshopper plague the following year. After the grasshoppers devastated his fields, Matt doggedly planted a late crop of potatoes and corn—and stuck it out. Many of his neighbors on the ridge overlooking Willow Creek didn't. They abandoned their farms and went back east or the optimists among them trekked farther west.

Perhaps Matt Hawkinson was made of sterner stuff than most of his fellow settlers. Instead of going back to Indiana in defeat and despair, he went to Grand Island and persuaded the officials of the land bank there to lend him enough money for lumber to build a wooden frame house. Hawkinson would defy the elements and stay put. After building his house, the first wooden structure in what he insisted on calling Wheatridge, as though the verbal talisman would flesh out his dream of a bountiful countryside, he filed a claim on the adjoining 160 acres and planted ten of them with box elders, thus enabling him to expand his farm to a half section under the provisions of the Timber Culture Act. At least the government was beginning to reward those who were willing to improve the open lands allotted to homesteading. Then that new marvel of technology, barbed wire, was introduced, and Hawkinson and his surviving neighbors could fence in their wheat fields against the roaming cattle herds. Windmills came into fashion, making some productive use of those eternal blasts from the south in summer and the north in winter, and allowed the drilling of deep wells for water to carry them through periods of drought. There were even rumors that the railroad would build a branch line to Willow Creek.

Wheatridge became a reality, the square tower of the Farmers' Mutual grain elevator loomed over the prairie, and a town grew up around it, just as Matt Hawkinson had envisioned. Enoch Strong opened a general store, and Emil Dutcher hauled in an anvil and forge one day to establish a blacksmith's shop, and by 1880 Wheatridge was a village yearning to become a town. Within a decade it grew to include a railway depot, a two-story hotel, two churches, a school, a lumberyard, and a livery stable. Wheatridge was on its way, a viable community despite the droughts and blizzards, despite the rates charged by the railroad for hauling away the thousands of tons of wheat produced on the surrounding prairies. Or was it? Wheatridge, it seemed, was still at the mercy of unpredictable factors.

It was hard hit by the depression of 1893, which was also a drought year, with both corn and wheat crops withered to half their normal size. By then Matt Hawkinson's son was a man of thirty. There was so little work to do around the family farm that in 1895 he went to work at the Mutual grain elevator on the weighing platform, degrading for a born farmer.

One morning in December he returned to the elevator's office from a trip to the post office to find his father and another old-timer sitting around the stove and talking about the days when there were only a few sod houses on Wheatridge, no railway and no grain elevator. Tom Hawkinson opened his mail, and out tumbled another railroad handbook—the same kind that sent his father westering from Indiana, but from a different railroad and heralding the glories of a farther frontier. Describing homestead lands newly opened for settlement in the Northwest, it proclaimed a paradise waiting to be broken by the plow, "sheltered by mountains and richly watered by their streams . . . regular rainfall and a long growing season . . . abundant yields as soon as the soil is broken. . . ."

Tom Hawkinson began restlessly pacing the floor of the tiny office, the walls of which seemed to be closer and more confining than the last time he'd noticed. Idaho . . . Oregon . . . Washington. Old Matt Hawkinson recognized that look in his son's eye; it was a reflection of his own a quarter century before. The process would start all over somewhere close to the Pacific shore, but where would Tom's son go in search of his own paradise? The railroads would sooner or later run out of promises.

The sagas of the Peter Bryants and the Matt Hawkinsons can be recovered now only in the collections of the various state historical societies, their agonies and privations as remote as the archives of the Nineveh Chamber of Commerce.

Their stories, by the tens of thousands, were essentially those of a whole generation of sod house frontiersmen. Who is there now to testify to the cholera epidemics which swept the Missouri River towns during the seventies or the destitution among settlers in 1871 so bad that the Kansas Relief Association had to be organized to alleviate the suffering?

The echo of those privations would be heard in the nineties when the populist movement gathered force largely through resentment of the railroads, their methods of *ad hoc* colonization, and their indifference to the fate of the colonizers they had lured out to territories which could be decently settled only after the most careful planning, preparation, and forethought. Instead of instituting an orderly process of exploiting the 155,000,000 acres of public land they had acquired, the railroads imported warm bodies by the carloads and left them in the wilderness with the pious hope that somehow they would make out all right. They took no responsibility for the lives they redirected with promises of a land ripe with grain, if not actually flowing with milk and honey. They acted only to protect their own property when cattle-forwarding centers like Hays City, Dodge City, Abilene, and Ellsworth sprang up along their rights-of-way and those towns were turned into maelstroms of cowboys and gunfighters battling it out on the streets.

Instead of slowly and efficiently settling the public lands, the railroads encouraged a rush of emigrants, and whenever there weren't enough coming west from the Eastern states, they redoubled their recruiting efforts in Western Europe. Fill up the country in a hurry, create markets overnight was the policy of the magnates in New York and Boston and San Francisco.

Those "short, dry, and invigorating" winters depicted in promotional literature took uncounted lives, particularly among those spending their first year out on the prairies, during the decade in which the major transcontinental railroads were built.

The winter of 1873 was neither short nor invigorating, as its survivors would testify. Easter morning was April 13, which dawned mild and sunny. Already the prairie was turning green. In hundreds of homesteads dotting the plains of Kansas and Nebraska people were rejoicing that the hard winter had finally loosened its grip. By noon the sky was darkening. Inside an hour the wind was blowing a gale, driving along a snowstorm that lasted for three days and nights. The wiser settlers simply holed up with their livestock, barricaded their doors, and waited for the blizzard to pass. Those who ventured outside, trusting to familiarity with their surroundings, often were lost less than 100 feet from their doors. One woman went out to feed her chickens, and five days later her neighbors found her body in a snowdrift. But most people survived by huddling around their stoves and keeping their fires going with twists of hay, chair legs, anything combustible.

Every year, it seemed, there was a natural disaster of some sort. If it wasn't a drought that seared half the planted crops, it was an insect plague or a prairie fire that wiped out scores of homesteads. In 1874 it was the swarming of billions of grasshoppers. That plague struck as unexpectedly as the April blizzard the previous year. On a sunny July morning the sky suddenly dimmed and

125

people heard the whirring of insect wings. Within minutes the grasshoppers covered everything, devastating the fields, chewing up gardens in a flash, even invading houses and eating Sunday dinners. From the Canadian border down to the Arkansas River they devoured the countryside. A Union Pacific train at Kearney, Nebraska, was stalled for hours until a three-foot drift of grasshoppers could be cleared from the tracks. For two weeks the hot July air was stirred only by the beating of billions of wings; then a wind came up, strong enough to send the grasshoppers whirring away from prairies as desolate as a newly made desert. Many farmers abandoned what was left of their farms that summer. Those who clung to their quarter sections sought out the sloughs and other wet plces where the grasshoppers had laid their eggs and burned them out.

Obviously there was little that was glamorous about pioneering out on the "sod house frontier" the railroads established on the Great Plains in the seventies. It was a dogged fight for survival, the sort that could be won only by people, stolid and phlegmatic, with generations and centuries of yeomen ancestors, the offshoots of English and European serfdom. People from the Eastern cities couldn't possibly carve out footholds for themselves in that hostile land with nothing but an ax, a spade, a plow, and a few other rude implements; it was a job for people whose fathers and grandfathers had cleared farms out of the Middle Western forests.

They found water scarce and no timber available for building houses except the cottonwoods and willows growing along the infrequent streams and therefore no fuel supply except buffalo chips (manure). It took years to save enough money to bring in lumber for a frame house. On the high plains most of the streams were brackish or bitter with alkali. About all they had going for them was the plentiful wild game. Shooting for the pot saved many a family from starvation.

They built dugouts into cutbanks or sloping hillsides, usually one-room affairs with slabs of sod for the front wall and a section of buffalo hide for the door. The roof was a layer of poles, a layer of brush, and finally a layer of tramped-down earth. "But no matter how well you did it," one expert on that form of habitation observed, "that roof was still a pain in the neck and muddy water in the soup, because, short of shingling it, you couldn't make the darn thing really leakproof in a heavy rain. It dripped muddy water over everything. If somebody was sick you might have to hold an umbrella over the bed, or bring in the wagon sheet. It was forever spilling grass roots, clods, bits of bark, and maybe even worms, mice, centipedes and scorpions into anything and everything below. The womenfolk hated it with a passion."

Sod houses built above ground weren't as snug against the winter winds, but at least their occupants didn't risk having a horse or cow fall through the roof. "To build one of these," the expert quoted above wrote, "you needed from one-half to one acre of heavy grass sod. You could handle this with just a spade, if you had to, but that was doing it the hard way. Usually a turning plow or sodbuster would be available, and you'd turn the sod, taking pains to keep the furrows even and the same depth. Then, with a spade, you'd cut big slabs, about 2 by 3 feet, or maybe square, 3 by 3, and these you'd haul to your house site in the wagon or on a sledge, which was called a go-devil by some folks." Water had to be obtained by digging wells or building cisterns to catch the inadequate rainfall. "Tank water," as that in cisterns was called, caused typhoid epidemics and had to be purified by boiling and adding alum to make the mud settle. Some settlers, unable to dig wells or build cisterns, had to bring their water from nearby streams in tank wagons or barrels on sledges.

The first settlers also learned very quickly that while an Eastern farm of 40 acres would support a small family, it took the cultivation of at least three times as much prairie land to supply the same amount of food. Eventually they acquired the techniques, some of them imported from as far away as the Russian steppes, of dry farming, selective seeding, crop rotation, the planting of drought-resistant maize, kaffir corn and Russian-bred wheat, by trial, error, and endless failures which broke the health and spirit of many—all on their own, without any county agricultural agent or university experimental station offering help and guidance.

Most of the sodbusters survived on their own, fighting their individual battles. All over the West, however, there were colonizing enterprises promoted by the railroads: the Chicago-Colorado Company, the St. Louis Western Colony, the German Colonization Company of Chicago, the Kentucky Emigration

127

Society, and many others. They bought lands, recruited people and established agricultural colonies (not, however, along the lines of communes or cooperatives for the most part). These groups dealt with the railroads through the National Land Company of New York, which was the sales agent for the Kansas Pacific and Denver Pacific in selling off their land grants, mostly in Colorado. Their agent and chief propagandist hymned the glories of Western farming in his grandly styled land-promotion magazine *Star of Empire*.

The fate of those various railroad-sponsored colonizations varied greatly, a few flourished, many eventually stagnated, and others collapsed within a few years of their establishment.

Perhaps the most fascinating chronicle was that of the Greeley Colony which was partly inspired by the go-west-young-man evangelism of Horace Greeley, the editor of the New York *Tribune*, who kept saying for decades how frightfully sorry he was that he couldn't take his own advice. Even more interesting was the fate of the man who promoted and led the enterprise, an idealist whose eventual reward was violent death at the hands of the people he was determined to help.

The colony at Greeley, Colorado, which became a model for agricultural communities and irrigation projects throughout the West, was the dream-child of Nathan Cook Meeker, a native Ohioan who for many years before the Civil War was a wandering newspaperman. One of the few nonalcoholics in the newspaper business, he devoted himself to reading various classic works on the building of ideal communities, particularly the books of Charles Fourier, the French Socialist, who advocated cooperatively governed phalanxes. He and his young wife joined the phalanx at Warren, Ohio, which finally broke up because of incompetent leadership and constant visitations of the ague. There Meeker learned "just how much cooperation people would bear."

During the Civil War he served as a correspondent at General Grant's headquarters for the New York *Tribune*, then was brought to New York to become the newspaper's agricultural editor. That duty took him on a tour of the West in the fall of 1869; he traveled on the Union Pacific to the end of its tracks. Already he was conceiving the idea of colonizing those empty spaces, but along more realistic lines than those which had misgoverned the Warren phalanx. Thus, in a dispatch sent back to the *Tribune* from Sheridan, Wyoming, he was candid about the sort of people who pushed out beyond the edges of civilization:

> The men are able-bodied and strong; few are more than 35 . . . they speak as good English as any people in the states, using many common household expressions. But they have a restless, uncertain look and quickness of movement both strange and suspicious. . . . Of course they are well armed and ready in a moment for attack or defense. . . . I have every reason to believe that they would commit murder on what we would call the slightest provocation. . . . Men of property have been obliged to resolve themselves into a vigilance committee and hang fifteen or twenty.

He also reported that in a Sheridan hotel's dining room one of those touchier citizens had asked the man sitting opposite him to pass the butter, drew his pistol when his fellow diner ignored him, placed the barrel against the man's forehead, and repeated, "Please pass the butter."

When he returned to New York, Meeker was determined to establish his own colony in Colorado but to take care that it did not include any persons who taught etiquette at gunpoint. Greeley encouraged the idea because it coud provide an experimental station for the Greeley "safety-valve" theory that shipping "landless millions" from the overcrowded city tenements would prevent social and political pressures from building into anarchy. A hundred years later city planners might agree that Greeley was showing considerable foresight. The hitch was that not enough people were willing to detach themselves from the miserable but familiar atmosphere of the cities to face the unknown hazards of pioneering in the wilderness.

"I understand you have a notion to start a colony to go to Colorado," Greeley remarked to Meeker one night late in 1869 at a press-club dinner. "I wish you would take hold of it, for I think it will be a great success." And as usual on such occasions, he beamingly added, "If I could, I would go myself."

The project got under way with surprising speed and momentum. On December 14, 1869, Greeley wrote an editorial, which bolstered Meeker's article on the subject, urging the feasibility of a Colorado agricultural community. More than 3,000 people wrote in expressing various degrees of interest. Nine days later at a meeting held in the Cooper Institute it was decided to send a locating committee composed of Meeker and several other men to find a townsite and adjoining tracts of farmland. Fifty-five persons signed up immediately and put down $150 each against the cost of buying land. Meeker was elected president of what would be called the Union Colony at first, with Greeley as treasurer.

Byers of the National Land Company and *Star of Empire* sped Meeker and the locating committee on their way, via the Union Pacific and Denver Pacific, hoping and trusting that the expedition would prove profitable for one of his railroad clients. It was. The committee bought almost 10,000 acres of the Denver Pacific land grant on the Cache la Poudre halfway between Denver and Cheyenne, plus several thousand acres from private interests, and also acquired 60,000 acres of government land.

Only four months after it was founded at the Cooper Institute meeting the colony had acquired 400 members, and half of them were already building the town of Greeley, Colorado, on the vast tract which would support it. A number of the original colonists quit within a few months, largely because the surroundings did not live up to the idyllic prose of the *Star of Empire* magazine. "No trees are within sixty miles," wrote one disgusted ex-colonist, "except a few stunted cottonwoods upon the banks of the stream. The soil is alkali, and poor enough. The thing is a humbug. There is nothing to induce a sane man to plant himself on that desert. If it shall serve the purpose of cooling the brains of a few hot-headed reformists [by which he evidently meant Greeley and Meeker] by showing them the impracticability of their theories, it will serve a good purpose. . . . Many have left it, and soon its last hovel will be deserted." Another departing colonist wrote a Missouri newspaper that most of the settlers had exhausted their capital in paying for their land, that the only crops were prickly pears and the population was composed of "disappointed men, weeping women and squalling young 'uns," and warned his readers "don't ever dream of doing such a wild and foolish thing as striking out for the great colony of Greeley, Colorado Territory."

Even one of the enthusiasts on the scene admitted that it

seemed a "vain hope of building up a paradise in the sands of the desert," that he and his fellow colonists were "evidently cranks and fools." One of Meeker's chief associates and a member of the locating committee, General Robert A. Cameron, "looked a good deal like a seedy, cast-off, played-out, third-rate politician."

Meeker was inclined airily to dismiss problems like the aridity and alkilinity of the soil and talk instead of a population of 10,000, set amid flourishing farms, inside of a few years. The first task was irrigation; there would be no farming until the parched lands were watered. Canals were dug from the Cache la Poudre, with connecting irrigation ditches, but the ground was so dry it soaked up the water faster than it could be brought from the river. By then the colony's funds were exhausted, and more canal building could be undertaken only after its surplus lands were sold off. The practical farmers among the colonists, who fortunately outnumbered the theorists and social reformers, often had to inveigh against "buncombe speeches filled with desert rose bushes, buncombe statistics of production that lie, and buncombe ditches on paper that can never be filled." They worked out a system of irrigation that satisfied their needs, without growing any rose gardens among the prickly pear, and their laws governing that system were so ably drawn up that Colorado itself, Wyoming, and Nevada used them as a model for their own. A certain amount of reformism was tolerated and extended to a fairly stringent prohibition of alcoholic beverages. When a German tried to open a saloon in Greeley, a committee bought up his lease and ushered him to the town limits. Lyceums were established to discuss all matters under the sun, particularly from the radical viewpoint, and it was said that the Hotel de Comfort, where the bachelor members of the community lived, held discussions that entitled it to be called "the Jacobin Club." On the other (or right) hand, there was an Army and Navy Club where those of a less radical disposition could gather. Women's suffrage was not a popular cause as yet in the rest of the country, but in Greeley it was encouraged. Writing in the Greeley *Tribune,* of which he was naturally the editor, Nathan Meeker informed his flock: "As to intellect, the women are fully equal to men and they only lack drill and wider means of obtaining information. Many of the females are remarkable for large perceptive and reflective

131

powers, and these, often, are in excess of their vitality."

Greeley within a few years was a viable and growing enterprise. Still, it did not live up to the claims made for it by the imaginative Byers in his *Star of Empire*, which probably printed more agricultural and scenic nonsense than any publication in the United States. Not since the first rumors of abundance leaked out of the land of Canaan had there been such hyperbolic bulletins as Byers published on the Union Colony at Greeley. In addition to bumper crops of various grains, the *Star of Empire* reported it was growing turnips 42 inches in circumference and cabbages often weighing 50 pounds each. Actually in most Greeley cabbage patches the first crops were too small to harvest. Besides, there was no market for the vegetables. Byers also neglected to mention that the colonists' tracts, formerly open cattle range, were repeatedly invaded by roaming herds, and herders had to be employed to ward off the incursions. Eventually it became necessary to fence in the whole colony at an expense of $400 per mile. Grasshoppers, too, were a recurring menace. For four years they ravaged the Greeley farmlands despite counterattacks of smudges, fire, and water. Finally the ichneumon fly was imported to combat the scourge, and that was the last of the grasshopper plagues.

Greeley after a half dozen hard years finally began to prosper, and before its first decade ended it was indeed a New Eden. Lateral canals laced the formerly barren ridges and valleys, which were now covered with fields of wheat, oats, alfalfa, and potatoes.

The only exception to the general prosperity was its moving spirit. Worn and aging, Nathan Meeker had sunk his money into building a large wooden house and into establishing the Greeley *Tribune*. The paper did not pay its way. He had not tried to make money on real estate speculation, as some of his associates did, and his only reward from the Union Colony itself was a deed to 40 acres in scant recognition of his services. He told a friend that "although the enterprise yielded me nothing in return, in a worldly sense, yet I am proud to have been the leader in such a movement." The finishing touch came when the executors of Horace Greeley's estate sued him for $1,000 which Greeley had lent him to keep the Greeley *Tribune* from folding.

So Nathan Meeker had to leave the colony and take the post of

132

government agent at the White River Indian Agency in northwestern Colorado. Like so many men who built the enduring parts of the West, he found there was no longer a place for him in the New Eden he had created out of borrowed philosophies and his own conception of what America should be.

All that unquenched idealism was poured into a new enthusiasm, bettering the lives of the displaced Indians. Like many of his breed, Meeker found his principles tending to coagulate into a brittle doctrine; he could not see that the Indians did not want to become white men with a darker complexion, that they wanted to return to a life of nomadic freedom, and more than anything they yearned for all the works of the white man—good and bad—to vanish from their part of the earth. Meeker took up his new duties in the spring of 1878 and immediately rounded up a sullen labor force, which demanded $15 a month and double rations, to dig a system of irrigation ditches on the reservation.

Civilization, as he saw it, was a strong medicine which would have to be forcibly administered to the Indians. Soon after becoming the agent at White River, he wrote:

> A great mistake was made at an early day, in supposing the Indians capable of civilization equally with whites. The proper course to pursue was to teach them to engage in common industries . . . for it is only upon rural life and its duties and cares that civilization and Christianity can rest, and if I were going to start a new religion I would make this the first article of the creed. Treated as if they were children, for they are little more, and entirely dropping the notion of their awful poetic character, and the sacredness of the land of their fathers; in short, coming down to the common sense of things, and in a few years they are bound to become as decent human beings as the average of us.

Playing the stern father, he was confronted several times by rebellions against his authority. The Ute, their chief informed him, wanted to give up plowing, leave the reservation, and take up hunting again. His followers pulled off the shoes the government had given them and threw them in a pile at the agency headquarters. Meeker kept them on the reservation by handing out extra rations. A short time later in the summer of 1879, a year of threat and cajolery having failed to make much impression on his charges, the Ute protested against further plowing on the reservation. Several warriors showed up with rifles and stopped other Indians from continuing to work under Meeker's direction. Meeker settled that dispute by promising to build one of the families a house with a well and exulted in a dispatch to the Greeley *Tribune*: "This stopping plows by bullets is by no means a new thing in America, for so to speak, the plow has plowed its way from the Atlantic to the heart of the Rocky Mountains, through showers of bullets, and the American plow is yet to turn the furrows across China and the Steppes of Tartary, and even invert the soil around sacred Jerusalem—'Speed the Plow!' " Like many other visionaries of the time, he saw America striding across the Pacific and peacefully conquering the Asian mainland. On the White River Reservation, however, speeding the plow soon proved beyond the powers of an elderly idealist more accustomed to dealing in theories than with the intransigence of human nature.

Only in the last tragic weeks of his life did he come to realize the glacial slowness of social reform, that impatience for progress can rarely prevail against deep-seated human desires. The situation at the White River Agency became so menacing that in September, 1879, he had to ask the Army to send troops to the reservation. A column of cavalry sent from Fort Steele was ambushed, its commander and 12 troopers killed, and the survivors surrounded by Indians. That same afternoon other Indians advanced on the agency headquarters, killed Meeker and mutilated his body, then slaughtered everyone who had cooperated with him and burned down all the agency buildings. A strong force of more than 500 cavalry and infantry had to be dispatched from Cheyenne. When it arrived at White River, Major General Wesley Merritt, a hardened veteran of Indian campaigns, wept at what he saw.

Nathan Meeker was one of the Old West's really great men, and the hundreds of thousands of irrigated and cultivated farmlands around Greeley, Colorado, would stand as his memorial. If there was one enduring thing about the conquest of the West, it was the reclamation of the arid plains through irrigation, and Meeker was the undisputed pioneer of that effort.

* * *

The high hopes with which Peter Bryant's Holton, Kansas, Matt Hawkinson's Wheatridge, Nebraska, and Nathan Meeker's Greeley, Colorado, were settled and protected against everything a hostile environment and an embittered aboriginal race could hurl against them—those hopes and countless other pioneer aspirations shriveled within a generation. In not much more than a decade they realized that somehow they were being betrayed; usually the inimical forces were given such shadowy designations as "Wall Street" or "Eastern capitalism." The pioneer knew that he had been sold out. He had been encouraged to turn the American West into one of the world's great granaries; then prices on the international wheat market fell so low that he could hardly make a living. And there were always the damned railroads. Even when wheat prices went up, he could count on being diddled by transportation costs. The juggling of freight rates on the Union Pacific, Kansas Pacific, Santa Fe, and other carriers became so outrageous that Congress finally was forced to pass the Interstate Commerce Act, but that didn't prevent the ruin of thousands of farmers squeezed between falling wheat prices and rising freight rates. As the Western farmer saw it, he was always at the mercy of the Chicago, New York, and Liverpool grain pits, the railways, the grain elevator operators, the steamship lines, and the utterly corruptible politicians.

Behind the frontier the railroads pushed westward at such an incredible speed there developed what sociologists would call a "stockade mentality," which at times approached the intensity of a psychosis. The people of the Middle Border and beyond felt themselves besieged by forces they could only vaguely identify and at which they could seldom strike back. A closed society, vehement in its opinions and attitudes, rapidly developed. Smart, sophisticated Easterners would later sneer at the Bible Belt, at the American Gothic style, at the narrowness of vision, at the phoniness of the pioneer legend with all its simpleminded Indian killers and long-jawed yokels and sunbonneted heroines. But never mind that: The pioneers and their descendants knew that Protestantism was the true religion, that the Republican Party (at least until the Populist movement arose) was the savior of the Union, that the farmers were the backbone of the country, that the Eastern cities were full of crooks and libertines and dirty

135

foreigners. Atheism and adultery were the greatest crimes. They saw themselves as an honest yeomanry which would always be the salvation of the nation.

Yet this defensive self-anointment did not make for happier lives, and self-righteousness did not lead to self-fulfillment. A class structure as rigidly stratified as any in the East developed; the successful citizen of Quality Hill overlooking Atchison, Kansas, priding himself on having shared the prosperity brought by the Santa Fe Railroad, looked down upon the surrounding farmers as haughtily as any resident of Louisburg Square, Boston, surveying the ignorant bogtrotters massed in the south end.

It was no accident that some of the country's most iconoclastic writers sprang from that soil. In their works there is little maundering over the American Dream. Nor is there much exclamation over the glory of pioneering, which they saw as unrewarded drudgery. The whites had their own Wounded Knee, one without storied martyrs, only obscure victims; it was a slow bleeding of hope, rather than a massacre by Gatling guns. They did not even have the satisfaction of enemies against whom they could direct their fire, until the Populists defined and identified them in the nineties.

The literature they produced, along with letters and unpublished memoirs preserved by state historical societies, tells the story of their disillusionment. Henry George described the pioneers as "flies in a pool of tar." From Hamlin Garland to Sinclair Lewis, the pioneer's plight was described as that of a drudge, a prisoner who could not hope for the remission of his sentence.

That little gray home in the West was an illusion cherished by Easterners and those who had made their escape from the wide open spaces.

Hamlin Garland described the prairie home with a silent yell of despair:

> It was a human habitation.
> It was not a prison. A prison
> Resounds with songs, yells, the crash of gates,
> The click of locks and grind of chains.
> Voice shouts to voice. Bars do not exclude

The interchange of words.
This was solitary confinement.

The sun upsprang,
Its light swept the plain like a sea
Of golden water, and the blue-gray dome
That soared above the settler's shack
Was lighted with magical splendor.

To some worn woman
Another monotonous day was born.

An even more sardonic observer of the pioneer settlements was Ed Howe, who took over as editor of the Atchison *Globe* in 1877, assumed the mantle of prairie philosopher, and made himself nationally famous as the "Sage of Potato Hill." His writings, in particular the savage compression of *The Story of a Country Town*, must have persuaded many a city dweller not to sell out, pack up, and head for the advertised splendors of the frontier. He attacked the sentimental falsities of the "cult of the yeoman" and described a world bound together by a savagely Fundamentalist religion, families grimly stuck with each other out of economic necessity, communities in which malicious gossip was the only available amusement.

Even more definitively harrowing was Hamlin Garland, "a son of the Middle Border" as he identified himself. He was born in 1860 and reared on a series of homesteads in Wisconsin, Iowa, and South Dakota. Each family farm was established farther west as his father, like so many others, tried to find more productive land to offset the steady decline in crop prices. Garland fled from the entrapment of his father's existence and headed for Boston, which he visualized as the opposite of all the hardship and intellectual privation he had experienced in his boyhood.

In his late twenties Garland began writing the stories and novels which expressed the squalor and bitterness of life on the prairie farms, "an everyday history of a group of migrating families from 1840 to 1895," as he summed them up, "a most momentous half-century of Western social development."

His masterwork on the subject was *Main-Travelled Roads*, a collection of twelve stories, whose theme, as Garland stated it, was:

The Main-Travelled Road in the West (as everywhere) is hot and dusty in summer, and desolate and drear with mud in fall and spring, and in winter the winds sweep the snow across it. . . . Mainly it is long and wearyful, and has a dull little town at one end and a home of toil at the other. Like the main-travelled road of life it is traversed by many classes of people, but the poor and the weary predominate. . . .

The characters in Garland's novels and stories "live in hovels and their wives wind up in insane asylums." Their only reward is "a hole to hibernate in" during the winter and to "sleep and eat in in the summer." It was the suffering of the pioneers' wives which particularly engaged Garland's sympathy, a plight which he epitomized in one stanza of one of his *Prairie Songs*:

> "Born an' scrubbed, suffered and died."
> That's all you need to say, elder.
> Never mind sayin' "made a bride,"
> Nor when her hair got gray.
> Jes' say, "born 'n' worked t' death":
> That fits it—save y'r breath.

Garland directed his literary voice, later more stridently as a good Populist, at the Easterners in the cities who battened off the labor of the prairie farmer and at the fugitive (like himself) who had escaped the drudgery and despair of his birthplace. The man from the Middle Border was poignantly reminded of the farm mother who bore him, picturing her as waiting in a country store, embarrassed by the questioning look of the clerk, who expects her to buy something, while her husband finishes his business with the townspeople. The reader with such a background was also driven to recollections of his gaunt father working year after year to build up a farm, fence it in, acquire a few cows, only to have it snatched away under the terms of a bloodsucking mortgage held by the bank.

But it was the pioneer's wife who figured as the emotional fulcrum of Garland's strongest writing. Usually she was worked to death; widows were rare but widowers plentiful in the prairie country. Even those women who survived incessant child bearing and grueling labor could not escape the barrenness of their circumstances. In "A Day's Pleasure," a careworn farm wife accompanies her husband to the nearest town because even its drab streets, its false-fronted stores, are more attractive than her own surroundings. The young wife, with her bawling baby in her arms, walks the streets while her husband goes about his business. A lawyer's wife, watching from her window, takes pity and invites the farm woman in, admires her baby, serves her tea, and "the day has been made beautiful by human sympathy." The memory of that hour in a decent home will, as Garland makes clear, be one of the few bright moments in the farm wife's existence, one to be looked back on and treasured.

He endlessly sounded the theme of how women's lives were ruined by the unending monotony of their days, which exactly matched the bleak sameness of the prairie world outside their windows, halved by sky and land, the horizon bisected as neatly as though it had been done by a gigantic scalpel. Men had the glory of the struggle, for what it was worth, but women were the true victims of a frontier advanced so swiftly there was no time for human values or consideration of the special requirements of the female psyche. The poet Eugene Field commented that Garland's heroines "eat cold huckleberry pie and are so unfeminine as not to call a cow 'he,' " but that was an Eastern city fellow's unfeeling view. To Garland they were, though drab and workworn, figures in an epic tragedy. He noted in one of his novels:

> Most of the girls were precocious in the direction of marriage and brought all their little girl allurements to bear with the same purpose which directs the coquetry of a city belle. At sixteen they had beaux, at seventeen many of them actually married, and at eighteen they might often be seen with their husbands, covered with dust, clasping wailing babies in their arms; at twenty they were not infrequently thin and bent in the shoulders, and flat and stiff in the hips, having degenerated into sallow and querulous wives of slovenly, careless husbands.

The soul-destroying quality of life on the prairies, again particularly for women, was illuminated with even greater artistry by O. E. Rolvaag in his novel *Giants in the Earth*. His story was centered on Per and Beret Hansa, Norwegian emigrants to the Dakota plains. At the outset Rolvaag's near-classic novel brings out the difference in the way the Great Plains affected men and women. Per Hansa fell in love with their starkly primitive splendor, but his wife, Beret, like most women, found herself in a world full of menace and mystery; she was crushed by the immensity, the obliterating monotony, of a prairie world that seemed to stretch into infinity.

"Was this the place?" Beret Hansa asked herself when she and her family arrived on their Dakota claim. "*Here!* Could it be possible? . . . She stole a glance at the others, at the half-completed hut, then turned to look more closely at the group standing near her; and suddenly it struck her that *here something was about to go wrong.* . . . A great lump kept coming up in her throat; she swallowed hard to keep it back, and forced herself to look calm. Surely, surely, she mustn't give way to her tears now, in the midst of all this joy. . . . After they had bustled about for a little while the others left her. The moment they had gone she jumped up and crossed the tent, to look out the door. . . . How will human beings be able to endure this place? she thought. Why, there isn't even a thing that one can *hide behind.*"

The literature of the prairies has, in fact, something of the monotony of its setting in the general agreement that the frontier might test and strengthen manhood, that men could make themselves part of their environment, if they were not overly sensitive souls, but women could never adjust themselves to it. In Vardis Fisher's *Toilers of the Hills*, Dock and Opal Hunter struggle to make a living at dry farming in Idaho. At the end he glories in sheer survival, in not letting himself be conquered in the brutish combat with nature, but Opal can see only the futility of their struggle. "She was old now, and it was little she cared what he said, what he did. These hills had got her, broken her, and she would never care now."

The style in which the Great Plains were settled simply didn't allow for the amenities, the social ambience which made life worth living for women. If they were lucky, such things as domestic comforts came with the years, but there was nothing that could be done to alleviate the loneliness of those endless empty plains. A prairie farm wife, it was said, always knew by

140

sunup if she was going to have visitors that day. If there was a dust cloud on the dawn horizon, company would arrive by noon.

When Hollywood began to produce the films glorifying the pioneer experience, some of its aged survivors were still around. It was interesting to note their differing reactions to such film epics as James Cruze's *The Covered Wagon* and *The Iron Horse* as they silently flickered on the screen of the local opera house. The men enthusiastically accepted the glorification—sure, that's the way it was. But the women, watching some dimpled ingenue playing Sunbonnet Sue, her golden hair carefully coiffed despite the incessant wind, dainty and perfectly groomed in the midst of prairie fires and Indian attacks, looked as though they had swallowed a tablespoon of alum. Not all the cinematic arts at Hollywood's disposal could persuade those bent and leathery old ladies that their lives had been charged with glamor or romance.

6.

Gold from the Russian Steppes

. . . when a daughter of the East is once beyond the
Missouri she rarely recrosses it except on a bridal
tour.
—Burlington road pamphlet

A hundred years ago the United States was what is now
termed an underdeveloped country. It was built up with
foreign capital, which was required in large amounts for the
development and exploitation of the West, particularly the construction of the railroads. Most of this venture capital was returned to Europe, with interest, when the United States became a
creditor country. Europeans soon learned, however, that invest-
ing in the Western railroads was a tricky business; they had a
distressing tendency to tumble or be tumbled into bankruptcy.
Americans of later years were outraged by Latin American
countries which expropriated their holdings. In a sense, and in a
more polite guise, we had pioneered the practice of expropriation.
Thousands of Europeans lost their savings or had their capital
depleted by the manipulation of American railroad securities. We
didn't call it expropriation, but the money stayed in the United
States, and financially, to the ruined investor in Amsterdam or
Munich, the effect was the same. In many a European household
the name of Union Pacific or Memphis & El Paso was mentioned
in the same sorrowful tone a resident of Johnstown, Pennsylvania,
might use in referring to a certain dam.

143

Europe was the indispensable rear base which provided not only the capital, but the emigrants to fill up the lands opened to settlement by the extension of the railroads.

When Jay Gould at the height of his career as a manipulator of Western railroads urgently needed a large block of Denver Pacific bonds to obtain control of that line, he knew where to get them in a hurry: not on Wall Street but on the Amsterdam bourse. He caught a fast steamer, and as he later testified before an investigating committee, "I went over to Amsterdam in the morning; washed up and had my breakfast. I saw the Dutch brokers at eleven; bought them out at twelve, and started back home in the afternoon."

German investors were so involved in the capitalization of the Kansas Pacific and other lines that they had to employ representatives to go over to the States and act as watchdogs over their interests, but nevertheless, they and other Europeans lost hundreds of millions in their American ventures.

European capital was attracted to the Memphis & El Paso largely because of the international fame of General John Charles Frémont, who as "the Great Pathfinder" had surveyed many of the Southwestern rail routes, in addition to other topographical missions. Frémont assumed the presidency of the Memphis & El Paso and sank his own fortune of more than $1,000,000 into the railroad. In the early seventies, while Frémont was in Washington exerting his political influence (having been the first Presidential candidate of the new Republican Party in 1856) on the problem of extending the company's right-of-way, unscrupulous agents were selling millions of dollars' worth of Memphis & El Paso bonds in various European countries. The company collapsed, and not only his foreign admirers but Frémont himself were wiped out. The bailiffs seized his home at Tarrytown, and Frémont had to take a $2,000-a-year post as governor of Arizona Territory.

Actually, as few people realized at the time, the Western railroads could hardly have paid worthwhile dividends even if they had been efficiently managed and honestly financed. The facts of economic life—regardless of the bumper crops of grain, the cattle, and the minerals requiring transportation to the Eastern markets—were all against them: the long hauls over rugged

144

terrain; the inordinate cost of construction (even if not swelled by the award of crooked contracts); the operating expenses, which were increased by the haste of construction over routes that disdained the topography.

Foreign and domestic investors might have saved themselves a lot of anguish if they had consulted an obscure monograph titled *The Economic Theory of the Location of Railways*, published in 1877. Its author was Arthur Mellen Wellington, a Massachusetts man with practical experience in locating railway lines and later the editor of the *Engineering News*. Wellington deplored the bravura with which the first Western railroad builders selected their routes. True, they could be built where a mountain goat hesitated to wander, and were, but there was a price to be paid in the future for such headlong, damn-the-grades, full-speed-ahead methods. Hasty and reckless location of the tracks, he pointed out in his monograph, which became the Bible of all locating engineers, could bleed a company to death through operating expenses. As Wellington described the financial hemorrhage, it was a "gentle but unceasing ooze from every pore which attracts no attention, albeit resulting in a loss vastly larger than any possible loss from bad construction."

In his classic study of human development on the Great Plains, Walter Prescott Webb also pointed to definitive causes of the Western roads' poor financial prospects. In the East, he wrote, railroads prospered because they "followed the population." By contrast, in the West the railroads preceded settlement:

> There was nothing, comparatively speaking, in the Plains country to support them—practically no population to travel on them, few supplies to be shipped, and, aside from cattle and hides, little produce to be sent to market. Hence the problem was to get *somewhere* as quickly as possible; consequently the railroads shot *across* the Plains and through the mountains in as straight a line as the topography would permit. There were no cities to draw them aside, to make them wander about and form irregular patterns, such as the railroad map of the East presents. The Western railroads had to get *across* the Plains. To stop on the Plains would have been fatal, because there was nothing to stop for. It follows, then, that a railroad on the Plains was almost inevitably a losing financial venture in so far as it depended on the Plains for revenue.

145

The throwing of a railroad across the Plains meant the tying up of enormous sums of capital from which by the very nature of things there could be expected no immediate return. Therefore it became necessary for society to subsidize the railways of the West. . . . There came into existence in the West a fever of railroad construction as a general public exercise to which all were expected to contribute in one way or another. . . .

Contribute they did, though the public and private money that went into the glorious enterprise was often diverted through subterannean financial channels to personal enrichment rather than public benefit.

Time after time, insiders generally headquartered in Wall Street used the Western roads as objects of manipulation. They regarded such enterprises as a collection of balance sheets, bundles of expensively engraved bonds and stock certificates, rather than human institutions on which so many livelihoods depended, on which so much energy, blood, and sweat had been expended.

They were unabashed predators, nurtured on the amorality of the post-Civil War years, who brought about the collapse of railroads as blithely as they would knock down a house of cards, who engineered panics and depressions without a twinge of conscience. A meek-looking, black-bearded little man named Jay Gould was easily the "smartest" of those predatory operators, at a time when "smartness"—outwitting your fellows by any means possible—was a greatly admired trait. As early as 1873 a New York newspaper was warning the public that Gould, who had learned the art of railroad financing and definancing as one of the wreckers of the Erie Railway, was a national menace. The editorial noted:

> There is one man in Wall Street today whom men watch, and whose name, built upon ruins, carries with it a certain whisper of ruin. He is the last of the race of kings, one whose nature is best described by the record of what he has done and by the burden of hatred and dread that, loaded upon him for two and one-half years, has not turned him one hair from any place that promised him gain and the most bitter ruin for his chance opponents. They

146

that curse him do not do it blindly, but as one who massacres after victory.

That newspaper changed its tune in short order when Gould bought it up. Its cautionary regarding Gould, before he silenced its criticism by becoming its proprietor, was well timed.

Gould just then was eyeing the possibility of seizing control of Western transportation. His first move was to conduct a raid on the financial position of the Pacific Mail Steamship Company, whose president had risen from supercargo on a Mississippi riverboat to control of the Pacific Mail through his wife's sewing-machine fortune. When Gould, his chief collaborator, Russell Sage, and other members of the raiding party got through with him, A. B. Stockwell delivered a wry summation of the comeuppance any amateur could expect from Gould and his group. "When I came to New York and bought stock by the hundred shares, they called me Stockwell. By the time I was trading in thousand-share lots I was known as Captain Stockwell. They promoted me to Commodore Stockwell when word got around that I had gained control of Pacific Mail. But when Jay Gould got after me and booted me out of the concern, all they called me was 'that redheaded son of a bitch from the West.' "

Early in 1874 Gould had acquired enough shares of Union Pacific stock to demand a seat on the board of directors, and he immediately formed an alliance with its president, Sidney Dillon. Most of the former insiders had been banished or had departed in the belief that the UP could never be plundered again. They left the railroad with a floating debt of $5,000,000, not to mention $10,000,000 in income bonds maturing immediately. Undismayed, Gould proceeded to buy 200,000 shares and take control of the company with Sage and Dillon as his chief collaborators. The $15,000,000 indebtedness, which threatened to sink the company into receivership, was converted into sinking-fund bonds, a printing-press maneuver which allowed Gould to defer payment of the road's obligations. Receipts began to rise rapidly when California produced a bumper grain crop and there was a heavy volume of shipments from the Western silver mines.

Merely making the Union Pacific a paying proposition was not enough to satisfy Gould's Napoleonic ambitions. His aim was to monopolize all Western railroad traffic. The first step toward that goal would be to acquire control of the Kansas Pacific, whose line paralleled much of the Union Pacific's; UP's route was Omaha-Cheyenne-Ogden, the Kansas Pacific's was Kansas City-Denver-Cheyenne. From Cheyenne westward, therefore, the KP had to rely on the goodwill of the UP with its linkage to the Pacific coast.

Now Gould bought stock in the Kansas Pacific to gain power over its affairs and subsequently force a merger of the two lines. The Kansas Pacific, having been looted for years, was now in receivership. Its receiver was Henry Villard, a native of Bavaria who had migrated to the United States before the Civil War and served as a correspondent for the New York *Herald* during the Civil War. Villard was an intelligent, able, and honest man, who would battle Gould for four years even after the latter acquired a controlling interest in the Kansas Pacific. He had been appointed receiver at the request of two groups of Kansas Pacific bondholders, one in Germany, the other in St. Louis. Gould, as Villard later recorded in his memoirs, tried to bribe him by offering "a profitable participation in the syndicate to be formed for the reorganization of the Kansas Pacific."

When Villard turned aside all attempts to cajole or bribe him, Gould employed other weapons. Newspapers under his influence heaped "slander and abuse" on the Kansas Pacific's receiver. He also persuaded the directors representing the St. Louis group to join him. Then Gould produced his master stroke by announcing that the Union Pacific would form a new subsidiary, the Colorado Central, which would build a line from Cheyenne to Denver, paralleling the Kansas Pacific's trackage between those two cities and draining off much of the KP's freight business.

Villard's supporters on the Kansas Pacific board panicked, and he was removed from the receivership. But he clung to a certain amount of power as representative of the German bondholders. Gould needed complete control, and Villard was an invincible stumbling block. After four years of infighting, Gould sent for Villard, told him he was "tired of fighting," and made the concessions which Villard insisted were necessary for the protection of his German investors.

Gould then proceeded to swing his weight in all directions,

acquired a controlling interest in the Missouri Pacific, bought up majority holdings in the Texas & Pacific, and was well on his way to monopoly over Western railroading. The Missouri Pacific's main line ran from St. Louis to Kansas City and was essential to the success of his operations. By these maneuvers he had built up a system to rival the Union Pacific's, one which he would use to bludgeon his fellow directors on the UP's board into accepting an outrageous proposition. Like the "shadow government" of certain European parliamentary systems—the loyal opposition—there was a new transcontinental line created through corporate maneuvers on Wall Street. Gould had strung together the Missouri Pacific (St. Louis to Kansas City), the Kansas Pacific (Kansas City to Denver), the Denver Pacific (Denver to Cheyenne). First he had acquired control of the Kansas Pacific by threatening it with extensions of the Union Pacific; now by a masterpiece of jugglery he was using the Kansas Pacific as a weapon against the Union Pacific. He presented an ultimatum to his fellow Union Pacific board members. The two railroads were to be consolidated, though the UP was paying dividends and its stock was selling at $60 a share while the KP was on the rocks and its stock was selling at $13. If they didn't agree, Gould said, he would wreck the Union Pacific by building a link between the KP's terminus at Cheyenne and the Central Pacific's at Salt Lake City, thus giving the KP an outlet to the Pacific coast.

It may have been the boldest steal in railroad history, but his fellow directors of the Union Pacific caved in. The merger was investigated by the Pacific Railway Commission (in 1887, long after the damage was done, various stockholders impoverished, and the Gould maneuver a *fait accompli*), and after listening to Gould and other witnesses, one of the commissioners estimated that Gould had made off with $40,000,000 simply through juggling stock, exchanging the Kansas Pacific's cheap paper for the Union Pacific's more expensive certificates.

The success of Jay Gould's machinations illuminates whole areas of Western railroad history. They were typical, though other machinators were not quite so gaudily successful in their operations. Built partly with public funds, subsidized in various ways by the government, favored by state and federal legislation, railroads occupied a special position, which was enjoyed by no

149

other form of industrial endeavor, and thus were beholden to the people for whom they were supposed to be operated. They could have functioned in a decent, modestly profitable manner, but instead, they were subjected to successive waves of corporate looting. To offset all that thimblerigging, stock watering, and other devices perfected by Wall Street, they had to resort to ruthless methods of colonization—bringing in hordes of people ill equipped and ill prepared to withstand the hazards and privations of frontier farming—and then victimize those clients further by imposing inordinately expensive freight rates. The West was swiftly and ruthlessly exploited in the physical sense, but so were the people who were the tools of that exploitation.

To keep the railroads afloat and a continuingly juicy proposition for the New York and Boston financiers, it was necessary to recruit hundreds of thousands of innocents, some of them halfway around the world, to keep stocking the West with human beings. It would take much too long to convert the original settlers into docile customers; the Indian psyche, as viewed by nonexperts in Wall Street, was not suited to building an agrarian economy and providing a work force for the mines. The Indians had to be compressed into reservations and replaced by whites whose peasant ancestry had proved them capable of eternal drudgery, much as domestic cattle filled the ranges on which the buffalo had once roamed. If the melting pot seemed to be accomplishing the process of amalgamation in the Eastern cities, where the social pressures were greater, it would work all the better out in the open society of the new West.*

By far the most aggressive departments of the various Western railroads were the colonization bureaus which stationed agents and spread Golden West propaganda throughout Europe. Those promotional seedlings fell upon especially fertile soil in Germany, with all its political and religious dissension. America had long been a gleam in the Teutonic eye. Reading clubs in hundreds of German villages, usually sponsored by the local pastor or priest, listened avidly to readings of James Fenimore Cooper's *Leather-*

---

*An indication of the ethnic mixture that resulted was provided by the 1877 municipal election in Leavenworth, Kansas, where the mayor was German, the city marshal Scottish, the weightmaster Irish, the city health officer French, and the street commissioner Danish.

stocking Tales (translated into German as early as 1830), Karl May's Western stories (which involved a hero named Old Shatterhand who fought on the side of the Indians), and the works of such travelers as Gottfried Duden, who lived on a Missouri farm for three years and described the American frontier as overflowing with wild game and bountiful harvests. All this encouraged such an exodus from the Fatherland that the idea of separatist New Germanys being established on North American soil had to be firmly discouraged by the Anglo-Saxon majority.

A great shower of pamphlets and brochures describing the new Canaan (variously titled *Views and Descriptions of Burlington and Missouri River Railroad Lands, B and M Railroad—750,000 Acres of the Best Lands for Sale, Guide to the Union Pacific Railroad Lands, North Platte Lands of the Burlington*, and so forth) descended upon the various countries of Western Europe, all of them fittingly translated.

People who would never be able to hope that even their grandchildren would save enough money to buy their own land in their native countries were urged to start over in the American West. The Union Pacific suggested a mass migration to the Platte Valley, "a flowery meadow of great fertility clothed in nutritious grasses, and watered by numerous streams." Judging by the rhetoric of the railroads' pamphleteers, the land itself was edible. The Burlington claimed for its Nebraska land grant: "Many fields of properly cultivated wheat have yielded *over thirty bushels of grain per acre, and many fields of corn over seventy.*" The pamphlets told of men who had come west with nothing and within a few years made themselves wealthy. Sometimes the "scientific" basis for the claims made for the climate and fertility of the Western plains was more than a trifle wobbly, one pamphlet citing the records kept by a Plattsmouth, Nebraska, physician to show that rainfall there between 1866 and 1879 was heavier than in Illinois.

The letters of satisfied customers were liberally quoted. A Burlington client wrote of making a "fortune of ten thousand dollars" in seven years. Another wrote gratefully: "Nature seems to have provided protection and food for man and beast; all that is required is diligent labor and economy to ensure an early reward." Another grateful settler attracted to Nebraska by Burlington propaganda enthused over the "wonderfully cheap

151

homes in the west" and "people living almost in affluence on their prairie farms."

The pamphlet writers dangled all sorts of bait before prospective settlers, not neglecting those with anxiously marriageable daughters on their hands. Males, as a Burlington copywriter pointed out, greatly outnumbered the females in the Western states, and "accordingly, when a daughter of the East is once beyond the Missouri she rarely recrosses it except on a bridal tour."

Equally florid and shrewdly varied promises were made by Burlington propagandists abroad. The Burlington promotional apparatus was so abundantly talented that it could afford to turn down the application of one Augustus Dickens, of Chicago, for a post as circular writer. "As a brother of Charles Dickens, the English Author, I have picked up a smattering of literary 'ability' that might be useful in getting up land pamphlets, etc.," he wrote the Burlington, "and I might be able to 'gild up the frame without spoiling the picture.' " Obviously Dickens knew what was required of a Burlington pamphleteer. Apparently, too, the railroad had read or heard of the maledictions his brother had placed on the American rail system during an earlier journey to the States.

Its English land agent circulated thousands of pamphlets, brochures, and broadsides, in addition to advertising heavily in rural weeklies and agricultural journals. Specimens of crops raised in Iowa and Nebraska were displayed at fairs and exhibitions. The ancient grudges of Western Europe were also exploited. France had recently lost the provinces of Alsace and Lorraine to the Prussians, so Burlington pamphlets published in French and German flooded those provinces and urged the dissidents to "escape from the crushing heels of the German Empire's militarism" by migrating to the American prairies. In Germany itself the railroad's Hamburg agent, Frederick Hedde, found that his campaign to enlist German emigrants was being undermined by newspapers owned by the aristocracy, which hated to see its farm laborers slip away from Pomerania for a more abundant life promised in the States, but reported to the company headquarters that Chancellor Bismarck was "smart enough to know that stopping emigration means favoring revolution."

Pamphleteers for the various Western roads did not hesitate to deprecate each other's claims. The Santa Fe drumbeaters boasted that southwestern Kansas, where their land grant happened to be located, was so lushly profitable for cattlemen that an investment of $8,000 would bring an annual return of $11,000, while the Chicago, Milwaukee & St. Paul crooned over its Dakota acreage as "the land of promise" in which thrived "every cereal, vegetable and flower grown in this latitude in the United States." But the Burlington and the Union Pacific, with their own swatches of territory in mind, warned emphatically against "going too far north" (the Dakotas) or "too far south" (southern Kansas). Nebraska was just about right for making agriculture pleasurable and profitable. It also happened to be where the UP and Burlington were peddling their land grants.

Those pamphlets are mere dust-gathering curiosities in the Union Pacific railroad museum in Omaha and other repositories, but to a generation of European peasants they offered the "home of the free" to the politically oppressed and cheap land to the landless.

Colonizers were particularly active in England during the early 1870's when competition between the railroads for land buyers approached the stage of internecine warfare. The Northern Pacific, with 43,000,000 acres of land grants creating a huge vacuum in the northern tier of states, was especially aggressive and inspired its rivals to undertake sneaky methods of reprisal. English settlers were coveted above all others, and the Northern Pacific's competition was outraged by its success with what became known as the Yeovil Colony. In 1872 George Sheppard, the European agent for the Northern Pacific, employed the Reverend George Rodgers of Stalbridge, Dorsetshire, to recruit a group of "good and prosperous persons" to colonize part of the railroad's Minnesota land grant. A party headed by the Reverend Mr. Rodgers came to Minnesota and selected a tract at Hawley in Clay County.

The first batch of English settlers arrived at Yeovil Colony in March, 1873, at the end of a harsh northern winter. People accustomed to the relatively milder temperatures of an English winter were appalled by the Minnesota climate; certainly it would have been wiser to have brought them over when the

153

prairies and meadows were green and blooming. Those first settlers and others intending to join them received an anonymously published pamphlet titled *Advice from an Old Yeovilian*, otherwise unidentified. It warned that the lands located along the Northern Pacific right-of-way were unfit for civilized habitation. Only savages could survive. Besides, the growing season was too short to provide crops. The land was and always would be worthless.

Northern Pacific, perhaps rightly, charged that the pamphlet had been produced by other railroads competing for settlers. It was, however, effective in persuading a number of the first group of Englishmen to drop out of the project. Those who stayed in defiance of the "Old Yeovilian's" predictions made out all right. So did another Northern Pacific group, about 200, who founded the Furness Colony in Wadena, Perham, and Audubon, Minnesota.

Some of the smaller railroads took better care of the people who colonized their land grants than the big transcontinental carriers. The Wisconsin Central, for instance, specialized in importing Germans from the state of Saxony. Since Saxons were said to be a sturdy folk likely to resent bad treatment, the Wisconsin Central made arrangements for the emigrants which the Union Pacific and other human importers might have emulated. The railroad established a receiving depot at Medford, Wisconsin, where the newcomers were allowed to live for two weeks after arrival to acclimate themselves. There was no charge for their food and shelter, and in addition, they were provided with cooking stoves and free fuel before being dispatched into the northern woods to clear their farms.

Perhaps because it was a late starter in the colonization game, the Atchison, Topeka & Santa Fe tried harder and went to greater geographic lengths to fill up its holdings. Like the Northern Pacific, too, it ran through a section of the country even less hospitable to settlement than the plains and mountains traversed by the Union Pacific-Central Pacific. It followed the old Santa Fe Trail which had long been used between the Missouri River and New Mexico by pack trains, oxcarts, and stagecoaches. There were many obstreperous Indians along that route, and beyond the Kansas border the land wasn't of much use except for grazing.

154

It was a long time, in fact, before the project got off the ground.

The prime mover of the enterprise was a Pennsylvanian named Cyrus Kurtz Holliday. A lawyer, he allied himself with the Free Soil Party on migrating to Kansas and was one of a group of men who staked out Topeka and made it the capital. Like many other ambitious men, he became infected with the railroad-building fever several years before the Civil War. In 1859 he obtained a state charter for the Atchison & Topeka Railroad with a modest land grant of 3,000,000 acres. There was a condition attached to the grant: It became the railroad's only if the line was extended to Colorado within ten years.

Holliday spent years trying to raise the money to build his railroad, watched helplessly while the Union Pacific streaked across the landscape and the bankers kept rejecting his applications for financing. The map in Holliday's office showing his projected road stretching across the territory to Colorado, then down to New Mexico, became a local joke.

It wasn't until 1868 that Holliday had collected enough money to break ground at Topeka and start building westward. Some of it came from the more prosperous citizens of Topeka, some from bonds sold through a Cincinnati securities firm. He also began selling off pieces of his land grant by running excursions for prospective buyers late in June, before the parching of the high summer, when the corn was waist-high and the fields at their greenest with growing wheat.

Despite its late start, Holliday's Santa Fe rapidly became a competitor in the transcontinental stakes. Other railroads had laughed it off as "two streaks of rust," but within a few years it reached Colorado and began heading through New Mexico and eventually to Los Angeles. There was a stroke of luck in 1872–73 when the Texas ranchers began sending their cattle herds to Dodge City on the Santa Fe line. The long stock trains trundling east from Dodge meant a windfall of half a million dollars to the Santa Fe. Further expansion was indicated when the Santa Fe bought up the government franchise for the projected Atlantic & Pacific Railroad, which was never built, and obtained access to Southern California. The grasshopper plagues drove hundreds of settlers out of lands they had bought from the Santa Fe, and the railroad came close to bankruptcy until a group of Boston finan-

155

ciers pumped in fresh money. Thereafter it was known, pejoratively, as the "Yankee road." The new financing had been provided by the Boston bankers Joseph and Thomas Nickerson and the brokerage of Kidder, Peabody & Company; Thomas Nickerson thus became president of the Santa Fe in 1874, replacing Holliday, who lived comfortably for another quarter century on his dividends. By then the Santa Fe had 12,000 miles of track and was a billion-dollar giant of the transportation industry.

Before it reached that status, it was engaged in rate wars with the Southern Pacific, which resented its intrusion on California soil, and a real shooting war with the Denver & Rio Grande. The Santa Fe reached Needles, California, and Guaymas, the Mexican port, in 1882. William B. Strong, formerly the general manager and a hard-driving executive favored by the Boston financiers who had taken control of the road, had just been appointed president to succeed Nickerson, and he was determined to elbow aside the Southern Pacific on its own territory. He bought the California Southern and thereby gained access to the port of San Diego. By threatening to establish a steamship line between San Diego and San Francisco, he forced the Southern Pacific to lease the Santa Fe trackage to Los Angeles and San Francisco. Eventually Santa Fe obtained direct access to Los Angeles by buying the short line Los Angeles and San Gabriel Railroad.

Now in direct competition with the Southern Pacific, having linked itself to four principal ports on the Pacific, the Santa Fe tried to bulldoze the Southern Pacific into cutting it in for 50 percent of the freight traffic in Southern California and 27 percent in Northern California. A rate war broke out, with all California cheering on the sidelines. Freight rates were cut from $5 to 30 cents a ton. The rate cutting was extended to passenger fares, and at one point it was possible to buy a ticket from Chicago to Los Angeles for $10, from New York to Los Angeles for $23. The throat-slashing tactics reached the ridiculous stage when Santa Fe cut the fare from St. Louis to Los Angeles to $1, upon which the rate war was called off. During those years, in the mid-1880's, the rate war brought on a new kind of migration, the rival roads having advertised California as an earthly paradise.

Iowa farmers tired of fighting the hard winters came in search of orange groves; invalids in search of a balmy climate and prosperous Easterners looking for palm-shaded haciendas all joined in the rush for the California coast.

Aside from its aggressive methods, the Santa Fe shouldered its way into the transcontinental competition with the Union Pacific and the Southern-Central Pacific by occasionally giving some thought to the comfort of its patrons. Palace cars, later known as Pullmans, had early been developed for the cozening of the well-heeled, those who didn't travel in their own private cars. Travelers of lesser rank, however, were treated with not much more concern than cattle. One of the greater hazards of traveling out west in the seventies, particularly for anyone with a delicate stomach, was the "eating houses" along the way. The quick-lunch counter in a depot out on the plains, to which passengers resorted during stops for coal or water (the locomotive's nourishment was more important than that of the people it hauled), was an everlasting monument to dyspepsia and heartburn. The passengers would be given seven and a half minutes, say, while the engine was coupled to the hose at the water tank, to grab a leathery sandwich, a slice of moldering apple pie, and a deplorable mug of coffee before the conductor herded everyone back on board.

The Santa Fe ordained more humane feeding of its patrons when Fred Harvey, a Scottish immigrant who had established a chain of small restaurants in Kansas, came up with the revolutionary idea that the railroad passenger should be preserved from the perils of ptomaine poisoning. By then the depot lunch counter had become such a menace to the American digestive system that it was the subject of a whole literature and a school of comic art. Harvey's idea was that passengers could be fed quickly and nourishingly without disrupting the railroad's timetable. He was allowed to build the first Harvey House in the Topeka station, which with its walnut furniture, its clean linen and unchipped plates, not to mention plain but substantial fare, became one of the wonders of Western travel. Next he took over a run-down hotel in Florence, Kansas, with a population of 100, refurnished it and installed the former head chef of the Palmer House in Chicago as superintendent of the kitchen. The Florence House

157

was soon known as the finest place to eat in Kansas—not, perhaps, an overwhelming distinction, given the state of the cuisine anywhere west of Chicago—and travelers often made a point of stopping overnight in that hamlet just to remind themselves that civilization still existed. Harvey eventually built up a chain of forty-seven restaurants and fifteen hotels, as well as operated thirty dining cars, along the Santa Fe's right-of-way. His waitresses, known as the Harvey Girls, were imported from the East through advertisements calling for "young women of good character, attractive and intelligent"; they lived in dormitories under supervision of a matron and were dressed in black uniforms with white bows in their hair. Soon they provided respectable competition for the dance hall girls out West, and 5,000 of them were said to have contracted suitable marriages.

One stroke of venturesome management early in the Santa Fe's history enabled it to gain the financial footing to build its line to the Pacific ports and become a major transcontinental carrier. That was in the mid-seventies when its colonization bureau reached halfway around the world, plucked a whole wandering Germanic tribe out of the steppes of Asian Russia, literally stole them from the Czar of All the Russias, and deposited them on the plains of Kansas to work for the greater glory of their Mennonite God and the greater profit of the Atchison, Topeka & Santa Fe. It was one of the strangest migrations in American history and incidentally produced incalculable benefits for Western agriculture.

In the early seventies, with its tracks being pushed through the desolate barrens of the Southwest and not much revenue to be expected until they could reach the Pacific ports, the Santa Fe was desperate for cash income. It had to sell off its land grant and people it with producers of agricultural freight. A. E. Touzalin, the railroad's land commissioner, set up a colonization department like that of the other Western railroads but much more venturesome. Touzalin had advertised widely in the United States and organized a network of agents in Europe, but those measures brought only a trickle of emigrants.

His master stroke was to hire a footloose journalist rather uninspiringly named C. B. Schmidt. His name should have been

Errol Flynn or Scaramouche. Born in Saxony, he happened to be traveling out west when Touzalin hired him as an immigration agent. Schmidt immediately returned to Germany, where he heard that there was a large colony of Germans in Russia who wanted to get out and find a new place of settlement.

Schmidt's adventures in Russia as a Santa Fe secret agent would have made a stirring novel. First he devoted himself to considerable research on that wandering Teutonic band of religious outcasts. There was plenty of material in the German libraries. The research proved useful because the people he was seeking were a branch of the Mennonites, a touchy and contentious sect, whose hands-off attitude had been reinforced by centuries of persecution.

To outsiders, or Philistines, all Mennonites may seem alike, but actually there are many sects within the sect, endless schisms having occurred after quarrels about marriage regulations, preaching in other languages than German, four-part singing, and even the style of the preacher's dress. They were followers of a sixteenth-century prophet named Menno Simons, who broke away from the Anabaptists at a time when Germany was a religious battleground. A type of neurasthenia, as it appears to the non-Mennonite, seems to have afflicted the faith. In the United States alone, according to one authority, there are at least fourteen different Mennonite congregations: the Mennonite Church, the Hutterian Brethren, Conservative Amish Mennonites, Old Order Amish, Church of God in Christ Mennonites, Old Order Wisler Mennonites, Reformed Mennonites, Mennonite Brethren in Christ, Mennonite Church of North America, Krimmer Breuder Gemeinde, Mennonite Kleine Gemeinde, Central Conference of Mennonites, Stauffer Mennonites and Conference of Defenseless Mennonites.

In 1786, as Schmidt learned from his researches, a group of 400 Mennonite families moved to Russia at the invitation of Catherine the Great, who offered them free transportation, loans, and the promise of freedom from persecution. The Russian empress wanted to fill up the empty steppes to the south and east which had been acquired through conquest of the Tatars and Turkomen, and the Mennonites were known to be hardworking, skillful farmers who might quarrel among themselves over doc-

159

trinal differences but otherwise were law-abiding and docile. Their history in Russia was, to say the least, colorful and exotic. Settled in the Chortitz and Meltschna regions, they endured the searing summers and brutal winters of the steppes and made them flourish with crops of wheat that astounded the czar's officials. Schismatic differences also flourished. Small and beleaguered minority though they were among the mass of the Russian Orthodox, whose pogroms against the Jews indicated a minimal tolerance in religious matters, the German Mennonites in Russia still indulged themselves in endless schisms, one of the many traits they brought with them from Germany. One split, it was recorded, developed over the rental of a barley field. Another subsect, the Kleine Gemeinde, which was transported bodily to America, broke away from its brethren because its leader was opposed to such worldly customs as smoking tobacco, hilarious conduct at weddings, education, and socializing at funerals.

By the time C. B. Schmidt appeared on the scene the Russian authorities had wearied of Empress Catherine's bargain with the German Mennonites. They found many things wrong while admitting that the Mennonites raised tremendous crops where nothing but grass had grown before. The Mennonites refused to be converted to the Orthodox faith or be assimilated with their Russian neighbors in any way; they also refused to spend their money but insisted on exchanging their produce for gold coins, which they kept buried in chests to the detriment of the Russian economy. Taking counsel with the Orthodox archbishops, the czar decided to proscribe their religious practices and sent Cossacks to harass the German communities. The knout, it was felt, might accomplish conversions where theological argument failed, but it didn't. At the same time the Russian government was determined to keep the Mennonites on their steppe lands; it couldn't afford to lose so many thousand diligent farmers.

The Russians had succeeded in keeping colonization agents from other countries away from their Mennonites until C. B. Schmidt, regarding himself as an updated Scarlet Pimpernel, arrived in southern Russia. Just an innocent tourist, he told the Russians. The Ochrana did not believe him and assigned agents to shadow him. He gave them the slip and headed across country, riding by night and lying low in the daytime, until he reached the German settlements.

Schmidt's proselytizing was more successful than that of the Orthodox missionaries. He went from farm to farm spreading the Santa Fe gospel of cheap but fertile lands in a country that guaranteed absolute religious freedom and ruled without an Ochrana or Cossack regiments. (More specifically, the Santa Fe would sell its land at $5 to $10 an acre, with five or ten years to pay.) He did not, of course, say anything about hostile Indians or grasshopper plagues.

After spreading his propaganda throughout the Mennonite colonies, which then numbered more than 15,000 members, Schmidt slipped out of Russia and went back to the United States to wait for the seeds to sprout. Instead of appeasing their diligent but autonomous colony, the czar and his government announced that the Germans would have to Russianize themselves, stop using German as a first language, join the Russian Orthodox Church, and be subject to military service like any other citizens. They were given ten years to convert themselves into Russians, and those who balked would be exiled.

The Mennonites opted for the freedom they were promised in America, but it was months before the first group of 1,900 began the mass movement to the States. They had to sell most of their possessions and devise a means of bringing their hoards of gold coins out of Russia. In 1875 the first detachment landed at Ellis Island and was forwarded to Kansas. All along the way from the Russian frontier, knowing the Mennonites would send word back to their coreligionists of how they were treated, the network of Santa Fe agents in Europe had facilitated their passage, protected them from being fleeced by ticket brokers for the steamships and from thieves and confidence men. Stateside agents met them at Ellis Island and escorted them across the country to Topeka.

There was a good reason for that careful shepherding: Every time an adult Mennonite took a step there was a clinking of the gold coins they had sewn into their clothing.

Another reason was the practical methods of competing railroads. Despite all their precautions, the Santa Fe several times lost whole trainloads of gold-bearing Mennonites to its rivals.

161

Carl J. Ernst, the head of the Burlington road's land department, also sent a representative to Russia, as did the Union Pacific. In a confessional article many years later he recalled:

> I met them [the Mennonites] several times by the trainload and on one occasion swiped a whole trainload from the two Kansas roads, each of which had a special train waiting their arrival at Atchison, but I stole the whole bunch, except less than a, dozen unmarried young men, and carried them all by special train, free, to Lincoln, Nebraska. Those were certainly strenuous days for settling up our prairie states. . . . We located large settlements, not only of the German colonists from Southern Russia, but many other settlements of Germans, Swedes, Norwegians, Danes, Hollanders, Bohemians and Polanders, most of them coming from other states where land was too expensive to enable them to acquire farms of their own.*

At Topeka the vanguard of the Mennonite emigrants were given an official welcome, the warmth of which fairly dazzled them. The governor himself addressed the group, with C. B. Schmidt providing the translation. It must have been a curious confrontation, officialdom in claw-hammer coats, the Mennonites in fur hats, Russian blouses and mujik boots; refugees from the world of Tolstoy and men who had shaken the hand of George Armstrong Custer; Old World and New staring at each other across a cultural chasm that still has not entirely closed. The Mennonites found the religious tolerance they had been promised, but their way of life sometimes has come into conflict with the commonweal; their belief in pacifism, for one thing, and the reluctance of some Mennonite factions to send their children to public schools in which they would be indoctrinated in more worldly attitudes.

The vanguard pushed on west as soon as the governor of Kansas finished his address and fell to work with an energy that amazed and delighted the Santa Fe sponsors. Fortunately they

---

*Ernst also reported that the Burlington alone spent the rather surprising total of $969,500 on advertising the railroad's land in Nebraska. The Union Pacific spent about $100,000 less on the same project.

had just missed the worst grasshopper plagues. Eventually 15,000 Mennonites, practically the whole colony in Russia, joined the migration to Kansas, Colorado, and the Dakotas. Their dryland farming techniques, necessarily developed in the similarly arid plains of Southern Russia, greatly forwarded the agricultural development of the plains states.

A sizable splinter group of Mennonites, the Hutterian Brethren, came over about the same time under the sponsorship of the Burlington road, which settled them in what became the state of South Dakota. The Hutterian Brethren differed from other Mennonites not only in matter of doctrine but in their belief in a sort of nonpolitical communism. To the amazement of their new neighbors in the Dakotas, they lived a strictly communal existence, collected in large households called *Brüderhöfe*, eating in a common dining room and rearing their children in collective nurseries. The men wore uniforms without buttons, fastened together with hooks and eyes. Sixteenth-century hymns were sung at their services. During World War I they resisted the authorities and refused to support the war effort in any way; the government retaliated by seizing their sheep and cattle and selling them to buy $20,000 worth of Liberty Bonds, at which time many of the Hutterian Brethren migrated to Canada.

It was estimated that the Mennonites who migrated to Kansas brought $2,200,000 worth of czarist gold coins secreted in their clothing. The hoard was soon exhausted in their struggle against the fickle American climate. Several years after their arrival in 1879 and 1880 there was a series of droughts which shriveled the southern plains—an early warning of the dust bowl conditions which developed a half century later. Hundreds of settlers were wiped out and had to be carried out of the stricken region without charge by the Santa Fe. But not the Mennonites. Their neighbors could return to Ohio; the Mennonites couldn't go back to Russia. They stuck it out, survived, and prospered.

They had brought something much more valuable than gold coins minted by the Russian imperial treasury: the seeds of various types of wheat new to the American continent. The seeds were of turkey and durum wheat which needed little moisture,

163

were impervious to wheat rust and other plant diseases. One day those packets of seed, planted, replanted and adapted to their new environment, would stave off famines on the other side of the world. They would even return to their Russian birthplace under the terms of a contract supplying the Soviet Union with American wheat.

7.

The Invasion of the Indian Territory

Pickin' up bones to keep from starving,
Pickin' up chips to keep from freezing,
Pickin' up courage to keep from leaving,
Way out West in No Man's Land.
—*Song of the Oklahoma pioneers*

M ORE than six decades after the railroads spearheaded the invasion of Oklahoma, formerly Indian Territory, the dust bowl created by overly intensive colonization was sadly but compellingly evoked by John Steinbeck:

To the red country and part of the gray country of Oklahoma, the last rains came gently, and they did not cut the scarred earth. The plows crossed and recrossed the rivulet marks. The last rains lifted the corn quickly and scattered weed colonies and grass along the sides of the road so that the gray country and the dark red country began to disappear under a green cover. In the last part of May the sky grew pale and the clouds that had hung in high puffs for so long in the spring were dissipated. The sun flared down on the growing corn day after day until a line of brown spread along the edge of each green bayonet. . . .

The great rush to Oklahoma, encouraged by the railroads which penetrated a vast territory supposedly set aside for the evolution of a promising Indian civilization, was duplicated in reverse in the 1930's, when the ravaged land was abandoned by jalopy-borne columns of the grandsons of the pioneers heading westward for inhospitable California.

Viewing their departing backs, the surviving members of the Five Civilized Tribes whose birthright had been plundered, many of them enriched by oil revenues unforeseen by the plunderers, must have felt a sardonic amusement. The Cherokee, Creek, Chickasaw, Choctaw and Seminole who formed the "nation" titled the Five Civilized Tribes were all uprooted tribesmen who had been guaranteed a permanent home by the federal government in the Indian Territory, which included all of what is now the state of Oklahoma minus the Panhandle. They had lived in close contact with the whites for more than a century and were evolving into a copper-colored mirror image of Anglo-Saxon society.

Many were farmers, cattle ranchers, planters, and millwrights; they had their own churches and schools and governmental structure. Some were wealthy plantation owners and kept black slaves. Most of them were settled on the timbered hills and rolling prairies of the eastern half of what was designated as Indian Territory, moderately prosperous, guaranteed a permanent home, in the words of so many broken treaties promulgated by Washington, "as long as the grass shall grow and the waters flow." Each of the tribes tried offenders against its laws in its own courts, administered its own government and conducted parliamentary debates in its legislature with meticulous regard for the rules of order.

The Civil War, however, interrupted the process by which Indian Territory was evolving into an isolated but successful protectorate of the United States, with a position somewhat like that of the commonwealth of Puerto Rico. Secession ended its isolation when the Five Civilized Tribes, coming originally from Tennessee, North Carolina, and the Gulf states, sided with the Confederacy. Oddly enough they joined forces with the white men who had expelled them from their homelands. Stand Watie became a brigadier general in the Confederate Army. Chief John Ross of the Cherokee, who tried to keep his tribe neutral, was forced to flee from the territory. During the war Indian Territory became a battleground of partisan bands.

After Appomattox the federal government declared that the

Five Civilized Tribes had been guilty of "rebellion" and detached the western half of Indian Territory for settlement by other Indian tribes. Unfortunately the plains tribes supposedly resettled in Indian Territory merely used it as a base for hunting expeditions to the north and raids on the white settlements of Kansas and Colorado. This provided Washington with the excuse to build Fort Supply near the western boundary and Fort Sill on the eastern slopes of the Wichita Mountains, supposedly to protect white settlements, and supplying the forts gave the railroads an opening wedge into Indian Territory. The Five Civilized Tribes did their best to stave off the incursion. They not only built up an educational system under which neighborhood elementary schools were taught by Indians and secondary boarding schools were staffed by white college graduates, but in a council at Okmulgee (the Creek tribal council) tried to persuade the representatives of the plains tribes to take up farming and stop raiding white settlements as the only way of keeping what the Indian race had left.

Indian Territory could have been what high-minded proclamations from Washington maintained it was: a pilot model for the solution of the Indian problem. It could have been kept as a protectorate, a haven for Indian aspirations, a proving ground for the ingenuity and adaptability of the Indian race, a social laboratory in which the more advanced tribes educated and assimilated those closer to the Stone Age. But those lush ranges already were coveted by Texas ranchers to the south and homesteaders from all over; the Cherokee Strip alone contained more that 6,000,000 acres of rich grassland, and bills were constantly introduced in Congress to liquidate the tribal governments and throw the land open to white settlement.

In the case of Indian Territory, rails followed the flag. The Army decided it was necessary to establish Fort Gibson deep in the territory in 1869, and Congress quickly passed legislation authorizing land grants to whichever railroad was first to lay track connecting Fort Gibson with the great western supply depot of Fort Leavenworth in Kansas. The grants would go to the railroad whose track first reached the boundary of Indian Territory.

A helter-skelter contest, familiar to railroad construction his-

167

tory, ensued. Everything was turned into a competition, with speed more essential than sound engineering practices. Three railroads entered the race, the Kansas & Neosho Valley, the Leavenworth, Lawrence & Fort Gibson, and the Missouri, Kansas & Texas Railway (always to be endearingly known as the Katy).

It may have appeared that the Missouri, Kansas & Texas was a regional enterprise, both from its name and the fact that two sons of the Middle Border, Levi Parsons and George Denison, were president and vice-president respectively. But the company organized expressly to lay hands on the Indian Territory land grants, was another Wall Street creation, with the financial backing supplied by such familiar figures as J. Pierpont Morgan, August Belmont, Levi P. Morton, and John D. Rockefeller, Sr., all names which pop up continually in the backstage areas of the exploitation of the West.

The tracklaying race began in May, 1870, with the Leavenworth, Lawrence & Fort Gibson dropping out of the competition within a few weeks because of inadequate financing. That left the field to the Katy and the Kansas & Neosho Valley, both captained by men who did not flinch at skulduggery and violence as means of winning the race to the Indian Territory boundary. The two railroads, in fact, came into armed conflict which required intervention from the White House; the tendency of such enterprises to consider themselves independent principalities, with small standing armies privileged to conduct operations against each other, provided a number of bloody footnotes to the history of nineteenth-century capitalism.

Levi Parsons, as president of the Katy, knew that the New York and Cleveland financiers backing his company would expect nothing less than total victory and was perhaps a trifle more desperate in his methods than his rivals. At the outset of their competition he sent a large crew of workmen and a wagon train laden with rails to the Kansas-Indian Territory border. There they began laying a section of track across the boundary. By that maneuver, Parsons evidently believed he could seize the land grants: the Katy's tracks were the first to reach into Indian Territory, no matter that they were unconnected and served no useful purpose. The officials of the Kansas & Neosho Valley were

168

so outraged by Parsons' end run that they organized a gang of thugs to descend on the Katy's track gang. A battle with ax handles, picks, and shovels followed, with the outcome bloody but indecisive. Before the border battle could be renewed, however, President Grant issued an executive order directing the Katy to halt its activities in the Indian Territory, go back to square one, and start laying track in an orderly fashion.

The Katy and Kansas & Neosho Valley crews then returned to their railheads and began a giddy contest in rail building. They weren't building railroads, they were engaged in a tracklaying race. Ties were plumped down on the prairie soil, and no matter how uncertain the footing, the rails were laid on top of them. For years afterward Katy passengers would pay for that race in jarred vertebrae, bruised rumps and shattered nerves as Katy trains jolted over the uneven roadbed. (Pioneer passengers claimed that riding the Katy from St. Louis to Galveston was a more grueling ordeal than making the same journey on muleback.) During the crucial spring of 1870 the rival track gangs often worked around the clock, laying track by the light of the prairie moon or huge bonfires.

One June dawn the Katy workmen, having labored through the night, suddenly became aware of hundreds of silent, bemused Indians wrapped in blankets and watching them from a nearby hillside. They had crossed into Indian Territory. By noon that day a diamond-stacked Katy locomotive bucked and reared down the last stretch of quivering track and triumphantly blew its whistle.

At almost the same moment the Kansas & Neosho Valley was crossing the Indian Territory boundary farther up the line. Its officials were preparing to contend that they had won the race when it was discovered that a ghastly geographic error had been made by its locating engineers. The land grant legislation specified that rails had to be laid into the territory of the Five Civilized Tribes. But the Kansas & Neosho Valley tracks had been built into the Quapew Indian reservation, where no railroad had any right to be.

The chagrin of the Kansas & Neosho Valley group was considerably alleviated a short time later when the appellate courts ruled that the whole tracklaying race had been an exercise in

169

futility. Congress, the courts held, had exceeded its authority in granting land that belonged to the Five Civilized Tribes.

Victorious but emptyhanded, the Katy's masterminds pondered what to do next. A railroad without millions of acres of land to sell was regarded as a surefire loser. Parsons and Denison, however, urged that the railroad be extended southward and their Wall Street supporters reluctantly agreed. So while the Five Nations won their court battle, they lost the larger issue of preventing white penetration; it was inevitable that the Katy, and soon enough other roads arrowing east and west as well as north and south, would construct the webbing that ensnared their development as a culturally, socially, and economically independent entity. The trains brought in the cavalry by the regiment to railheads from which the "wild" tribes could be subdued. The very existence of the railroads and the accessibility they offered increased the political pressure to allow white settlement in Indian Territory. The Germans were not the first to discover that treaties could be regarded as scraps of paper when overriding considerations appeared.

The Indians of the Five Nations knew what the extension of the railroads would mean to their way of life. When the Missouri, Kentucky & Texas began moving in the direction of Fort Gibson, the hitherto-peaceful Cherokees became so warlike that the Katy was forced to divert its line, head instead for what is now Muskogee, and cross the Red River to the newly established town of Denison, named for the Katy's vice-president. Denison attained municipal dignity on Christmas Day, 1872, when an engineer named Pat Tobin drove the first flag-decked Katy locomotive across the Red River bridge and into the new railhead. It was then a mere huddle of false-fronted saloons and boardinghouses in which, it was observed by a passing moralist, there seemed to be a chambermaid for every room.

Three months later Denison could be regarded as a monument to white civilization as represented by its more venturesome elements, also as a thing of wonder to the observant Cherokee, who had been encouraged to build such solid and worthwhile institutions as churches, schools, courthouses. In three months Denison had grown to a town of 3,000, but without any of the attributes which whites had always told Indians were the hallmarks of Anglo-Saxon culture and all-conquering Christianity. The only temples raised were those dedicated to drinking and fornication. "Every third building is a drinking saloon with gambling appurtenances," a resident admitted. "Robberies are frequent occurrences in these gambling hells, but in the primitive hotels where passengers from the M. K. & T. Ry. await transfer by stage to Sherman, they are as safe from robbery or outrage as in any first-class hotel." Crime became so rampant, in fact, that a celebrated town tamer named Red Hall, who dispensed summary justice with a Colt revolver in one hand and a Winchester rifle in the other, had to be imported to maintain order. Mr. Hall shot the more unruly characters, arrested those deemed worthy of redemption, and drove a number of others out of town before he was satisfied with his labors.

Farther north on the main line, another Katy town, this one named for its president, Levi Parsons, was a junction point in which keno joints and brothels flourished. Violence seemed to strike wherever the Katy established a terminal. At Muskogee, Indian Territory, one man was shot, killed and buried before the first train arrived; three others were similarly defunct before the first streets were laid out. The Katy towns, as the railroad's official historian noted, seemed to attract all the hard cases who had been kicked out of such centers of refinement as Dodge City and Cheyenne. They became so numerous that the badmen of the Katy towns were given the title of "terminuses" because they seemed to cluster around the end of steel and possibly also because their activities tended to have a terminal effect on their victims. In playful moods the "terminuses" got their kicks by tampering with switches and derailing trains. The Katy was forced to arm all its trainmen, which terminated a number of lively careers. A short time later, however, President Grant ordered the Tenth Cavalry into Indian Territory to drive the rest of the "terminuses" out of the region.

Viewing the brawling, boozing, frequently homicidal vanguard of white civilization, the membership of the Five Nations, so often abjured by emissaries from Washington to emulate the sobriety and refinement of Caucasian society, must have been utterly bewildered. A band of Comanche whooping it up on the warpath seemed models of gentlemanly deportment compared to

171

the exemplars of gracious living which had been thrust into their midst. The Five Civilized Tribes had been told endlessly that they must establish and abide by a system of laws, that they must respect each other's property rights, that they must build their society on a foundation of order and communal peace.

Yet within a few years the whites who came coursing into the Katy towns and other settlements made the territory a synonym for lawlessness; the towns of Parsons and Denison provided material for Sunday-supplement spreads on shootouts for a generation, and the term "Oklahoma trainrobber" stood for a demiprofession in itself. The James, Younger, and Dalton gangs all operated profitably on the Katy right-of-way. The Dalton brothers and their confederates, in fact, chose the Katy town of Coffeyville, Kansas, for their farewell appearance, and the bodies of four members of the gang were dumped into a single grave along the Katy tracks.

Undismayed by all the violence and disorder it attracted, the Katy continued pushing southward, became the first railroad to cross the Texas line from the north, and plastered the West with posters under the slogan "Gateway to Texas" with a cowboy riding a longhorn followed by a Katy locomotive. Their work parties had to be guarded by riflemen against the growingly hostile Indians as well as white predators, but eventually the Missouri, Kentucky & Texas reached from its northern terminus at Sedalia, Kansas, all the way to Galveston on the Gulf of Mexico.

Once the railroads had penetrated Indian Territory, Washington made only the feeblest gestures toward preserving the sworn, documented, oft-attested, and much-boasted concession of the Indians' right to self-development in their prairie enclave.

Late in the seventies, by the time the railroads had created the possibility of rapid settlement, there were hundreds of prospective homesteaders poised on the borders of Indian Territory for the rush to claim quarter sections, and the Texas cattle barons were clamoring for grazing rights on the ranges of the Cherokee Strip. Naturally they were encouraged by the railroads, not only the Katy but the St. Louis & San Francisco (Frisco), which began building the first east-west line across Indian Territory in 1871,

172

and later the Santa Fe, which extended south from Wichita to Galveston, and still later the Rock Island, with its tracks running from the Kansas line to the border of the Chickasaw Nation.

From 1879 on, determined efforts were made to penetrate Indian Territory by various means. Some used as their model for the settlement of the "forbidden land" the recent invasion of the Black Hills of Dakota Territory, which had shown how the impasse could be overcome. The Black Hills, despite the fact the government had ceded them to the Sioux, were simply overrun by gold prospectors and their camp followers. Cattle drovers using the Chisholm and other trails kept propagandizing for settlement of the lush farming and ranching country they passed through on their way to the Kansas railheads. Western newspapers kept demanding to know when the federal government was going to open up the territory to vigorous white settlers and stop coddling the "indolent Indians." The Kansas City *Times,* for instance, charged that a corrupt "Indian ring" was responsible for defeating various bills designed to open up the territory for settlement, that the membership of the ring was composed of Indian leaders who handled the tribal annuities. "All opposition," the newspaper charged, "comes from this ring of Indian sharpers admitted to have spent over $300,000 in Washington during the last two years, of money sacredly designed for schools and other territorial purposes, simply to defeat any legislation which by opening the Territory would end their pelf and power."

In 1879 came the self-discovery of one David L. Payne as a prophet, a new Moses, who would lead his people into the land of Canaan/Oklahoma. Endowed with a talent for oratory and showmanship, with an imposing and inspiring presence and an instinct for attracting public notice, Payne within a few years would make himself a national figure. He would advertise himself as Old Oxheart, the Scout of the Cimarron.

Actually, in 1879, Payne had come no closer to the Cimarron than the maps of Indian Territory he studied so feverishly in a Washington office, and any oxheartedness he had displayed during a long and picaresque career on the fringe of various military and commercial ventures had been in scrounging a precarious living. Laying claim to the questionable rank of major, he had served for six months as a member of Custer's Seventh Cavalry.

173

Early in the seventies he had been the proprietor of Payne's ranch, on the banks of Dry Creek, which served as a stop on the stagecoach line between Humboldt and Wichita. His establishment was a dugout on the creek catering to stray travelers, the stock of which, according to a contemporary, was "a bale of hay, a box of crackers and a keg of whiskey." That dubious enterprise petered out, and Payne drifted to the national capital, where his glib tongue won him a sinecure as assistant doorkeeper of the House of Representatives gallery.

Payne's sense of opportunism was ignited early in 1879 by the discovery of what were termed "unassigned lands" by a fellow bureaucrat. The discovery on which Payne would capitalize was made by Elias C. Boudinot, a clerk employed by the House Committee on Private Land Claims. A former Confederate colonel, Boudinot had a natural interest in the subject. He was a member of the prominent Cherokee family who during the Civil War had served as a staff officer under General Stand Watie and as Cherokee representative to the Confederate Congress in Richmond. After Appomattox he had lost his standing with the tribe and apparently decided that he might as well throw in with the whites. Besides his Congressional clerkship, Boudinot moonlighted as an agent for the Missouri, Kansas & Texas Railroad. The Katy's attorney and Washington lobbyist, Judge T. C. Sears, admitted as much when he stated, shortly before Boudinot publicized his discovery of the "unassigned lands," that "Colonel Boudinot and myself have received within the last few weeks, scores of letters from all sections of the country making inquiries as to the status of the lands of the Indian Territory and the prospect of opening them for occupation."

As a sort of Cherokee turncoat and a secret operative for the Katy, Boudinot published an article in a Chicago newspaper, which Western journals eagerly reprinted, pointing out that there were 14,000,000 acres of public lands west of the Cross Timbers which belonged to neither the Five Nations nor the "wild" tribes who had been ceded territory. It was a vacuum, Boudinot held, rightly attracting the attention of the thousands of whites looking for an opportunity to homestead. Taking notice of this new lunge at the Indian enclave, Marshall M. Murdock, the editor of the Wichita *Eagle*, wrote a few weeks after Boudinot's article appeared that the Katy and other interested railroads for years had been exerting pressure on the Cherokee, Creek, and Choctaw to open their borders to white settlers. Despite a large expenditure of money and energy, the railroads had failed to move the leaders of the Five Nations. "Time and again during the years the writer served in the State Senate," wrote Murdock, "were efforts made to gain the consent of Kansas to the scheme. Stevens [a railroad lobbyist at Topeka] at one time took the whole state government by special train into the heart of the Territory where he feasted and wined the members in a manner nothing short of royal." Murdock, incidentally, was one of the few Kansas editors to oppose the invasion of Indian Territory—not as a matter of principle but because he feared that Kansas would lose its sturdiest citizens to Oklahoma.

After reading Boudinot's article, and undoubtedly discussing it with Boudinot and receiving his encouragement, David Payne decided to make himself the man of the hour. There were thousands of landless waiting for a leader, and Payne considered himself admirably suited for the role. Various associates described him as a "stalwart young man, 35 or 40 years of age, pleasant and sociable in manner," with curiously magnetic gray eyes flecked with yellow. With his expansive personality and his command of bureaucratic expertise, he figured that enough political pressure could be built up to persuade Washington to yield up a principle. He had observed that principles withered rather quickly under political duress.

When Payne went out west to organize his colonization venture, however, the federal government was still stubbornly maintaining that the so-called unassigned lands were designed only for occupation by members of the Indian race. If the "wild tribes" hadn't claimed them, then they still belonged to the Creek, Seminole and other members of the Five Nations. Besides, white colonization was forbidden in any part of Indian Territory; that was the whole idea of the enclave. Separatism had always been quelled by the federal government when it cropped up among the whites (one instance being the aspirations of German immigrants to establish New Germanys in Missouri, Texas and southern Illinois), but Washington still felt that the Indians deserved the right to attempt their own development in at least

175

one large and fertile territory. The cramped life of the reservations wasn't sufficient for that purpose.

Further, the federal government warned that it would employ the cavalry to keep white invaders out of Indian Territory and would also drive off the Texas cattlemen who, without any legal sanction, had divided the ranges among themselves, built corrals, and fenced in parts of the Cherokee Strip.

David Payne paid no attention to the warnings from Washington. With $200 borrowed from a sister in Indiana, he proceeded to Wichita and organized what he called the Oklahoma Colony and what other people soon began calling the Boomers. In such southern Kansas towns as Baxter Springs, Caldwell, Independence, and Coffeyville the invasion forces were gathering by the thousands, a symptom of the national "land hunger." Donning buckskins and a tall hat, ranging the Kansas border and making endless speeches, Payne enrolled trekkers who swore they would follow him into the wilderness and, if necessary, into the mouths of the army's howitzers. Soon he was claiming to have 10,000 dedicated followers.

"If David Payne hadn't been such a handsome man," the daughter of one of Payne's Boomers later recalled, "Oklahoma would never have been settled. He was exciting to look at, he was so handsome. He had the kind of voice that got you all stirred up, just listening to it. It wasn't just women who were willing to follow him anywhere. It was the men too. You had to trust him, because of his looks and his voice."

The eventual trekking of Payne's Boomers, and their countertrekking when United States troops caught up with them, became part of American folklore, a colorful (if somewhat discreditable) chapter in the pioneer saga. There were several false starts, however. President Hayes in his message to Congress had expressed doubt whether the government could keep the Boomers out of Oklahoma. This weak-kneed attitude in Washington encouraged Payne to launch a premature invasion in the spring of 1880. He could persuade only twenty-one men to follow him across the line, and they were soon driven back to Kansas by the cavalry.

No doubt funded by the sympathetic railroads, Payne managed to keep his following intact and ready for massive ex-

176

cursions into Indian Territory. In 1883 and 1884 the Boomers made two determined thrusts into the "unassigned lands." One group traveling in wagons with all their possessions moved into the country west of Arcadia on the North Canadian River, where they established Camp Alice on February 8, 1883. They were quickly driven back to the Kansas line by the U.S. Cavalry. In the following year Payne made several more determined efforts to occupy land in Indian Territory.

For those ventures Payne began attracting national support and sympathy early in 1884. His propagandizing was abetted by the fact that most white Americans didn't know an educated, frock-coated Cherokee from a war-painted, ferocious Comanche; they were all red-skinned savages, weren't they? The concept of Indian self-development simply hadn't been explained by the government, which apparently believed that it was a matter of interest only to the Department of the Interior's bureaucracy.

Washington's vague idealism didn't stand a chance when David L. Payne took to the platform—or when he appeared with Buffalo Bill's Wild West Show in the spring of 1884 billed as "Old Oxheart, the Scout of the Cimarron." With reckless hyperbole the show's program declared that Payne's "Oklahoma Raiders" were advancing the cause of civilization. In their foray across the border of Indian Territory, Payne and his colonists had been carefully ignored by the Indians, yet the program asserted that the Indians "have surrounded his cabin in the lonely solitude of those primeval forests, threatened his life, tried to burn down his house, and watched day and night for opportunity to murder him. . . . With his trusty Winchester he had defended his cabin against scores of his wily foes." All balderdash, of course. The only harassment of the Boomers had come from the cavalry obeying orders to evict them from places they had no legal right to be. "While waiting for certain developments in his still continued contest," the show's program added, "Captain [sic] Payne will accompany, for recreation only, his old friend Buffalo Bill's 'Wild West,' to renew again the cherished object so dear to the progressive spirit of the Oklahoma Raiders."

Later that year, after being cheered by hundreds of thousands of his fellow citizens in the Wild West arenas of a dozen cities, Payne renewed his efforts to occupy the heart of Indian Territory.

Despite what he bellowed from Buffalo Bill's podium, he knew that the cavalry, not the Indians, constituted the opposition. To thwart the cavalry (and the law of the land), he divided his colonists into several groups and sent them pell-mell across the Kansas line to dig in and defy the dictates of Washington. It would be more difficult for the cavalry to round up scattered groups of his Boomers. And sooner or later, he was certain, the government would grow weary of resisting the pressure from the Western states to allow homesteading on the Oklahoma prairies.

One group of Boomers moved into the area west of Council Grove, near the future site of Oklahoma City, and began breaking the soil on the northern bank of the Canadian River. The Boomers brought their families and were quick to build shanties or sod houses to establish their squatters' rights. One Boomer girl, wearing a sunbonnet to keep her fair skin from freckling, drove a four-hourse team of the family's wagon on the ninety-day trek to Council Grove. "Oh, sugar," she said, "it wasn't nothing, driving that team. It was a sight easier than washing clothes on a fire in the yard, back in Kansas. It was fun. And clean! My lands, you never saw a country was so clean. Until you've walked on land that's never been broken, and smell air that's never been breathed, you don't know what clean is. If you cut your finger in those days, you didn't get blood poisoning. There weren't any germs. It would just heal right over." It was just possible that the girl who marveled over the "cleanness" of Indian Territory before it was overrun by the white man was still alive, a grandmother with memories of a pristine past, when that same section became part of the dust bowl; that she was one of those lean and leathery survivors who rejoiced in being called one of the Boomers but who lived long enough to take part in the flights to California and be opprobriously labeled Okies.

It was only two generations from stalwart Boomer to unwanted and despised Okie, less than half a century from verdant Indian Territory to parched red-brown Oklahoma, from blue prairie skies to towering dust clouds. . . .

The settlers at Council Grove were soon visited by a detachment of cavalry from Fort Reno. Its captain politely suggested that the Boomers had better move on, that they were occupying Indian lands, and that he would probably receive direct orders to evict them. The soldiers, most of them naturally sympathetic to their fellow whites, were in for a long struggle with Payne's followers. No sooner would they evict a group than it settled elsewhere on the prairie, or their attention would be diverted by another incoming column of Payne's doggedly determined homesteaders.

"We got to know the soldiers real well," the girl quoted above recalled. "The ones from Fort Reno would move us south of the river, and keep us drifting southwest until we got to the Fort Sill area. Then they'd go on back and the soldiers from Fort Sill would come out and start shifting us north and east till we were back around Fort Reno again. That way we kept the soldiers too busy all summer to notice what was going on east of us, in the Sauk and Fox country. Payne and his bunch managed to get some crops in, and even harvested. Yes, you might say we got to know some of the soldiers *real* well. I married one myself."

A mad sort of checker game ensued through the summer and autumn of 1884. On Sundays, pursuing soldiers and chivvied Boomers would gather around the itinerant preacher's wagon and sing hyms to the accompaniment of his portable piano. In October Payne himself led a large caravan of wagons and cattle to a site on the Canadian, along what became Lake Overholser formed by the damming of the river to provide Oklahoma City with a water supply. They quickly established a camp, laid out a townsite, and set aside one plot for the State Capitol they planned to erect. Inside two weeks the colonists had staked out farms and begun plowing.

Another colony was planted where the town of Blackwell now stands. On the Chikaskia River 25 miles northwest of Ponca City, Payne set up his propaganda center, even importing, printing presses and all, his journalistic mouthpiece, the *Oklahoma War Chief.* That periodical was published at various places along the Kansas border from 1883 to 1886, but from June 14 to August 7, 1884, is was issued from the Boomer settlement of Rock Falls, a town of several hundred tents and plank houses on the Chikaskia. Payne imported printers, too, who were willing to run off his paper for hazardous-duty pay. The *Oklahoma War Chief* was printed in a hastily built shack, the door of which defiantly displayed a placard distributed by the federal government and warning that any person attempting to publish a newspaper in the Cherokee Strip was guilty of trespassing and subject to fine and imprisonment. Freedom of the press, as interpreted by Payne, was suddenly expunged when a company of infantry descended on Rock Falls, arrested Payne and other leaders of the colony, burned down the office of the *Oklahoma War Chief*, and escorted his followers to the Kansas line. Another infantry outfit moved on Payne's other colonies, uprooted the illegal settlers, and sent them trekking back to Kansas.

The Boomer cause was temporarily crushed but not destroyed by news of David Payne's premature death in Wellington, Kansas, on November 28, 1884, only a few weeks after the Army had carried out its eviction proceedings. For several years the Boomers clung to their springboard along the Kansas border, waiting until their lobbyists in Washington suceeded in changing the government's mind about its Indian Territory policy.

The urgent land hunger of the whites was like a river at flood stage eroding the banks of the levee. Though the initial penetration had been no wider than the few yards of the Katy right-of-way, it had been enough eventually to funnel in settlers by the tens of thousands.

Railroad lobbyists and Boomer propagandists never wearied of pointing out that the population of the United States had swollen from 3,000,000 to 63,000,000 since the signing of the Declaration of Independence. Their pressure on Congress was unremitting, and they secured the passage of the Railroad Act of 1886, which was promoted by the Katy and other Western roads. As a contemporary historian noted, it "laid the territory open to further railroad encroachment under the right of eminent domain," and it was no longer necessary to ask permission to lay steel through the Indian preserves. No matter that the Indians strongly objected. For years the Cherokee Nation fought bitterly against the extension of the Kansas and Arkansas Valley Railway westward from Fort Smith, Arkansas, and up the Arkansas Valley to Kansas. The Cherokee refused permission for cutting ties along the right-of-way, but lost their battle in the courts.

Early in 1889 the Creek and Seminole were persuaded to sell their title to their tribal lands to the government for a total of less

180

than $4,200,000. This was an area covering six present Oklahoma counties.

On April 22, 1889, less than two months after the transaction was completed and with no time for preparation, came the famous "run" for 160-acre homsteads. Instead of devising some orderly process for allotting the new land, the authorities presided over one of those helter-skelter spectacles which epitomized the heedless rush, competitive elbowing, and frantic reaching with which the West was colonized. Many opportunists called Sooners sneaked over the line to grab the choicest land before the "run" officially began. Thus, when a trainload of settlers arrived at the tiny Santa Fe depot on the site of Oklahoma City, they found several hundred Sooners staking out the better locations. Many of the First Families of Oklahoma are descended from some spry fellow who "beat the bugle" in April, 1889.

The law-abiding majority, however, had to take their chances on fast footwork. On the appointed day a long wavering line of settlers was assembled on the Kansas border for the race across the prairies. They stampeded southward when a signal gun was fired. The prizes would go to the fleetest, as always, rather than the neediest or most deserving. On horseback, in covered wagons and buggies, and some unfortunates on foot, they plunged into the heart of Indian Territory to claim the tracts. After staking his claim, a homesteader often had to fight off men slower of foot but quicker of trigger. For the next thirteen months a state of near anarchy prevailed until Congress got around to passing legislation providing a governmental structure for the newly occupied land.

White Oklahoma, as the territory would be named when it achieved statehood, soon engulfed the tribal lands. The various tribes moved onto reservations after selling their surplus land to the government, and the former preserves of the Sac, the Fox, the Iowa, and the Shawnee-Potawatomi were occupied by whites.

Almost yearly one tribe or another yielded up its lands, and even the vast countryside around Fort Sill, occupied by the Kiowa, Comanche, Kiowa-Apache, Wichita and Caddo, was thrown open to another "run" by white settlers. This time the government decreed that the homesteaders must register, along

181

with Indians who were given first choice of the allotments, having opted for 160-acre farms instead of living on a reservation. Then lots were drawn to decide which settlers got the choicer tracts.

It was an amazing spectacle to a cavalry captain named W. S. Nye who was stationed at Fort Sill. He wrote;

> Free land! When the good news spread through the surrounding country, homesteaders began rushing to Fort Sill and El Reno to register. Just why they were hurrying no one knew; every person stood an equal chance of drawing a lucky card in the lottery, irrespective of the order in which he registered. But no one wanted to be last. During the last part of July the roads and trails leading across the prairies were filled with caravans of homesteaders. Some were in wagons, some in buggies, others on horseback. A few rode bicycles and there were many who trudged along with packs on their backs. It was like the migration of a people. One might see a covered wagon drawn by a team composed of a dispirited pony and a placid cow; wagons piled with household goods, here a crate filled with chickens, there a pig squealing in a box. . . .

After the drawing, the town of Lawton was staked out and the benefits of Anglo society quickly followed, Captain Nye recalling in his colorful memoirs the "throngs of sharpers, gamblers, cattlemen, honest farmers mingled in the dust which lay ankle deep in the streets. Water sold at fancy prices. Sanitation was elementary. All the lively entertainments of a boom town were present in quantity. . . .

"The day of the Indian was over," he added with a note of regret. "He was now an insignificant minority in a land settled by white people."

Within a year two railroad lines converged on Fort Sill, where the post interpreter, Horace P. Jones, who "remained unreconciled to the delights of civilization," often declared in his old age that he did not intend to live long enough to see the first train come in. On his deathbed Jones could hear the sledges of the track gangs approaching Fort Sill. The Indians living around the fort viewed the coming of the first train with equal distaste, according to Captain Nye. They had heard that the old Comanche chief, Tabananica, had died of heart failure while running to catch a train over in Anadarko, and believed that signified the evils of

182

modern transportation. The iron horse could only take them off to places where they would be confronted by the dangerous complexities of the white man's civilization. Yellow Bear, another Comanche leader, had blown out the gas light on retiring in his Fort Worth hotel room and had been asphyxiated. Such incidents tended to convince the Indians that they were fortunate in not having invented the wheel.

They made one last attempt to preserve something of their heritage, to reclaim part of what Washington had always promised them. With a few white sympathizers collaborating, the leaders of the Five Civilized Tribes met at Muskogee in 1906 and drew up a constitution for a new state to be named Sequoyah in honor of the Cherokee who taught his people to read and write in their own language. Congress, however, rejected the Indian plan for statehood—it would have created a separate state for the Five Nations, with the rest of Indian Territory left to the whites—and insisted that whites and Indians both become Oklahomans.

The Katy and other railroads could claim a large share of the credit for converting Indian Territory from tribal isolation, from inward-looking obsession with the old way of life, to the modern and integrated state of Oklahoma. Along with most whites, they urged that the communal preserves of the Five Civilized Tribes be broken up and the land distributed as individual farms to the members of the tribes. That brought them all under the sway of the state government rather than their tribal councils.

The Indians could hardly help feeling that they had literally been railroaded into the condition of an inferior minority dominated by the Anglo-Saxon majority.

Yet the prime contractor on that project, the Katy railroad, ironically was also the victim of the Eastern capitalism which manipulated the encroachments on their territory.

Jay Gould had looked upon the Katy balance sheets and found them attractive. In 1880 he and his collaborators, principally Russell Sage, bought up a controlling interest in the railroad at small cost to themselves. They secured control when Gould acquired 34,000 shares of Katy stock and Sage 16,000 shares. In moved the Gould plunderbund, with Gould himself as president and a board which included Sage and other such veterans of the

Union Pacific-Crédit Mobilier operation as Sidney Dillon, former UP president; Oliver L. Ames, the brother of the late Oakes Ames; and General Dodge, who had somehow managed to spend $100,000 a mile building the Union Pacific.

With that group in control, financial disaster for the other stockholders could not be far behind. Gould intended to loot the Katy on behalf of the Missouri Pacific, the linchpin of his system of Western railroads. One of his earliest moves was to buy the bankrupt East Line & Red River Railroad for $800,000 and sell it to the Katy for $2,852,000 as part of link to Texas. The East Line & Red River was a three-foot gauge line operating with the general efficiency of a Toonerville Trolley. Daniel Upthegrove, president of the Cotton Belt Railroad, described a journey over its tracks:

> When this train reached a speed of fifteen miles per hour the passengers insisted that the company was tempting Providence and if by any chance the engineer had to blow the whistle at a Texas longhorn and it was on the upgrade, the engine would stall, as it did not have sufficient boiler pressure to pull the three freight cars and a passenger coach up a hill and whistle at the same time.

Missouri Pacific equipment was repaired in the Katy shops at Sedalia, Parsons, and Denison, and worn-out Missouri Pacific rolling stock was exchanged for new Katy locomotives and engines after being newly stenciled and relettered. By 1888 the Katy's stockholders began worrying about what the "Gould wrecking crew" was doing to their investment and launched a joint effort to reclaim the company. But Gould and his associates had begun clearing out two years earlier when the Texas attorney general, James S. Hogg, filed suits against the Katy and other Gould lines operating in Texas. Hogg had been elected on a promise to compel all railroads operating in Texas to maintain their general offices in the state and abolish control of Texas roads by "foreign" corporations. When the Katy's other stockholders closed in on Gould and his collaborators, they found the battlefield deserted by the enemy. Gould and Sage no longer owned a dollar's worth of Katy stock, which they had quietly dumped in the past few years. Fattened by having nourished itself

184

at the Katy's expense, Gould's Missouri Pacific, however, was flourishing—and that was how the nineteenth-century conglomerate operated.

The Katy, under more objective and honest management, survived the Gould treatment and in the following decade offered the public one of the more spectacular events in its lively history—a deliberately staged train wreck. That event must have been viewed by the Indians in the audience with wry and ironic reflection.

To enliven interest in the Katy during the depression of the mid-1890's, W. G. Crush, the aptly named general passenger agent of the railroad, decided to stage what he advertised as a MONSTER WRECK between two passenger trains.

The collision would take place on September 15, 1896, at a place on the Katy tracks between Waco and Hillsboro, Texas. The temporary town of Crush would be hammered together to accommodate the 20,000 people for whom tickets were printed in Kansas, Indian Territory, Missouri, and Texas. Given the safety standards of the Western railroads, many of the customers had been inadvertently involved in train wrecks, but this was a glorious opportunity to witness one from a less subjective standpoint.

As it turned out, Mr. Crush had underestimated the appealing qualities of a train wreck. On the day his spectacular took place, more than 30,000 people, "the largest crowd in Texas history" according to the Dallas *Morning News*, assembled to watch the collision at $2 a head.

At five o'clock in the afternoon, with the spectators ranged on the low sandhills overlooking the designated point of collision, two trains composed of an outmoded locomotive and six passenger cars approached each other at speed. The crash was more than anyone, including Mr. Crush, had bargained for. "Words bend and break in the attempt to describe it," wrote the Dallas *Morning News*. "It is a scene that will haunt many a man . . . the air was filled with flying missiles from the size of a postage stamp to half a drive-wheel falling indiscriminately on the just and the unjust, the rich and poor, great and small." For once a Texas journalist was not exaggerating. The impact was so great that the two locomotives went right through each other, and one of the

185

smokestacks landed a quarter of a mile away. Falling debris killed three persons and injured scores of others, and a farmer named Theodore Millenberger was so astounded by the spectacle that he fell out of his tree and broke his leg,

With a harvest moon lighting the scene, the tracks were cleared for business as usual the next day, the dead and injured were hauled away, and any philosophers present could reflect that the man-made disaster epitomized much of Western railroading history.

8.

Railroad War in the Rockies

I don't build railroads; I buy them.

—Jay Gould

THE image of those two Katy trains butting each other in a staged collision over in Texas, with the fallout killing or maiming the onlookers, could have been superimposed as a legend over the history of the Western railroads. In the expansive period of main-line construction the Western railroads collided over routes through the most lucrative territory, fought each other with private armies levied with scant regard for the law, and often resembled prehistoric monsters battling over territorial rights to a primeval swamp.

Railroad building was capitalistic competition at its hottest; the builders had to contend not only with the inhospitable topography of the West and its violent extremes of climate, but with rivals aiming to extend their lines through the same territory. And when their labors were finished, and the casualties counted, they often found that the rewards were snatched away through corporate maneuvers 2,000 miles to the east. That craftiest of railroad financiers, Jay Gould, who at one time controlled more Western railroad trackage than anyone else, once smugly remarked, "I don't build railroads; I buy them."

Gould wisely preferred the Wall Street arena to the internecine

187

warfare out on the plains and in the mountains, possibly because he had studied the career of Thomas A. Scott, who had built up the Pennsylvania Railroad as its president and then taken the plunge into Western railroading. Scott knew everything there was to know about railroad construction and operation; he was charged with energy and ambition, and yet his career ended with a disastrous attempt to build a line from Texas to the Pacific. One of his chief rivals, in fact, hinted that Scott worked too hard at his monumental task. "Tom Scott," Collis P. Huntington of the Southern Pacific summed him up, "was as clever a man as ever lived but he died from turning night into day and day into night. No man can live and do hard work transposing night into day. He started from an office boy—swept out the office; he grew up and died worth six or seven millions." Huntington and his associates were the men who thwarted Scott's ultimate ambition.

Scott, who had been Assistant Secretary of War during the Civil War and later built the Pennsylvania into one of the two strongest Eastern railroads, rightly believed that there was room for a major carrier from Texas to Southern California, but he underestimated the jealous determination of the Central Pacific and its offshoot, the Southern Pacific, to monopolize all rail traffic into California. The one thing Scott had going for him was California's detestation of the Central Pacific-Southern Pacific and its monopolistic practices, particularly in establishing freight rates, and its high-handed contempt for public opinion. Californians, referring to their homegrown enterprise as the "octopus," welcomed anyone who would give the Big Four a run for their money.

Scott began promoting his new enterprise with great vigor. He obtained a charter for the Texas & Pacific Railway early in 1871 and proceeded to build two lines in Texas, the northern starting from Texarkana with direct connections to the north and east, the southern starting from Marshall with connections to New Orleans and Vicksburg, and both converging at Fort Worth. From Fort Worth he planned to build a main line, roughly along the thirty-second parallel, to San Diego. He employed General Grenville M. Dodge, the builder of the Union Pacific, to take charge of construction. In 1872 he and General Dodge journeyed to San Diego, where they were welcomed as saviors, to forward a plan to build east from San Diego as well as west from Fort Worth. "All San Diego drew a breath of relief and hope," a local newspaper said, when it appeared that the struggling little port on San Diego Bay might escape the clutches of the Southern Pacific. The latter was just then building south of San Francisco. The Santa Fe had not yet entered the California picture. It seemed to Scott that, with a little help from Congress and a lot from foreign financiers, he would be able to push the Texas & Pacific into Southern California before the Southern Pacific could muster its forces against him.

Scott worked fast. While his construction crews were building west from Fort Worth, he obtained a land grant from San Diego and a right-of-way from the Colorado River to the ocean and in April, 1873, watched while grading begain on the first 10-mile section east from San Diego. They gave him a foothold in California, as he believed, and he was able to turn his attention to raising the necessary funds. Scott hurried to New York and sailed for Europe to peddle his Texas & Pacific bonds. A Parisian triumph awaited him. The financiers of the bourse wined and dined him and the newspapers hailed him as the Railroad King. Within a few days the Paris bankers agreed to finance the Texas & Pacific's construction. Well satisfied with his progress, Scott journeyed to Brussels for a dinner with the King of Belgium. During the thirty-six hours that side trip took, news arrived in Paris that the Jay Cooke banking house had failed because of overextension in financing the Northern Pacific. The Paris bankers, throwing honor to the winds, refused to sign the agreements they had verbally pledged to Scott.

He could fall back only upon the overtaxed financial resources of his own country. Knowing his way around Washington through his wartime service, Scott obtained subsidies from Congress for his railroad, while Huntington, who spent much of his time as the Southern Pacific's chief lobbyist in Washington, did the same for his company's line from San Francisco to Yuma. The battleground had now shifted to the nation's capital. Huntington was determined to prevent Scott from receiving the full ($68,000,000) subsidy he was seeking from Congress. A horrifying insight into the way Huntington and his fellow railroad magnates operated and their ability to bribe, suborn, and cajole the membership of the national legislature was later afforded a shocked public when Huntington's correspondence with David C. Colton, the financial director of the Central Pacific, was published by a New York newspaper. It was made plain by those letters, published in 1883, that the Western railroads thrived or failed in direct proportion to their influence on Congress

In one letter to Colton written during the several years the two men fought for Congressional favor, Huntington reported:

> Scott is prepared to pay or promises to pay a large amount of money to pass his [subsidy] bill but I do not think he can pass it, although I think that this coming session of Congress will be composed of the hungriest set of men that ever got together, and the devil only knows what they will do. . . . Would it not be well for you to send some party down to Arizona to get a bill in the Territorial legislature granting the right to build a R. R. east from the Colorado River, have the franchise free from taxation on its property and so that the rates of fare and freight cannot be interfered with until dividends of the common stock shall exceed ten percent? I think that would be as good as a land grant. . . . If such a bill was passed I think there could at least be got from Congress a wide strip for right of way, machine shops, etc. . . .

Early in 1876 Huntington was writing Colton that he had just been summoned back to Washington on receiving word that Scott was close to getting his subsidy bill passed. As usual Huntington had journeyed to Washington with a valise packed with his emergency kit: a Bible, a set of spare collars, and sheaves of U.S. currency. "It costs money to fix things," Huntington advised his colleague, "so that I would know that his bill would not pass. I believe with $200,000 I can pass our bill, but I take it that it is not worth that much to us."

Only a few years after the Crédit Mobilier scandal had infused its odor into the Potomac mists, it was still possible to buy up a sizable block of Congressmen for cash on the barrelhead. Yet Huntington complained a few months later that "Scott has several parties here that I think do nothing else except write against the Central Pacific and its managers and get them published in such papers as he can get to publish them at small cost, and there is no doubt that he has done much to turn public sentiment against us." He also groaned over Scott's knavery in spiriting away a member of a crucial committee by "getting some fellow to ask him to take a ride to New York, or anywhere else, of course on a free pass, and away they go together."

A year later Huntington was confiding to Colton his suspicions that Jay Gould had become interested in the Texas & Pacific and was collaborating with Scott in trying to obtain the full subsidy for the Texas & Pacific, meanwhile working to defeat Huntington's own claims on the pork barrel. Several months later he reported that he had obtained exact information on how much his rival was paying for a Congressman's political honor. "The Texas & Pacific folks are working hard on their bill, and say they are sure to pass it, but I do not believe it. They offered one M. C. one thousand dollars cash, five thousand when the bill was passed, and ten thousand of the bonds, when they got them, if he would vote for the bill."

Huntington became so alarmed by Scott's campaign that when both men appeared before a Senate committee to press their proposals, he offered to build the Southern Pacific to its eastern terminus without any subsidy from the Congress. Later he told Scott that "you are beating me out of nine things and I shall only beat you in one. You will beat me in demoralizing the press, you will beat me in sending colporteurs over the United States to get petitions to your bill; you will beat me in getting Boards of Trade; you will beat me in this and that, but in building the road, that is one thing I shall beat you."

Scott was mortally weary of the contest. He seemed to be losing out in the Congressional contest, and the Southern Pacific, with superior financial resources, was building east from Yuma even while waiting for the subsidy question to be decided. Meanwhile, Huntington's Big Four colleague Senator Leland Stanford was haranguing Californians on the destiny of the Southern Pacific: "We are toiling for the greatest prize this continent affords. Magnificent destiny awaits us when we shall have brought to our doors the vast trade of Arizona, New Mexico, Sonora, Chihuahua, for it is nothing less than this we are striving for."

Shortly, however, a far more sinister figure than Thomas A. Scott interposed himself between Leland Stanford and his vision of a "magnificent destiny."

191

Scott had journeyed to Switzerland to recuperate from his six-year campaign against Huntington and the Southern Pacific when Jay Gould, on one of his quick round trips to Europe, just happened to run into him in Berne. Scott, as Gould later told the story, "was very much depressed and broken up. . . . I felt a profound sympathy for him. He asked me as a favor to take his Texas & Pacific Railroad off his hands and I concluded to do so."

Rather than being overwhelmed by compassion, Gould had sensed that the time was ripe for a more vigorous and ruthless exploitation of the Texas & Pacific's possibilities. Scott had done the donkey work, and Gould would reap the benefits.

A different sort of enemy now confronted Huntington, one far more resourceful in financial maneuvering and legislative combat, as Huntington realized. "I wouldn't go into the stock market against Gould," the still-confident Huntington remarked, "for he would whip me at that game. That is his business. When it comes to building and operating railroads in the most efficient and economical way, I can beat him, for that is my business."

He soon learned that Gould was suppler as well as tougher than Scott. When the Southern Pacific kept building eastward and was reaching out from the Colorado River toward El Paso, Gould's sense of the territorial imperative was thoroughly aroused. In 1881 he learned that the Southern Pacific was laying track over land granted to the Texas & Pacific. He blocked that intrusion by obtaining an injunction from the New Mexico Supreme Court.

Gould also had begun employing the diversionary tactics which had destroyed earlier rivals. Sensing that the Big Four would be panicked by a road which would compete with their Central Pacific and force a lowering of passenger and freight rates by breaking their monopoly, Gould extended a Union Pacific subsidiary, the Utah Central, westward from Ogden and bought a controlling interest in a feeder line, the California Central, which possessed the prime assest of a right-of-way into San Francisco. The Utah Central and the California Central would be linked on the Nevada border, thus fulfilling a transcontinental railroader's dream of an outlet to the Pacific, as fervent as any Russian czar's yearning for a warm-water port. But wasn't it all a bluff? Huntington and his associates asked each other. They became even more alarmed, however, when word leaked out that

Gould was suggesting to the Santa Fe that they combine in their efforts to reach California: the Texas & Pacific to be dominant east of El Paso, the Santa Fe to build the western extension to San Diego or Los Angeles. The Santa Fe just then was looming as the Southern Pacific's chief rival. Both to the north and south the Southern Pacific would be outflanked.

Gould and Huntington, however, were not romantics but hardheaded businessmen. Their scuffling was merely a test of wills, a preliminary to the peace which would be much more profitable to both parties. Both groups sat down at a conference table in Huntington's New York offices late in 1881. It took them only a few days to hammer out an agreement. Gould would halt the Texas & Pacific at El Paso (thus making its title sound a trifle vainglorious), and the Southern Pacific would stop building a line parallel to the Texas & Pacific's through New Mexico and Texas. The revenues from through traffic on the two systems would be prorated. In addition, the Texas & Pacific would surrender its land grant west of El Paso to the Southern Pacific. Thus Gould was spared the unfamiliar task of building a railroad, yet could share in the profits of the southern route to California and return to the more congenial work of manipulating securities.

While the contest of the Texas & Pacific and the Southern Pacific for the thirty-second parallel route was confined to bluffing, bribery, and psychological warfare, the struggle between the Santa Fe and the Denver & Rio Grande for a north-south line to serve the Colorado mines developed into a mountain war on the scale of a conflict between two Balkan kingdoms.

It brought into conflict not only two corporations but two empire builders of equally strong wills and combative dispositions—William B. Strong, the chief executive of the Santa Fe, and General William J. Palmer, the founder and president of the Denver & Rio Grande—and behind them hundreds of armed and equally aggressive workmen and gunmen.

Palmer had been one of those young cavalry commanders who won fame and high rank in the Civil War. A railroad surveyor in Pennsylvania before the war, he had joined the Army of the Cumberland and within two years was commanding a division, though he was still in his twenties.

After the war he conducted surveys to determine whether the

193

thirty-fifth or thirty-second parallel (the latter originally advocated as the most feasible by Jefferson Davis when he was Secretary of War) would be the best route for a transcontinental line. He favored the thirty-fifth parallel, and his whole subsequent career would range the plains and mountains of Kansas and Colorado. He saw for himself that the section, then inhabited only by nomadic Indians, could be turned into an agricultural paradise, covered with grazing lands and wheat-covered fields, that the mountains undoubtedly were rich in minerals.

He became the drive wheel of the Kansas Pacific enterprise during its construction phase and before Jay Gould could lay hands on the company. The railroad was largely financed abroad, but Palmer was its builder, fund raiser, and chief lobbyist in Congress. Money was always short, but Palmer's executive ability and his resourcefulness as an engineer, combined with a genius for leadership, kept the construction going forward. Not yet thirty years old, he attacked the engineering problems with the vigor of a general launching an all-out offensive. A contemporary journalist observed:

> At the time of entering upon the work of construction of the Kansas Pacific railroad no material was in sight and yet General Palmer graded the road bed, procured ties and rails, laid the tracks and constructed the bridges for one hundred and fifty miles of road in ninety-two days. This masterly achievement in railroad building was accomplished in the face of serious obstacles other than those placed by impersonal forces, as the workmen were greatly harassed by hostile Indians, and eight of their numbering including the principal contractor were scalped. In order to accomplish this work in the time desired he was compelled to inspire his men with his own earnestness and determination, pushing them to the very limit of their strength, but with such courtesy and tact that they remained willing workers to the last and were his friends as well as his workers. . . .

An utter pragmatism governed the man. He saw the West as something to be exploited as quickly and relentlessly as possible. Feeding his construction gangs—a total of 1,200 men—was one of his larger problems. He solved it by contracting with a Kansas City meat-packer to hire buffalo hunters to provide fresh meat for his workmen; thus, the Kansas Pacific literally lived off the land. Young William F. Cody was paid $500 a month to kill at least twelve buffalo a day, supervise the meat cutting and dressing, and see to it that the slabs of buffalo meat reached Palmer's camps in time for dinner. In eighteen months Cody killed 4,280 buffalo to nourish the Kansas Pacific's workmen. But Palmer still wasn't through with extracting the last dollar of profit out of the buffalo surviving the meat hunters' onslaught. Since the Kansas Pacific badly needed passenger revenues during its early years, he began running excursion trains on his completed trackage for sportsmen of the type that later would hunt wolves from helicopters. Those city fellows, yearning to reinforce their sense of manhood by destroying something on four legs, were encouraged to ride the KP excursion cars potting buffalo from their seats as the train moved slowly over a prairie. The buffalo was a huge but helpless target. Dropped by one of the cheap-jack sportsman's bullets, it was simply allowed to lie there and rot. Those potshot excursions also served, of course, to reduce the Indians' food supply so drastically that they would soon be forced to live off government rations on reservations, where they would be kept out of the path of rail-borne progress.

The ruthlessly practical General Palmer built the Kansas Pacific arrow straight westward into Denver. He had favored a different route, based on his personal reconnaissance of the southern Colorado region and his optimistic estimate of its farming and mining potentialities, but was overruled. Palmer had recommended that the KP take a route 100 miles to the south, establishing a division point at Pueblo, then proceed to Denver through the passes and deep valleys of the Rockies. From that Pueblo-Denver line, feeders could be sent in all directions like taproots drawing sustenance from the farms, ranches, and mines.

If the Kansas Pacific was too shortsighted to take on the project, Palmer would do it on his own. Late in 1870, when he had pushed the railroad into Denver, he resigned and within a month organized his own company. The Denver & Rio Grande would follow the base of the Rockies southward from Denver and ultimately, it was hoped, would extend farther south in Mexico and westward to Southern California. Whatever his methods, he had

195

to be credited with great clarity of vision. In 1870 he would be building a railroad through a towering wilderness, against all but insuperable engineering obstacles. Between Denver and Pueblo there were only a few gold-mining camps and fewer than 500 (white) people. The triweekly stage between Colorado City and Denver averaged only 5 passengers a trip.

Yet he was able to raise the necessary financing, largely through the help of William A. Bell, the young Englishman who had joined his staff and kept a photographic and verbal record of his achievements with the Kansas Pacific. The funds were subscribed largely by Palmer and Bell's friends in Philadelphia and England.

Then Palmer proceeded with the construction, undeterred by the advice of surveyors and locating engineers that his chosen route would require all but impossible feats of engineering over mountain ranges two miles high and through canyons half a mile deep. The route would cross back and forth over the Continental Divide with sharp curves and a grade of 211 feet to the mile, literally over the spinal column of the North American continent.

Palmer's only reply to objections and adverse expert opinion was: "The decision is made. It's going to be done." He disdained to obtain land grants or subsidies and had acquired from the government only a 200-foot wide right-of-way with 20 acres allotted for stations every 10 miles. And his first trackage was of a narrow-gauge variety. His researches showed that the Fastinog Railway in Wales had used tracks only 2 feet wide through the mountains, that in India a railway had been built with 1-meter (39.37 inches) tracks. He decided on a 3-foot gauge which would allow for cheaper and easier construction on the steep grades and hairpin curves on his route, which later and justifiably was advertised as the most scenic railway in the world.

Some indication of the spectacular efforts required to build the Denver & Rio Grande south to Pueblo was provided in a description of the construction crews at work in Animas Canyon:

> The smooth vertical wall was 1,000 feet deep. From that height were seen hanging spider-web like ropes, down which men seeming not much larger than ants were slowly descending while others perched upon narrow shelves in the face of the cliff, or in trifling niches from which their only egress was by dangling ropes, sighting

196

through their theodolites from one ledge to the other, and directed where to place the dabs of paint indicating the intended roadbed. Similarly suspended, the workmen followed the engineers, drilling holes for blasting, and tumbling down loose fragments, until they had won a foothold for working in a less extraordinary manner. Ten months of labor were spent in this canyon-cutting—months of work on the brink of yawning abysses and in the midst of falling rocks and yet not one serious accident occurred.

In 1878 Palmer considered that his position in Colorado was secure, with his line between Denver and Pueblo completed and extensions planned to the south and west. To the west of Denver great quantities of silver had been discovered around Leadville. In the absence of any rail service, 12,000 horse teams were freighting into Leadville daily, and 100,000 pounds of bullion were being hauled every day to Colorado Springs at $18 a ton. In his original plans for the Denver & Rio Grande, filed when he obtained the federal charter, Palmer had declared his intention of building westward from the main line at Pueblo, through the Royal Gorge of the Arkansas River. Such a line would go through Leadville. He had also proclaimed his intention of building south into New Mexico through the Raton Pass just south of the Colorado-New Mexico border.

He seemed to have a patent on those routes south and west of his alpine railway to Pueblo. But his ambitions now had come into conflict with those of William B. Strong and the Santa Fe, which not only had earned a net profit of $4,000,000 in 1878 but had a whole battalion of lawyers and some brilliant schemers back in Boston. The Santa Fe was stretching westward but continually found itself running into legal roadblocks thrown up by agents for the Southern Pacific. When Strong journeyed to the New Mexican capital to obtain enabling legislation, he learned that the Southern Pacific had slipped in ahead of him and persuaded the territorial legislature to pass a law making it mandatory that the majority of board of directors of any railroad operating in the territory be residents of New Mexico. To bypass that inspired legislation, Strong organized the New Mexico & Southern Pacific Railroad Company overnight and incorporated it to build from the Raton Pass to the Arizona border.

Hastily returning to his advance headquarters, Strong urged

his engineers to survey the Raton Pass immediately and get started on construction. Chief engineer Albert A. Robinson was instructed to push the line through the southern outlet from the Rockies by force if necessary. At Pueblo he boarded a Denver & Rio Grande train, the only available transportation to El Morro, the point nearest the Raton Pass. Passing through the smoker, he spotted chief engineer J. A. McMurtie of the Denver & Rio Grande with several of his aides. The two men nodded coolly, each suspecting what the other's presence meant.

On arrival at El Morro, Robinson and McMurtie each proceeded to levy forces necessary to secure the vital pass. McMurtie had a work crew already assembled and believed he would have no difficulty in leisurely occupying the strategic ground. He did not reckon, unfortunately, on Robinson's youthful energy and enthusiasm. Robinson rode hell for leather to Trinidad, a settlement on the Colorado side of the border where there was considerable sentiment against the Denver & Rio Grande for having bypassed the place. In a few hours Robinson recruited a force of several hundred men armed with rifles or equipped with shovels and led them on a forced march toward the Raton Pass. McMurtie and his crew had arrived first in the neighborhood, but they had complacently made camp and bedded down for the night. Robinson and his followers worked through the night driving surveyor's stakes through the pass and establishing a flimsy sort of legal claim to the route.

The first skirmish between the Santa Fe and the Denver & Rio Grande went to the former, but it was a mere curtain raiser to the hostilities between Strong and Palmer. The Santa Fe had seized the Raton Pass in February, 1878, and before the year was out, it had built a tortuous roadbed through the cleft with a maximum grade of 316 feet to the mile, which subsequently was reduced to 185 feet by construction of a 2,000-foot tunnel.

Meanwhile, in April of that year, the two railroads began their contest for the Grand Canyon of the Arkansas, the Royal Gorge route leading from Pueblo to Leadville and westward. The gorge, with walls 2,000 feet high and only 30 feet apart in places, the river itself a rushing thread of water rarely touched by sunlight, was so daunting it had never been traveled by man or beast.

Another race for strategic territory began. The Denver & Rio

Grande controlled all the telegraph lines in the area, and General Palmer did not scruple to intercept messages sent to and from his rival, Strong; thus, he learned that Strong was planning to execute a *coup de main*. Late in April, 1878, the Santa Fe president ordered one of his engineers, William R. Morley, to occupy the route. Morley set out on horseback for the 63-mile ride across rugged terrain from Pueblo to Canyon City. Having learned of his mission through his telegraphic eavesdropping, Palmer ordered his own forces to counter the Santa Fe thrust. His men, as yet unaccustomed to the imperatives of competition, were again outflanked by the Santa Fe.

Engineer Morley's horse dropped dead under him en route to Cayon City, and he had to finish the journey on foot, but he found Canyon City's citizenry in a sympathetic mood as Robinson had found Trinidad's a few months earlier and for the same reason. Canyon City had been bypassed by the Denver & Rio Grande, and it willingly supplied a few hundred men to help the Santa Fe's cause. Morley and his supporters marched to the mouth of the Royal Gorge about two miles away. They were the first on the ground, and Strong was so pleased with his engineer's efforts that he presented Morley with a repeating rifle with gold mountings.

Palmer's crew arrived a mere half hour later, but found that Morley had already dug in and placed a rifleman behind every boulder to repel the opposition.

Palmer was enraged by the way he had been outmaneuvered. A mere civilian had twice flanked a veteran cavalry commander. Palmer swore it wouldn't happen again. He would fight Strong on all fronts until one group or the other was destroyed. First, he sent an armed force into the canyon several miles above Morley's camp, built several stone forts in which men armed with Winchester repeating rifles were posted, and ordered his grading crews to begin work.

The Denver & Rio Grande also opened up a legal front, obtaining from the Colorado court an injunction prohibiting the Santa Fe from building through the Royal Gorge. On the Santa Fe's appeal, however, the matter was transferred to a federal court. The federal judge made a very curious ruling: Both railroads would be permitted to build roadbeds through the canyon, "neither to obstruct the other." How two railroads could be built through a gorge 30 feet wide in many places, the jurist did not say. Palmer appealed that ruling to the United States Supreme Court.

By then it was December, 1878, and Palmer's financial backers thousands of miles to the east—like rear-area troops in any combat situation—were the first to succumb to panic. His bondholders did not believe Palmer could prevail against his much stronger rival and ordered him to make a humiliating deal with the Santa Fe. A lesser man's pride would have been broken by its terms. The Santa Fe was granted a thirty-year lease of all the Denver & Rio Grande's trackage. The only inhibiting proviso, and a fortunate one it turned out to be for Palmer, was that the Santa Fe would not raise freight rates out of Denver in a discriminatory fashion.

Very unwisely, but with characteristic arrogance, Strong proceeded to violate the terms of the lease. He raised freight rates on Denver shippers to favor those in Kansas City, allowing the latter to gain control of Southwestern trade.

That was all Palmer needed to get back in the game. He charged that Strong had broken their agreement and moved to reclaim all the Denver & Rio Grande's property. While still awaiting a ruling from the U.S. Supreme Court, he also obtained from a local judge a writ declaring the railroad was to be restored to its original owners.

Already Palmer had moved back into the Royal Gorge in force, and a shooting war was in prospect.

He sent a tough young man named James R. De Remer, his assistant chief engineer, into the disputed canyon with several hundred armed men. De Remer, who had enlisted in the Union Army at the age of fifteen, was more than a match for the Santa Fe's minions. He soon proved himself so adept at seizing the initiative that the Santa Fe posted a $10,000 reward for him—"dead or alive," as the posters put it. One man who aimed to collect that reward was the sheriff at Canyon City, who naturally was a Santa Fe partisan. The sheriff had posted twenty deputies at the mouth of the canyon with orders to arrest any Denver & Rio Grande employee trying to slip into town for mail or supplies. One day a member of De Remer's crew ventured into town and was promptly arrested; the legalities of such actions had long

200

been discarded as frivolous. De Remer immediately rode into town to demand bail for his employee. Just as the sheriff came into the justice's court to arrest him, De Remer dashed outside, cut the reins of the sheriff's horse with one slash of his knife and escaped into the wilderness. The Santa Fe now held the mouth of the canyon, but the Denver & Rio Grande occupied its interior. De Remer built seventeen stone forts commanding all the strategic heights. The gorge was so well fortified, in fact, that it would have taken a small army equipped with alpine troops and a battalion of mountain howitzers to root out the Denver & Rio Grande occupation forces.

The Santa Fe began pushing into the gorge, but at the 20-mile post its work force was halted by De Remer with fifty riflemen at his back. That was on April 19, 1879. De Remer had just received word that the Supreme Court had ruled in the Denver & Rio Grande's favor and given it the sole right to build through the Grand Canyon of the Arkansas.

Meanwhile, Palmer had made a quick trip to New York to finance what he foresaw would be an expensive campaign of wresting his property back from the Santa Fe, which was disposed to defy the law of the land on the ancient pseudoprinciple that possession was nine points of the required ten. He hoped to raise $2,000,000 or $3,000,000 on Wall Street, but recent publicity given the river of molten silver flowing out of Leadville made investors so enthusiastic that they subscribed a $10,000,000 fund. Possibly some of the enthusiasm was fermented by the New Yorkers' delight in poking a figurative stick in the eye of the Boston financiers who controlled the Santa Fe. Anyway Palmer took $7,000,000 of the amount subscribed and hastened back to Colorado to direct the operations, often more military in essence than corporate, against the equally determined men of the Santa Fe.

Palmer had the law on his side now, all the way from the Colorado courts, often conducted on a plank between two barrels in a saloon, to the black-robed majesty of the Supreme Court. But just as there was said to be no God west of the Pecos, there was no law west of the Arkansas unless it was reinforced with money and power. Despite a blizzard of writs, the Santa Fe still occupied and held by force the Denver & Rio Grande's property from the

201

Pueblo roundhouse to the Denver passenger station. Each bit of real estate and equipment would have to be wrenched away by force or the threat of force.

Thus began what one Denver newspaper called, with considerable accuracy, "strife between two feudal lords," Strong and Palmer.

At six o'clock in the morning of June 9, sheriff's deputies began serving writs ordering the Santa Fe to return the Denver & Rio Grande's property. They appeared at every station and office along the road from El Morro to Denver, but in every case the Santa Fe's men refused to yield up possession.

Strong, in fact, had made urgent preparations to resist the law, apparently holding that the Santa Fe was a higher power than any governmental institution. His position was different only in degree and nuance from that of an outlaw holed up in a cave with his loot and standing off a sheriff's posse.

The key point, Strong's cave, was the Pueblo roundhouse, which had to be held at all costs. Strong sent his agents to Dodge City, which was a Santa Fe town and had a surplus of unemployed gunmen, and quickly enlisted recruits for the Santa Fe's private army. "Twenty of our brave boys," Robert Wright, the merchant-historian of early Dodge, sardonically observed, "promptly responded, among whom might be numbered some of Dodge's most accomplished sluggers and bruisers and dead shots." The first echelon proceeded to Pueblo early in April under the command of a redoubtable frontiersman named Captain John Joshua Webb, with Ben Thompson, a Texas desperado whose mettle had been tested in many shootouts, and Doc Holliday, the gunman-dentist even handier at drilling his enemies than rotten molars, as his chief lieutenants. Holliday tried to recruit Eddie Foy, a young actor stranded in Dodge who later became a celebrated vaudevillian, but Foy demurred on the grounds that he was more familiar with punch lines than six-shooters. "Oh, that's all right," Holliday assured him. "The Santy Fee won't know the difference. You kin use a shotgun if you want to. Dodge wants to make a good showin' in this business. You'll help swell the crowd, and you'll get your pay anyhow."

The first contingent of twenty gunfighters was followed up by a group captained by William Barclay "Bat" Masterson, the former sheriff at Dodge and a virtuoso with a Colt .45. The movement of the Dodge City irregulars to Pueblo was presented as an example of local patriotism, with the Dodge City *Times* boasting: "We will bet a ten-cent note that they will clear the tracks of every obstruction." The Dodge City bravos were strictly mercenaries, however, too sensible to risk their skins for anything less substantial than hard cash.

Bat Masterson arrived at Pueblo, wangled a commission as a deputy United States marshal to lend a fictitious air of legality to his mission, and assumed command of the Santa Fe forces, which had barricaded themselves in the roundhouse. They fortified the place with bridge timbers and were supplied with a Gatling gun, in addition to their personal armament. A few days later it appeared that the Pueblo roundhouse might become the Alamo of the railroad wars and live forever in glory. Down the tracks came a Denver & Rio Grande special train with General Palmer, James De Remer, about 200 men inspired to a homicidal pitch and armed with rifles, shotguns, and revolvers, and, most importantly, treasurer Robert F. Weitbrec carrying a satchel stuffed with greenbacks.

The Denver & Rio Grande special halted. Viewing the bristling barricade ahead, Palmer felt his military ardor reborn; it was like the dawn of a second Chickamauga. Treasurer Weitbrec was coolly reckoning the cost of an armed clash, however, and argued, "It is possible that you can storm that roundhouse and capture it. But it is also possible that you may be repulsed. In any event, if you resort to violence there will be bloodshed. Before you attack, let me try to negotiate with those Santa Fe gunmen."

Palmer reluctantly gave his consent, and Weitbrec, carrying his satchel, advanced under a white flag. Masterson tipped his derby to the envoy, was shown the contents of the satchel, and conferred briefly with his associates. It was marvelous to note the cooling effect on the Dodge City partisans, who had left their Kansas bailiwick swearing to hazard their very lives in defense of the Santa Fe's interests. "Our boys didn't smell any powder," the Dodge City *Times* remarked a few days later. "Their vote was for peace." Masterson accepted the contents of Weitbrec's satchel, reportedly about $10,000, and surrendered the roundhouse to the Denver & Rio Grande.

Elsewhere, up and down the line from El Morro to Denver, the Palmer forces violently recovered railroad property from the Santa Fe. The newspapers reported that Palmer's gunmen were patrolling the streets of El Morro, Pueblo, and Trinidad and that no one dared express a sympathetic word for the Santa Fe without risking a bullet. A task force of about 200 armed Denver & Rio Grande partisans climbed aboard a train at El Morro under the command of Alexander Cameron Hunt, a former governor of Colorado and presently a director of Palmer's railroad, whom the newspapers characterized as a "whirlwind of energy and indiscretion." Hunt's train stopped off at every depot and made prisoners of any Santa Fe loyalists they found. At Cuchara the Santa Fe hirelings resisted, and two were killed, two more were wounded. Hunt paused at Pueblo to capture the dispatcher's office, where a number of Santa Fe men were holed up. There was a great deal of shooting before the citadel fell, but no one was hurt. Hunt and his band whirled on to Canyon City, a Santa Fe stronghold. They captured the town in a blaze of gunfire, but the Santa Fe men there fled up the tracks in four locomotives before they could be captured.

The Denver & Rio Grande had recaptured its property, but President Strong of the Santa Fe continued to demonstrate a truculent attitude.

Several months of guerrilla fighting between the two railroads followed. The fact that the highest court had ruled in favor of the Denver & Rio Grande made little impression on railroad men who had become accustomed to thinking of themselves as performing work which placed it above the maunderings of mere Supreme Court Justices. Both railroads continued to maintain private armies in the field which spied on each other, cut each other's telegraph wires, and beat up each other's employees. Acts of sabotage were committed almost daily, and public officials who had displeased one side or the other were kidnapped or had their families threatened. Santa Fe trains crews were fired at by Denver & Rio Grande pistoleros, and the rival forces attacked each other's roundhouses and depots. One good thing came of all the fighting. A Santa Fe freight conductor named Charles Watlington, who like all trainmen on the line wore a revolver to work, became a highly proficient marksman and one day used his

204

ability with the six-shooter to prevent a train wreck. His west-bound train had been stalled by a washout near Cimarron, Kansas, at dusk, and he went up the tracks with a lantern to flag down an eastbound passenger train. The visibility was poor, and the engineer of the passenger train didn't see his signal. The train was hurtling past him, toward derailment, when Watlington recalled his training in the Santa Fe-Rio Grande war. He pulled out his revolver, shot out the air hose connecting the last two passenger cars, and brought the train to a sudden halt.

In January, 1880, the Eastern executives of the two roads confronted each other in the Santa Fe offices in Boston. Unlike the horny-handed Santa Fe partisans of Canyon City or the Denver & Rio Grande supporters of El Morro, the manicured fingers of those well-bred gentlemen did not curl around a trigger as a means of settling their differences; they swapped cigars and small talk instead of bullets. Their dispute over territorial rights had caused the death and injury of scores of simpleminded men, but they would no more have considered exchanging blows than sending their sons to a Western landgrant college instead of Yale or Princeton. How quick and easy it was to come to terms in the polite atmosphere of industrial diplomacy. The Denver & Rio Grande agreed not to extend its lines to St. Louis or El Paso, the Santa Fe that it would stay out of Denver and Leadville. The former also agreed to pay the Santa Fe $1,400,000 for the track it had laid in the Royal Gorge.

It is not recorded that the bullheaded William B. Strong and the combative General Palmer ever shook hands, but Coloradens celebrated the completion of the Denver & Rio Grande line through the Royal Gorge to Leadville with a hoedown that lived long in Western history. Leadville, which was sitting on $2 billion worth of silver, lavishly welcomed the first train to arrive in Leadville. The former President, General U. S. Grant, rode in with Palmer on that first train and was greeted by 30,000 people, most of them waving either flags or whiskey bottles. They rode from the depot to the Tabor Opera House in an open barouche drawn by four black horses whose gleaming backs had been sprinkled with gold dust. That night an incredible amount of whiskey and champagne flowed down throats hoarse from cheering the destiny wrought by thick veins of silver ore and enhanced by the coming of the railroad.

Palmer himself became not only the railroad magnate of the Rockies, extending his system to link up with the Union Pacific at Salt Lake City, but the leading real estate developer and town promoter as well. Even before he built the railroad, he had organized the Mountain Base Investment Fund and bought twenty-five tracts of land between Denver and Pueblo, including coal-mining property near Canyon City and the site of Colorado Springs at the foot of Pikes Peak. He was endowed with the split vision few railroad men had, could foresee not only the opening up of the country through which his lines traversed, but the possibilities of sharing in that exploitation. He built and promoted the city of Colorado Springs, where he ordained the prohibition of alcoholic beverages because, as he wrote, "At Sheridan [Wyoming], where I had the privilege of a residence of some eight months in 1870–71, while directing the construction of the railroad to Denver, the most noticeable suburban feature, notwithstanding the salubrity of the air and the brevity of the settlement, was a fat graveyard, most of whose inhabitants, in the language of the 100th meridian, had died 'with their boots on.' " Colorado Springs, as dry as its mountain air during its early years, prospered and grew. Its founder sold his railroad interests to Jay Gould and retired to Glen Eyrie, an immense graystone castle surrounded by gardens. Once on a camping trip to the Sierra Blanca, where Palmer owned 700,000 acres, Hamlin Garland came across "the Lord of this Desmesne and his three daughters encamped, attended by a platoon of cooks, valets, maids and hostlers."

Palmer was one of the big winners of the Western sweepstakes and was magnificently rewarded for his efforts.

No doubt many others blessed his name and his achievements for the prosperity he brought them, but as in all such chronicles of exploitation, there were thousands of losers and victims to every winner—thousands who were worked to death, whose lives were no richer than those of the blind mules condemned to the lower levels of the mines which could not have been fully exploited without the railroads to haul in equipment and work forces and haul out the gold and silver ore, the coal and iron.

206

Before one is blinded by the glory of a Palmer's achievements, so necessary to the development of the West, yet which could have been shaped in a more humane fashion, it seems appropriate to examine their effects. The argument that such massive and ruthless empire building was necessary has always been with us. But where was the urgency, the need for haste and the reckless expenditure of human lives—except in the egocentricity, the acquisitive depths of the psyches of the empire builders? The West could have been wooed instead of raped.

The impact of those imperial methods would be felt for generations, nor has time entirely dissipated their effects, because the New West is only the Old West with an overlay of modern technology. Their success, in the limited sense of profit and loss, promoted their longevity. It is diminished only by the reflection of what the West might have been under the shaping of gentler and less prehensile hands.

Several generations comprising tens of thousands of miners and their families would not join in the hosannas to the Palmers and their successors. Their history is as grim as their sufferings were obscure to the rest of the nation. The Western Federation of Miners believed they had won a great victory when, after years of pleading and threatening, they forced the owners of the forty mines in the Cripple Creek district to agree to an eight-hour-day six-day week, for which hard and dangerous labor the miners were paid $18 a week.

That agreement with the miners' union was to have a disastrous effect on the whole country. To make up for what they regarded as an overly generous pay scale, the larger mine operators speeded up production through methods that prefigured the Stakhanovite system in Soviet Russia. Carelessly disposing of what seemed like inexhaustible resources, they overproduced and brought on a calamitous glut in the international silver market. Naturally they had cheered on the advocates of free silver. For many years the Republic had been distracted by a clamor for the "free and unlimited coinage of silver" from the Western states. The Colorado mines produced so much silver that one day in June, 1893, the mints of India shut down on the issuance of silver coins. The effect of that measure on the other side of the world was felt immediately in America, where the price of silver plum-

207

meted. The principal bankers refused to consider further financing of Western enterprises, and a panic exploded on Wall Street, which was heavily involved in those enterprises. Directly traceable to the refusal of Western mine operators to cut down on production, the resultant depression gripped the country for several years and sent General Coxey's boxcar armies converging on Washington, as well as encouraged the growth of an indigenous radicalism.

One of General Palmer's creations was the Colorado Fuel and Iron Company, which developed coal and ore lands around Trinidad, Canyon City, and Ludlow and became an empire in itself for which such moguls as John T. Gates, Edward H. Harriman, John D. Rockefeller, Jr., and George J. Gould contended at various times. Eventually Rockefeller shouldered aside his rivals and acquired a 40 percent controlling interest; the coal and iron lands became a Rockefeller principality, piled on top of the family's near monopoly of oil production and distribution. Perhaps it was indicative of the quality of absentee ownership that John D., Jr., in one ten-year period never visited his Colorado properties or even attended a board meeting of Colorado Fuel and Iron.

The company which Palmer founded, then sold to Eastern financiers, imported 30,000 miners of Italian, Slavic, Greek, and Mexican descent and ruled their lives from cradle to grave through a private army of sheriff's deputies and private detectives. Whenever the miners attempted to loosen the company's domination even slightly, there was a swift and brutal crackdown from the bosses and their armed forces.

Year after year the Rockefeller-controlled company maintained its dictatorship over the work force, until in 1913 the United Mine Workers moved into the region with scores of organizers. Some months later the mine operators were alarmed by reports that most of their employees were armed with shotguns and rifles. They were also angered when a large number of miners and their families moved out of a dozen settlements where the company rented them slabwood shanties and furnished unfiltered water pumped up from the mines and set up a tent colony at Ludlow. Hitherto the Colorado Fuel and Iron had regarded them

208

as ignorant and docile immigrants; now they were demanding wages equal to those paid in the Wyoming coalfields, an eight-hour day, and the right to trade at other than company stores. Nine thousand miners went out on strike and established themselves in tent cities like the one at Ludlow. What they called the "Death Special," an armored car mounted with a machine gun, patrolled the strikers' colonies, but they refused to be cowed even after the armored car killed a striker and seriously wounded a child. Mother Jones, an eighty-year-old Irish-born radical, was arrested three hours after she arrived to stir up more trouble, was thrown in a cellar under the Walsenburg courthouse and kept incommunicado for nine weeks, during which she fought off sewer rats with a beer bottle.

The governor of Colorado was persuaded to call out the National Guard, which had recently been beefed up by professional gunmen and other adventurers. On April 20, 1914, two companies of the Colorado National Guard, equipped with machine guns, attacked the Ludlow tent colony. When the machine guns stopped chattering, forty-five persons were dead and another score wounded. A New York *Times* correspondent reported:

> The Ludlow camp is a mass of charred debris, and buried beneath it is a story of horror unparalleled in the history of industrial warfare. In the holes which had been dug for their protection against the rifles' fire the women and children died like trapped rats when the flames swept over them. One pit, uncovered this afternoon, disclosed the bodies of ten children and two women. . . .

The nation was outraged. It had always thought of Colorado as the garden spot of the Rockies, not as a medieval fiefdom ruled by a great corporation's hired gunmen. The pressure of public opinion forced Colorado Fuel and Iron to provide housing and schools, better pay, and full recognition of their civil rights to the miners. A happy ending. But it could not ameliorate the tragedy of two generations which had endured a death rate in the Colorado mines twice as high as the national average. Nor could it make up for the thousands of lives stunted by privation, brutalized throughout their short duration, in which there had never been one ray of hope.

In 1929 a number of bronze plaques were struck off and placed in railroad stations and other public places in Colorado and other Rocky Mountain states. They memorialized General Palmer, "pioneer railroad builder, prophet of Colorado's greatness." It is evident that the plaque left much unsaid and was notable for its discreet omissions.

9.

A Vision of What Might Have Been

I hate all the white people. You are thieves and
liars. You have taken away our land and made us
outcasts.

—Chief Sitting Bull

WITHIN a decade the main lines of the Union Pacific,
Kansas Pacific, Santa Fe, the Katy, the Missouri Pacific,
the Texas & Pacific, the Southern Pacific, and a webbing of
feeder lines between them placed a steel grid over Indian
Country. The Northern Pacific and the Great Northern were
being extended over the northern tier of territories.

The Indians could combine on occasion to fight regiments,
could summon up the courage to face Gatling guns and rapid-fire
cannon, but they could never cope with the iron horse. The first
railroads stretching across the plains had suddenly created a new
market which would make terrifying inroads on the buffalo herds.
Buffalo tongues were pickled in cast-off whiskey barrels and
shipped east, where they were featured on the menus of every
decent restaurant. The hides were cut into strips for use as power
belting in the factories springing up during the period of great
industrial expansion. When the price of a hide shot up from $2 to
$5, hundreds of white hunters descended on what had been the
Indians' main source of food. Treaties guaranteeing the Indians'
territorial rights were broken almost before the ink was dry. In the
three years after the whites moved down to the Arkansas and

211

preempted the Indian hunting grounds, the government estimated that 4,300,000 buffalo were shot. Seventy-five thousand buffalo were shot in a few months around Dodge City, where the daylong booming of .50-caliber rifles made it sound as though the settlement were under siege. At every station along the railroads there was a mountain of buffalo bones. "There followed," as one Western historian has written, "the most disgraceful slaughter of animals the world has ever seen." Buffalo hunting had become an industrial operation. Each hunter was attended by supply wagons, a half dozen skinners, wagon drivers, a cook, and a camp boy.

The Indians could only watch helplessly as their ancient freedoms shriveled with each mile of railroad constructed. Occasionally they managed to teach the whites a sharp lesson. At Adobe Walls down in the Canadian River country a large outfit of Dodge City hunters was attacked in June, 1874, and narrowly escaped being wiped out. Some years earlier General Patrick E. Connor's Powder River Expedition had come to grief in Wyoming. When the whites wanted to fortify the Bozeman Trail from Fort Laramie to the Montana goldfields, and incidentally protect the Union Pacific line to the south and the Northern Pacific to the north, the great Sioux Chief Red Cloud and his allies placed Forts Phil Kearney and C. F. Smith under siege for two years and forced their abandonment in 1868. Later the plains tribes combined to prevent an invasion of the Black Hills, the land sacred to them as the dwelling place of the Great Spirit but also the repository of thick veins of gold-bearing ore, and slaughtered one squadron of the Seventh Cavalry at the Little Bighorn. But those victories were barely enough to keep the flame of resistance from guttering out, and their effects on white encroachment were transitory.

Eventually gold rushers overran the Black Hills, followed by the steel-fingered reach of the railroads, and the place where the plains tribes gathered every summer to commune with the Great Spirit and seek his blessings and invoke his presence—their Jerusalem, their Mecca—was desecrated beyond recall.

The Cheyenne could make a desert out of western Kansas during the summer of 1868, when in protest against the extension of the Union Pacific through their hunting grounds they conducted twenty-five raids on white settlements and killed 117 settlers without losing a single tribesman, but they could not prevail against the increasingly numerous and growingly mobile white regiments. Everywhere the railroad was employed as a military weapon. Combined with the telegraph, it enabled the bluecoat generals to transport whole regiments, with their horses and supplies, from one threatened point to another. When the proud Northern Cheyenne had been reduced to 79 warriors after a few years of exile to Indian Territory and made a mass break for the north and their old hunting grounds, the Union Pacific was General George Crook's ready-made line of defense. The massive campaign launched in the mid-eighties to hunt down the Apache chief Geronimo was constantly reinforced, supplied, and facilitated by the southern transcontinental railroads. Again, when the Sioux were finally crushed at Wounded Knee, the Indians could only watch helplessly as regiment after regiment was brought from all over the West, from as far away as New Mexico, on the railroads which had penetrated the southwestern corner of Dakota Territory.

The Indians recognized the iron horse as their enemy when it made its first appearance in the hunting ranges, snorting and whistling and pouring black smoke as it frightened away the game in the Platte Valley of western Nebraska. During the summer of 1867 the Oglala Sioux and the Cheyenne several times crossed the Union Pacific tracks behind the construction crews and puzzled over how to deal with this monstrous creation introduced by the whites. They were also greatly curious over what those little wooden houses drawn by the black engines could contain. Some of the cars were entirely wooden-sided, others had windows at which pale or bearded faces could be seen.

The first recorded attempt by an Indian to tackle the iron horse was that of a nameless Cheyenne warrior. One day he decided to rope an iron horse and drag it off its tracks. He raced his pony alongside a puffing locomotive, tossed the loop of his lariat around one of its brass fittings, was jerked off his pony's back, and dragged for several hundred feet until he disengaged himself from the lariat.

Another Cheyenne named Sleeping Rabbit, surely a misnomer in consideration of his ingenuity, hit upon a better scheme for catching one of the monsters. "If we could bend the track and spread it apart," he told his companions, "the Iron Horse might fall off. Then we could see what is in the wooden houses on wheels." Sleeping Rabbit and his band lay in ambush for the next train after pulling the rails apart. The engine was derailed, and the train crew fled. The Cheyenne broke into the freight cars, snatched up some of the food they were carrying, drank whiskey from broken barrels, then tied bolts of cloth to ponies' tails and fled across the prairie with long multicolored streamers following them, before the soldiers could be summoned on what the Indians called the "singing wire." Future confrontations with the iron horse were not so successful, once the whites learned how to combat the sabotage attempts, and the fight against the iron horse was as short as it was bitter.

The depths of the Indians' resentment could be sounded in the sardonic attitude of Sitting Bull, the Hunkpapa Sioux who had rallied the plains tribes for the ephemeral victory at the Little Bighorn. Seven years after that battle Sitting Bull was living on the agency at Standing Rock. The Northern Pacific completed its main line in the summer of 1883 and incidentally formed one of the walls of the Sioux's prison. One of the railroad's officials, demonstrating that lack of comprehension which, as much as brutal indifference, characterized the whites' outlook on the Indian problem, decided that an Indian must deliver the welcoming address. After all, the railroad would haul in the Indians' rations and farming equipment. No one but Sitting Bull was considered for the welcoming role.

A young Army officer who understood the language was detailed to work with Sitting Bull on the speech. It would be delivered in Sioux, and the officer would translate.

On September 8, 1883, the railroad officials and other dignitaries assembled at Bismarck. Sitting Bull and his blue-coated mentor rode at the head of the parade, were seated on the speakers' platform and watched solemnly while the last spike was driven. Then Sitting Bull was introduced.

"I hate all the white people," he was saying, in Sioux, to his translator's horror. "You are thieves and liars. You have taken away our land and made us outcasts. . . ."

214

And so on, with no trace of emotion on his broad, blunt features. Occasionally, as instructed, he paused for applause. Then he would bow, and smile, and continue upbraiding the whites in Sioux. The officer rose and delivered a translation of what Sitting Bull *should* have said, and no one but he and the chief realized that Sitting Bull had told off his hosts in the most blistering terms. There was an ovation. The Northern Pacific executives were so pleased by Sitting Bull's performance, as they understood it, that they carried him off to St. Paul to appear at another self-congratulatory ceremony.

Years before that symbolic spike was driven into the Northern Pacific's track, a white man had formulated a program by which the Indians' violent dispossession need not have happened and the West might have been settled with a civilized regard for all men and for their new environment.

It was almost too late by then, in 1878, but a geologist named John Wesley Powell, in charge of the United States Geographical and Geological Survey of the Rocky Mountain Region, produced a document titled *Report on the Lands of the Arid Region* which was published by the Government Printing Office. Its dryly factual title concealed one of the most important and controversial reports ever submitted by a civil servant. We have endlessly relived the homicidal affray at the OK Corral, but Major Powell's survey of the real possibilities of the West has been forgotten by all but historians.

It was not that Powell lacked eloquence or literary talent in addition to his scientific knowledge. The titles of his monographs were deadly dull, but the verve and grace of his style conveyed in the fullest measure his love of the vast Western lands he labored to preserve. Under the scholarly but off-putting title *The Tertiary History of the Grand Canyon*, he would soar into lyricism when he wrote of that time-sculptured region:

> Standing among evergreens, knee-deep in succulent grass and a wealth of Alpine blossoms, fanned by chill, moist breezes, we look over terraces decked with flowers and temples and gashed with canons to the desert which stretches away beyond the southern horizon, blank, lifeless, and glowing with torrid heat. To the southwest the Basin Ranges toss up their angry waves in

characteristic confusion, sierra behind sierra, till the hazy distance hides them with a veil. . . .

Those familiar with western scenery have, no doubt, been impressed with the peculiar character of its haze—or atmosphere, in the artistic sense of the word. . . . The very air is then visible. . . . The Grand Canyon is ever full of this haze. It fills it to the brim. Its apparent density, as elsewhere, is varied according to the direction in which it is viewed and the position of the sun . . . we are really looking through miles of atmosphere. . . . The canyon is asleep. Or is it under a spell of enchantment which gives its bewildering mazes an aspect still more bewildering. Throughout the long summer afternoon the chasm which binds it grows in potency. At midday the clouds begin to gather, first in fleecy flecks, then in cumuli, and throw their shadows into the gulf. At once the scene changes. The slumber of the chasm is disturbed. The temples and cloisters seem to raise themselves half awake to greet the passing shadow. . . .

John Wesley Powell was a remarkable combination of the man of intellect and the man of action. Perhaps the keynote of his career as protector of the West was his repudiation of that school of Darwinian thought which held that man was the helpless pawn of evolutionary forces; he believed that man had the capacity to escape from the prison which confined other forms of life, to use his will to shape his environment.

He was born in upstate New York in 1834, the son of a Methodist minister, and brought up on a farm in southern Wisconsin. Various Midwestern colleges provided him with a semblance of scientific training, though he was too restless to stay at one institution for more than a term or two. Young Powell was adrift, unable to find any suitable occupation, when the Civil War broke out. The Union Army provided the touch of discipline he needed. Enlisting as a private, he was commissioned a lieutenant and then promoted to captain of artillery and attached to the staff of Major General U. S. Grant. At Shiloh he lost his right arm to a Confederate minié ball. After recuperating, he insisted on returning to active duty and rejoined Grant's army as chief of artillery, XVII Corps. Swamp fever and dysentery laid him low during the siege operations against Vicksburg, but he followed Sherman on his march through Georgia and was discharged as a brevet major.

Though he had to make do with only his left arm, Powell refused to consider a sedentary career. Two years after the war ended he organized and raised funds for the Colorado Scientific Exploring Expedition and led it westward, via the Union Pacific from Omaha to Cheyenne, to conduct a scientific survey of the Rocky Mountain region. The West was still swarming with hostile Indians, but Powell persuaded the military to allow the expedition to proceed. It included not only a variety of scientists equipped to study the geology, topography, and other aspects of the unexplored territory, but his wife and sister, who officially were listed as ornithologists and also served as camp cooks. The party explored the canyon of the Colorado, the Green and White River valleys, and Powell became fascinated with the language and customs of the Ute.

During the next decade Powell led a number of surveys, generally supplied with funds cajoled from Congress. Largely self-educated, he made himself familiar with every aspect of the Western environment, yet his scientific detachment often dissolved when he considered the problem of providing a decent and humane life for the Indians. His sympathy for their plight was fully engaged when he was appointed to a special commission charged with resettling the Indians of Utah and Nevada and introducing them to the agrarian way of life. The report of the special commissioners, probably written by Powell, rings with his conviction that the Indians had to be given a decent start in their new life:

> The Indian in his relations with the white man rarely associates with the better class, but finds his companions with the lowest and vilest of society—men whose object is to corrupt and plunder. He thus learns from the superior race everything that is bad, nothing that is good.
>
> The commission does not consider that a reservation should be looked upon in the light of a pen where a horde of savages are to be fed with flour and beef, to be supplied with blankets from the Government bounty, to be furnished with paint and gew-gaws by

217

the greed of traders, but that a reservation should be a school of industry and a home for these unfortunate people.

No able-bodied Indian should be either fed or clothed except in payment for labor, even though such labor is expended in providing for his future wants. . . . Each Indian should be supplied with a cow, to enable them to start in the accumulation of property. The Indians now understand the value of domestic cattle . . . it is interesting to note, that as soon as an Indian acquires property, he more thoroughly appreciates the rights of property and becomes an advocate of law and order.

The military must relinquish its control over the Indians and maintain a low profile, he urged, because:

They regard the presence of a soldier as a standing menace to them; the very name of soldier is synonymous with all that is offensive and evil. To the soldier they attribute their social demoralization and the unmentionable diseases with which they are infested. The Indians object to going on reservations for two main reasons: "We do not wish to dessert the graves of our fathers," and "We do not wish to give our women to the embrace of the soldiers." Some hungry Indian steals a beef, some tired Indian steals a horse, a vicious Indian commits a depredation and flies to the mountains. No effort is made to punish the real offender, but the first Indian met is shot at sight. Then, perhaps, the Indians retaliate and the news is spread through the country that war has broken out with the Indians. Troops are sent into the district and wander around the mountains and return. Perhaps a few Indians are killed, and perhaps a few white men.

He pointed out that $2,000,000 currently was being budgeted for military pacification while "much less than two hundred thousand dollars is being spent through the Indian Department for feeding, clothing, and civilizing the Indians."

Various surveys were undertaken by the War and Interior Departments as they contended for funds during the last years of the second Grant administration, and Powell's Geographical and Geological Survey of the Colorado River of the West and Its Tributaries, as it was formally designated, struggled for its existence. Powell himself had made almost thirty trips out west and produced two notable reports, *The Exploration of the Colorado River*

218

of the West and *The Geology of Eastern Portion of the Uniata Mountains.*
Powell was an obscure laborer in his chosen vineyard; his fame
did not approach that of General John Charles Frémont, whose
genius for publicity had won him the title of "The Great
Pathfinder," but he was beginning to fashion a unified theory to
govern the settlement of the West. The postwar stampede for
cheap Western lands must be succeeded by a pause in which the
nation considered how to use the lands with respect for their
fragile nature. A place must be found for the Indians in what
Powell envisioned as a new and improved sector of American
democracy. The greed of the railroad promoters and land
grabbers had to be curbed while there was still time. His geologic
studies and topographical surveys had developed into something
more significant in the long run: planning how to use the land for
the benefit of everyone rather than the inordinate profit of a few.
He compiled new temperature and precipitation tables to
debunk the claims of railroad land agents and local boosters that
the dry plains could be infinitely exploited. And he tried to view
the whole vast region between the 100th meridian (bisecting
North Dakota, South Dakota, Nebraska, Kansas, and Texas) and
the Sierra Nevada as a whole but with separate climate and soil
problems in each section.

Powell knew that his reports on these matters could be muffled
in the Interior Department bureaucracy, and he avoided that by
expressing his opinions and popularizing his findings in *Scribner's*
and other magazines with a general readership.

His testimony before the Committee on Public Lands in
Washington during the spring of 1874 stated the main thesis of
what became his crusade:

> About two-fifths of the entire area of the United States has a
> climate so arid that agriculture cannot be pursued without irriga-
> tion. When all the waters running in the streams found in this
> region are conducted on the land there will be but a small portion
> of the country redeemed, varying in the different territories
> perhaps from one to three percent. Already the greater number of
> small streams such as can be controlled by individuals who wish to
> gain a livelihood by agriculture, are used for this purpose, the
> largest streams which will irrigate larger areas can only be
> managed by cooperative organization, great capitalists, or by the

General or State Governments. It is of the most immediate and pressing importance that a general survey should be made for the purpose of determining the several areas which can be redeemed by irrigation.

In his magazine articles and on the lecture platform, Powell used the available media to promote himself as the man to conduct that survey in depth. He was setting himself up as a prophet. And he was attracting unfavorable attention from those who understandably took alarm at such phrases as "cooperative organization," those who profitably carried the banner of "rugged individualism" and resented any implication that private enterprise should not be allowed to operate unhindered forever. One of the capital's acidulous satirists observed in his newspaper:

> Major Powell has but a superficial knowledge of geology. He picks up a bone here and there and gets some terminologist to put a name on it when he gets it back to Washington. That is paleontology. He enriches the Smithsonian Institution with a few pieces of shattered earthware of which there is already a supererogation, which is archeology. He makes an annual report with an express view to another appropriation, and that is art. There is no exaggeration in this. At the hands of the educated ninny-hammers of Congress he gets an annual $25,000 to $50,000 to go anywhere he pleases, employ whom he pleases, do as he pleases and write and publish what he pleases with no official accounting to anybody. This is high art. . . .

Another Washington journal rose to his defense, proclaiming:

> His abilities are considered by the most eminent scientists in this country, and his studies of the aboriginal races of America will one day win for him golden fame. He is an enthusiastic worker in the field, and a careful writer and compiler of his researches. His marked powers will one day cause him to be as well known to the general public as he now is to the distinguished scientific men of the United States.

Major John Wesley Powell was rapidly becoming a controversial and, to some people, an intellectually suspicious character in

220

the Washington of the new Rutherford B. Hayes administration. He had attracted little attention so long as he confined himself to geology, geography, topography, paleontology and archaeology, but when he began to venture into fields which would bring him into conflict with the prevailing economic and social system, when the logical extension of his theory about the fragility of the Western environment was far-ranging reforms in the administration of the Western territories, he was treading on a minefield.

For those who watched for such storm signals in the intellectual community, Powell was beginning to be identified as a dangerous radical, a man determined to rock the economic boat so recently righted after the panic and depression of '73. Certainly he was blunt enough about his views on the exploitation of the West—the basis of prosperity during the last third of the nineteenth century—when he wrote in an article for *Century Magazine,* "In the East, the log cabin was the beginning of civilization; in the West, the miner's camp. In the East, agriculture began with settler's clearing; in the West, with the exploitation of wealthy men." Or when he declared in an address before the National Academy of Sciences:

> The present land system of the country, whether as to the purchase, preemption, or homestead plans, is not at all suitable for the area of the arid region. If it offers, for instance, title to timber lands on the homestead plan, the result is that nobody can make a homestead on such lands, the timber is simply stolen, except in instances where it was worth while to dig a mine.
>
> In the whole region, land as mere land is of no value; what is really valuable is the water privilege. Rich men and stock companies have appropriated all the streams, and they charge for the use of water. Government sections of 160 acres that do not contain water are practically, or at all events comparatively worthless.
>
> All the good public lands fit for settlement are sold. There is not left unsold in the whole United States, of land which a poor man could turn into a farm, enough to make one average county in Wisconsin. In the pasturage area of the West, a stockman must have available to him a great number of acres, for the grass is thin and poor, and no man can make a living by pasturing a few cattle upon a tract of one or two hundred acres.

*   *   *

All this defied conventional wisdom, not to mention the incessant propaganda of the railroad magnates and land barons. He was talking like a bear in a bull market. The great myth of his time was the concept of the West as the "garden of the world," an inexhaustible treasure house of agricultural and mineral sources. Infatuated with this concept, the American people felt they could be casual about the way the West was settled and exploited. And here was Powell trying to destroy that most cherished of myths which was chiefly responsible for the inveterate American optimism. Powell, as Wallace Stegner has written, was not only "challenging political forces who used popular myths for a screen, he was challenging the myths themselves, and they were rooted as the beliefs of religion."

It may have seemed to Powell that the climate was right for issuing his bold challenge. Hayes had taken office promising reforms to a country disenchanted wth the recurrent scandals and revealed corruption of Grant's eight years in the White House. Congress, sensing the public temper, was also inclined to push for reforms, at least until it was safe to drag its heels. Perhaps the most frightening action of the new administration to those who had been fattening themselves at the public's expense was the appointment of Carl Schurz as Secretary of the Interior, then perhaps the most important of Cabinet posts. A Rhinelander who had been forced to flee Germany after the collapse of the '48 revolution, a Civil War general and intimate of Lincoln, Schurz was the leader of the liberal wing of the Republican Party, as fearless and dedicated politically as Powell was socially and intellectually. Schurz could not be corrupted, bullied, or blackmailed, and he chose a like-minded man, J. A. Williamson, as commissioner of the General Land Office.

Schurz and Williamson immediately announced that the land laws henceforth would be enforced—and reinforced. They knew, however, that those laws as written were ineffective and new legislation would have to be drafted despite the angry backlash in Congress, which saw its biggest source of graft endangered. The land laws had been fabricated for the protection of those who owned large tracts, the railroads, the timber and mineral companies, the larger ranchers and others who controlled the water resources. There had been no legal protection for the homesteaders, two-thirds of whom had been ruined by drought, blizzards, insect plagues, and cyclones in the country west of the 100th meridian. The Homestead Act, supposedly designed to provide small farms in a checkerboard over the prairies, had become a farce. It simply allowed land companies to acquire tracts ranging from 100,000 to 600,000 acres at $1.25 an acre; one mining company had obtained 50,000 acres from the General Land Office for $14,000, and a few years later, following the discovery of iron ore, it was worth $25,000,000.

By the time Powell began his save-the-West campaign it was estimated that more than half a billion acres of public domain in the West had been acquired by the exploiters and monopolizers, 181,000,000 by the railroads alone.

To reverse that trend, at least to the extent that it was politically and economically possible without expropriation, Powell through most of 1877 labored over a report to Schurz which would enable the Secretary of the Interior to press for legislation to conserve what was left of the Western lands and resources. Powell would make the cannonball, and Schurz would fire it. It became Powell's masterwork: *Report on the Lands of the Arid Region of the United States.* Into it went everything Powell had observed during his thirty field trips, his researches in various scientific fields and the observations—particularly those on rainfall, soil conditions, water tables—of his colleagues on the various surveys he had undertaken. Most of all, it was informed by his witnessing, through an eye that was poetic and historic as well as scientific, the whole movement west. He would recall, and compress, images of the great migrations just after the Civil War, the steady decimation of the buffalo herds, the extension of the railroads and the mushrooming of cow towns at the railheads of the cattle trails from Texas, the search-and-destroy missions of the cavalry, the gold and cattle rushes, the growth of the big ranches, the wars of nesters and cattlemen, the losing fight of homesteaders against land speculators and land grabbers—and all the time the despoliation, the overrunning and ravaging of the pristine West he had first viewed as a one-armed Civil War veteran operating his surveys on a shoestring.

In his mind's eye he saw the prairies covered, then abandoned, then recovered by generations of failed farmers on those

223

seemingly (not really) endless prairies broken only by an occasional stream with its bordering of cottonwoods and a hillock of buffalo bones. The great question that hung over that 1,400-mile strip of land between the Dakota-Nebraska-Kansas frontier and the Sierras was whether it would become a rich empire, whose resources would be distributed with a reasonably equal hand or the forcing bed of a revolution powered by the frustrations and resentments of a horde of losers and victims, that two-thirds proportion of homesteaders who were in peonage to the banks. It was time that a voice be raised for the men bent under the burden of a mortgage and further weighted down by the cost of rail transporting his crops, chancy as they were, to the marketplace.

In 200 manuscript pages, which he revised to make as cogent and clarifying as a flash of heat lightning, he would explain that a national disaster was in the making if present practices continued, that the homsteaders flooding westward would be ruined and the land itself turned into a desert of blowing dust.

Instead of that predictable tragedy, he offered a blueprint for the orderly development of the "dryland empire," the arid region which could stand just so much settlment, in which the "mean annual rainfall is insufficient for agriculture." That two-fifths slice of the United States could support a large population only if its grasslands, water, and timber were judiciously utilized. "It is thus that a new phase of Aryan civilization is being developed in the western half of America," he pointed out, under "the physical conditions which exist in the arid lands."

An opportunity was waiting to be seized, but already it was vanishing. The key in all the three sections of the arid region (which he classified as irrigable, timber, and pasture) was water rights. Equal access to water in those drylands, instead of being controlled by a few land barons, had to be arranged. The accepted wisdom of riparian rights would not obtain in the West. A settler might wake up one morning and find that the stream which watered his soil had been diverted by others living above him on the creek. Without new laws governing land use, he wrote, "water will become a property independent of the land, and this property will be gradually absorbed by a few. Monopolies of water will be secured, and the whole agriculture of a country will be tributary thereto. . . ."

He pointed out that while a state like Iowa was almost totally arable, Utah had less than 3 percent of its area suitable for farming. Three of his associates on the survey had spent two seasons in Utah measuring rainfall and testing water tables, and their conclusion was that only 2,262 square miles were even potentially irrigable. (Eighty years later their findings were confirmed as accurate. In 1945 only 3.3 percent of the state was cultivated.)

If the arid region were to be homsteaded, he wrote, "general laws should be enacted under which a number of persons would be able to organize and settle on irrigable districts . . . the people should not be hampered with the present arbitrary system of dividing the lands into rectangular tracts. If there be any doubt of the ultimate legality of the practices in the arid country relating to water and land rights, all such doubts should be speedily quieted through the enactment of appropriate laws by the national legislature."

Orthodox thinking on the subject of the size of homesteads necessary to support a family was shocked by Powell's recommendations, which were qualified by the differing soil and water conditions in, say, a central Kansas section and one in the near desert country of Utah or Wyoming. The standard homestead of 160 acres, he said, could not support a family in the arid region without irrigation. With irrigation, 80 acres was a large enough farm. What really shook the orthodox, however, was his insistence that farms dependent on pasturing livestock, without irrigation, must be much larger than anyone had thought necessary. As he put it:

> The grasses of the pasturage lands are scant and the lands are of value only in large quantities. The farm unit should be not less than 2,560 acres. Pasturage lands need small tracts of irrigable lands, hence the small streams of the general drainage system and the lone springs and streams should be preserved for such pasturage farms. The pasturage lands will not usually be fenced and hence, herds must roam in common. All the pasturage lands should have water fronts and irrigable tracts and as the residents should be grouped and as the lands cannot be economically fenced and must be kept in common, local communal regulations or cooperation is necessary.

225

Almost a quarter of the arid region was covered by timber, large areas of which were being destroyed by fires set by the Indians. That practice must be stopped and conservation measures adopted not only to save the trees but to prevent erosion of the invaluable watersheds.

The New West he envisioned might be a paradise, but it would be a limited and controlled one, organized to allow comparatively little leeway for individual enterprise. It would have a scanty population, no more than the drylands could support:

> The homes must necessarily be widely scattered from the fact that the farm unit must be large. That the inhabitants of these districts may have the benefits of the large social organizations of civilization—as schools, churches, etc., and the benefits of cooperation in the construction of roads, bridges and other local improvements, it is essential that the residents should be grouped to the greatest possible extent.

Powell was proposing a revolution in land tenancy and water rights to form a cooperative society on the prairies. Cooperative methods were necessary because beyond the 100th meridian more than individual initiative was required to make the land productive. Powell's revolution, he made it clear, would be accomplished through access to the available water. "Monopoly of the land is not to be feared. The question for legislators is to solve some practical means by which water rights may be distributed among individual farmers and water monopolies prevented. . . . The right to use water should inhere in the land to be irrigated and water rights should go with land titles. . . ."

He proposed a law providing for the organization of any nine bona fide settlers into irrigation districts which would be self-governing. A second bill proposed in his report provided for organizing pasturage districts for the communal grazing of cattle.

With all that constant sounding of the cooperative theme, the reiteration of words like "communal" and the pejorative "monopolies," Powell's report, as transmitted by Secretary Schurz, was certain to plunge through the dome of the Capitol like a cannonball and create havoc in the houses of Congress.

226

A Vision of What Might Have Been

More than one statesman, well larded by years of patronage from the railroads and land companies, would catch whiff of the unholy doctrines broadcast during the communard uprising in Paris, which had been dissipated, but apparently not vaporized, by the blasts of French artillery only a few years before.

The report, one historian has observed, went "far beyond the social and economic thinking of the period that popularized the pork barrel as a national symbol and developed to its highest and most ruthless stage the competitive ruthlessness of American business" to the extent that "it seems like the product of another land and another people." The folklore of generations of farmers, who had survived and often prospered in Eastern states with plentiful rainfall, would be held invalid for the new "dryland democracy." The cherished image of a frontier farmer clearing his own patch of land and triumphing over the environment through his individual efforts would be effaced by a new reality. There would be no continuation of the pioneer legend; it would be replaced by the unpicturesque structure of an ant colony.

Americans of his century abhorred the idea of interdependence, were infatuated with the mathematically improbable theory that every man was a potential millionaire. Popular acceptance of his recommendations would be greatly inhibited by the feeling that nothing was worthwhile unless it was accomplished by individual effort—a feeling that endured well into this century and certainly has not been entirely extinguished. Sensing the innate American attachment to individualism, Powell some years later argued that interdependence was an essential fact of civilization:

> By the division of labor men have become interdependent, so that every man works for some other man. To the extent that culture has progressed beyond the plane occupied by the brute, man had ceased to work directly for himself and come to work directly for others and indirectly for himself. . . . For the glasses I wear, mines were worked in California. . . . As I sit in my library to read a book, I open the pages with a paper cutter, the ivory of which was obtained through the employment of a tribe of African elephant hunters. The paper on which my book was printed was made of rags saved by the beggars of Italy. . . . Thus the enmity of man to man is appeased, the men live and labor for one another;

individualism is transmuted into socialism, egoism to altruism, and man is lifted above the brute to an immeasurable height. . . .

But the America of a century ago was psychologically unprepared for any transmutations of "individualism into socialism," though he probably was not speaking in any Marxist sense, and it would be a long time before any sizable part of the citizenry was ready to consider giving up the joys of reaching for the top prizes of a capitalist economy.

Powell's *Report on the Lands of the Arid Region* was a bomb with a delayed-action fuse. Its very title indicated that it was a dusty-dry academic treatise, and it was months before the enemies of all that Powell proposed awoke to the fact that it called for a reversal of the conditions under which the West had been and was being settled.

Rather casually, Secretary of the Interior Schurz passed it along to the House of Representatives on April 5, 1878. It was referred to the Committee on Appropriations, which routinely ordered that it be printed by the Government Printing Office. The reluctance of Congressmen to do any serious reading, particularly during the summer months, kept it in the status of an open secret.

But Powell and his supporters knew that a storm would break once the report's implications were grasped, and they prepared for a defense of its findings. One bastion was the newly organized Cosmos Club, which became Washington's most prestigious club. Its nucleus was an intellectual circle which had gathered in the Powell parlor on Saturday nights for feasts of reason accompanied by mild tippling. With Powell as its first president, the Cosmos Club enlarged its membership to 300 and rented rooms in a downtown building. The support of the National Academy of Sciences, which had been chartered by Congress in 1863 to advise it on scientific matters, was also enlisted. The new president of the academy was Professor O. C. Marsh of Yale, the celebrated paleontologist, who had exposed the corruption of the Indian Bureau during the Grant administration after observing its agents at work in the Sioux lands. Marsh became one of Powell's most vocal and powerful supporters. The intellectual community in the United States, though rudimentary by present standards,

228

commanded a certain amount of attention in the available media, and it generally rallied to the same cause.

For sheer wind force, however, the scientists and intellectuals could not hope to match the efforts of the Western political bloc and its phalanx of self-interested parties, the railroads, the land and water companies, the timber companies, the mine operators. When the 1,800 copies of the first edition of Powell's report and its second printing of 5,000 copies achieved a wider distribution and made their expected impact, the Western politicians rose almost to a man to denounce Powell and his masterwork. Powell came under assault by a whole brigade of railroad propagandists and land promoters, who charged that he was an enemy of progress, that his ivory-tower vision of an orderly development of Western resources would wreck the economy and crush individual enterprise.

The leader of the anti-Powell Congressional chorus was Representative Thomas M. Patterson of Colorado, who, with some accuracy, characterized Powell as "this revolutionist." Powell and his supporters, he charged, were "theorists who knew nothing about the practical problems of the public lands." Powell was a "charlatan of science and intermeddler in affairs of which he has no conception."

The Western newspapers, echoing Patterson, branded Powell a visionary, a revolutionary, a dreamer, and a mad idealist. They pointed out that recent years, when thousands of homesteaders were ripping up the grasslands of Kansas, Nebraska, and Colorado, had seen heavy rains and bumper crops on the great plains. They quoted their own prophet, the publicist William Gilpin, author of *The Mission of the North American People,* who had proclaimed that the western half of the continent could support hundreds of millions of people, and whose fervently mystical style was indicated in this passage from one of his speeches: "What an immense geography has been revealed! What infinite hives of population and laboratories of industry have been electrified and set in motion! The great sea has rolled away its sombre veil. Asia is found and has become our neighbor. . . ." The idea of providing a dryland homesteader with 2,560 acres was ridiculed. State legislatures in the West adopted resolutions denouncing the Powell report.

Powell and his friends lobbied vigorously and enlisted the support of several powerful Congressional figures: John D. C. Atkins of Tennessee, the chairman of the House Appropriations Committee; Abram S. Hewitt of New York; and James A. Garfield of Ohio. They pushed for legislation Powell had advocated in his report and his recommendation that the various Western surveys be consolidated. But the Western bloc was strong enough to constitute a formidable obstacle to any program which would revolutionize settlement and curb exploitation. The old myths were invoked, the old gospels quoted, and the battle over the report went on for months, as one observer said, "to the point of exhaustion, and beyond exhaustion to stalemate and compromise."

Powell's urgent plea for a reform of the land laws in effect was stifled in the acrimonious controversy they aroused. The measures he advocated were pigeonholed in the Public Lands Subcommittee of the House Appropriations Committee and there died an unnatural death. All that Powell's Congressional supporters could save from the wreckage of his program was a bill providing for the consolidation of the Western surveys and the appointment of a commission to study the public land question. Only in time did bits and pieces of the Powell program emerge in legislation; his ideas were revived in the Newlands Reclamation Act of 1902 (passed shortly before Powell's death), the 1933 legislation establishing the Tennessee Valley Authority, and the Taylor Grazing Act of 1934, as well as other laws creating national forests and interstate water-sharing agreements.

Powell emerged from the legislative battles at least partly triumphant. At his urging Clarence King was named director of the newly consolidated United States Geological Survey, in which Powell became King's second-in-command. At the same time Powell was named director of the Bureau of American Ethnology, which would be under the control of the Smithsonian Institution instead of the politicians and bureaucrats.

Even before his death his theories would be vindicated, but meanwhile, he devoted himself largely to defining and improving the position of the Indians in American life. The role he conceived for the Indian would fit in with the new society, in which individuals acknowledged their responsibility for each other in a harsh and difficult land, which he hoped would arise in the West. The Indians of the northern plains must not be crushed out of existence through the greed and stupidity of the more numerous whites. Indian culture, or what was left of it after the vengeance exacted in the year following the Little Bighorn, must be preserved. In the new Western society the Indians would have their rightful place but with the hardships of primitive life eliminated as much as possible. The Indians would be allowed to evolve gradually and become an independent part of the larger community.

In urging his fellow whites to attempt an understanding of Indian mores, he wrote:

> [the Indian] looks upon our whole system of property rights as an enormous evil and an unpardonable sin, for which the gods will eventually punish the wicked and blasphemous white man. . . . In this matter, and many others of similar character relating to their customs and belief, we must either deal with the Indian as he is, looking to the slow but irresistible influence of civilization to effect a change, or we must reduce him to abject slavery. The attempt to transform a savage into a civilized man by a law, a policy, an administration, or a great conversion, in a few months or a few years, is an impossibility clearly appreciated by scientific ethnologists who understand the institution and social conditions of the Indians.
>
> Again, we have usually attempted to treat with the tribes through their chiefs, as if they wielded absolute power; but an Indian tribe is a pure democracy; their chieftaincy is not hereditary, and the chief is but the representative, the speaker of the tribe, and can do no act by which his tribe is bound without being instructed thus in due and established form. The blunders we have made and the wrongs we have inflicted on the Indians because of a failure to recognize this fact have been cruel and inexcusable, except on the ground of our ignorance.

Powell systematized the study of the Indian past to find clues to their future development, and he worked endlessly to spread his personal gospel that most of the trouble between whites and Indians was caused by the former's lack of comprehension. He argued:

Savagery is not an inchoate civilization; it is a distinct status of society with its own institutions, customs, philosophy, and religion; and all these must necessarily be overthrown before new institutions, customs, philosophy and religion can be introduced. The failure to recognize this fact has brought inconceivable mischief in our management of the Indians.

Eventually his observations of what had happened in the West and his prophecies of what could happen took on a wider range and encompassed the national destiny as a whole. He foresaw "a whole chemical industry based upon the uses of petroleum." He also predicted the need for antitrust laws and the regulation of commerce and industry: "Modern civilized society is based on property—the unit being the individual. The social unit will eventually be a business corporation, and there will be a hierarchy of corporations, the highest of which will embrace all the rest and constitute the government. The basis of society will then cease to be property, and will become industry." To those who accused him of espousing Socialism, he would reply that he did not advocate government ownership of the means of production or the abolition of private property, but only legislation to ensure that any person had the chance to improve himself. Obviously he had been thoroughly alarmed by the monopolies created by the exploitation of the West and their control over so many lives.

It would take the passage of generations before Powell's pleas for evolutionary development of the Indians, in a humane and intelligent fashion, could be seen as truly prophetic, but the accuracy of his warnings against the haphazard, headlong exploitation of the dryland belt from North Dakota to Texas was proved long before his death—most strikingly, in fact, just eight years after Congress refused to heed those warnings.

The proof of his jeremiads against overpopulation of the American steppe was visible in the mid-eighties when a prolonged drought turned the earth to powder under endlessly brassy skies. Hot winds tore away at the topsoil and whirled it away in sky-blackening dust clouds. Then came the Great White Ruin of the winter of 1886.

Shortly after New Year's, 1886, a calamitous blizzard came

howling down from the north, devastating the eastern slopes of the Rockies, the short-grass plains, all the country between the Dakotas and Texas. Whole herds of cattle were wiped out. About 500 people lost their lives, and for years afterward their skeletons would be found out on the prairies. All along the sod house frontier the people, many of them German, Russian, or Scandinavian immigrants, huddled for days, then weeks, as successive storms swept down from the north. Many cattlemen lost from 50 to 90 percent of their herds as the cattle went unfed on the deep-drifted prairies, and one western Nebraska combine lost 100,000 head.

The catastrophic winter was followed by an early spring, a blazing summer, and a late autumn, with October days as hot as was midsummer usually. And the violent extremes of weather continued. Late that autumn, a Nebraska historian recorded: "The real uneasiness hit the old cowmen of the North when they noticed curious and unusual movement among the wild life. Prairie dogs holed up early. Elk moved in determined march southward. Suddenly almost all the birds were gone. . . . Instead, Arctic owls came flying on silent wings, the first seen in the Judith Basin so far as any white man could remember. Old Indians followed their ghostly flight with narrowed eyes and drew their blankets closer. . . ." Such omens were followed by the screech of the first blue northers, then snowstorm after snowstorm, and once again the grasslands were devastated. With pardonable hyperbole it was said that a man could walk from the Black Hills to the Bighorn Mountains without stepping off the carcasses of cattle perished during the winter. The Indians had seen such things before, when the white men killed off all the buffalo and left their carcasses heaped on the ranges.

That was the end of the great cattle bonanza, the breaking of the "cattle bubble" which had caused wild speculation in the American and English commodity markets. Cattle were being sold at giveaway prices. Not only cattlemen but homesteaders, the squatters, the nesters who had been encouraged to overcrowd the Great Plains on their checkerboard of quarter sections, were brought to the realization that there was nothing but a few barbed-wire fences between themselves and the North Pole. A few years later, in a speech at Bismarck, North Dakota, Powell

233

warned the settlers, "You hug to yourselves the delusion that the climate is changing. This question is 4,000 years old. Nothing that man can do will change the climate. . . . There's almost enough rainfall for your purposes, but one year with another you need a little more than you get. . . ."

The graphic testimony to the accuracy of Powell's warnings was provided by the caravans of prairie schooners—100,000 of them in one year, according to contemporary accounts—reversing the traditional course of empire. Careworn, ragged, near-starving, those ex-pioneers trekked in long trains back to the Middle Western states, leaving whole counties depopulated and towns deserted.

It was our first taste of the dust bowl. A collective tragedy for thousands of people, but it would be repeated in less than a generation when a feverish railroad promotion sent other thousands similarly overpopulating the plains of Montana.

All those now-forgotten tragedies could have been averted if his country had listened carefully to John Wesley Powell, if his warnings had not been muffled by the counterpropaganda of the private interests which thrived on the conditions which led to such large-scale disasters. As the late Bernard DeVoto wrote, Powell's *Report on the Lands of the Arid Region* was:

> one of the most remarkable books ever written by an American. In the whole range of American experience from Jamestown on there is no book more prophetic. It is a scientific prophecy and it has been fulfilled—experimentally proved. Unhappily the experimental proof has consisted of human and social failure and the destruction of the land. . . . The twist of the knife is that meanwhile irreversible actions went on out west and what we did in error will forever prevent us from catching up with it altogether.

Powell offered a vision of what might have been, it was rejected, and we continue to pay the price of that rejection.

10.

California's Octopus (I)

> The Overland Express arrived at midnight last night, more than nine hours late, and twenty passengers descended from the snow-covered cars. All were frozen and half-starving, but thankful they had escaped with their lives.
> —AMBROSE BIERCE in the San Francisco *Examiner*

MORE than a year before California's railroad linked up with the Union Pacific, a literary periodical called the *Overland Monthly* was founded in San Francisco, with the as-yet-obscure Bret Harte as its first editor. One purpose of the monthly was to glorify the state's future, now that it was about to have an overland transportation system connecting it with the East. The most striking feature of the first issue was its logotype, which showed a grizzly bear with one paw planted between the railroad tracks. Originally the logotype showed only the bear, California's sacred emblem ever since the days of the Bear Republic, but according to Mark Twain, one of the *Overland Monthly*'s early contributors, Harte was seized by an inspiration during an editorial conference and "took a pencil and drew those two simple lines under his feet and behold he was a magnificent success!—the ancient symbol of California savagery snarling at the approaching type of high and progressive Civilization, the first Overland locomotive!" It was, Twain wrote, "the prettiest fancy and the neatest that ever shot through Harte's brain."

There was no doubt of young Mr. Harte's cleverness, but within half a dozen years of that day most of his fellow Californians would have designed a different logotype for the *Overland Monthly*.

It might have shown a mangy old bear swaying with exhaustion as it battled for survival against an octopus, biologically illogical though such a confrontation might have been.

The Octopus soon became the state's designation of the Central Pacific-Southern Pacific railroad system, one tentacle stretching over the Sierras toward Utah, the other extending southward to Los Angeles and then eastward across the southern deserts. Not only the *Overland Monthly* but most of the state's citizenry heralded the completion of the Central Pacific and the construction of feeder lines to bring the farm and ranch crops to market and the ores to the smelters and the San Francisco Mint. Almost everyone agreed that it was the greatest thing that ever happened to California.

Within a few years, however, many began to have their doubts about the Big Four who had built the railroad. Their collective arrogance, their public-be-damned attitude were obnoxious to a society founded on the egalitarian principles of mining-camp democracy, and the rapidly accumulating power of their wealth and the political influence it bought them were becoming more alarming every year. The ego of Charles Crocker, who superintended the Central Pacific construction, expanded to fit his 230-pound hulk. He as well as two of his partners, Hopkins and Stanford, began building magnificent new homes on San Francisco's Nob Hill which were obviously intended to overawe their fellow citizens. Crocker bought up a whole block on the city's stateliest hill, bounded by California, Tyler, Sacramento, and Jones streets, except for one small parcel owned by an undertaker named Yung. His attempts to squash Yung seemed to typify his character. He grew more enraged daily as his ornate wooden palace, which a local esthete defined as "the delirium of a wood carver" and which featured a 76-foot tower from which Crocker could look down on the whole city, was being completed and undertaker Yung still refused to sell his lot. The modest Yung house, crouched at the foot of his mansion, was a cinder in the new tycoon's eye. Finally, in towering exasperation, Crocker ordered drays laden with lumber and a large crew of workmen up Nob Hill to build a 40-foot "spite fence" around Yung's property.

Yung's house was cast in perpetual shade by the immense palisade, but the undertaker still refused to sell out.

It was a bad time for Crocker or any magnate to be flaunting the power of his wealth. The depression of 1873 had thrown thousands out of work. Three years later the city, always one of the most volatile in the country, was seething with protest. Just about the time Crocker's spite fence was finished, a young Irish drayman named Denis Kearney, who had educated himself at the Lyceum of Self-Culture, was making himself into a highly effective demagogue. On the sandlots around the City Hall Kearney every Sunday rallied thousands of listeners as he exhorted his Workingmen's Party—now so considerable a force in California politics that it had attracted the support of two of the leading San Francisco newspapers—to "lynch and burn out the thieving millionaires, the hell-born, the hell-bound villains, the bloated bondholders."

Crocker's feud with Yung had been reported in detail in the newspapers, and Kearney seized upon this as an issue. Clearly, he proclaimed, it was a contest between capital and labor. He promised his followers that he would lead them on a march to Crocker's mansion and tear down the spite fence, board by board, then use one of the planks to chastise Crocker himself.

The fence, however, was only a side issue. The real quarrel Kearney and his followers had with Crocker and his fellow railroad builders was that they had employed "cheap Chinese labor" to build the Central Pacific; they disregarded the fact that Crocker had imported thousands of Chinese only because no Caucasians, not even Mexican peons in Sonora, could be found to swing picks on the Sierra grades. Now San Francisco's Chinatown had a population of 116,000, and they were taking jobs away from the unemployed whites.

"The monopolists who make money by employing cheap labor had better watch out," Kearney shouted one Sunday night to his sandlot following. "They have built themselves fine residences on Nob Hill and erected flagstaffs upon their roofs. Let them take care that they have not erected their own gallows."

During the next year Crocker and the other lordlings of Nob Hill faced the possibility that all they had might be swept away in a rising from the city's lower depths. Kearney began leading marches up Nob Hill, with himself mounted on a horse and addressing his cohorts from the saddle, and holding meetings outside the Crocker and Stanford mansions at which he demanded that the residences be taken over by the people and turned into asylums for the homeless. "Judge Lynch," he shouted, "will decide the fate of capitalism!"

Some of his more moderate sympathizers began to back away from Kearney as his prescriptions for violent reform of the social and economic system grew wilder and more outrageous. Many agreed with him that the Big Four had formed an oppressive monopoly, that the Chinese were a formidable threat to the white workingman, but was it necessary to level the city to prove his point? Mass destruction seemed to be the only panacea Kearney offered. It was one thing to suggest lynching a few wealthy malefactors—vigilante law had figured in the city's history from the beginning—but another to demand that most members of the state legislature be hanged from the lampposts. Kearney also urged that all his followers arm themselves with rifles for the day of reckoning and proposed that bundles of dynamite be dropped on Chinatown from balloons.

One summer evening in 1877 it became apparent that there was more than demagogic flourishes to Denis Kearney. Mobs inflamed by his oratory took to the streets, invaded Chinatown, beat up Chinese, and wrecked their homes and business establishments. Then they set fire to the wreckage. It took a desperate effort by the city's fire fighters to keep the Chinatown flames from spreading to and destroying the rest of the city. A strong reaction to Kearney resulted from that incident. Kearney was arrested on charges of inciting riots, and during his months of imprisonment his following was leaderless. A Businessmen's Vigilance Committee was organized by the wealthy residents of Nob Hill and formed a "Pickhandle Brigade" to confront Kearney and his draymen, steamfitters, longshoremen, and hod carriers if they ever ventured up Nob Hill again. Crocker himself installed a rack of Springfield rifles in the library of his Victorian monstrosity and announced that he personally would shoot Kearney if he appeared on Nob Hill again. He and his fellow magnates also backed a weekly titled *The Argonaut* with instructions to "let the Irish have it." The associate editor was one

Ambrose Bierce, who in the near future would become, not the chastiser of the Irish working classes, but the gadfly who devoted much of his sulfurous literary career to attacking the California railroads.

The threat posed by Kearney and his Workingmen's Party soon evaporated as the radical movement split into factions and Kearney himself lost influence when economic conditions improved and the jobless found employment.

Neither Crocker nor his partners had learned a lesson from the threatened uprising of 1876–77 and continued to exercise their transportation monopoly in the most ruthless manner. They had come to regard California as a near-medieval fiefdom. They had aroused hopes which titillated even the intellectuals with a promise of a better life for everyone, causing Henry George to write in 1868 that the railroads would be "the means of converting a wilderness into a populous empire in less time than many of the cathedrals of Europe were building," which inspired the poet Joaquin Miller to observe that there was "more poetry in the rush of a single railroad train across the continent than in all the gory story of burning Troy." Popular songs sounded the same theme, and any play which insinuated a·railroad scene (the hero throwing a switch and saving the night express from derailment) was assured of success.

Merely by building their first railroad, the Big Four had accumulated an enormous reserve of goodwill. They dissipated it entirely within a few years. For forty years, from the finish of construction to the inauguration of the first real reform administration to take over the statehouse, the history of California was, to an almost incredible extent, the struggle between the Southern Pacific-Central Pacific and the people, between the Octopus and the Bear. A hundred years ago, of course, there were few restraints on a monopolistic enterprise; those which were self-imposed by the monopolists, those few who apprehended that their power might one day be diminished, were so rare as to appear miraculous. There was no necessity then for an enterprise to adopt a public relations policy or cloak itself in even an assumed benevolence.

The owners and operators of the California roads established an economic dictatorship protected by an unbreakable control of the state legislature. Neither the Republicans nor the Democrats, not even the violent idealists sent to Sacramento by the Workingmen's Party, were impervious to the Central Pacific's methods of suborning the legislature. Lesgislators were given passes on the railroad, of course, and cash subsidies in addition. Despite all the public pressure on them to curb the power of the railroad, they doggedly defended its interests session after session, decade after decade. In 1881 a Republican-Democratic fusion ticket obtained control of the legislature on its pledge to throw the rascals out—by which, everyone understood, they meant Collis P. Huntington's bagmen and lobbyists—but the Central Pacific's satchels opened wide and cash poured into legislative pockets. Surveying that session when it adjourned in April, Ambrose Bierce, by then the leading performer at the bitterly anti-railroad periodical *The Wasp*, wrote:

> If nonsense were black, Sacramento would need gas lamps at noonday; if selfishness were audible, the most leathern-lunged orator of the lot would appear a deaf mute flinging silly ideas from his finger tips amid the thunder of innumerable drums. So scurvy a crew I do not remember having discovered in vermiculose conspiracy outside the carcass of a dead horse—at least not since they adjourned.

The helplessness of Californians, not only those on marginal farms shipping their crops to the city but merchants and wholesalers, mining and industrial magnates, to defend themselves from the railroad they had hailed as a benefactor is difficult to understand in today's context, with all the regulatory laws and agencies established since the Big Four were at the height of their power. From the early 1870's on, the Huntington-Crocker-Stanford-Hopkins combine controlled the shipment of all goods not only within the California borders, but to and from California. Their freight schedules were based on the principle of the nutcracker. "It was perhaps the nation's choicest example of a complete and sustained monopoly," one historian has observed, "an almost ideal demonstration of the power of a corporation to control for its own profit the economic resources of a region comprising one sixth of the area of the nation." For many years the Southern Pacific-Central Pacific combined, in fact, monopolized transportation in all the coastal states, with the result that from the middle seventies to 1910 the profit margins of almost every business and industry on the Coast were controlled, not by market conditions, but by the dictates of the railroad. The prosperity of each entrepreneur was directly controlled by the officials at the railroad headquarters at Fourth and Townsend streets who drew up its freight-rate schedules.

Rate fixing was a delicate art considerably enchanced by an intelligence system which kept watch over every business's fortunes. In San Francisco agents of the Central Pacific even demanded, and were given, the right to make periodic inspections of the shippers' books. A merchant's rates were raised if he was prospering, lowered if bankruptcy was looming. Farmers and manufacturers were similarly kept under constant surveillance. The railroad did not want to ruin anyone, because that cost it a customer, but was determined that it would take the hog's share of all profits flowing into the state. To assure this, it established a system of economic surveillance which has hardly been equaled by the present Internal Revenue Service with all its computers.

What should have been a general prosperity for people along the Pacific littoral, once the depression of '73 waned, instead became an outrageous bonanza for the railroads and their little clique of major stockholders.

It was all but incredible how nakedly authoritarian the Southern Pacific had become (the Central Pacific, though the parent company, was soon submerged).

The horror stories abounded. One later disclosed by its participants once they escaped the Southern Pacific's stranglehold concerned the development of a gold mine near Shasta in the northern foothills. The developers, who had to ship their quartz to a stamping mill near San Francisco, asked the Southern Pacific to fix a rate for the 300-mile haul. Fifty dollars a car, the railroad replied. The mine operators soon were shipping three cars of ore daily, upon which the Southern Pacific raised the rate to $73 a car. When the mine stayed in business, it was raised again to $100 a car. The mine operators then traveled down to San Francisco to inform the railroad that the new rate would force them to shut down. Very well, a railroad official replied, show us your books

241

and we'll set a price that will keep you afloat. The mineowners could only comply. The Southern Pacific was, in effect, running hundreds of enterprises in that fashion.

Occasionally of course the railroad's rate fixers miscalculated, as they did in the case of the California lemon growers. The latter found a good market in the East, and their prosperity encouraged landowners to plant whole new lemon groves. This boomlet came to the attention of the Southern Pacific with its hound-dog alertness for any new source of profit. Its freight division upped the rate on lemons by 15 cents a box despite bleats of protest from the orchards. The railroad refused to believe that the 15-cent rate increase was exactly the amount netted by the growers on each box. It was somewhat taken aback when the lemon growers uprooted their trees and planted their acreages in other crops; poor-mouthing was the only defense its customers had against the Southern Pacific, and railroad officials always took that into account. In the case of the lemon growers, they lowered the freight rate and persuaded their old customers to replant the lemon groves.

Even the railroad's official historian would admit a dozen years after the Interstate Commerce Commission forced the Southern Pacific to behave in a less vampirish fashion that during its forty-year period of unchecked rapacity it always exacted "the utmost possible profit." The late Stewart H. Holbrook, a railroad buff, wrote that all the railroads of that period were merciless in gouging profits out of their customers, but the Southern Pacific operated "with a cynicism and often with a brutality that it would be hard to match."

There were several places along the Southern Pacific system where the pincers of monopoly were especially painful, along the San Pedro and Oakland waterfronts, which were then controlled by the railroad. It owned a 21-mile spur line between San Pedro, the port of Los Angeles, and the Los Angeles freightyards, the main purpose of which was to discourage shippers from using the sea route from the Atlantic to the Pacific coasts. The rate on the San Pedro-Los Angeles line, including wharfage costs, was $3.50 a ton. It cost almost half as much to ship goods from San Pedro to Los Angeles, a forty-five-minute journey, as from a Chinese port to Los Angeles, which took many weeks.

242

Besides its monopolistic prices, the Southern Pacific's hapless clientele had plenty of other reasons to complain. The railroad's safety record, for one thing, was deplorable; its timetables were approximate at best, fictitious at worst. Southern Pacific passengers, noted Ambrose Bierce when he began writing a column for William Randolph Hearst's San Francisco *Examiner*, were "exposed to the perils of senility." Like most of the state's newspapers (with the notable exception of the Los Angeles *Times*), the *Examiner* always prominently reported the lateness of every Southern Pacific passenger train; it was a standard feature like the Wall Street quotations and the weather forecast. But Bierce was its chief railroad watcher, and on one occasion observed in his column that the Overland Express, one of the Southern Pacific's much-advertised "crack" passenger trains, "arrived at midnight last night, more than nine hours late, and twenty passengers descended from the snow-covered cars. All were frozen and half-starved, but thankful they had escaped with their lives."

Reading through files of the San Francisco newspapers, one gathers the impression that traveling on the Southern Pacific was at least as adventurous as going on an African safari. Like most railroads, the Southern Pacific was laggard in adopting the safety devices which had been available for years. George Westinghouse had invented air brakes in 1868, a year before the Central Pacific was linked to the Union Pacific, Eli Janney patented his automatic coupler the same year; but it wasn't until the early 1880's that those devices and automatic signals were generally installed. To Ambrose Bierce it was all part of "the methods devised by the railroad company to punish the Demon Passenger," but it was more likely due to Southern Pacific parsimony.

Hearst's *Examiner* always had a crew of reporters, photographers, and sketch artists available to rush to the scene of a Southern Pacific wreck and provide graphic details of the disaster. Often the newspaper exaggerated; no public utility could have functioned in as slipshod a manner as Hearst claimed, but the Southern Pacific's safety record was bad enough for the public to believe such *Examiner* items as this: "Last week in Petaluma a man withdrew to his hay-loft, tied one end of a rope to a rafter and the other about his neck. He then stepped through a trap door. Petaluma is not on the line of the Southern Pacific

243

Railroad. The citizens that enjoy that privilege can commit suicide with far less fuss and bother."

Traveling over the Sierras to Nevada doubtless was something of an adventure. Because of hasty construction, the roadbed was shaky, the crossties were too widely spaced, and the trains bucked and reared. Often the locomotive jumped the tracks, and the passengers would be cooped up in their cars for half a day until the engine was righted. But they traveled at a speed of about 20 miles an hour through the foothills, and a derailment usually wasn't disastrous. In the high Sierra, however, a derailed locomotive might plunge over a 1,000-foot cliff, as at the famous Cape Horn curve, and many passengers traveling from the East preferred to return via steamer and through the fever zone at the Isthmus of Panama rather than face again those hairpin curves above the Sierra canyons. Once over the hump, having passed through the long snowsheds built to protect the tracks from the mountain drifts and avalanches, a passenger could breathe easier.

It would never be forgotten, however, that in its early days one of the Central Pacific's mountain-division trains, the Grizzly Bear, collided with a cow on the tracks near Dutch Flat and immediately turned over on its side.

Nor would most Californians disagree when Ambrose Bierce delivered his magisterial opinion of the Southern Pacific's first twenty years of operation:

> The worst railroads in America are in the west. The worst railroads on the Pacific Coast are those operated by the Southern Pacific Company. The worst railroad operated by the Southern Pacific Company is the Central Pacific. It owes the government more millions of dollars than Leland Stanford has vanities; it will pay fewer cents than Collis P. Huntington has virtues. It has always been managed by rapacity tempered by incompetence. Let Leland Stanford remove his dull face from the United States Senate and exert some of his boasted "executive ability" disentangling the complexities in which his frankly brainless subordinates have involved the movements of his trains.

You could hardly open a California-based periodical during the 1880's without being confronted by a cartoon showing a particularly aggressive octopus, its head bearing the features of

Collis P. Huntington, its tentacles coiled around the State Capitol, hapless farmers, ships and stagecoaches, the Oakland and San Pedro waterfronts. Generally the writhing beast was labeled "Railroad Monopoly."

Not only such zoological images, but the rallying cry "Remember Mussel Slough" would animate the antirailroad partisans for three decades.

The Mussel Slough incident bathed the Southern Pacific and its method of operation in a garish light, an event it would take many years and enormous public relations efforts to efface. Nothing better demonstrated the "rapacity" charged by its unrelenting critics.

During the 1870's the Southern Pacific began building its line south from San Francisco, having been subsidized by land grants on either side of its right-of-way. The railroad immediately advertised throughout the Middle West for settlers to come out and buy railroad land at bargain prices. Thousands thus were encouraged to migrate to the San Joaquin Valley and the Tulare Basin; sometimes whole communities packed up and joined the movement to the cheap land promised by the Southern Pacific.

Potentially, as events proved, the land was as fertile and bountiful as the Southern Pacific proclaimed, but it became an agricultural paradise only after years of effort. When the first settlers arrived, in fact, they found themselves in a hot, dry trough, struggling to survive in their board shacks against the searing summer winds sweeping down the valley, the winter floods, the sudden spring frosts, the autumn sandstorms that buried their crops. Their only hope was to build an irrigation system by damming foothill streams and bringing the water to their parched fields through canals and ditches. In those years it was known as Starvation Valley, which came close to being the literal truth.

By the end of the 1870's, however, the settlers in the San Joaquin Valley had begun to solve their problems. Word that they had achieved a measure of prosperity inevitably reached the Southern Pacific headquarters at Fourth and Townsend in San Francisco, whose sensors signaled every change in the state's economic life.

Accordingly, to the railroad's executives, it seemed time to bring up the matter of paying for the Valley lands. The settlers had come out more or less on trust; they would be required to pay for the land they staked out and improved when the railroad (which, of course, was dealing in land conveyed to it by the state government) got around to running surveys and validating titles. They had been promised that the sales price would be "moderate." In the Southern Pacific's promotional literature it pledged an average price of $2.50 to $5 an acre, with only the best land going for as high as $10 an acre. The railroad also promised: "In ascertaining the value, any improvement that a settler or other person may have on the lands will not be taken into consideration; neither will the price be increased in consequence thereof. Settlers are thus assured that in addition to being accorded the first privilege of purchase, they will be protected in their improvements."

Late in the seventies the Southern Pacific began informing individual farmers that the purchase price of their lands would range from $25 to $40 an acre instead of the $2.50 to $10 the railroad had promised when it urged them to populate the valley.

When the settlers refused to accept the outrageous markup, the Southern Pacific began advertising in newspapers throughout the state to sell land in the San Joaquin Valley—land which the first settlers had irrigated. Newcomers moved in, having bought land from the railroad at $25 and $30 an acre, and prepared to share in the fruits of the pioneers' labors. One night, however, the sky turned red over the Tulare Basin, and the railroad's protégés were burned out and sent packing.

The settlers, knowing they were in for a long hard fight against a corporation with all the political and judicial influence it could buy, organized themselves for a legal battle. The Settlers' Rights League, led by a lawyer named John J. Doyle, attacked the Southern Pacific's title to the lands along its right-of-way. Doyle appealed for help to the California delegation in Congress, which of course was wearing the Southern Pacific colors to a man. None of the state's politicians would help. Doyle took a test case to the federal court and also appealed directly to the Interior Department. At every turn he was defeated. The federal court ruled in favor of the railroad, giving it clear title to the lands it had offered for settlement and now intended to repossess.

246

Given the favorable court decision and the hands-off attitude
of the state government, the Southern Pacific proceeded to throw
what it called "the squatters" off the lands they had cultivated,
irrigated, and made to flourish. The railroad sent in two men
named M. D. Hartt and Walter J. Crow as agents provocateurs;
they were to receive free farms in return for holding them, come
what may, against the settlers of the Mussel Slough district of
Kings County.

The railroad's agents had been dispatched to a particularly
militant neighborhood. In other parts of the valley, the settlers
either paid the price demanded by the Southern Pacific or
allowed themselves to be dispossessed. Around Mussel Slough the
Settlers' Rights League was determined to hold out despite the
adverse rulings from the courts. Their leader, Major Thomas J.
McQuiddy, had always counseled his followers to "go it slow,"
not respond to provocation, because the railroad had the state
and federal governments on its side. Now McQuiddy was beginning to believe it would be necessary to resist by force.

On May 10, 1880, he called for a mass meeting and barbecue to
be attended by all the settlers in the Mussel Slough district. They
were to be addressed by a professional firebrand named David
Smith Terry, who had gained considerable renown as a jurist,
duelist, politician, and upholder of lost causes. That morning all
the roads in the district led to Hanford, where the mass meeting
was to be held, with hundreds of farmers coming into town with
their families in buckboards and buggies. Even before the meeting they were all but unanimously resolved to hold out until their
case had been appealed to the United States Supreme Court.

The night before, Major McQuiddy had sent a message to A.
W. Poole, the U.S. marshal of that district, warning him against
any attempt to evict the settlers:

> We hereby notify you that we have had no chance to present our
> equity in the case nor shall we be able to do so as quickly as our
> opponents can complete their process for a so-called legal eject-
> ment, and we have therefore determined that we will not leave our
> homes unless forced to do so by a superior force. In other words, it
> will require an army of 1,000 good soldiers against the local force
> that we can rally for self-defense, and we further expect the moral

247

support of the good, law-abiding citizens of the United States sufficient to resist all force that can be brought to bear to perpetrate such an outrage.

McQuiddy's proclamation pointed out:

These lands were never granted to the Southern Pacific Railroad Company.... We have certain equities that must be respected and shall be respected.... The patents they hold to our lands were acquired by misrepresentation and fraud, and we, as American citizens, cannot and will not respect them without investigation by our government.... The Southern Pacific Railroad Company have not complied with their contract both with our people and with our government, and therefore for these several reasons we are in duty bound to ask you to desist....

Undeterred by this warning, the Southern Pacific made its move against the dissidents of Mussel Slough. On the morning of the mass meeting, Marshal Poole, accompanied by W. B. Braden, the railroad's local land agent, arrived in Hanford with writs ordering the dispossession of a number of farmers in the region. He rented one buggy for himself and Braden, another for Hartt and Crow, who were designated to occupy the farms of at least two of the displaced settlers. In the second buggy with Hartt and Crow was a small arsenal of rifles, shotguns, and revolvers and a supply of ammunition, including shotgun shells in which the birdshot had been replaced by slugs.

The two buggies rolled down the dusty road to the Branden farm, whose owner was in Hanford to attend the Settlers' Rights rally. Unable to serve their writ, the party left four rifle cartridges on Branden's doorstep as their calling cards. Then they continued down the road for three and a half miles to the Brewer farm. By then word had spread over the countryside that the Southern Pacific was taking action.

It was on the Brewer farm that the power of the Southern Pacific, backed by legal sanction, confronted that of the settlers, and moral right collided with judicial process. Brewer was working in the fields when the United States marshal and his companions appeared. The marshal and the SP land agent drove out ahead to serve Brewer with their writ while Hartt and Crow followed in their buggy about 30 yards behind. Curiously, the marshal, though he embodied the power of the federal government, apparently was unarmed. If there was any shooting, it would have to be done by those two unofficial and shadowy members of his party, Hartt and Crow.

Suddenly about a dozen settlers appeared to back up Brewer, some on horseback, about half of them (as later inquiry showed) armed with pistols.

The marshal, writ in hand, approached Brewer and his friends. A spokesman for the settlers suggested that Poole delay service of his writ until the Supreme Court ruled on their appeal, but the latter insisted that Brewer had to get off his farm immediately. The settlers, some of them apparently displaying their pistols, demanded that the marshal surrender to them, which he wisely did, on the promise that he and the land agent would be escorted to the Hanford railroad station and be put on the first train bound for San Francisco.

The marshal and the land agent were just being led away when one of the settlers, James Harris, rode over to the buggy in which Hartt and Crow were waiting. He demanded that they surrender their weapons. Crow's reply was to raise his double-barreled shotgun and shoot Harris in the face. Harris fell dead from his saddle.

A general shootout ensued. A farmer named Henderson rode up to Harris' assistance and shot Hartt in the stomach. Crow killed Henderson with the other barrel of his shotgun, then picked up a revolver and began firing at the other farmers, some of whom were unarmed. Obviously Crow, whatever his background, was an expert gunman. He shot Daniel Kelly three times in the body, killed Iver Kneutson with one shot, drilled Edward Haymaker through the head, and plugged the unarmed Archibald McGregor twice in the chest. McGregor ran screaming across the field while Crow dropped his empty revolver and picked up a rifle, then shot McGregor in the back and dropped him for good. Certainly the Southern Pacific got its money's worth out of Mr. Crow; single-handed he had cut down six men in the space of about two minutes.

The gunsmoke was just drifting away when the local Settlers' Rights leader, Major McQuiddy, galloped up. He suggested that

249

the federal marshal order the shooting to stop. It already had, with half the farmers dead or wounded and Crow fleeing through an adjacent wheat field.

"Don't let that man escape," McQuiddy shouted to the survivors among his followers, who had been paralyzed by the swiftness of the tragedy which overtook their neighbors. One of the men, whose name was never disclosed by his companions, obeyed McQuiddy's order. He trailed Crow through the wheat fields and over the irrigation ditches to a nearby farm. There was to be one more killing that warm spring morning. The settler caught sight of Crow on the bank of an irrigation canal. Crow raised his rifle to fire at the settler, but the latter fired first and killed Crow with one shot.

The Brewer farmhouse that noon was turned into a casualty station. The bodies of Harris, Henderson, and Kneutson all were placed on the porch. Inside the tiny parlor two doctors summoned from Hanford worked over Kelly, McGregor, Haymaker, and Hartt. That night Kelly and McGregor died. Hartt, the Southern Pacific hireling, died the next day. Only Haymaker, among the six men shot by Crow, survived.

The Southern Pacific did its best to muffle the echoes of those gunshots. It had won a great victory, thanks to the trigger finger of the late Mr. Crow, which convinced the settlers of the San Joaquin Valley that resistance would only bring in more gunmen, but it seemed best not to brag about it. The Southern Pacific's first measure was to clamp a censorship on the area after announcing that all traffic through the valley was being halted because of an "armed insurrection." Only Southern Pacific telegrams were accepted at the Goshen telegraph office, and in Hanford, as the company explained to the press in San Francisco, the telegrapher had been driven away from his key by "outlaw farmers." The Southern Pacific's accounting to the public was somewhat depreciated when the Hanford telegrapher turned up in San Francisco and told newspapermen that the company had ordered him to close down the office.

Thus the first accounts of the "battle of Mussel Slough" all were biased reports filtered through the Southern Pacific's executive suite. A phalanx of SP executives, with the burly figure of Charles Crocker himself at their head, toured the newspaper

250

offices and explained that their emissaries had been attacked by "gangs of ruffians" down in the San Joaquin Valley. For lack of any other, their version was published. Most of the San Francisco newspapers, however, sent their own men down to investigate, and the truth of the matter began to appear in print. By strict interpretation of the law, the Mussel Slough farmers had acted lawlessly. On the other hand, they had been gunned down by a hireling of the Southern Pacific, who may or may not have been deputized on the spot by the U.S. marshal. Furthermore, there was strong legal doubt of the sanctity of the Southern Pacific's franchise. Even if it was not prepared to keep its word with the farmers it lured out to the hot barrens of the San Joaquin Valley and set a fair price for the land after the farmers' efforts had made it valuable, the railroad could have restrained itself from acting against them until the Supreme Court had ruled on their appeal. From the public relations standpoint alone, the company's course of action had been deplorable, though shaping public opinion would not be regarded as a necessary corporate tool until the antimonopoly agitation of later years.

On May 12 the settlers of the Mussel Slough district buried their dead. A two-mile procession of buggies and farm wagons followed the hearses to the cemetery. Less than a month later the families of the raiload's victims were evicted. And that was not the end of the railroad's campaign to quench the spirit of resistance among the valley's settlers. Seventeen men were charged with the "murder" of Hartt and Crow, though the Southern Pacific's agents had fired first and there were not more than a dozen men present on the Brewer farm when the shootout occurred. Five of the defendants were convicted and sent to prison.

The settlers were beaten. They dropped the appeal to the Supreme Court for lack of funds, partly, and because many of their leaders were in prison. If they had persevered, they probably would have won their case. Years later in another county a similar situation arose, and the settlers carried their appeal to the Supreme Court, which ruled in their favor.

The settlers of the Mussel Slough region, like others in the valley, either paid what the railroad demanded or surrendered their holdings. Their bitterness against the Southern Pacific was not ameliorated in the decade following the killings; every May

10 was observed in Tulare County for a score of years with public memorial services for the martyrs of the Mussel Slough. Farm prices were depressed during the eighties, but the railroad continued to gouge the farmers through inflated freight rates.

For the Southern Pacific the Mussel Slough affair would serve as a Banquo's ghost even as its profits multiplied and its corporate and political influence waxed inordinately. A young Californian named Frank Norris published a highly successful novel titled *The Octopus*, in which the railroad was the antagonist and the battle of Mussel Slough was the dramatic climax. The gunfight on Brewer's farm, as Norris reconstructed it from newspaper accounts, became one of the more striking passages in modern American literature.*

Indirectly, too, the killings at Mussel Slough and the events surrounding them created the railroad-hating climate in which a pair of hyperactive train robbers made themselves statewide heroes and were the subjects of the greatest manhunt the state had seen since the legendary Joaquin Murietta. The two men, in fact, achieved the status of Robin Hoods—not because Californians were so susceptible to lawless exploits, but because they operated against the widely detested Southern Pacific. For four years the train-robbing exploits of Chris Evans and John Sontag, and their phantomlike ability to elude the hundreds of amateur and professional man hunters sent against them, would keep presenting the Southern Pacific in an unfavorable light. Almost the entire state, with the exception of Southern Pacific stockholders and those with qualms about canonizing a pair of lawbreakers, constituted a cheering section; it was generally understood that Evans and Sontag were acting out of principle, not for illicit gain, as avengers of the Mussel Slough affair.

Legend says that Evans was one of the settlers dispossessed by the railroad, but objective research indicates this was not true. Several of his wife's relatives, however, were among those evicted from their holdings in the valley.

Evans himself was a short, slight, mild-mannered fellow, born in Canada but reared in Vermont, who was thirty-three years old

*Coincidentally, *The Octopus*, as the first of Norris' celebrated trilogy, was published the same year as Collis P. Huntington's death and the beginning of the decline of the Southern Pacific as an oligarchic power. It sold 60,000 copies.

when the Mussel Slough killings occurred. An intelligent and determined man, he had served as an Army scout in Dakota Territory during the seventies. In the early eighties he retired from the Army and settled down with his wife and three children as an employee of the Bank of California. Evans was in charge of three of the bank's warehouses at Goshen, Alila, and Pixley, where the bank stored grain it took from farmers in payment of their mortgages. In that post he heard plenty of tales about the Southern Pacific's dealings with its hard-pressed shippers. Evans subsequently moved to Modesto and opened a livery stable; that enterprise failed when the stable burned down, and Evans began farming a tract near Visalia.

While trying to make out as a farmer, he formed a friendship with John Sontag, who had even more powerful grievances against the Southern Pacific. Sontag was the son of one of the German farmers who had settled the Minnesota Valley and in his youth became a "boomer," that is, a wandering railroadman working for various Western lines. While working as a brakeman on a Southern Pacific train, he had been badly injured in one of the line's frequent accidents. Workmen's compensation had not yet been devised, nor had the company's responsibility for such misadventures been established in principle or practice. Sontag therefore had no recourse but treatment in the Southern Pacific hospital in Sacramento. Most company hospitals in those days offered treatment on a level with a Dickensian workhouse, regarding such care as pure charity on the part of the employer. Sontag came out of the institution with a bad limp, unable to perform the heavy work the railroad assigned him, and a brooding sense of grievance against anything connected with the Southern Pacific.

The tall and muscular but lamed Sontag and the short, quick-witted Evans, though an ill-assorted pair, got to know each other around Visalia and evidently decided on a partnership in retribution. The railroad which ran past their parched little tracts would be made to pay for its oppressions. Evans would provide the brains, Sontag the muscle.

They were to be credited, if that is the word, with five train robberies, followed by a four-year manhunt with all the elements that encourage the writing of pulp stories and popular ballads.

253

On the cloudy night of February 22, 1889, two masked men boarded the coal tender of the SP's No. 17 near Pixley, which is in the Mussel Slough neighborhood. Armed with pistols, they forced the engineer to halt the train, then ordered the Wells Fargo messenger in the express car to throw out the safe. The messenger refused until the two bandits threatened to kill the engineer and fireman. He heaved the safe onto the right-of-way, at which time there was a melee and the bandits killed one trainman and wounded another. They made off with about $5,000. One of the pair was described as a short man who gave the orders, the other as a six-footer.

At the time no one suspected Evans or Sontag, who were discreet enough not to flaunt their sudden wealth. A year later the southbound No. 19 was held up near Goshen, and this time the bandits got away with $20,000 without having to do any shooting. Railroad detectives converged on the district but found the residents, still sullen over the Mussel Slough killings and the high freight rates, unanimously unwilling to help in their investigation. The third foray occurred on February 6, 1891, when No. 17 was held up again, this time without producing any loot. The express messenger defied the two robbers and began shooting through the grating of a side door, killing the train's fireman and driving off the bandits. The Southern Pacific, getting desperate, offered a $10,000 reward and had undercover men by the score snooping around the countryside. All the robberies occurred in the same area and evidently were committed by the same two men. Bill and Grant Dalton, members of the infamous Dalton train-robbing gang, were living quietly on a San Joaquin farm at the time. On little or no evidence, they were quickly arrested and convicted. This was proved a miscarriage of justice a few months later when Evans and Sontag boarded a train near Modesto, tried to dynamite the express car, and shot it out with two Southern Pacific detectives hidden in the car. One of the detectives was wounded, but the two bandits had to flee emptyhanded. Their last foray occurred at midnight on August 3, 1892, just west of Fresno when the No. 17 was held up for the third time. They blew open the express car and made off with 125 pounds of silver coins which they hauled away in a waiting buggy.

Five holdups in three years, engineered by the same two men

handy with pistols and dynamite, had thoroughly alarmed the railroad, the express company, and the law enforcement agencies. All those forces now combined: Southern Pacific detectives (a hard-bitten crew greatly unloved by most of the citizenry), Wells Fargo agents, and sheriff's officers thirsting for that $10,000 reward. Those bloodhounds, now numbering several hundred and coursing all over the central valley and the foothills to the east, got their first break in the case when rumors reached them that John Sontag's dudish and boastful younger brother George had been heard discussing details of the Fresno holdup. After questioning George Sontag, Will Smith, a Southern Pacific detective, and a deputy sheriff went to Chris Evans' home and arrived just as John Sontag was slipping in the back door of the farmhouse. Chris Evans' sixteen-year-old daughter, Eva, a pretty blonde soon to be the heroine of the saga, came to the door when the officers knocked. Eva ran back into the house to warn her father. A gun battle in the Evans parlor ensued, Evans and Sontag vs. the two lawmen. Smith and his companion both went down with bullet wounds, and Evans and Sontag escaped in the wagon which had brought the lawmen out from Visalia.

After that it was up hill and down dale for two years, with Evans and Sontag leading a man-hunting force totaling 3,000 men on a chase alternately grim and merry. They made fools out of their pursuers time after time, but obviously they could not have survived so long without the help and sympathy of the countryside. For months they moved from hideout to hideout in the Sierra foothills to the east of their home territory. Whenever they needed a square meal, they showed up at one of the mining or logging camps, were fed, reprovisioned, and sent on their way with the best wishes of their hosts. Whenever large parties of man hunters ventured into the hills, Evans and Sontag were kept advised of their movements by their network of sympathizers.

Occasionally the two fugitives had a close call as they dodged around the hill country ahead of posses equipped with Indian trackers and packs of bloodhounds. Late in 1892, wearying of their own cooking, they went down to the cabin of a friend named Jim Young on Pine Ridge and invited themselves to supper. While the meal was being prepared, they sighted an approaching posse, which had been tipped off by a lookout stationed to keep an eye on a known friend of the fugitives. Evans and Sontag came charging out and firing their sawed-off shotguns. Two of the man hunters were mortally wounded, but one of them shot Sontag in the arm as the pair hightailed it back to their hideout.

The Southern Pacific was considerably irked when, at the height of the manhunt, which was costing the company a small fortune every month, a San Francisco reporter managed to contact and interview the fugitives. The enterprising journalist was the lean and dapper Petey Bigelow of the San Francisco *Examiner*, who went to Visalia with five $100 bills in his pocket and persuaded somebody to guide him to Evans and Sontag's current hideout, which Bigelow in his subsequent account vaguely described as "in the vicinity of the Kings River." A few days later, having descended from the fugitives' mountain lair, Bigelow was able to report that Evans and Sontag were hauling in the "last of their winter stock of provisions on the backs of tiny burros." There was an awkward moment at the start of the interview, he recalled, when he opened his jacket and inadvertently displayed the nickel-plated press badge pinned to his suspenders. "Sontag scowled and said something about 'detective,'" but Evans managed to calm him down. The gist of Bigelow's story was that Evans and Sontag stoutly denied having pulled any train robberies and maintained they were victims of Southern Pacific persecution. The *Examiner* crowed that "what the sheriffs and their posses and innumerable detectives, stimulated by great money rewards and animated by a desire for vengeance, have so far utterly failed to do, an *Examiner* reporter has done."

The Southern Pacific urged a redoubling of the effort to capture Evans and Sontag and demanded to know why the combined forces of the law were unable to accomplish as much as a mere journalist. Ambushes were laid along most of the trails leading down from the foothills, the man hunters suspecting that Evans, a devoted family man, sooner or later would attempt to visit his farm near Visalia.

Accordingly the man hunters staked out a cabin at Stone Corral on one of the foothill trails. There U.S. Marshal George Gard and four deputy sheriffs were hiding in ambush. One day early in June, 1893, Evans and Sontag came down the trail. There was no attempt to take them alive; it was a simple case of at-

256

tempted assassination. Gard and the four deputies cut loose with everything they had, wounded Sontag a half dozen times in the arms, legs, and chest, and Evans' left arm was shattered and a load of buckshot blinded his right eye. Evans crawled away into the woods, Sontag tried to commit suicide and succeeded only in plowing a bullet through his temple. The deputies hauled Sontag down to the jail at Visalia, where he died soon after, weighted down, the attending physician said, by more lead than he had ever seen in a human being. Evans, with one arm hanging by a few shreds of flesh and his right eye shot out, somehow managed to stagger six miles up into the foothills. He sought shelter with a family living in a cabin and sent word down to Visalia that he was willing to surrender. His left arm was amputated in jail while he awaited trial.

But that wasn't the end of Chris Evans' saga. One of his sympathizers smuggled a gun into his cell, and once again Evans escaped. He had been at large for weeks and might never have been recaptured until someone suggested leaking word into the foothills that one of his four children was seriously ill. That brought Evans out of hiding, and he was recaptured by a score of riflemen staked out at his farmhouse.

To raise funds for his legal defense, a San Francisco playwright concocted a six-act melodrama titled *Evans and Sontag; or, the Visalia Bandits*, with Mrs. Chris Evans and her comely daughter, Eva, playing themselves. Eva brought down the house opening night when she rode onstage on a black horse to warn her father and Sontag that the dastardly Southern Pacific detectives were coming to arrest them. Even the sympathetic San Francisco *Examiner* admitted the play was an example of the "blank cartridge school of drama," but public support of Evans' cause was so strong that it ran for months at the National Theater, then played one-night stands in the California interior, with 25 percent of the proceeds going to Evans' defense fund. Neither money nor public opinion, however, could save a man who had earned the enmity of the Southern Pacific. Evans was sentenced to life imprisonment at Folsom. Seventeen years later, when the first real reform administration took office, he was promptly pardoned.

Not until John Dillinger came along many years later during

257

the bank-hating 1930's and was occasionally sheltered during his bank-robbing career by Middle Western farmers, was there so great an outlaw folk hero. It was a measure of how much Californians hated the Southern Pacific.

11.

California's Octopus (II)

Before this good man [Collis P. Huntington] shall
long be in the New Jerusalem he will undoubtedly
find an opportunity to pull up a packload of blocks
from the golden pavement and retire to Hades to
enjoy them like a gentleman.

—AMBROSE BIERCE in the San Francisco *Examiner*

ALMOST deliberately, it seemed, the Southern Pacific's arrogant directorate courted public disfavor. The art or science of public relations had not yet evolved, of course, and the blatant crudity of its methods were not concealed by a fog of publicity handouts. The Big Four—which dwindled to the Big One when Crocker retired, Hopkins died, and Stanford contented himself with pompous vaporings on the floor of the United States Senate, leaving Collis P. Huntington as the sole man in charge —were limned in a mercilessly revealing light. Perhaps the trouble was that they got rich so quick and acquired so much instant stature that they never had to learn how to deal with public opinion.

Their reckless disregard of contemporary opinion was strikingly illustrated by their actions following the death of David D. Colton and the unnecessary unlatching of the Pandora's box of Huntington-Colton correspondence which revealed in detail how the Southern Pacific acquired and used its political influence.

Colton was a dynamic redhead who rejoiced in the unearned title of "General." One of his early business ventures was helping organize a $10,000,000 corporation to exploit the "diamond fields" of northern Colorado. Two men described as "honest prospectors" had claimed discovery, received $600,000 for their interests, and then disappeared. It was then disclosed that the field had been "salted" with a few thousand dollars' worth of diamonds bought in Antwerp, and that general manager Colton and some of the coast's most illustrious financiers had been taken in by a barefaced swindle. Colton recovered from that blow, made a sizable fortune in San Francisco real estate, bought into Southern Pacific, and became the financial director of its subsidiary, the Central Pacific. Actually his role was more that of a political fixer who operated on the Coast while Huntington was busy lobbying in Washington. His mansion on Nob Hill was located near Crocker's and Stanford's; his close association with Huntington was attested by the letters he received, frankly stating Southern Pacific's methods of dealing with the legislative branch of government, some of which his widow caused to be published to the utter embarrassment of his former associates.

His brusque and often brutal manner made him many enemies, and one morning in early 1878 early arrivals in Montgomery Street, the financial district, found posters tacked to the telegraph poles near Colton's office. Addressed to Colton, they warned: "There is a BLOOD HOUND on your track you little dream so near, who will have justice, slow but sure. Lawyer, Priest, or Doctor, you cannot, shall not escape calumny, and were you in any city but San Francisco, your DAMNABLE LOOKS would hang you. Meddle no more in business not your own, or you will reap a bitter but well-merited punishment, fit for scoundrels such as yourself." It was signed "Justice."

The vaguely menacing poster was recalled months later under the rather mysterious circumstances surrounding his death.

Late on the night of October 8, 1878, a carriage rolled up in front of Colton's mansion at California and Taylor streets. Several men accompanying him were seen to carry his apparently unconscious form into the house. Two doctors, his secretary, and his law partner were summoned immediately. The city rooms of the *Examiner* and *Chronicle* were galvanized by an anonymous tip that Colton had been stabbed. Reporters arriving at his mansion were told, however, that he had been injured by a fall from his horse out at the Mount Diablo ranch and that his injuries were not serious. Two days later Colton died amid persistent rumors that he had been murdered.

Colton's death caused only the expectable speculation about the Southern Pacific and its management, which now included a second-generation echelon of Huntington's nephew and the sons of his partners. Public interest in the matter expanded when Colton's widow filed suit charging that the Big Four were trying to cheat her out of a large part of her husband's estate and had refused to return securities belonging to him.

The Southern Pacific and its directorate had not lost a court battle in fifteen years, and small hopes were held for the widow's suit, which, after the usual delaying tactics, finally came to trial in Santa Rosa. It took almost two years to try the case. The Big Four fought dirty and claimed they were holding Colton's securities because he had been guilty of embezzlement. Mrs. Colton's side retaliated by introducing the batch of letters Huntington had written her husband as evidence of his importance as an executive of the corporation.

Those were the Colton Letters, as they were headlined. They were first published by the New York *Sun*, which somehow obtained an advance look at them through Mrs. Colton's attorneys. Three years later those candid dispatches from Washington, relating how Huntington bought and bullied support of Southern Pacific legislation, were read into the record of the Pacific Railroad Commission's investigation and created a national surge of indignation. Some of them have been quoted previously in this account, but there was particular outrage over Huntington's coarse but forthright contempt for the near-sacred office of the Presidency. In one letter to Colton, he referred to the spineless character of President Rutherford B. Hayes and boasted that "he was not big enough" to veto a bill Huntington wanted to pass.

To no one's surprise, the Southern Pacific's directorate won the case, but they lost a lot more in the intangibles. A corporation, as they would learn, lived on more than profit alone. As a commentator assessed the cost of the legal victory, "Even journals friendly to the railroad and enjoying subsidies from the corporation did not claim that the Huntington-Stanford group emerged with credit to themselves. Shrewdness, the ability to drive a close bargain, to press an advantage for all it was worth, were qualities still highly regarded among California businessmen, where there was no more coveted distinction than to be known as a 'smart trader.' " Applying such talents to the widow of a former partner, however, proved distasteful even to hardheaded businessmen. Huntington, Stanford, and Crocker may have won a court battle, but they lost more in the respect of their contemporaries than they gained in dollars.

Worse yet the publication of the Colton Letters made the Southern Pacific a marked corporation and Collis P. Huntington a marked man in Washington. His own correspondence identified him as a blatant corruptionist. No public servant anxious about his reputation—one, that is, facing a reelection campaign—could risk being seen talking to Huntington in public; it was said that Congressmen were "known to dodge down Washington alleys" rather than meet him on the street. And this semiostracization occurred just as the Southern Pacific needed all the political help it could get in refunding its public debt.

Huntington and the founding fathers of the railroad may have been too old to acquire suppleness in adapting their policies to accommodate public opinion. They were so blindly self-righteous that a few years before his death Huntington would boast that "we have served California better than any other set of men have ever served any other state in the union." But the second generation of the founders' sons and nephews were seemingly as obdurate as their seniors.

As long as the four original families stayed in control of the corporation, it was operated with a stupid and brutal disregard for public sentiment or the rights of individuals. Thus it maintained an ironhanded control of the Oakland waterfront. With considerable foresight the Big Four had acquired ownership of the property rimming the harbor even before the Central Pacific had crossed the High Sierra. They wanted not only to control the rail and ferry traffic between San Francisco and the East Bay cities (Oakland, Alameda, Berkeley, Richmond), but to prevent any other line from acquiring a deepwater terminal. The city of Oakland also owned a strip of waterfront land, but the Southern Pacific's influence at City Hall prevented industries settling on any but the railroad's property, where they could ship only by grace of the Southern Pacific.

California's Octopus (II)

The Southern Pacific's method of ruling its enclave on the Oakland waterfront was dictatorial, as in all other of its spheres of influence. Although it did not own all the land bordering the bay and its estuary, a sleeve of deep water that extended almost to the Oakland business district, it assumed control over its usage.

One man, a storekeeper and wholesaler named John L. Davie, decided to defy the Southern Pacific. He was a versatile man whose career had ranged from cowpunching to opera singing and who had turned to the mercantile trade in his middle years—a hardy and independent spirit. His defiance of the railroad came about one day in 1894 when a salesman talked him into buying two schooner loads of salt. To shelter his mountain of salt, he would need a warehouse. He applied to the Oakland board of public works for permission to build a warehouse and wharf on a site along the estuary, on land controlled by the city government. Tom Carrothers, the chairman of the board, was a loyal SP man and kept delaying action on Davie's application.

Finally Davie gave up on the estuary site and leased two acres of tideland at the foot of Webster Street. This property was owned by an oyster company, which held title under the Oyster Bed Act, a state law, and thus legally was beyond the control of both the city and the Southern Pacific. It was a tough, polyglot section surrounded by the masts of North Pacific whalers, Chinese junks, Greek fishing boats, South Sea schooners, rusty tramps from all over the world and rows of ramshackle houseboats.

Davie shrewdly foresaw that he might make allies of the ruffianly residents of the section, none of whom professed any abiding love for giant corporations. When he filled in his tidal acres and built his wharf and warehouse, he was careful not to disturb a gang of oyster pirates who convened in a shack on a corner of his property. One of them was the teen-aged Jack London, future literary eminence, one of whose works was *Tales of the Fish Patrol.* London and his fellow rascals used the shack as a headquarters when they were not raiding the state-leased oyster beds down in the Lower Bay and selling their loot to peddlers and saloonkeepers at the market behind the Oakland waterfront. The oyster pirates and other waterfront desperadoes would come in handy when Davie defended his foothold against overwhelming forces.

263

In recounting his long fight with the Southern Pacific (*My Own Story*, published many years later), Davie recalled that shortly after his wharf and warehouse were finished, he decided to go into the coal business, ordered 3,000 tons, and built wooden bunkers near his wharf. That move evidently spurred the Southern Pacific into action; its executives decided Davie would have to be smashed or all sorts of independent operators would encroach on their asserted domain, since its lawyers warned that Davie's niche on the tidelands might jeopardize the railroad's title to the rest of the waterfront.

Just after Davie's coal was delivered, he was tipped off that the Southern Pacific was preparing to strike back. He knew that he couldn't count on police protection against the railroad so he went to a sporting goods store and bought up its stock of rifles and ammunition. The weapons were "lent" to his oyster-pirate friends, who were equally ready to fight for "their" waterfront.

Over that weekend, as Davie learned when he went to the foot of Webster Street to check on his property Monday morning, the Southern Pacific's minions had stolen a march on him. He found a 12-foot fence built around his property, and inside the fence he heard the sounds of axes and sledgehammers being employed with vigor. Ripping down a board from the fence, he saw that a crew of railroad hirelings were tearing down his warehouse and throwing the lumber into the bay, from which men in fleet rowboats were towing it away.

Davie charged through the fence and confronted the boss of the wrecking crew, who ordered him off his own property. While the merchant roared his protests, someone slipped around behind him with a two-by-four, which he brought down on Davie's skull. When Davie came to, he was lying in the street outside the fence.

Most men would have reckoned the odds against them and written off that warehouse, but Davie's spirit was as durable as his skull. He tottered to the nearest saloon, revived himself with a shot of whiskey, and went home to arm himself. Returning to the arena with a small crowd of the curious at his heels, he slipped through the fence and again confronted the half dozen men demolishing his warehouse. This time he backed up his protest with a shotgun cradled in his arm and two revolvers strapped to his waist.

264

With the crowd cheering him on, he nudged the Southern Pacific wrecking crew over to the wharf with the barrel of his shotgun and then forced them to take the deep six over the edge and into the water. Davie then appealed to the crowd to help him tear down the fence, using the tools abandoned by the Southern Pacific men. In half an hour the fence around the two-acre plot was torn down. Before the day was out reporters from the San Francisco papers were streaming across the bay, and their accounts of the "Oakland Waterfront War" not only made Davie a local hero but rallied public support for yet another struggle against the Octopus. Once again front pages featured a tentacled monster reaching out to crush a victim.

The "waterfront war," in fact, was just beginning. Davie, encouraged by the support of Hearst's *Examiner* and a majority of his fellow citizens, was prepared to defend his wharf and warehouse by any means. Goaded by the railroad, the Oakland chief of police and a squad of patrolmen marched down to arrest Davie. They found themselves confronted by a belligerent crowd numbering about 500 and including the oyster pirates, who hated the police only a little less than the Southern Pacific. The police chief ordered a nightstick charge. It was poor strategy, since the police were greatly outnumbered. The oyster pirates took away the cops' batons and enthusiastically belabored constabulary skulls. After a melee lasting several minutes, the police were forced to retreat in disarray. They were even more discomfited when the morning papers hailed Davie's victory, with the Hearst paper suggesting it paralleled Concord and the Alamo as a struggle for human rights.

Even the Southern Pacific, with its contempt for public opinion, recognized that it was stymied so long as Davie could rally street mobs to defend his interests. One alternative was to seek court action forcing Davie off his leased acreage on the waterfront, but the railroad was not eager to test its claim to total control of the section. Its attorneys advised that, with the judiciary becoming less amenable to the Southern Pacific's dictates, it might lose the case and suffer accordingly. (They were right about that; the railroad did go to court finally, and its claims to control the whole waterfront were denied in succession by state and federal courts and ultimately by the U.S. Supreme Court.) Reluctantly, therefore, the Southern Pacific tried to make

265

a deal. It sent its chief Oakland operative, Tom Carrothers, who was chairman of the Board of Public Works in his spare time, to Davie with what it regarded as a generous offer. Davie was offered a blank check and told to write in any conscionable amount, then take off for a ten-year sojourn in Paris (as he recalled in *My Own Story*).

Davie decided that Oakland was more interesting than Parisian boulevards at the moment. He and the oyster pirates, armed with their rifles, stood guard over his waterfront property day and night waiting for the railroad's next move. It was not long in coming. Hitherto its tactics had been brutally simple and direct, now they became a trifle too intricate. The new Southern Pacific stratagem was to claim possession of Davie's tiny parcel on the waterfront by landing a grain barge there at high tide. This would take some doing, so two locomotives attached to flatcars loaded with chain were run up to the embattled sector on tracks that extended almost to the tide line. The chains were attached to the grain barge. When the tide crested, the barge would be hauled ashore and serve as a massive squatter.

It was an explosive situation. The railroad had brought in a considerable force of railroad police and other hard-nosed characters to back its play. On the other side were Davie and his oyster pirates itching to tangle with their old enemies. Both groups were armed. On neither side, except for Davie himself, and even he was a trifle overeager to take the law into his own hands, were there any noble or public-spirited characters. The oyster pirates, as described by Jack London from the vantage point of respectability, were a murderous crew; they were simply fighting for their turf against outsiders.

As the tide rose, the locomotives began hauling in the grain barge. Davie's cohorts wanted to attack the railroadmen then and there, but he restrained them. Instead he and several of his allies put out in a skiff. They attacked the chains with hacksaws. The last chain was cut, in fact, just as the barge touched Davie's property. Then a battle royal began, though fortunately no one fired a shot. With fists and clubs, the waterfront toughs boarded the barge and forced its defenders to jump overboard. Others attacked the railroad police guarding the locomotives and chased them through the waterfront streets.

266

By then Davie had lost control of his allies. Their blood was up, and they surged out of the waterfront district on the scent of total victory over the Southern Pacific. Aside from its domination of the Oakland waterfront, the railroad had made itself thoroughly detested by building a spur between its Oakland and Alameda lines right through the city plaza, over the protests of most of the citizenry. The oyster pirates, other waterfront hoodlums, and a swelling crowd of volunteer railroad wreckers stormed into the plaza at Fifth and Harrison streets. Equipping themselves with crowbars and sledgehammers looted from a Southern Pacific toolhouse they passed on their way to the business district, they burst into the city center. Hundreds of the sans-culottes brandishing rifles and wrecking tools were swarming everywhere. The Oakland police had sounded the alarm and gathered reinforcements, but one look at that seething mob and they decided not to interfere. Most of those waterfront characters would never work so hard in their lives as they did that afternoon for the pure joy of destruction. They ripped up the Southern Pacific's tracks through the heart of Oakland, burned the wooden ties in huge stacks, and threw the rails into the estuary.

Night fell, but the mob stayed on the job. Main-line trackage was destroyed as the ringleaders urged further demolition. One symbol of the Southern Pacific's overlordship remained: the quaint little wooden passenger station with its bell tower, which in any case had been slated for replacement by a larger and more modern structure. A huge dray was commandeered, and willing hands hoisted the station off its foundation and onto the wagon. It was then hauled through the plaza to the City Hall with the company's passenger agent, scared witless, peering from one of its windows. The station was dumped off the dray and onto the steps of City Hall as a warning to the city fathers that they had better stop serving two masters. Somehow the heavy bell broke loose from its tower and crashed into the crowd, just as the station was toppling over, and one of the mob was killed. With that sobering event, the mob dispersed to their warrens on the waterfront.

Vox populi and a certain amount of lawless mob action had confirmed John Davie in his lodgment on the Oakland estuary, but that doughty ex-cowhand wasn't through with his assaults on the majesty of the Southern Pacific. No doubt the publicity was more than satisfying; within a few months, portrayed as one man standing against a giant corporation, David slinging stones at Goliath, he had made himself into the No. 1 folk hero of the cities around the San Francisco Bay.

His next objective was another Southern Pacific monopoly. The railroad claimed the right to being the sole operator of ferries across the bay which brought thousands of commuters to San Francisco offices and stores every morning. The SP ferries charged 15 cents a head, provided slipshod service, and maintained the ferries on a level with cattle boats or coastal tramps.

To remedy this situation, Davie organized a group of Oakland men to inaugurate a new ferry service which would charge only 5 cents a ride. The "nickel ferry" was a swift and comfortably appointed new ship called the *Rosalie*. Naturally transbay traffic was immediately diverted to the *Rosalie*, and its operators announced the addition of other boats to the "nickel fleet."

Instead of lowering prices and improving the service of its own ferries, the Southern Pacific retaliated in characteristic fashion. The San Francisco waterfront came under the jurisdiction of the State Board of Harbor Commissioners, who were beholden to the Southern Pacific and who discovered that they could not provide regular docking facilities for the *Rosalie* and her sister ships. Instead the nickel ferries were shunted to remote and ramshackle piers where their passengers found, on disembarking, that they had to fight their way through a dense collection of drays and wagons which seemed to show up just as they docked. Davie as usual found an activist solution to the problem. He engaged a phalanx of longshoremen to clear the pier, heaving drays and draymen into the water if a path for the passengers wasn't cleared quickly enough. On the Oakland side, too, the nickel ferries' passengers were harassed for patronizing the railroad's rival service. Just as they came down the gangplanks, the railroadmen would dump a ton of coal dust in a nearby bunker and sent the passengers home looking like the members of a stranded minstrel show.

There seemed to be no end to the Southern Pacific's determination to monopolize the traffic between San Francisco and the East Bay cities. Unwisely, as it turned out, they took their guerrilla war against the nickel ferries a step further. One day the

Southern Pacific ferry *Alameda*, undoubtedly on orders from Fourth and Townsend, tried to force the *Rosalie* aground in the Oakland estuary. Instead, she was rammed by the *Rosalie*'s prow, and her captain beached the *Alameda* because he feared she might sink with the 15-foot hole in her stern. Thus *Alameda*'s passengers were forced to trudge through estuarial mud while the *Rosalie*'s patrons lined her railings and hooted at them.

The Southern Pacific became so desperate that it slashed the price of ferry rides to two for a nickel. There were a number of skirmishes between it and Davie and his partisans, one of them resulting in Davie's arrest. A sympathetic grand jury refused to indict him. His role as Southern Pacific baiter was just about played out. The Souhern Pacific, realizing that Davie's group was operating its ferry service at a loss, simply outwaited its opponents. The *Rosalie* and her sister ferries, unable to compete with the SP's two-for policy, went out of business within a few months. Its monopoly on transbay traffic restored, the Southern Pacific then raised the price of a ferry ticket back to 15 cents. But the corporation had been damaged in intangible ways by the Davie grudge fight as it had been in the long headlined contest against the Widow Colton, in the Mussel Slough killings, and in so many other abrasive campaigns against the public interest.

Late in the nineties the Southern Pacific had begun slipping badly. Its monopoly on transportation within the California borders had been broken by the Santa Fe. The latter had acquired the so-called Valley Road, the stock of which was sold through public subscription; it ran through the San Jacinto Valley to Point Richmond, 10 miles from San Francisco, and was designed to provide competition for the Southern Pacific. The Santa Fe finished the line and became the first "outside" railroad to reach San Francisco Bay.

The Southern Pacific's influence was eroding at a rate alarming to its management, even in the political sector. Of the California delegation to Congress, only one man, Representative Grove L. Johnson, was accounted a Southern Pacific supporter. There was no doubt of Johnson's fealty; he had always spoken up loud and clear for Southern Pacific legislation. But in the election of 1896 the Representative was snowed under by a landslide and returned to Washington as a lame duck. He had finally been defeated largely because Hearst's *Examiner* had hammered away at his loyalty to the Southern Pacific. The railroad had even lost its magic touch at the Oakland City Hall. When a unit of Coxey's Army gathered in Oakland and demanded free boxcar passage to Sacramento from the Southern Pacific, the railroad had refused and suggested that they be dispersed by the National Guard. Determined to rid themselves of troublemakers, who were bound for Washington to make their protests against economic conditions heard, the Oakland authorities simply commandeered Southern Pacific freight trains and loaded their unwanted guests aboard.

All this slippage occurred just before the Southern Pacific was mustering its forces for a legislative battle crucial to its financial structure. Festering away for years had been the matter of the corporation's public indebtedness. That debt amounted to somewhere between $60,000,000 and $75,000,000, depending on who was doing the calculating; it included money borrowed from the government for construction of the Central Pacific, as well as $28,000,000 worth of subsidy bonds (then approaching maturity) and interest charges for thirty years. The Southern Pacific, of course, had always hoped its due bill would never be called for payment. Now, with the tidal surge of antitrust and antimonopoly sentiment throughout the country, the government and the public were demanding repayment. The railroad would have foundered, of course, if it had been required to pay up in full on the barrelhead. Through the years the SP treasury had been drained to buy mansions, pay for lavish excursions to Paris, endow Stanford University with $30,000,000, acquire a vast collection of paintings and sculptures and rare books, and other outlays, not all of them of a purely selfish nature.

The aged Huntington, last of the Big Four, his own death only a few years away, summoned all his energies, collected on all his political debts, to avoid or at least delay paying off the mortgage. Anyone inclined to pity the poor old fellow had only to reflect on how he had treated the Mussel Slough settlers or that his San Francisco residence on Nob Hill was formerly the home of the Widow Colton, to choke back a sob, but it could be said that old Huntington put up a gallant struggle to wriggle out of the dilemma.

270

First he boldly proposed that the government cancel the indebtedness on the wholesome theory that the Southern Pacific had done so much to develop the Pacific coast. When that didn't wash, he urged that the debt be drastically reduced. Finally his Washington lobby proposed a funding bill. Under its provisions the entire debt would be refunded, with the corporation given eighty-three years to pay it off at 2 percent interest.

The proposal was greeted by denunciation in California. Just as Huntington went all out for the funding bill, Hearst's *Examiner* devoted columns daily to campaigning against it. The *Examiner* had prospered greatly through the years and became the foundation of the Hearst newspaper chain largely through circulation gained by crusading against the Southern Pacific. Ambrose Bierce, as the most brilliant polemicist on its payroll, was sent to Washington to supply the Hearst cannonade with fresh ammunition. Bierce was so important a literary figure that other newspapers interviewed him when he arrived in Washington to pit his rhetorical skills against the Huntington lobby. He was quoted as saying:

> At a meeting to voice San Francisco's opposition [to the funding bill], there were fully 13,000 persons who could not secure admittance to the big hall. The great majority of those actively concerned folks knew, of their own knowledge, how much of wicked greed was centered in the group of which Collis P. Huntington is now the only surviving figure; they knew how the directors of the Central Pacific Company had transferred to themselves, as directors in a closely related organization [the Southern Pacific], everything that could be regarded as worth having; they knew that this conscienceless gang had entered upon the work of railroad construction as poor men and had somehow or other—the details read like the report of a grand larceny trial—acquired fifteen to twenty million each; they knew that competition in freight-carrying had been and is still systematically and murderously choked out of existence. . . . One of the surprising features of the campaign is the unwillingness of the average legislator to admit testimony bearing upon the moral phase of the controversy. It ought to be plain that those who unrighteously possessed themselves of $60,000,000 thirty years ago, and who have never given up one cent of either principal or interest, have

271

no claim upon which to base a demand for an extension that would continue the outrageous condition for a hundred years to come. . . .

Huntington's struggle to unshoulder the Central Pacific debt, in effect by arguing that the parent company should not be responsible for its subsidiary's obligations, would go on for three years, during which the fighting between Hearst and the SP got dirtier with every charge and countercharge exchanged.

Huntington kept appearing before Congressional hearings to press his case, on one occasion tripling his estimate of what it had cost to build the Central Pacific. In 1887 he had testified before the Pacific Railroad Commission that $36,000,000 had been spent on construction. Ten years later he was telling a committee that the figure was $122,000,000—more than enough to cover what the government claimed it was owed.

Bierce's gadfly attacks became more and more irksome. They not only were personally penetrating—even to one with Huntington's armadillolike hide—but were helping incite those mass meetings in San Francisco, sponsored by the *Examiner*, which whipped up sentiment against the railroad. In his last years Mr. Huntington was beginning to acquire a certain amount of respect for public opinion; disregard for that elusive and volatile element had cost him the California Congressional delegation.

When Huntington testified before a committee that the Southern Pacific prided itself on providing employment for women, Bierce riposted:

It is cheering to note that new "avenues" are being constantly "opened" to women; Mr. Huntington, for example, employs thirty or forty female spotters to travel over his several railways and afflict dishonest conductors. A noble "mission," truly—that of sewing up the holes in Mr. Huntington's pocket to keep other persons' money from flowing down his leg.

When a woebegone Huntington appeared before another committee and pleaded that the Southern Pacific would be ruined if it was forced to repay the government through a short-term loan, Bierce commented:

272

The Senate Committee listened to his tale of woe with the respect due to his wealth and the sympathy compelled by his reluctance to die and leave it. The sympathy, it may be remarked, is wasted on imaginary disaster. Before this good man shall long be in the New Jerusalem he will undoubtedly find an opportunity to pull up a packload of blocks from the golden pavement and retire to Hades to enjoy them like a gentleman.

Day after day Bierce assailed Huntington in the columns of the *Examiner*, with his articles reprinted throughout the United States, and variously termed him "a promoted peasant with a low love of labor and an unslakeable thirst for gain," as the "surviving thirty-six of our modern Forty Thieves," as an "old pigskin" who "knows neither how to enjoy nor to whom to bequeath" his wealth. Yet, he added, "Mr. Huntington is not altogether bad. Though severe, he is merciful. He says ugly things of the enemy, but he has the tenderness to be careful that they are mostly lies."

Huntington had an even lower opinion of journalists than he had of politicians. Experience had taught him that they could be bought off rather cheaply. With his devilish pride, Bierce's price might be a little higher than most, but Huntington was confident that he could be silenced.

One day he met Bierce on the steps of the Capitol and asked him how much he wanted to soften his blows. He mentioned figures, but each time Bierce shook his head.

"Well, name your price," Huntington said impatiently. "Every man has his price."

Bierce replied in tones loud enough to be heard by a group of colleagues standing nearby. "My price is seventy-five million dollars. If, when you are ready to pay, I happen to be out of town, you may hand it over to my friend, the Treasurer of the United States."

Bierce, of course, published the story of the bribe offer. When questioned about that highly indiscreet gesture, Huntington replied, "Oh, I just wanted to see how big he was. I know now."

At the second session of the Fifty-fourth Congress, which convened early in 1897, Huntington counterattacked vehemently. To implicate Hearst in his charges that the California press was generally venal and corrupt, Huntington confessed his own role in the corruption. The San Francisco *Bulletin* was receiving a "subsidy" from the Southern Pacific that ranged from $250 to $375 a month. The *Call* was also in Huntington's pocket and obligingly published his charge that Hearst, too, had been "subsidized" through advertising contracts. In a four-column story headed PAID TO SILENCE HIS BLACKGUARDISM; HEARST'S SECRET COMPACT WITH THE SOUTHERN PACIFIC COMPANY, the *Call* declared that in 1892 the *Examiner* received a $30,000 advertising contract from the Southern Pacific with the proviso that "The [Southern Pacific] company is to enjoy immunity from hostility in the columns of the *Examiner*, and is not to be the victim of malicious attacks or criticisms or misrepresentations; that the *Examiner* will not seek to create hostile sentiment in the minds of the community against the Southern Pacific Company. . . ."

Purportedly that contract was signed by a member of Hearst's business department when Hearst was vacationing in Egypt, but the *Call* charged that he bore the ultimate responsibility: "He may have been listening to the crocodiles on the Nile or listening to the bulbul in Cashmere [*sic*] when his agents were selling the *Examiner* to the Southern Pacific, but when he personally hypothecated that contract . . . Hearst could not be ignorant of the conditions of the sale nor of the time lock it had upon his lying and blackguardism for the space of thirty months."

Hearst may have accepted a bribe by proxy from the Southern Pacific, but the files of the *Examiner* during the period of the advertising contract show that his attacks on the railroad were unabated. His theory, as he once expressed it, was that it was all right to accept a bribe so long as you didn't comply with its conditions.

The Huntington assault on Hearst became more vituperous as Huntington felt his funding bill losing ground in the Congress. His only remaining mouthpiece in Congress among the California delegation, Representative Grove L. Johnson, who had his own reasons to hate Hearst, got up one day and delivered an attack that could only be described as a masterpiece of libel:

> We knew that he was erotic in his tastes, erratic in his moods, of small understanding and smaller view of men and women, but we thought "Our Willie" with his English plaids, his cockney accent,

274

and middle-parted hair, was honest. We knew that he had sought on the banks of the Nile relief from the loathsome disease contracted only by contagion in haunts of vice, and had rivaled the Khedive in the gorgeousness of his harem in the joy of restored health, but we still believed him honest, though low and depraved. We knew that he was debarred from society in San Francisco because of his delight in flaunting his wickedness, but we believed him honest, though tattooed with sin.

Continuing perhaps the most scurrilous address ever made in the libel-free zone of the congressional floor, Johnson characterized Hearst as "a debauchee, a dude in dress, an Anglomaniac in language in manners." Then with the pretense of sorrow Johnson brought up the matter of that advertising contract and charged that Hearst was "simply fighting the railroad funding bill because he could get no more blackmail from the Southern Pacific Company. . . . With brazen effrontery only equalled by the lowest denizen in the haunts of vice 'Our Willie' knows so well in every city of the globe, he unblushingly admitted he had blackmailed the railroad company, but pleaded in extenuation that he did not keep his contract, but swindled them out of their money. . . ."

The violence of Johnson's assault not only was counterproductive, but brought a devastating reply from the Hearst forces, whose spokesman was Representative James C. Maguire. Hearst's reporters had been digging into Johnson's background and came up with the dirt they were looking for. Maguire not only defended Hearst's honesty on the floor of the House, but inserted in the *Congressional Record* the information that Johnson thirty-four years before had been indicted for forgery in Syracuse, New York.

The nastiness of the methods used by Huntington, and those against him, was a measure of the stakes at hazard. Huntington was discovering the power of public opinion when it was marshaled by the increasingly influential daily newspapers. One miserable scrivener could challenge a hundred-million-dollar monopoly when his voice was magnified by the mass circulation of the dailies. A dozen years later Charles Edward Russell, one of a later generation of what would become categorized as muckrakers, credited Ambrose Bierce's crusade against the "railrogues" (Bierce's favorite term) with humbling Huntington and his associates. "When Mr. Bierce began his campaign, few persons imagined that the bill could be stopped. After a time the skill and steady persistence of the attack began to draw wide attention. Within six months of incessant firing, Mr. Bierce had the railroad forces frightened and wavering; and before the end of the year, he had them whipped."

Eventually the Congress dictated a settlement without being unduly influenced by Mr. Huntington's crocodile tears. The Central Pacific-Southern Pacific debt was refunded, but the corporation was given only ten years to pay at interest of 3 percent. During that decade it coughed up $6,000,000 a year without going into receivership, despite Mr. Huntington's anguished forebodings, and justice was done the U.S. Treasury.

Huntington died a year after the matter was finally settled and suffered the ultimate indignity of having his epitaph composed by Bierce:

Here Huntington's ashes long have lain
Whose loss was our eternal gain,
For while he exercised all his powers
Whatever he gained, the loss was ours.

One by one the tentacles of the Octopus withered and loosened their grip on the state. A controlling interest in the Southern Pacific was bought by E. H. Harriman, who had already taken over the Union Pacific; he rebuilt the system and improved its services, but its rates were still unconscionably high, thanks to the railroad's continued hold over affairs in the state capital. But the tide was turning. Newspapers which had been receiving "subsidies" from the Southern Pacific for years found it was costing them circulation to continue supporting the railroad. The ownership of the San Francisco *Bulletin* was persuaded to detach itself from the Southern Pacific payroll by its fiery new managing editor, Fremont Older, who had made a great reputation for himself and boosted his journal's circulation by crusading against corruption of all kinds.

Politically, however, the Southern Pacific maintained its dominance within the state's borders. Regarding its pervasive influence the San Francisco *Call* later observed: "In every county in California the railroad maintained an expert political manager whose employment was to see that the right men were chosen as convention delegates, the right kind of candidates nominated and elected, and the right things done by the men in office." Thomas Storke, the publisher and editor of the Santa Barbara *News-Press*, observed that the Southern Pacific "extended its evil influence to Sacramento and Los Angeles, up into Oregon, and as far East as Washington, D.C. . . . I saw the Octopus nominate and elect governors, U.S. Senators, judges, and even town constables owed their jobs to the machine. . . ." William F. Herrin, the chief attorney for the Southern Pacific, was the real political boss of California. "If a man wanted political preferment," Storke recounted, "he had to go to Herrin's headquarters at 4th and Townsend and, hat in hand, beg permission to become a candidate." The journalist Charles Van Devander recalled that "the bar of the Palace Hotel in San Francisco was the real state capital. Round-trip tickets from Sacramento to San Francisco were placed on each legislator's desk every weekend. Hotel bills were sent directly to the railroad company."

In 1906 the Southern Pacific overreached itself in arrogantly displaying its political power at the Republican state convention in Santa Cruz, the beach resort south of San Francisco. It had decided to replace the somewhat balky incumbent governor, George Pardee, with the more pliable James M. Gillat, a former mayor of Oakland. To round up the votes for Gillat, according to a contemporary historian, "even the higher judicial positions were traded like commodities." Abe Ruef, the San Francisco political boss, later admitted that he was paid $14,000 to swing votes he controlled in Gillat's direction. As Governor Pardee summed up the nomination of his rival, "We have met the enemy and we were theirs on the first ballot."

A dinner was held to celebrate the triumph of Southern Pacific's will. Unfortunately for some of the diners, a photograph was taken of the banqueting table which became a graphic document in the antirailroad campaign several years later. It was, in fact, one of the most embarrassing photographs ever taken in California. Among the acutely embarrassed was Joseph R. Knowland, the publisher of the Oakland *Tribune* (an enthusiastic defender of the SP fiefdom) and the father of the subsequent conservative U.S. Senator William F. Knowland.

Both the administration and the legislature were solidly prorailroad in 1907, and the air of corruption over Sacramento was as thick as a later Los Angeles smog. The legislature employed eighty-three "doorkeepers" to guard the chamber's three doors, according to an exposé published by the Fresno *Republican*. Stenographers placed on the state payroll were found to be illiterate. Prostitutes were receiving per diem compensation from the legislature as "committee clerks." "Scarcely a vote was cast," commented a Republican state senator, "that did not show some aspect of SP ownership, petty vengeance, or legislative blackmail." Another legislator observed that "you couldn't get the Lord's Prayer enacted in this administration without money." That legislature was so brazenly venal that it prodded the whole electorate into wakefulness. The Southern Pacific, under Harriman, had simply failed to quit while it was ahead.

In 1910, one decade after all the original Big Four had been laid to rest under an impressive tonnage of cemetery marble, a San Francisco attorney named Hiram Johnson ran for governor with a platform highlighted by the promise to "kick the Southern Pacific out of politics." Curiously enough, Hiram Johnson, who had come to prominence as the special prosecutor at the graft trial of Abe Ruef, was the son of ex-Congressman Grove L. Johnson, who had sacrificed his political career defending the Southern Pacific's interests in Washington.

Johnson, a future luminary of the U.S. Senate, not only won the governorship but carried like-minded candidates to victory with him in both houses of the state legislature. Furthermore, all three members of the new railroad commission were dedicated to the same principle of curbing the Southern Pacific's economic power just as the electorate had destroyed its political base.

The railroad commission, headed by a hard-nosed attorney named John Eshelman, proceeded to dismantle the rate structure which had squeezed Californians for so many years. R. L. Duffus, who had covered the commission's hearings as a youthful reporter for the San Francisco *Bulletin*, would recall in his memoir of those times:

The old commission had done what the railroads told them to do; this one took no orders from any railway or any other public utility. It was a pleasure to watch the old-fashioned type of railway attorney squirm in this unusual situation. . . . It is sad to think, now that railroads are the underdogs and at times a bit on the quaint side, how high they were then and how they have fallen. . . . But they were the lords of creation then, and when the State Railway Commission under Eshelman cut them down to size we underlings rejoiced. This was freedom, this was the day of jubilee. . . . John Eshelman was saying, in a proper and judicial way, that the rule of the Southern Pacific machine in California was over. It was. . . . I sat in at those hearings, and thought that democracy had been reborn in California. . . .

Most of Duffus' fellow citizens felt the same way and rejoiced accordingly as the railroad commission ordered total annual reductions in freight rates and passenger fares by $6,000,000.

For thousands of those who had been victimized by the railroad, however, the reforms came too late. There was no way of arranging retroactive justice for the dispossessed settlers of the San Joaquin Valley. They could only ask why it had taken forty years to accomplish that rebirth of democracy in California, why it had been thwarted by a handful of willful men.

12.

A Brandishing of Pitchforks

> There are but two sides in the conflict that is being waged in this country today. On the one side are the allied hosts of the monopolies, the money power, great trusts and railroad corporations, who seek the enactment of laws to benefit them and impoverish the people. On the other are the farmers, laborers, merchants, and all other people who produce wealth and bear the burdens of taxation.... Between these two there is no middle ground.
>
> —A Populist manifesto

By the early 1890's the American pessure cooker was whistling with the escaping steam of a volatile disillusionment. All the promises that had been held out to the American people since the euphoric post-Civil War years seemed to have been broken. Americans do not suffer disenchantment in silence.

The "conquest" of the West seemed to have turned into self-defeat for the foot soldiers as bitter as the fate of the conquered. Almost simultaneously there arose two movements among the red and white people of the West. The Indians hailed a new coming of the Messiah—an Indian Messiah this time—who would rid them of the whites, the iron horse, and other afflictions. Their desperate resort to mysticism as expressed in the rituals of the Ghost Dance ended when the rapid-fire weapons of the U.S. Cavalry, employed on the banks of a Dakota creek called Wounded Knee, proved their medicine men had not made them impervious to bullets.

At almost the same time the pioneers and their sons were as frustrated and embittered as the Indians they had displaced. Somehow, they felt, they had been cheated. The flamboyant promises of the railroad promoters, land developers and

281

westward-ho politicians proved to have been as false as the claims made by the Sioux medicine men. Their feelings of betrayal were condensed in a Jack London novel, not one of his best, titled *The Valley of the Moon*. London, who had turned from oyster piracy to Socialism and finally to literary capitalism, was himself a member of the most bedraggled segment of the postpioneer generation; he had seen them lining up in breadlines and at soup kitchens, the people whose fathers had gone west in wagon trains, found pioneering too rugged and wound up in the slums of the Western cities. His hero in *The Valley of the Moon* was one of the citified descendants of the pioneers, and as he sets out to find a piece of land of his own, following the same dream that betrayed his father, he says, "We're the white folks an' the children of white folks, that was too busy being good to be smart. We're the white folks that lost out."

That same righteous theme could be heard as an undertone in much of the agitation of the time. It was the "white folks" who lost out. They had failed because they were too "good" to connive and cheat their fellow men. The red, brown and black folks who lost out—heathens or only nominally Christian—were not included in the area of their concern.

There was plentiful evidence during the eighties that other men were busier being "smart," and generally at their expense. The Pacific Railway Commission's investigation, ordered by Congress after its members began feeling the heat from back home, was an eye opener for those who troubled to read the columns of testimony set in flyspeck type. Occasionally the railroad magnates summoned to testify spoke with the candor of men who had little to fear from anyone. There was Collis Huntington blandly admitting that he readily "lent" money to members of the state and national legislatures if they were hard pressed to maintain themselves in their respective capitals. And there was Jay Gould telling about how he juggled the finances of the wheat belt carriers with the casualness of a man recalling a hard-fought game of tiddlywinks.

Q. According to the ethics of Wall Street, do you consider it absolutely within the limits of your duty, while a director of the Union Pacific, to purchase another property and to design the extension of the road which would perhaps ruin the Union Pacific?

A. I don't think it would have been proper. That is the reason we let it [the Kansas Pacific] go.

Q. Did you consider your duty to the government?

A. I had considered it.

Q. How would the government claim have been affected by building a parallel line?

A. It would have been wiped out.

One of the commissioners estimated that Gould had made $40,000,000 personally out of manipulating the corporate affairs of the Union Pacific and Kansas Pacific. Regarding another of his stratagems to ruin the Union Pacific at a time when he had temporarily given up interest in the line, except as a sacrificial lamb, he testified:

Q. How great an injury to the Union Pacific would the extension of the Missouri Pacific [a Gould line] have been?

A. Extended through to where?

Q. To Denver and San Francisco.

A. It would have destroyed it.

To the thousands of people who depended on his carriers to take their grain and cattle to the marketplace, Gould was a remote and terrible presence brooding over their lives and fortunes, a devil figure, though in private life he was a home-living, churchgoing family man. They read all about his sinister machinations in articles reprinted from the New York newspapers. A few days before the election of 1884, for instance, when the New York *World* headlined a banquet Gould gave at Delmonico's for Senator James G. Blaine, the Republican Presidential candidate, as THE ROYAL FEAST OF BELSHAZZAR AND THE MONEY KINGS and "An Occasion for the Collection of a Republican Corruption Fund." The story confirmed the prairie farmer's view of Gould as a Babylonian emperor, reporting that Blaine and his friends "bowed and scraped and backed as if they were in the presence of a despotic foreign potentate." Gould and his fellow Wall Streeters pledged a half million dollars for the Blaine campaign chest, despite which, and partly because of which, Blaine lost the election to Grover Cleveland.

The people out on the wheat plains and short-grass country could only agree with the *World*'s editorial writer that Gould was "one of the most sinister figures that ever flitted bat-like across the vision of the American people" and with the sentiments of a New York mob which coursed through the streets looking for Gould so they could hang him to a lamppost (always nimble, Gould had fled to his yacht and was safely afloat in the middle of the Hudson River).

The thousands of men who worked for the Gould roads out west, particularly the Missouri Pacific and the Texas & Pacific, were as harshly oppressed by Gould's labor policy as the farmers were by his freight-carrying charges. In the years since the violent but unsuccessful railroad strike of 1877, which affected mainly the Eastern section of the country, the Noble Order of the Knights of Labor had been especially active in organizing the employees of the Gould lines. The New York *Sun*, which was stridently opposed to all forms of labor organization, warned that "communism and socialism" were infecting the hierarchy of the Knights of Labor and could "disable the railroads."

But Gould paid little attention to warnings that his labor force had become restive. In an uncommonly boastful mood, he replied to the demands of labor leaders for something better than a $10-a-week wage for hard and dangerous work that they should remember that he and his fellow railroad magnates had "made the Great West" by an act of will. He was especially proud of his "constructive labor" in the territory served by the Missouri Pacific. "*We* have made the country rich," he asserted. "*We* have developed the country, coal mines and cattle raising, as well as cotton. *We* have created this earning power by developing the system."

Few except his fellow capitalists were inclined to agree completely, and the Knights of Labor were among those who took the most violent exception. Gould lost heavily in the bear market of 1884, which was followed by a short recession. He followed standard practice in making up his losses, and hundreds of men were cut off the Missouri Pacific payroll while the other employees had their wages reduced. When Gould refused to restore the pay cuts, the Knights of Labor, who had organized the

284

shop workers and others not included in the railroad brotherhoods, called its membership out on strike.

The strikers were led by a magnetic organizer named Martin Irons and succeeded in paralyzing rail traffic throughout the Southwest. Public sympathy was all on the strikers' side in the sections served by the Missouri Pacific, where a "violent antagonism" to Gould was noted. Even the mercantile middle class supported the strikers. With the public against him, Gould saw that he couldn't win and accepted the mediation offer of the governors of Missouri and Kansas. The strike ended when Gould agreed to restore the pay cuts. It had only increased hostility to Gould and all his works. His only personal satisfaction was in seeing to it that Martin Irons was hounded from town to town by police and private detectives; Irons ended his days as a peanut vendor.

In the eighties labor rarely won an argument with the employers. A strike was still regarded as downright immoral by the majority. Thus, the defeat of Gould, the "strongest and wiliest of capitalists," only encouraged the unions' leadership. More thousands were enrolled by the Knights of Labor. In 1886 Terence V. Powderly, General Master Workman of the Knights of Labor, began agitating for a $1.50 minimum daily wage—nine whole dollars a week—for unskilled workmen. Soon there was trouble over this unseemly agitation on Gould's Texas & Pacific, particularly after Gould cut several hundreds of employees from the railroad payroll. He had an agreement with Powderly that "no strikes would be ordered until after a conference with the officers of the company." Powderly kept his promise but threatened a strike unless the Texas & Pacific rehired the men, gave the Knights of Labor full organizational rights and halted its practice of farming out shopwork to nonunion plants, where it could be done at lower cost.

Gould defied Powderly to call a strike and threatened to sue each of the union's officers for damages if the men were called out. Powderly replied that the Gould system must be defeated because it was "gathering in millions of dollars of treasure and keeping them out of the legitimate channels of trade and commerce."

Out went the Texas & Pacific work force, 9,000 of them, and this time the strike was as violent in the Southwest as the 1877 strike had been in the East. For forty-eight hours the situation was beyond control of the law or even of the Knights of Labor leadership. Trains were derailed, strikebreakers were chased off company property, roundhouses and depots were seized by the strikers, and hundreds of thousands of dollars' worth of property was destroyed.

After that outbreak Gould vowed publicly that there would never be a settlement of the strike except on his own terms. A letter from Gould to Powderly was widely publicized. "If, as you say," Gould wrote, "I am now to be destroyed by the Knights of Labor unless I sink my manhood, so be it." Powderly replied with an appeal to "bring this terrible struggle in the Southwest to a speedy termination."

At whatever cost to himself Gould was determined to smash the Knights of Labor. The strike went on for months while he craftily engineered a reversal of public opinion, which initially, as in the Missouri Pacific strike, had favored the strikers. He brought all traffic on the Texas & Pacific to a halt, and the Southwest began to suffer from a commercial paralysis. Public sympathy already was alienated from the strikers because of the widespread violence with which the strike had begun. Gould's agents worked skillfully to focus resentment on the Knights of Labor. Finally, he succeeded in breaking the union, whose members drifted away from the picket lines in search of employment elsewhere. Gould hired a new work force for his shops, and since the railroad brotherhoods had not joined the Knights in this strike, the trains began running again. Never again was there labor trouble on any of the roads of the Gould system. He was widely praised for having shown other employers how to "handle" the rising threat of unionism. Yet in the end Gould's tactics proved to be self-defeating as the less romantic American Federation of Labor assumed the role pioneered by the Knights of Labor. For decades the railroads would complain of featherbedding and other practices forced on them by the operating brotherhoods—practices which eventually would cripple the railroad industry—but they all dated back to Gould's illusory victory over the Noble Knights of Labor.

They also contributed to the feeling among the people of the

Western states, not only those employed at low wages by the railroads but those for whom the roads were the lifeline to the Eastern markets, that they were being crushed by shadowy, remote and sinister forces. To a great extent it was, of course, true that their lives were compressed, their incomes made marginal, by the oppresive policies of railroad management. It was also true that larger, more impersonal forces were at work on their individual destinies. For the past two decades there had been a quickening of international communications, beginning in 1869 with the opening of the Suez Canal and the completion of the first transcontinental railroad. The full effects of steam locomotion and steam navigation, together with the linking of cables between the United States, Europe, and South America, were now being felt. Immense new lands, largely given over to grain crops and cattle raising, were settled not only in the American West but in Canada, Australia, and Argentina. Mechanical cultivation and harvesting were being introduced. And the overproduction which naturally resulted brought prices down in the international markets. From the early 1870's to the early 1890's there was a steady decline in farm prices.

As William A. Peffer, an agrarian reformer, analyzed the farmer's dilemma:

> While one hundred dollars were the same on paper in 1889 that they were in 1869, yet by reason of the fall in values of products out of which debts were to be paid the dollars grew just that much larger. . . . In some counties from three fourths to seven eighths of the homes of the farmers are mortgaged for more than they would sell under the hammer.

The prime villain, according to Peffer, was the railroad industry.

> The railroad companies, after obtaining grants of land with which to build their roads, not only sold the lands to settlers and took mortgages for deferred payments, but, after beginning the work of building their roads, they issued bonds and put them upon the market, doubled their capital upon paper, compelling the people who patronized the roads to pay in enhanced cost of transportation all these additional burdens. The roads were built

287

without any considerable amount of money upon the part of the original stockholders, and where any money had been invested in the first place, shrewd managers soon obtained control of the business and the property. So large a proportion of the public lands were taken up by these grants to corporations that there was practically very little land left for the homestead settler. . . . The lands granted to the railroad companies directly, and to the States for building railroads indirectly, if sold at the Government price of $1.25 an acre, would be equal to three times as much as was received from sales of the public lands directly to actual settlers.

The railroads hogged the land, Peffer concluded, while "the money changer took possession of the farmer."

All the time that prices were steadily falling, their decline was only hastened by the fact that 600,000 new farms were established between 1880 and 1890, and 1,100,000 in the following decade, all with the fervent blessings of the railroads. There was a feverish land boom in progress during the eighties, nurtured in part by the fact that Kansas alone had more railroad trackage than all the New England states combined.

"Land fever" was reaching the crisis point by the mid-eighties. An artificial inflation in land values, originally caused by high prices for farm products, was occurring throughout the prairie states. Newcomers bought the land at ridiculously high prices and mortgaged themselves to the hilt. "Most of us," a Kansas state official later confessed, "crossed the Mississippi or Missouri with no money but a vast wealth of hope and courage. . . . Haste to get rich has made us borrowers, and the borrower has made booms, and booms made men wild, and Kansas became a vast insane asylum covering 80,000 square miles."

According to one survey of the speculative frenzy:

In a block of six counties in southeastern Nebraska, the price of land doubled in the years 1881 to 1887, achieving by the latter year a price of about $17.50 an acre. . . . Near Clifton, Kansas, a quarter section of land, once thought worthless, brought $6,000. A farm near Abilene in the same state that had cost $6.25 an acre in 1867 sold twenty years later for $270 an acre. Wild and unimproved land in Colorado was held at from $3 to $10 an acre and when slightly cultivated, at from $8 to $20 an acre. If newspaper advertisements are to be trusted, increases in value of from 400 to 600 percent from 1881 to 1887 were by no means unusual.

Until the land boom peaked in the spring of 1887, such prairie cities and towns as Omaha, Lincoln, Kansas City, Topeka, Atchison, and Wichita were the centers of a wild speculation. "Every train brings in additional scores to swell the boom," the Wichita *Eagle* exulted early in 1887. "Everybody is talking real estate and shouting for Wichita." A clerk invested his savings of $200 in a town lot, the newspaper reported, and two months later sold it for $2,000; a barber cleared $7,000 in a few months dabbling in the same sort of venture. Over in Nebraska about the same time the *Nebraska State Journal* in Lincoln was reporting that more than $200,000 worth of real estate had changed hands in one March day. That newspaper also jocularly noted: "Nothing causes the Nebraska farmer more dismay than to return from town after spending a few hours there, and find that his farm has been converted into a thriving city with street cars and electric lights during his absence. But such things will occur now and then and should be regarded with comparative calmness."

The railroads not only kept pace with the land boom but encouraged it by extending their lines to the point that the map of Kansas resembled a closely woven spider's web. From 1880 to 1890 the total trackage in Kansas increased from 3,102 miles to 8,810; the state had a mile of track for every 9⅓ square miles of land. During the same period trackage in Nebraska increased from 1,634 to 5,407, and in the Dakotas from 399 to 4,726.

The boom was punctured with dramatic suddenness. It had reached its crest just before the drought of 1887 (which extended through most of the following decade, with only two years in which most areas had enough rainfall to provide full crops). The hopes of thousands of new settlers on their heavily mortgaged lands shriveled under the hot, dry winds of that summer. "Week after week," wrote a regional historian, "the hot burning sun glared down from a cloudless steel-blue sky. The dread hot winds blew in from the south. Day after day they continued. All fodder, small grain, and corn were cut short. Where farming had been carried on extensively rather than intensively the yield amounted to preciously near nothing. The careful expert got some returns from his work, though small. . . ." Then a plague of chinch bugs finished off what was left of the seared fields.

Thus in a few months the boom encouraged by the railroads, the land speculators, the town promoters, the newspapers, and the politicians collapsed, because of not only crop failure, but declining prices on the international market and the evaporation of the self-generated confidence which had pushed the boom to its logical conclusion.

The population of the Western states was overwhelmed by the bitterest convictions of betrayal, which in a few years were to result in that general but orderly uprising known as the Populist Revolt. They listened to arguments that "overproduction" had caused their predicament and countered them with vexing questions: Why did a Kansas farmer sell his corn for 10 cents a bushel while a New York grain broker was demanding $1 for it? Why—demanded Kansas and Nebraska farmers—did it cost a bushel of corn to send another bushel to market? Why did the farmers of Minnesota and the Dakotas have to pay half the value of their wheat crop to transport it to Chicago?

A volatile resentment against the railroads was forming and soon would be built to the explosive point by diligent and skillful agitators. A homegrown radicalism, as indigenous to the Great Plains and the Middle Border as Marxism to the intellectuals of the European cities or Bolshevism to the plotters in Russian cellars, was flaring up and beginning to spread like a prairie fire. Perhaps the most curious development of that cause, as homely and Gothic as, and partaking of, the old-time religion, the Fundamentalist faith in helping God put things right, was that the burning issues of 1890 somehow became transmuted eight decades later into the modish philosophy of New York intellectuals, as well as the catchphrase of Governor Wallace of Alabama. Populism, obviously, was a portmanteau credo. Not surprisingly it was compounded of all sorts of dreams, philosophies, and panaceas, such disparate doctrines as those of the Single Taxers, the Greenbackers, the Socialists, the Knights of Labor, the Grangers, the Farmers' Alliances, and even the Prohibitionists.

What may have seemed like a motley collection of wild-eyed dreamers and parish-pump philosophers all came under the same umbrella as Populists, and the hundreds of thousands of dispossessed and disenchanted found a political and emotional outlet for their frustrations.

The focal point of all the rising wrath was the railroad industry, with the mortgage-holding banks, the land speculators, and "Wall Street" as secondary villains lurking in the background. The "grasping and domineering railroads," as Ignatius Donnelly would identify them, had, in the popular view, become hog-fat off overcharging their customers. American railroads in 1883 had made net earnings of $337,000,000 on an actual valuation of $3,787,000,000—almost 9 percent. Surely those excessive profits must have come out of the farmers' payment of shipping costs. Even those farmers who had prospered in the lush years just after the Civil War had reason to be outraged by the methods of railroad management. Many had invested their money in the Western railroads, as a sort of testament of faith, and now they learned that the companies had been vastly overcapitalized, had issued watered stock, and their securities had a real value much less than they had been led to believe. They could only nod grimly when the Populist agitator Sockless Jerry Simpson asserted that the Kansas roads had cost $100,000,000 to build but they were capitalized at $300,000,000 in stocks and an equal amount in bonds. They were hardly mollified when apologists for the railroads asserted that the overcapitalization was justified by "future earnings" and denounced as "impertinence" anyone questioning the right of corporations to issue as much stock and as many bonds as they saw fit.

But the crunch came over the matter of freight rates. The railroads claimed that average rates had steadily declined, but their figures included the rebates given to favored industrial shippers. A revisionist historian has also propounded the theory that the Western railroads were the benefactor of the prairie farmers and cattle shippers:

> Historians have repeatedly attributed the plight of the farmers, at least in part, to high freight rates, yet available figures show conclusively that rates dropped drastically during the last half of the nineteenth century, while the farmers' returns failed to show anything commensurate with the drop in rates. Many farmers attributed the sagging prices to these alleged extortionate rates,

291

but by doing so they overlooked the fact that it was these lower rates that made it possible for them to reach markets which were formerly considered incredible . . . rates that in many other countries would have been considered incredibly low.

All the farmer knew was that he was hurting and that meanwhile the railroad corporations reported 9 percent profit margins on their total valuation; that their children went barefoot while the railroad magnates' attended private schools and took the Grand Tour of Europe; that Iowa farmers were burning their corn rather than accept 15 cents a bushel; that it cost only 8.7 cents a bushel to ship wheat from Chicago to New York via the Great Lakes and the Erie Canal, and 14.6 cents to ship the same distance by rail, and even that figure would have been much higher if it weren't for the competition from the waterborne carriers.

There were all sorts of statistics to demonstrate how the farmer was being victimized by the capriciousness of the freight-rate system constantly juggled and revised by the railroads. It was regarded as significant that the railroads could manage to reduce those rates wherever they were confronted by competition.

In his cogent analysis of the farmers' marketing dilemma, Fred A. Shannon discovered striking discrepancies in the rates between various shipping points. There was no such animal as a standard rate; it all depended on whether you were fortunate enough to be farming in a section served by more than one railroad. Shannon found:

> The wheat rate from Fargo to Duluth, on the Northern Pacific railroad, was sometimes almost twice that from Minneapolis to Chicago, though the latter distance was twice the former. But Minneapolis shippers had more than one railroad to choose. Suppose the farmer tried to beat the game by shipping to the first competitive city, and then reshipping to the ultimate market. He found the cards stacked against him. If the wheat grower of the Northwest decided to ship his grain to Minneapolis, in order to get the lower rates from that center to Milwaukee or Chicago, his crop would not be hauled unless he paid the full through rate to the lake port. . . . The cost all the way from Chicago to Liverpool was less than some Dakota areas to Minneapolis. Again, local rates were

often outrageous. Iowa farmers, shipping in feed corn from the next county, had to pay as much freight as though buying from Chicago. But Nebraska farmers, paying half again as much, thought the Iowa brethren were getting by famously.

It hardly soothed the farmers' outraged feelings when their complaints, growing more strident in the late 1880's, were haughtily brushed aside by the railroad executives.

President Sidney Dillon of the Union Pacific declared that the farmers were guilty of ingratitude when they grumbled about the freight rates. "What would it cost for a man to carry a ton of wheat for one mile?" he demanded. "What would it cost for a horse to do the same? The railway does it at a cost of less than a cent."

Such simplistic arguments no longer were acceptable to the farmers, who were kept fairly informed by the growing number of farm journals and bulletins from the Farmers' Alliances. They knew they were being squeezed because the railroads were over-capitalized and had to keep their revenues at a high level. They knew all about the rebates given the larger shippers and the favoritism shown the grain elevator owners.

The farmers were aware of the fact that the system linking elevators and railroads was rigged against them. It was simpler and much less profitable to sell their wheat to the elevators, those monolithic structures which dominate the prairie skyline. Many of them openly or covertly were owned by the railroads; others had secret arrangements which provided them with rebates for their bulk shipments and preferential treatment in obtaining the cars to move their wheat. The Northern Pacific was one of the principal carriers for the wheat plains, and its president, James J. Hill, decreed that farmers must ship through elevators with a capacity of at least 30,000 bushels or "cars will not be furnished." Partly, of course, it was a matter of convenience for the railroads. Frequent and easily regulated shipments from collecting stations were easier to handle than a large number of small, irregular carloadings.

Supposedly the Western railroads had been built, largely with the infusion of public funds, to serve all the people, whether they had 1,000 bushels of wheat to ship or 100,000. They were a public

293

utility. Yet the railroad commissioners apparently were unable to exercise their regulatory powers effectively enough to compel the roads to provide an even-handed service. "The railways," the railroad commissioner of Minnesota protested in 1883, "cannot have a choice of customers. Railways, like inn-keepers, must take all that come until the quarters are full. If it is an inconvenience to furnish cars to flat-houses or merchants, the answer is, that is just what the railways are paid for; to serve the public generally is their proper function."

If the wheat grower complied with the railroads' wishes and sold his wheat through his friendly local elevator, he often found himself cheated through the grading process. The grading was done arbitrarily by the elevator operator. The grain elevators, in effect, were just another monopoly. They paid the highest prices for No. 1 wheat, "sound, plump and well cleaned"; then came No. 2, which had to be of "good milling quality," and finally No. 3, "inferior, shrunken, dirty." A farmer either had to accept the grading given his wheat by the elevator or haul his grain back home and let it rot. Generally the elevator downgraded the wheat it received, then sold it in Chicago as a higher grade. The Minnesota railroad commissioner estimated that the growers were cheated out of an average of 5 cents a bushel through the arbitrary grading system. A group of Minnesota farmers who claimed they rarely had their wheat graded No. 1, no matter how fine it was, organized a committee to do a little detective work in that field. They appointed three members to trace a shipment of thirty cars from their elevator to Duluth. The grain in all the cars had been rated as inferior by the elevator operator and paid for accordingly. Yet a miraculous thing happened to that shipment en route to Duluth. When it arrived at the terminal, fourteen of the thirty cars were graded No. 1, and nearly all the rest received higher prices than their local elevator had paid them. The difference went into his pocket.

A "price-fixing plutocracy" had come into existence, as the editor of a Farmers' Alliance bulletin argued, "the logical result of the individual freedom which we have always considered the pride of our system." Those who formed the monopolies which were squeezing the life out of the Western farmers had taken advantage of the American ideal of the "very least legal re-

A Brandishing of Pitchforks

straint." Eventually the corporations "absorbed the liberties of
the community and usurped the power of the agency that created
it, and 'individualism' congealed into 'privilege.'"

The grievances of the Westerners were political as well as
economic; there was a widespread conviction that most state
legislators and Congressmen were beholden to the railroads. They
felt that their political representatives existed only to trumpet the
propaganda of the railroads and the traders in Chicago and New
York who controlled the market place. As one outraged farmer
put it, shortly after the Kansas land boom ended:

> We were told two years ago to go to work and raise a big crop,
> that was all we needed. We went to work and plowed and planted;
> the rains fell, the sun shone, nature smiled, and we raised the big
> crop that they told us to; and what came of it? Eight-cent corn,
> ten-cent oats, two-cent beef and no price at all for butter and
> eggs—that's what came of it. Then the politicians said that we
> suffered from over-production.

Railroad influence, it was generally believed, was stronger in
the statehouses than the combined will of the electorate. The
Santa Fe controlled Kansas, the Burlington and the Union
Pacific shared power over Nebraska, and one or more railroads
similarly dominated other states. Railroad money and influence
were highly visible at the nominating conventions, and railroad
lobbyists prevented the state legislatures from equitably taking
railroad property.

William Allen White, the future editor and publisher of the
Emporia *Gazette* and oracle on all things Kansan, was just starting
his notable journalistic career in 1888 as editor of Thomas Benton
Murdock's El Dorado *Republican*. Publisher Murdock was running for state senator that year, and young Mr. White soon
gained valuable insights into how the railroads dominated the
state's political life. Murdock wore the colors of the Santa Fe and
therefore was opposed by the Missouri Pacific, which had extended its lines into the county five years earlier. Each railroad
struggled to become dominant in the territory it traversed. But, as
White observed, "when two railroads crossed a county, often in
those days the railway overlords struggled for domination, which

295

was both unethical and wasteful. Even worse, it became revealing. For people, lined up on each side, knew the masters on the other."

The young rural editor observed how the Missouri Pacific supported another Republican journal in his county, which attacked Murdock on the grounds that he was a sissified type who bought his clothes from a New York tailor and kept his fine-cut chewing tobacco in a silver case. His opponent took care never to attack Murdock on the grounds of his Santa Fe sponsorship because if he had, as White noted, it would have highlighted the growing suspicion that Kansas was no longer a "republican democracy but part of a plutocratic republic." Murdock won his legislative seat despite the opposition's charges that he bought his suits from Brooks Brothers.

The Farmers' Alliances, as a future component of the Populist movement, began offering their own candidates, but at the moment they were generally regarded as members of an underclass which included the town drunk, the village atheist, and the crankier of the cracker barrel philosophers. By 1890, however, those Farmers' Alliance candidates, campaigning against the railroads and their overweening influence, had become so popular that State Senator Murdock and his friends began demanding that the Republican Party of Kansas "clean house" and free itself of corporate domination or it would face a calamity.

Until now the chief lobbyist of the Santa Fe had been the head of an invisible government in Kansas, sort of a second and unofficial governor. The Santa Fe's chief fugleman at the legislature was George R. Peck, who was also its general counsel. He presided over a suite at the Copeland Hotel in Topeka, where there was always whiskey and cigars for any legislator who voted as Mr. Peck suggested. Ten or twelve members of the legislature were on the Santa Fe payroll for yearly emoluments—never, never referred to as bribes—of from $500 to $2,000 a year, depending on the sensitivity of their committee assignments. "If they were lawyers, they got it to help them with their expense money. . . . When Mr. Peck distributed his largesse, nothing was said of any return from any recipient. It was just a pleasant social gift. . . ."

One of Peck's henchmen was a picturesque state senator named

Bill Blivens, who as a committee chairman rated an annual subsidy of $2,000. Once, as White recalled, Blivens ran out of money before the session ended and went to Peck with a demand for more money. Peck protested that this was a violation of whatever ethics governed bribe givers and bribe takers.

"Well, George," Blivens replied, "I have had to buy some of my own whiskey and I have had to sit in some poker games to keep my standing. Now you know how it is with these girls around the capital here. That accounted for fifteen hundred of it. I may have spent the rest of it foolishly. But anyway it's all gone. I tell you, George, it's all gone!"

Peck remonstrated that he would not be able to explain to the Santa Fe's treasurer why he had to bribe a state senator twice.

"George," Blivens said, putting his arm around Peck's shoulder, "you go back to your fellers and say sort of mysterious: 'Old Bill Blivens is acting queer.' Just that! And see what they say."

A more subtle and equally effective method of influencing legislation was the genial custom of presenting legislators, editors, judges, and other influential citizens with annual railroad passes. For decades politicians throughout the country rode the cushions free of charge; it was the rarest of sights to see an elected official or any member of his family lining up at a depot's ticket window. Two Congressmen—Ignatius Donnelly of Minnesota and Lemuel "Calamity" Weller of Iowa, both highly vocal opponents of the railroads—did finally turn in their passes in 1886. Various farmers' organizations campaigned against the practice, charging that annual passes were a "railroad invention for corrupting state officers." A publication of the Farmers' Alliance pointed out that "the man who will accept railroad transportation, which may be worth hundreds of dollars every year, and feel under no sort of obligation for it is a very contemptible sort of man, and as rare as he is contemptible."

Antirailroad sentiment was reaching into the towns, most of them founded on high hopes of the prosperity that the railroads were supposed to bring, as well as into the farmlands. William Allen White, from his observation post in the heart of the rebellious countryside, noticed that one or two nights a week the schoolhouses were lit up. In Kansas the schoolhouses were used for political meetings. Since the Republicans had not started campaigning as yet, it was obvious that the meetings were being held by the Farmers' Alliance. Evidence of the success of their agitation soon made itself apparent. "Right square in July, almost without notice, certainly without any clamor from the Republican papers, a procession two miles long moved down Main Street in El Dorado. It was made up of protesting farmers, their wives and their children." The hay wagons were covered with signs reading DOWN WITH WALL STREET and LET US PAY THE KIND OF DOLLAR WE BORROWED. To the young El Dorado editor it signified "a mass psychology which manifested itself in the growing Populist movement."

Townspeople were staggering under the load of public debt incurred through supporting the railroads with direct contributions and bond issues. In Kansas alone, during the year 1890, the railroads received almost $75,000,000 from state and local sources. Eighty percent of the municipal debt of Kansas, it was estimated, was incurred through helping finance the railroads. There were horror tales aplenty. Often fly-by-night railroad promoters conned a community into floating a bond issue for construction, pocketed the proceeds, and walked away from their pledges. It was not until the red-letter day of May 4, 1938, that the treasurer of St. Clair County, Missouri, made the final payment on a $585,000 bond issue floated in 1871 for construction of the Tebo & Neosho Railway, on which no train whistle was ever heard; its franchise, though not its financial obligations, was taken over by the Katy line.

Then came the Populist movement. It began with a coalescing of various farmers' organizations—the Grange, the Farmers' Alliances, and others—which in the late eighties began veering toward the goal of political action. In various combined meetings they began campaigning for government ownership of the railroads, the abolition of the national banks, and the substitution of greenbacks for bank notes. They also formed an alliance with the Noble Knights of Labor and linked up with other reform movements, no matter how outlandish their philosophies. It was this goulash of lost or faded causes, this mixture of aspirations and grievances dating back to the foundation of the Republic, this willingness to accept as followers of the Populist banner anyone with a grudge or cure-all or obsession that resulted in certain regrettable extravagances. Among them was a strong undercurrent of anti-Semitism.

More than a score of dissident and semirevolutionary causes seeking reforms without number were welcomed into the Populist fold. It is perhaps needless to add that many of the prophets who rose to lead the Populist multitude toward a new utopia were obsessed with conspiratorial theories of history and addicted to frequent references to shadowy powers at work destroying various versions of the American Dream. In general, however, as the late Richard Hofstadter (perhaps the most perceptive historian of such movements) wrote, "The Populists looked backward with longing to the lost agrarian Eden, to the republican America of the early years of the nineteenth century in which there were few millionaires and, as they saw it, no beggars, when the laborer had excellent prospects, when statesmen still responded to the mood of the people, and there was no such thing as the money power."

The theorists and propagandists of Populism may indeed have been looking backward toward a lost Eden, but most of their followers were more concerned with getting a fairer deal out of the railroads and banks and with making the various echelons of government more responsive to their needs. They were motivated more by present bitterness than nostalgia for times that few of them ever heard about.

The bind in which they found themselves at the end of the eighties was expressed by a part-time editor and farmer in a Farmers' Alliance bulletin:

> There are three great crops raised in Nebraska. One is a crop of corn, one a crop of freight rates, and one a crop of interest. One is produced by farmers who by sweat and toil farm the land. The other two are produced by men who sit in their offices and behind their bank counters and farm the farmers.
>
> The corn is less than half a crop. The freight rates will produce a full average crop. The interest crop, however, is the one that fully illustrates the boundless resources and prosperity of Nebraska. When corn fails the interest yield is largely increased.

To give voice to their despair and to counsel them on how to make it heard from their state capitals to the halls of Congress and the White House, there sprang up a wonderfully eloquent if sometimes intellectually warped band of prophets, orators, soothsayers, propagandists, and office seekers. Some of them possessed a literary talent of the apocalyptic school, principally Ignatius Donnelly, whose career has been outlined above and whose best-selling *Caesar's Column* foretold a plutocracy established in 1988 which crushes democracy and forces a decent remnant of the American people to begin all over in Africa. As Donnelly became one of the Populist leaders and his short, plump figure appeared on hundreds of platforms throughout the Middle Border, *Caesar's Column* took its place in prairie homes where the only other reading matter was the Bible and a stack of dime novels.

Another work widely circulated among the Populists' following was Mrs. Sarah Emery's *Seven Financial Conspiracies Which Have Enslaved the American People*, which was published in 1887. All their troubles, Mrs. Emery told her readers, stemmed from the "money kings of Wall Street," whose control of the currency held prosperity in check at their whim.

Women were at the forefront of the Populist leadership. Indubitably *La Pasionara* of the movement was the mellifluous Irishwoman Mary Ellen Lease, whose slogan "Raise less corn and more hell" caused a brandishing of pitchforks and inspired visions of an overalled army marching on the seats of power. Born in Ireland, she had come to Kansas in 1873, married, raised four children, passed her bar exams, and at the age of forty took up a career as a political crusader. Recalling her from his days as a young Kansas journalist, William Allen White believed that her voice more than any originality of thought was her principal asset as an agitator:

> I have never heard a lovelier voice than Mrs. Lease's. It was a golden voice—a deep, rich contralto, a singing voice that had hypnotic qualities. She put into her oratory something which the printed copies of her speech did not reveal. They were dull enough often, but she could recite the multiplication table and set a crowd hooting or hurrahing at her will. She stood nearly six feet tall, with no figure, a thick torso and long legs. To me, she often looked like

a kangaroo pyramided up from the hips to a comparatively small head. . . . She had no sex appeal—none!

But her following wasn't looking for sexuality—that, if anything, would have turned it off—but for magic, instant and potent remedies for the despair which had enveloped their lives for the past several years. And certainly her speeches were not "dull" to the audiences she attracted, who came to regard her as a Joan of Arc of the cornfields. She made 160 speeches during the year 1890, and her set piece was strong medicine indeed for the national and regional ills:

> Money rules and our Vice President [Levi Morton] is a London banker. Our laws are the output of a system which clothes rascals in robes and honesty in rags. . . . The politicians said we suffered from overproduction. Overproduction when 10,000 little children starve to death every year in the United States and over 100,000 shopgirls in New York are forced to sell their virtue for the bread their niggardly wages deny them. . . . Kansas suffers from two great robbers, the Santa Fe Railroad and the loan companies. . . . The people are at bay, let the bloodhounds of money who have dogged us thus far beware!

In her boldly titled book *The Problem of Civilization Solved*, Mary Ellen Lease revealed that curious mixture of near Socialism and near Fascism which marked the thinking of many Populists. The Populists were generally anti-imperialist but at the same time jingoistic. In her book Mrs. Lease proposed a reshuffling of the world's population in which the lands of the Southern Hemisphere would be taken over by a white planter class acting as overseers of a mass of black and Oriental "tillers of the soil." The racial and religious prejudice which tinged the Populist movement was strikingly evident in Mrs. Lease, who wrote that "through all the vicissitudes of time, the Caucasian has arisen to the moral and intellectual supremacy of the world" and believed that the white race should be appointed to the management of all the colored races. The United States, according to her prescription, would take over Central and South America and turn them into vast plantations while North American soil would be tilled by "vast swarms of Asiatics."

Something of the same sort of chauvinism was revealed by Ignatius Donnelly in his *The Golden Bottle*, published as a follow-up to *Caesar's Column*, in which he urged that the United States halt all immigration:

> We could, by wise laws and just conditions, lift up the toilers of our own country to the level of the middle classes, but a vast multitude of the miserable of other lands clung to their skirts and dragged them down. Our country was the safety-valve which permitted the discontent of the Old World to escape. If that vent was closed, every throne in Europe would be blown up in twenty years.

All this indicates the volatile nature of the movement which came into being largely because of the monopolistic practices of the Western railroads.

Those wild-eyed prophets, inspired by the thousands who gathered around them at mass meetings amid the rotting wheat and burning corn of the American steppe, began inflaming a dangerous, semireligious passion among the desperate people of the Middle Border. Kansas farmers who burned corn in their stoves because it was cheaper (at 10 cents a bushel) than coal, gaunt men and women of the Nebraska and Dakota plains, townspeople overburdened by public debts mainly incurred through helping finance the railroads which now treated them like ignorant helots—all were ready to listen to the most demagogic appeals. And they were combining with other restive legions in the Southern states, where Tom Watson of Georgia and Pitchfork Ben Tillman of North Carolina were organizing a holy war against what they termed an industrial oligarchy. Neither the Republicans nor the Democrats, even by making leftward turns in their party policies, were able to deflect or redirect the popular wrath.

Inevitably there arose from all the mass meetings, all those Sunday gatherings in the trampled corn at which Donnelly, Mrs. Lease, and other prophets spoke to the multitudes from the tail-gates of farm wagons, an urgent movement toward the formation of a third party. The People's Party was its official designation. It began presenting candidates for state, local, and national offices, many of whom were successful in their appeals to the electorate. There was William A. Peffer of Topeka, editor of the *Kansas Farmer* and author of *The Farmer's Side*, in which he advocated the "destruction of the money power," at which time "the death knell of gambling in grain and other commodities will be sounded." He won election to the United States Senate. And there was Sockless Jerry Simpson, perhaps the most charismatic figure of all the Populist ideologues. Simpson had been a Great Lakes sailor, a Civil War veteran, and a farmer near Medicine Lodge, Kansas, before being seized by political ambition. William Allen White, who knew all the Populist leaders at close-up range, considered him the most impressive intellectually despite his clownish sobriquet. Aside from an oratorical talent which won him a seat in Congress from the Seventh Congressional District, White wrote, Simpson was a self-educated man who quoted Carlyle and the essayists and poets of the seventeenth century:

> He was smart. . . . He accepted the portrait which the Republicans made of him as an ignorant fool because it helped him to talk to the crowds that gathered to her him. . . . He was intelligent enough to know that the more his silk-stocking opponents portrayed him as "Sockless Jerry," the quicker the discontented and the underprivileged citizens of Kansas would give him their vote.
>
> He was opposed in his first victorious campaign for Congress by a Wichita railroad lawyer who went around campaigning in a private car and was known as "Prince Hal." In a contest wherein the bidding was for the farmer staggering under his mortgage, it is not strange that "Sockless Jerry" defeated "Prince Hal" in the race for Congress. "Sockless Jerry" became a national figure. The real Jerry Simpson profited by the fame of his own effigy.

The Populists gained national momentum, were reaching out from regional bases to the rest of the country, early in the nineties, despite White's conservative judgment of most of their leaders as "incompetents of one sort of another, sometimes moral misfits but more often just plain ne'er-do-wells, with here and there a

303

visionary staring at his utopia, wandering in a dream with the marching hordes of the discontented, the disinherited, the poor."

The marching song titled "Goodbye, My Party, Goodbye," began echoing far from the Great Plains, with its first stanza:

> It was no more than a year ago,
> That I was in love with my party so,
> To hear aught else I never would go;
> Like the rest I made a great blow,
> Goodbye, my party, goodbye.

Populists from all over the country convened in Cincinnati in 1890 to formulate a program acceptable to all its many factions. Two years later, in Omaha, they held a national nominating convention at which Ignatius Donnelly received a thirty-four-minute ovation when he took the platform as its presiding officer. Certainly he was its guiding spirit, if not its nominee, and he wrote most of the new third party's platform. The delegates convened in a lowering atmosphere. Something of the menacing spirit of many of them was suggested in a "grim warning to plutocrats" which had appeared in a Farmers' Alliance bulletin: "The twin of this oppression is rebellion—rebellion that will seek revenge with justice, that will bring in its Pandora's box fire, rapine and blood. Unless there is a change and a remedy found, this day is as inevitable as that God reigns, and it will be soon. . . ."

Such blood-and-thunderous forebodings were not reflected in the Populists' platform, which was modeled after the Populist Manifesto issued a few months earlier by the Kansas state central committee. It called for a democratic solution to the problem of overproduction through a fairer distribution of goods to benefit the poverty-stricken. "We hold these conditions are the legitimate result of vicious legislation in the interests of the favored classes averse to the masses of American citizens, and we appeal to the great body of the people . . . to rise above the partisan prejudices engendered by political contests. . . ." There was a "tumultuous ovation" for the antirailroad plank in the platform, as the Omaha *World-Herald* reported, and when the whole platform was adopted, a demonstration erupted with "a likeness to the enthusiastic Bastille demonstration in France." But this was Omaha, not,

304

Paris, and "the band played 'Yankee Doodle' and it lasted for twenty minutes."

Possibly to symbolize the Populists' presentation of themselves as the party of reconciliation and to mute the suspicion that they represented an American version of the Communard insurrection, they nominated a Union general for the Presidency and a Confederate general for the Vice Presidency. The Presidential candidate was James B. Weaver, an ex-Congressman from Iowa, a veteran of third-party campaigns who had run for President on the Greenback ticket back in 1880. His running mate was James G. Field of Virginia, a former Confederate general, who was to represent the Southern wing of the People's Party. "The Blue and the Gray," Ignatius Donnelly, always quick with a slogan, cried from the platform, "are woven together to make our banner."

They may have been an ingathering of enthusiastic amateurs when it came to national politics, but the Populists made a more than respectable showing in the 1892 campaign. Running against Grover Cleveland on the Democratic ticket and Benjamin Harrison on the Republican, Weaver received 1,027,329 votes and won North Dakota, Kansas, Idaho, Nevada, and Colorado with more than 48 percent of the vote in each of those states. They may have lost the White House to Cleveland, but they elected many governors, Congressmen, and state legislators. To Richard Hofstadter, however, the most impressive feature of the election was the "negligible chance they had to replace a major party. In 1892 General Weaver had 8.5 percent of the total vote—and it may help to gauge the dimensions of his support if we remember that this was much closer, say, to Debs's 5.9 percent in 1912 than it was to LaFollette's 16.6 percent in 1924." The election statistics also showed clearly that Populist sentiment was sectional, that General Weaver was strongly supported only in a few plains and mountain states and a half-dozen states in the South. He got more than a third of the vote in only nine states.

The Populist movement could not, however, be measured only by election returns. There were intangibles: the influence of Populist ideas on the two major parties; the fact that much of what the Populists advocated (the graduated income tax and other former heresies which were subsequently written into the national laws) was quietly taken over by the Democrats; and, most of all, the Populist theme that the government belonged to all the people, not to parties, special interests, or bureaucracies.

Even William Allen White conceded that "they abolished the established order completely and ushered in a new order." The political system would never be quite so rigid once Populism showed that a sizable part of the electorate could be roused to make themselves heard. Certainly we have not heard the last of one Populist slogan—"direct legislation by the people"—which in different terminology has been recently and resoundingly revived.

In the Congressional and state elections of 1894 the Populists reached their political apogee, particularly in Kansas, where they won control of the legislature but were lured into bickering with the Republicans and failed to pass any significant legislation. Out in California, where resentment of the Southern Pacific was boiling over, the Populist candidate Aldoph Sutro was elected mayor of San Francisco. But the Populists, with all those factions ranging from Socialism to women's suffrage to prohibition, never really coalesced again as a united party. They continued to hold national conventions but never fielded another Presidential candidate.

Perhaps one reason was the extremism of some of its elements, whose obsessions would always militate against any wide appeal among Americans. At times Populism seemed to be a patchwork of lunatic fringes. During the 1896 national convention in St. Louis an Associated Press reporter remarked on the "extraordinary hatred of the Jewish race" among the delegates. "It is not possible to go into any hotel in the city without hearing the most bitter denunciation of the Jews as a class and of the particular Jew who happened to have prospered in the world."

Among Populist writers and agitators there was also a notable strain of anti-Semitism. In Donnelly's *Caesar's Column* the leader of the vicious plutocracy was one Jacob Isaacs, Mary Ellen Lease described Grover Cleveland as "the agent of Jewish bankers and British gold," and Populist propagandists made frequent references to "Jews and the international gold ring." They were linked to the Populism's strong but undocumented suspicion that "the people" were being victimized by a conspiracy which

306

included the Eastern financial leadership, the major political parties, Jewish-American and Anglo-Jewish bankers. In those fever dreams of conspiracy, they often lost sight of their real enemies and their real problems.

Populism never managed to expand its base and appeal to the urban working classes, and in the cities it would always be regarded as a hallucination of the hayseeds. No effort was made to join forces with the dissident elements which composed Coxey's Army or other manifestations of urban protest. Farmers had to stay on their farms as a matter of necessity, and besides, there was the unspoken conviction that the purity of an agrarian movement would be endangered by contact with the cities, part of a strong and enduring American credo that innocence resided in the countryside while evil made the city its haunt.

By 1896 much of the political force of Populism was rechanneled into the Democratic Party when a country boy of certified purity, William Jennings Bryan of Nebraska, the "boy orator of the Platte," ran for the Presidency and created the striking metaphor of mankind being crucified on a cross of gold. That was Populist talk. Bryan held them enthralled in successive but unsuccessful Presidential campaigns. Yet the Populist idea did not simply vanish. It was strikingly evident in various Congressional acts which granted considerable regulatory power over the railroads to the Interstate Commerce Commission, in the federal income and inheritance taxes enacted in 1913, and various anti-trust laws. In 1914 Mary Ellen Lease could look back on her hell-raising career and say with considerable justification that it had not been in vain, that "the Progressive Republican Party had adopted our platform, clause by clause, plank by plank. Note the list of reforms which we advocated which are coming into reality. Direct election of senators is assured. Public utilities are gradually being removed from the hands of the few and placed under the control of the people who use them. Women's suffrage is now almost a national issue. The seeds we sowed out in Kansas did not fall on barren ground. . . ."

If those seeds did not develop into a whirlwind, if the Populist Revolt did not become a revolution, they still constituted the sternest of cautionaries to the Western railroads that their methods were intolerable. Ultimately they resulted in the regulation of all railroads. The magnates and empire builders of that industry were slow to learn, and many continued to create the conditions of discontent. They would have one last fling on the northern plains.

13.

"All Montana Needs Is Rain"

I owe the public nothing.

—J. Pierpont Morgan

Mastodonic grapplings over control of the Western railroads continued after the first generation of builders and promoters and thimbleriggers died off. By the turn of the century Jay Gould, all of the Big Four, and most of the original predators had been buried with pious reflections at their gravesides on how the great American West could never have been conquered and settled without their selfless labors. Now came the heyday of George Gould, eldest son of Jay, Edward H. Harriman, and James J. Hill. Directly or indirectly all three inherited the imperial visions of their predecessors, but only two had the will, the stamina, and the extraglandular ambition to accomplish their objectives.

Even the lordliest of the railroad magnates had been taken aback by the whiplash of Populist sentiment in their territories, but Populism temporarily talked itself out of existence. There was growing "interference" from the Interstate Commerce Commission and other regulatory agencies, but lobbyists and lawyers could always devise ways to outwit the bureaucrats. The depression beginning with the panic of 1893 started shock waves throughout the railroad industry, with the result that many fell

309

into receivership or went bankrupt. But there was still time and opportunity for a final round of railroad wars, this time largely fought in boardrooms and in stock exchanges, and a last splurge of empire building on the northern grasslands in which thousands of emigrant farm families were casualties and much of the state of Montana was turned into a disaster area.

One ambition of the original empire builders had eluded them. That was to establish a truly transcontinental railroad, one from the Atlantic to the Pacific. The so-called transcontinental roads like the Union Pacific, the Santa Fe, and others all terminated at various points in the midsection of the continent. Jay Gould, with all his inordinate skill at manipulating corporations, had not managed to achieve the goal of linking the Gould systems from New York to Los Angeles or San Francisco; hostile forces had always combined against him.

For about fifteen years after the elder Gould's death, his eldest son and designated successor, George, had been content to manage the family enterprises and play the country gentleman at his New Jersey estate. He had lacked even the drive to finish his college education. Shortly after the turn of the century, however, he was seized by unfortunate ambitions of his own, determined to make it come to pass that a passenger could ride from one coast to the other without stepping off a Gould-operated train. At great cost he managed to extend the Wabash, an old family holding, to the Atlantic. His next move was to try to push the Missouri Pacific from Colorado to the Pacific coast. As one of the lawyers involved in sorting out the wreckage caused by those grandiose ambitions later phrased it, George Gould "launched forth as a great railroad magnate with bombastic flourishes" but brought about "a wreck that was colossal."

For a time it appeared that Gould might succeed in carrying out his coast-to-coast project. He was on what he considered very friendly terms with Edward H. Harriman, who had acquired control of the Union Pacific in the mid-nineties. Much of the warmth of that relationship evaporated, however, when Harriman bought up a majority interest in the Southern Pacific in 1900 and refused to sell Gould half his holdings. Much annoyed, Gould decided to declare war on Harriman, thus promoting a classic contest, inherited wealth vs. the self-made

310

man, the outcome of which could have been foretold by any diligent reader of popular fiction. Gould was so confident of putting Harriman down, as one associate revealed, that he "developed the habit of suddenly going to Europe and leaving nobody with authority to make a business move. His entourage developed into a petty court, constantly filled with jealousies, bickerings and scandal-mongerings."

George Gould believed Colorado would serve as a firm base for his planned expansion to the Pacific, a move which would, in effect, make an end run around Harriman's monopoly. With control of the Southern Pacific and Union Pacific, Harriman now dominated the southern and central routes to California; he would be greatly displeased by any attempt to build a rival road to the Pacific coast. Gould's Missouri Pacific ran as far west as Pueblo, Colorado, where it connected with the Denver & Rio Grande, now also a Gould line. Gould's plan called for the construction of the Western Pacific from Denver to San Francisco. When Harriman heard of the project, he told Gould with the quiet forthrightness for which he was celebrated: "If you build that railroad, I'll kill you." Presumably, he meant "kill" in the financial sense.

Some of Gould's self-confidence may have sprung from his success in turning Colorado into a sort of Gould subsidy. In this venture he collaborated with the Colorado & Southern Railway, the Denver City Tramway, and the Denver Union Water Company, but Gould was the kingpin of the operation, being the owner of two of the state's principal railroads. In 1905 he and his allies secured the election of Governor Peabody. Several years later Judge Ben B. Lindsey of Denver, who later became celebrated for advocating "companionate marriage" and other theorems considered daring at the time, revealed in a national magazine that Governor Peabody had agreed, in return for his election, to let the Gould interests and their allies name the men to be appointed to seats on the State Supreme Court—a fairly startling instance of how much influence the railroads could still bring to bear. Judge Lindsey wrote:

> Does this seem incredible? Read the Colorado Supreme Court Reports, Vol. 35, page 325 and thereabouts. You will find it

charged that the Colorado and Southern Railway Company, the Denver and Rio Grande Railway Company, and the public service corporations of Denver had an agreement with Governor Peabody whereby those corporations were to be allowed to select the judges to be appointed to the Supreme Bench. You will find it charged that Luther M. Goddard had been selected as a proper judge by the public utility corporations, but that the two railroads objected to him as "too closely allied" with the interests of the Denver City Tramway Company and the Denver Union Water Company.

The statement quoted by Judge Lindsey from the high court's records continued:

> As a last resort the agent of the said Colorado and Southern Railway Company was induced to, and did, repair to the home of the said Luther M. Goddard, in a carriage, calling him out of bed, having then and there such conversation with the said Goddard that the said railway corporations, through their agents, withdrew their opposition to his confirmation, and they did on said morning at about three o'clock thereof announce to the remainder of the said corporations through their said agents and representatives, that their opposition had been withdrawn, and the withdrawal of the said opposition having been announced, the said senate of the Fifteenth Central Assembly did, almost immediately upon its reconvening on the morning of Monday, the ninth day of January, confirm the said nomination of the said Goddard.

In his magazine article Judge Lindsey related that the brief making the charges quoted above was signed "by Henry M. Teller, ex-Cabinet member and United States Senator, and by ex-Governor Thomas acting as counsel for Senator T. M. Patterson, who made the charges in his newspaper, *The Rocky Mountain News*. These gentlemen offered to prove the charges before the Court, but the Court, in a most amazing decision, refused the offer, held that no matter how true such charges might be, it was 'contempt of court' to make them, and fined Senator Patterson $1,000!"

Perhaps such triumphs over the democratic process went to George Gould's head and caused him to boast to his sycophants that he "wasn't afraid of Harriman or the devil" as he made his

Western Pacific plunge. He pushed all his chips on that number, forgetting his father's dictum that a cash reserve must always be held against the day that money got tight and stock prices fell. The senior Gould was enough of a pessimist to know that unforeseen disasters were always lurking, but as an associate said George Gould was "manifestly intoxicated by optimism."

The crash came almost overnight. Just when Gould needed all the credit he could raise to build his parallel and competing line to San Francisco, when in fact the biggest banking houses on Wall Street were lined up on Harriman's side, the panic of 1907 occurred. Gould was disastrously overextended. Not only was he unable to finish the Western Pacific, but most of the roads in the Gould system were thrown into bankruptcy or receivership. His lines in the East were sold to Harriman at the latter's price, which was not merciful; the Wabash and the Denver & Rio Grande were taken over by the Kuhn, Loeb & Company banking house and the Rockefeller interests; and Gould even lost control of the Missouri Pacific, the star in the Gould diadem. Within a few brutal months, George Gould was dealt out of the game. As a financial and industrial power the Gould dynasty, which had controlled so much of Western railroading for thirty years, and in which Jay Gould had invested so much paternal hope, survived its founder by less than a score of years. The writing of its obituary was left to the muckraking *McClure's Magazine*, which observed that the Goulds were dispossessed of their enormous holdings because "like the Vanderbilts, they have attempted to do two incompatible things—live lives of idleness and luxury, and at the same time control great enterprises. The complex forces controlling modern industrialism have proved too much for them." Another factor may have been the resentment which George Gould and his siblings inherited, along with about $100,000,000 worth of railroads, from their cordially hated father. The day Jay Gould died the Wall Street ticker recorded surprising advances in the prices of his stocks as an indication of how heartened his fellow financiers were by his death.

At least the man who vanquished the Goulds would never be accused of idleness. A small man with a walrus mustache and dolorous eyes, Edward Henry Harriman within less than twenty years built himself a railroad empire that included 18,000 miles of

313

trackage and employed 80,000 men, as well as Atlantic and Pacific steamship lines. While George Gould was playing polo, Edward Harriman was dreaming of making himself the czar of world transportation. The scope of his ambition was breathtaking. If he lived long enough—and this was doubtful because of his frail physique and failing health—he planned to dominate railroad transportation coast to coast, then around the world. A Harriman customer would be able to board a train in New York and travel all the way to Paris, via Asia on a Harriman train or ship. From one of the Pacific ports he would board a Harriman liner for China, take a train on the Chinese & Eastern to its connection with the Trans-Siberian, and travel all the way to Paris. Buying controlling interests in the Chinese and Russian railroads was part of his scheme, which came fairly close to fruition.

Harriman, a rare combination of dreamer and doer, was one of six children born in a parsonage at Hempstead, Long Island. His clergyman father received an annual stipend of $200. By the age of fourteen, when he was a $5-a-week office boy in a New York brokerage, Edward Harriman was making more than his father. Eight years later he was able to borrow enough money to buy a seat on the New York Stock Exchange. He became a specialist in railroad securities and financing. But he was middle-aged before he seized upon the panic conditions of 1893 to become an active railroader. By then he had obtained the backing of the Kuhn, Loeb banking house, without which his subsequent forays would have been impossible. With his aptitude for corporate infighting and Kuhn, Loeb's money he became virtually the railroad dictator in the next decade.

Harriman's first move was to secure control of the Union Pacific, stock in which had plummeted to 4 cents a share. The UP was in receivership. Harriman bought enough of its stock at bedrock prices to take over control. His next move as part of a syndicate including Kuhn, Loeb and banker James Stillman was to conduct a raid on the Chicago & Alton Railroad, which was capitalized at $34,000,000. In the next few years that stock was diligently watered, until its capitalization soared to $114,000,000. Harriman and his associates had acquired the railroad for $39,000,000 and turned a 200 percent profit simply by revving up

314

the printing presses and issuing stock certificates. The Interstate Commerce Commission investigated but, still a toothless tiger, could not exact penalties for that sort of stockjobbing. In 1907 it rather helplessly reported that "It was admitted by Mr. Harriman that there was about $60,000,000 of stock and liabilities issued against which no property had been acquired, and this is undoubtedly an accurate estimate," and declared that this was "indefensible financing."

In many ways Harriman's was the most spectacular of all the second-generation, robber-baronial figures in Western railroading. Like Gould, he was able to bring off one coup after another because of his insider's knowledge of stock market speculation and his ability to lay hands on large amounts of borrowed capital whenever he required it. He found another source of financing when he formed a useful friendship with young James Hazen Hyde, who had inherited control of the Equitable Life Assurance Company, with more than $400,000,000 in policyholders' money in the treasury. He made Hyde a director of the Union Pacific, upon which Equitable bought $10,000,000 worth of Union Pacific bonds. Hyde made him a director of Equitable, upon which he arranged a loan of $2,700,000 from Equitable.

The Interstate Commerce Commission frowned gravely; the newspapers denounced him as a "stock-jobber, looter and political corruptionist"; President Theodore Roosevelt was publicly breathing fire—a curiously nonincendiary flame—on the subject of "malefactors of great wealth"; the Congress was passing anti-trust laws. Yet no legal move was ever made against Harriman. He was able to brush aside the nit-picking of the ICC, which in its 1907 report noted that his network of railroads and steamship lines had enabled him to "eliminate competition between them [the Union Pacific and the Southern Pacific] in transcontinental business and in business to and from oriental ports." The report added, with a wringing of hands:

> . . . it is contrary to public policy, as well as unlawful, for railways to acquire control of parallel and competing lines. This policy is expressed in the constitutions and laws of nearly every state in the Union. We have examined the constitutions and laws of all of the states and we find in about forty of them prohibitions

315

against consolidation of capital stock or franchises of competing railways, or the purchase and acquisition by a railway of competing lines. . . . Mr. Harriman may journey by steamship from New York to New Orleans, across the Pacific to China, and returning by another route to the United States, may go to Ogden by any of three rail lines, and thence to Kansas City or Omaha, without leaving the deck or platform of a carrier which he controls and without duplicating any part of his journey.

Even Harriman, however, knew his moments of frustration. Mainly they were caused by one man, the short, stocky, one-eyed, equally self-made James J. Hill. If it was predictable that a Harriman would prevail over a second-generation Gould, it was also likely that a genius at railroad finance would find difficulty in coping with a practical railroader. To Harriman a railroad was a set of balance sheets. Hill, on the other hand, was the sort of rough diamond who sometimes swung a pick with his gandy dancers and reputedly knew every bend and grade on the Great Northern. Once during a Dakota blizzard Hill rode up on a special train to where a track gang was clearing away the drifts. "He grabbed my shovel," one of his workmen later recalled, "and started tossing snow, telling me to go back to his car and I'd find a pot of coffee there. Mr. Hill spelled first one man, then another. My, but he was tough! It has been told of Jim Hill that he knew all of his superintendents and chief foremen by name. Hell, he even knew the first names of all the older shovel-stiffs!"

In addition to his knowledge of practical railroading and an ambition which he admitted was Napoleonic, Hill had acquired the financial and moral support of J. Pierpont Morgan, who contemptuously referred to Harriman as "that little fellow," a judgment he rendered on the basis of Harriman's resemblance to an unemployed bookkeeper. Morgan's millions thus were backing Hill when he went up against Harriman in several contests which revived memories of the Union Pacific-Central Pacific and Santa Fe-Denver & Rio Grande wars.

Harriman and Hill had been making each other nervous for several years, principally over conflicting plans for the railroad development of Oregon. Harriman bought the Oregon Short Line and Oregon Railroad & Navigation Company, allowing him to penetrate the Pacific Northwest. That section, of course, Hill regarded as his turf. Obviously there would be a convergence of rival ambitions in the northwestern corner of the country.

Temporarily, however, their conflict moved to a new area: control of the long and profitable Burlington system. That rambling road first attracted Harriman's attention. His offer to buy a controlling interest was rejected by the Burlington's directors, so he and his associates, who now included William Rockefeller and H. H. Rogers of Standard Oil, as well as Kuhn, Loeb and Stillman of the National City Bank, began surreptitiously buying $10,000,000 worth of Burlington stock. That was in the spring of 1900, just when Huntington died and Harriman became more closely involved in taking over the Southern Pacific.

While his attention was diverted, Hill and his collaborators, who now included George F. Baker and the Vanderbilt interests as well as Morgan's banking house, themselves decided to pounce on the Burlington. It would make an admirable extension of Hill's northern system. The Burlington stretched between the Great Lakes and the Rocky Mountains. In its rambling fashion it connected Denver and Chicago, with enough trackage in Nebraska alone for a trunk line from New York to Salt Lake City. One branch traveled from St. Louis, through Nebraska, into the Black Hills of Dakota, across the Crow reservation in Montana, and connected with the Northern Pacific near Billings, Montana. Control of that crazy-quilt system would allow him to tap the cotton traffic coming up to St. Louis, the smelters in the Black Hills and Denver, the meat-packing houses of Omaha, Kansas City, and Chicago; it would also offer him access to the lumber-consuming prairie states, which would be supplied from the forest lands through which the Great Northern ran. It would also enable him to usurp the Union Pacific's agricultural-produce kingdom on the southern plains and compete with the Southern Pacific for hauling cotton.

Hill bought up a controlling share of the Burlington's stock and presented Harriman with a *fait accompli*. Harriman was coldly furious at being outmaneuvered. He demanded that Hill sell him a third interest in the Burlington, to which Hill replied with a wolfish grin. "Very well," was Harriman's reply, phrased in the starchy style of contemporary melodrama. "It is a hostile act and you must take the consequences."

The consequences, as Hill soon learned, could have been dire. His purchase of the Burlington was announced on April 20, 1901, and from that day forward Harriman devoted all his physical and financial energy to snatching control of the Northern Pacific away from Hill. He bought all the Northern Pacific stock, both common and preferred, he could lay hands on.

Hill was busying himself in Seattle during Harriman's ten-day buying spree and became aware of it only when he noticed that Northern Pacific's stock was shooting up on the New York Stock Exchange for no apparent reason. He ordered up a special train and sped east to investigate. Morgan was supposed to protect his rear, but when Hill arrived in New York, he learned that J. Pierpont had literally taken French leave of his responsibilities and was disporting himself at Aix-les-Bains, where a French noblewoman was helping soothe away the cares of financial genius.

Hill cabled Morgan immediately to order his banking house to take countermeasures on Wall Street. When the closing bell rang on Friday, May 3, he learned that Harriman had managed to buy up 370,000 shares of Northern Pacific common and 410,000 shares of preferred stock. There was still a narrow margin—30,000 shares of common—separating Harriman from gaining control of the Northern Pacific. Unaccountably Harriman dawdled for a few crucial hours and snatched defeat from the jaws of victory. He waited until Saturday morning to order his agents to buy the needed shares. It was necessary for him to obtain the approval of Mortimer Schiff of Kuhn, Loeb for the final purchase, but Schiff was at the synagogue. When the latter emerged from his Sabbath prayers, he advised Harriman to hold off buying any more Northern Pacific for the moment. The stock exchange in those years was open on Saturday mornings, and by then the Morgan machine had begun gathering momentum.

On Monday and Tuesday Morgan's agents crowded the floor of the stock exchange to buy up every available share of Northern Pacific. The stock was bid up from 110 to nearly 150, and the Morgan traders rounded up 150,000 shares, five times more than

318

was needed to guarantee control of the corporation. Speculators rushed into the game and promised to deliver 80,000 shares they did not own. To fulfill those contracts, they set off a wild bidding spree which sent Northern Pacific stock shooting up to 300, then 500, and finally to 1,000; the shock sent most other stocks tumbling, and the more avaricious bankers were offering loans at 40 and 50 percent to help those who were caught short in offering Northern Pacific stock they didn't own. The result was a short-lived but desperate panic in which thousands of smaller investors were severely damaged. Journalists who asked J. Pierpont Morgan in Paris why he had precipitated the disaster received a reply of characteristic arrogance. "I owe the public nothing," Morgan said.

As the self-proclaimed statesman of capitalism Morgan hastened back to New York to prevent any such raids in the future. The Northern Securities Company was organized by Morgan as a holding company for the stock of both the Great Northern and the Northern Pacific, a $400,000,000 corporation so powerful nobody could threaten it again. Morgan's arrogance, however, had begun to offend the public. President Theodore Roosevelt ordered his Attorney General to proceed against Northern Securities on charges of having violated the antitrust laws. A year later the U.S. Supreme Court ruled that the holding company was illegal and ordered it dissolved.

By then the electorate was thoroughly aroused and demanded stronger legislation to control the railroads. Their corporate image was lamentable. Every year 10,000 people were killed in railroad accidents and 80,000 seriously injured; it was generally known that the railroads granted enormous rebates to favored shippers, and the Interstate Commerce Commission was powerless to protect the public interest. As one of the ICC commissioners, Charles A. Prouty of Vermont, bluntly stated, "If the Interstate Commerce Commission were worth buying, the railroads would try to buy it. The only reason they have not tried to purchase the commission is that this body is valueless in its ability to correct railroad abuses." Partly because of Morgan's arrogance, three years after he declared that he owed the public nothing, the ICC was given some real teeth in the shape of the

Hepburn railroad-rate bill, which outlawed the free pass, made rebates a crime punishable by imprisonment, and empowered the ICC to fix maximum rates.

For the next several years the triumphant Hill, temporarily free of assaults on his southern flank from Harriman, occupied himself by imaginative extensions of his Burlington-Northern Pacific-Great Northern combine. The newly strengthened ICC did not bother him because he had always kept his freight rates as low as possible to encourage expansion, to increase traffic on his lines; he was a man of larger vision than the Goulds, Huntingtons, and Harrimans and saw that satisfied customers plus greater volume would eventually equal higher profits.

The Little Giant, as he had been known since he rammed through the final construction on the Great Northern, was a man who liked to think empirically as well as imperially. He saw that his railroads were not an entity existing in a vacuum but part of a greater design. Thus he invited Japanese industrialists to this country to interest them in mixing long-staple American cotton with the short-staple Indian cotton the Japanese mills were using. It proved to be a good idea, and soon Hill was shipping Southern cotton via the Burlington and Great Northern to Seattle for shipment to Japan. He also began sending flour from Minneapolis, metals from Colorado, textiles from New England mills to China and Japan. Hill's lines carried flour at bargain rates to Seattle, where a Japanese shipping line with which Hill had come to an agreement transported it to Far Eastern ports. He often said that if the millions in one Chinese province could be persuaded to eat an ounce of flour daily per person, they would use 70,000,000 bushels of American wheat every year. There may have been a romantic tinge to his Oriental visions, but Hill also used his rail network to ship lumber from Washington and Idaho to the treeless plains, again at rock-bottom freight rates, and encouraged the building of the sturdy farmhouses, barns, and silos which still stand as his unofficial monuments along the Middle Border.

From such constructive projects his attention was again diverted by the necessity of fending off Harriman in the Pacific Northwest. To counter the Harriman group's invasion of

320

southern Oregon, he began building the Spokane, Portland & Seattle as a subsidiary of the Great Northern and the Northern Pacific. His crews began laying tracks along the north bank of the Columbia, using the water-level route through the Cascade Mountains, despite court actions brought against him by Harriman. His trains began running into Portland in 1908.

Then the Hill-Harriman conflict sharpened and became more violent, the result of Hill's apparent intention of building down into California. Secretly Hill bought up the franchise of the Oregon Trunk, a railroad which existed only on paper but which had the right to build along the Deschutes River, a route which traversed the deep canyon of the Deschutes and a 165-mile stretch of sagebrush desert to end up in what was then the forsaken village of Bend, Oregon.

Harriman took alarm the moment that Hill's chief engineer, John F. Stevens, who had served in a similar capacity for the Panama Canal, announced that construction was beginning on the Oregon Trunk. He was certain that Bend would not be the real terminus of the line but would serve as a springboard to invade California and approach San Francisco from the north. Hill's crews were building along the east bank of the Deschutes. Instantly seized by a similar inspiration, Harriman announced the formation of the Deschutes Railroad and began building along the west bank of the river.

That was the beginning of the Deschutes railroad war, the last in the chronicle of Western railroading. Harriman sent a large work force into the Deschutes country under the supervision of George W. Boschke, who had built the famous Galveston seawall. It was rugged country for railroad construction, and all supplies and equipment had to be packed in. The two work forces came within range of each other in the deep and narrow Deschutes canyon, which had to be widened by blasting. Each side exploded charges of dynamite to bring down rock slides on the opposition. Men were also killed when huge boulders mysteriously started rolling down the escarpments. All sorts of dirty-trick maneuvers were tried. One day Boschke received a telegram from Galveston, evidently sent by a Hill agent, informing him that his seawall had broken and he was needed immediately to make repairs. Boschke, certain his wall would never break, shook his head and kept on pushing his crews. The issue, however, was decided in a more prosaic way than on the battlefield. Harriman's henchmen managed to buy a ranch which stood athwart Hill's right-of-way. Hill was forced to ask for a truce, during which it was agreed that he would build the Oregon Trunk no farther south than Bend. That agreement extended only to central Oregon, however, and Hill competed with the Southern Pacific by establishing an ocean terminal at Astoria, at the mouth of the Columbia, from which two large passenger ships operated to the San Francisco docks. In their long contest, which ended with Harriman's death in 1909, Hill could claim that he generally came out on top; he even enjoyed a postmortem victory over his dead enemy—if there is a Valhalla for railroad magnates—when the Oregon Trunk was extended from Bend to San Francisco a year after his own death.

Ambition still spurred Hill on after he had established his supremacy in Western railroading. It was no accident that the No. 1 train on his Great Northern was called The Empire Builder. In the castle he built in St. Paul, with its walls covered by a collection of French moderns, its library crammed with rare first editions, James J. Hill could reflect on an amazing and in some phases very constructive career. He was hardfisted and domineering, but there was more to him than the simple acquisitiveness of the robber baron school. He so prided himself on the esthetic strain in his character that he once fired a Great Northern clerk whose name was Spittles because he could not bear to see the name on his payroll.

He could also pride himself on having risen in the world through his own efforts. At eighteen he had migrated to St. Paul from his Canadian birthplace, had worked his way up from a clerk in a Mississippi steamship company to an independent forwarding agent and warehouseman.

Learning all he could about land and water transportation and what it could mean to the huge undeveloped country south of the Canadian border all the way to the Pacific—the heralded "inland empire"—he managed to secure the financial backing to take over the much looted St. Paul & Pacific when it fell into receivership after the panic of 1873.

This was accomplished with the assistance of the federal receiver appointed to take charge of the St. Paul & Pacific and the

322

backing of three old Canadian friends: Norman Kittson, of Montreal; George Stephen (the future Baron Mount Stephen), of Montreal; and Donald Smith (the future Baron Strathcona), of Winnipeg. The way in which Hill and his three fellow Canadians operated and took a large bite out of the American economy should do much to console modern Canadians embittered by the invasion of United States capital.

They formed what can only be termed a conspiracy, which they called the "Montreal agreement," with Jesse P. Farley, the receiver for the St. Paul & Pacific. Its details were revealed in open court only after Farley sued Hill and his three Canadian associates for his share of the boodle, which had been promised him in return for acting against the interests of the bondholders whose interests he had sworn to protect. No doubt it served Farley right that the courts rejected his claim to the reward he stated had been promised to him for betraying his trusteeship.

Farley had been promised a full one-fifth share, as he testified, in return for engineering an agreement by which Hill and his collaborators obtained control of the St. Paul & Pacific. The line, it was said, then "looked like a Virginia rail fence and nothing but a squirrel could run over its tracks," but its financial potential was enormous, as Hill & Co. proved.

In 1879 Hill and his friends formed a second company, the St. Paul, Minneapolis & Manitoba, to which they sold the St. Paul & Pacific's physical assets for a mere $3,600,000, although they were actually worth about $15,000,000. They then proceeded to sell the railroad's land grant for more than $13,000,000. And they issued $15,000,000 worth of bonds, the content of which was almost pure water. Kittson died before he could enjoy his share of the windfall. Smith and Stephen took their profits and embarked on social careers in England, but Hill plowed his back into railroading.

The single-minded Hill extended his railroad across the Dakotas and Montana to Puget Sound and restyled it the Great Northern. He imported thousands of immigrants from northern Europe, charging them only $10 a head if they would agree to settle along his right-of-way and refraining, unlike other railroad presidents with lines to the south, from burdening them with excessive freight rates—not, at least, until their prosperity warranted increases. And when the Northern Pacific tumbled into receivership, he bought control of that parallel system to the south, again largely with the help of Canadian financing.

His career dazzled even those like Charles Edward Russell, perhaps the most judicious and restrained among the muckraking journalists early in this century, who described him as the dictator of "approximately twenty-five thousand miles of track, traversing and dominating an area fitly termed the Inland Empire, of which, as he owns the highways, he is the practical ruler. When to these advantages you add newspapers, politicians, conventions, parties, houses, lands, farms, sycophants, praise-chanters, knee-crookers, legislatures, senators, and other matters, here appears one of the most colossal figures of the times." Russell regarded him as "the perfect type of the product of that free opportunity that America is said to offer to all men and of which we are so proud." To Russell, at least, some of that luster was diminished when at the beginning of 1909 Hill ordered a freight-rate increase on his roads ranging from 3 to 18 percent; it was time to start collecting on all those other, lesser careers Hill had sponsored.

Along his imperial progress, Hill rewarded his friends and punished his enemies. When a resort town on Lake Minnetonka objected to the whistling of the Great Northern expresses, he vindictively moved its station a mile away to Holdridge at considerable inconvenience to the complainants. On the other hand, he enabled his next-door neighbor in St. Paul, Frederick Weyerhaeuser, a German immigrant who had prospered as a sawmill operator, to become one of the richest men in America. Around the turn of the century Hill sold Weyerhaeuser almost 2,000,000 acres of the heavily forested Northern Pacific land grant in western Washington and made him a director of both the Great Northern and the Northern Pacific as an additional mark of favor. The Weyerhaeusers, cultivating what one historian has called "the studious art of reticence," built up a lumber fortune estimated at $300,000,000 at the time of Frederick Weyerhaeuser's death.

Hill's benevolence, as genuine as it was paternalistic, extended to the whole bleak and underpopulated "empire" of northern states which he believed his railroads would open up and make bountiful and prosperous. Riding his crack trains up and down the system, he viewed with a romantic's eye the wild and beautiful country his rails traversed, staring down at the foaming rapids on the Kootenai River, listening to the thunder of the train's passage through the Cascade tunnels, hearing the coyotes howl outside Havre, Montana, while the engines were being changed on a sub-zero night. At night perhaps even Butte, that corruscating plateau, looked beautiful as the North Coast Limited emerged from the high pass overlooking the "richest hill on earth." (It was anything but beautiful to its resentful citizenry, living atop 2,700 miles of tunnel from which copper was mined. The railroads enabled the copper kings to bring in heavy machinery and exploit the veins of ore and cause "more hell on earth," as Thomas Lawson wrote in *Frenzied Finance*, "than any other trust of financial thing since the world began." In the hot dark depths below the city, a miner was killed or crippled every day of the week, and all of them had their lungs rotted by the combination of rock dust and sulfuric acid. Drugstores regularly held sales on crutches and wheelchairs. Aboveground Butte was described as a "Dantesque wasteland, where no flower blossoms, no seed grows; there are acres of burnt slag, mountains of black boulders, mazes of chemical-encrusted iron. It is burnt-out, ravaged, raped and discarded. . . .")

In all his kingdom, there was only one element missing: sufficient population to farm those endless plains and make them bountiful. In one of the books he wrote during this reflective period, he produced an epigram which summed up his thinking on the subject: "Population without the Prairie is a mob, and the Prairie without Population is a desert." Of all "his" territory, Montana offered the widest, least populated open spaces; the Northern Pacific alone had a land grant of 20,000,000 acres yawningly unsettled.

Mr. Hill was not one of those tycoons who believed that he had prospered because he had found favor in the eyes of God. He was grateful for all he had gained and wanted to demonstrate his gratitude, once more, before he died. One of the most treasured possessions in his library was the transcript of a speech delivered in 1905 by the eminent Judge Thomas Burke of Seattle, which said in part, "Twenty-five years ago Mr. Hill found the Northwest, between Minnesota and Puget Sound, practically a wild,

325

uninhabited, and inaccessible country. A considerable portion of it used to be set down in the old geographies as a part of the Great American Desert." Yet through Hill's efforts "that region has, in less than fifteen years, given four new states to the Union with an aggregate population of more than one million five hundred thousand people."

Hill was a widely read man, but apparently he had not studied the findings of Major John Wesley Powell when he decided that the best thing he could do for Montana was to fill it up with farmers and small ranchers. Powell had undertaken specific studies of the Montana soil and climate. The state, he wrote in one of his monographs, was covered by "quasi-hay," but its grasslands would be ruined by overgrazing. Furthermore, Montana's average rainfall of 18 inches was 2 inches below the mark Powell deemed sufficient for crop farming. Small farms and ranches would ruin the state. "A quarter-section of land alone will be of no value. The pasturage it will afford will not suffice to maintain a herd that even the poorest man will need for support."

By 1909 Hill had started his campaign to populate Montana with homesteaders. The Secretary of the Interior had just opened up 1,500,000 acres for homesteading, and 1,000,000 acres of it were claimed by settlers in 1909. And all that influx had started before Hill began his campaign to attract settlers by the thousands. Most of those who settled in Montana in 1909 and 1910 had come in via the Northern Pacific; the new migration would be directed via the Great Northern to the northern counties of Montana up against the Canadian border.

One day, in Hill County, which had been named for him, Hill shared his vision with Montanans. He had been on an inspection tour, and a large crowd gathered around the depot at Havre to see him off. Climbing to the seat of the buckboard which had brought him to the station, he launched into a discourse on how he was going to make Montana one of the greatest states in the Union. With his grizzled leonine head he must have looked something like an Old Testament prophet, and certainly his message sounded more like something out of the Bible than the *Wall Street Journal*. He recalled that when he was building the Great Northern more than a score of years before people had repeatedly told him: "You'll never bring anything out of that country but buffalo bones." The warning, he said, had never ceased to grate on him; he was going to devote the last years of his life to proving it was false. Montana would be populated and would prosper as an act of one man's will. Within a few years, he roared, a farm family would be settled on every quarter section or half section in the public domain; dryland villages would grow into towns, towns into cities. Then Hill's special train pulled in, and he boarded it for St. Paul while the crowd went back to the annual fair they had been attending.

Perhaps many of his listeners dismissed the speech as so much oratorical blathering, but within a year they learned that Hill meant every word of his impromptu speech. One year later, in fact, the townspeople of Havre watched a line of prospective homesteaders standing in line for two nights and a day at the United States Land Office to file their claims. The men snatched a few hours' sleep or a meal while their wives or children stood in line for them. The first month 1,600 quarter sections were dispensed by that land office alone.

Hill had undertaken a massive international campaign to bring in settlers. In the Eastern and Midwestern newspapers there were flamboyant columns of advertising. Scores of Hill agents were dispatched with literature and lantern slides to enlist British and Scandinavian farmers in the come-to-Montana movement. His agents kept up a drumfire of propaganda for years, with the result that within the next decade 42 percent of the state was occupied by homesteaders.

Those little illustrated pamphlets and handbooks, which in the past had seduced so many millions into coming west and growing up with the country, were brought to a new plateau of promotional art by Hill's advertising people. Some of those published in foreign languages asserted that Montanans never became ill except from overeating. Preachers were favored as Hill recruiters, it was said, because people tended to believe the promises made by a man of the cloth.

Horseback surveyors, as they were called, quickly selected and allotted the 160-acre plots for the newcomers without taking time to consider whether those quarter sections—whether rich bottomland or arid steppe—would be sufficient to support a man and his family. A new Homestead Law expanded the amount of land a settler could claim, perhaps in belated recognition of John Wesley Powell's teachings, to 320 acres. The newcomers settled in a little more comfortably than those who had pioneered on the old sod house frontier. They built log cabins with roofs made of sod packed between two layers of boards. Often the houses were surrounded by small orchards and flocks of chicken, but few had any dairy cattle, and tins of condensed milk were a staple on their tables.

At least Hill, unlike the railroaders who had populated the Middle Border, did not abandon the people he brought in. He imported prize cattle, those which had the combined qualities of producing the best beef and the richest milk, and gave them to farmers along his right-of-way. He propagandized the virtues of diversified farming and sponsored the yearly Dry Farming Congresses at which farmers were instructed in "scientific farming" allegedly capable of doubling their wheat yields. He gave $1,000 prizes for the best wheat grown on dryland within 25 miles of the Great Northern's right-of-way. And as though to induce a state of self-hypnosis, as a means of wish-fulfillment, he erected billboards along the Great Northern route proclaiming that Montana was THE TREASURE STATE.

Native Montanans, more aware than Hill of the fraility of the prairie environment, of the dangers of intense cultivation causing the soil to blow away, watched all this with growing apprehension. They were beginning to take alarm when more than 20,000 people filed homestead claims in 1914. The last of the great land rushes had begun, and there were people who could remember what had happened to participants in the earlier ones.

The dinning of railroad propaganda dismayed, among many others, Charlie Russell of Great Falls, the celebrated "cowboy artist," who wrote a friend in 1913: "Bob you wouldent know the town or the country either it's all grass side down now. Wher once you rode circle and I night wrangled, a gopher couldn't graze now. The boosters say it is a better country than it ever was but it looks like hell to me. I liked it better when it belonged to God it was sure his country when we knew it."

But what was the grumbling of a few old-timers, with tobacco juice dribbling down their unshaved jaws, compared to the lyrical outpourings of Professor Thomas Shaw, "the well-known agricultural expert," as he was billed, who composed such panegyrics as *Montana: Homesteads in Three Years* and *More Free Homesteads: Another Big Land Opening,* both published by the Great Northern? Never mind that the professor was an expert on the soil of Jim Hill's native Ontario. Shaw wrote in those pamphlets that he had thoroughly examined the soil and climate conditions of Montana and come up with the following conclusions:

> The soil of this entire area is essentially a clay loam, very rich in mineral matter, and it has great staying power. The native grasses are more than ordinarily abundant and in fact this is evidence of producing power that can be relied on. The water supply is relatively good. [Professor Shaw did not say relative to what. The Sahara? The rain forests of Brazil?] In much of this area it is possible to secure a quarter section without a single foot of broken land on it. A portion of this region has been homesteaded for the past two or three years by persons who have prospered since they came. . . .
>
> The Winter climate is less cold than that of eastern Dakota. The snowfall is also usually considerably less than that of the Red River valley. There have been no records kept of the rainfall for any lengthened period, but it is safe to conclude that it is not far different from the rainfall of Williston in North Dakota. This would mean the average rainfall is about 15 to 16 inches in a year, sometimes running higher than 18, sometimes, but rarely, as low as 11 or 12. This is not high rainfall, but it is sufficient to grow crops fair to excellent on summer fallow land any season. . . .

Apparently Professor Shaw had not investigated the records kept at Glasgow, Montana, which had been updated since 1894. During those years there had been "average" rainfall of 15 to 16 inches only three years, there had been no 18-inch rainfalls, and in seven years the total had been 12 inches or less.

Happily for Hill's promotional experts, unhappily for those tens of thousands of new settlers attracted by their promises, the rainfall on the northern plains was above average from 1910 to 1918. In the decade from 1909 to 1919 the Montana wheat acreage increased from 280,000 to 3,417,000. With the rain so plentiful, wheat crops were soaring toward the 50,000,000-bushel mark, and prices were moving up toward the magic $2-a-bushel level. The boom was on, its later phase helped along by the war in Europe and the demand for wheat to supply Britain and France, their allies, and the neutral nations.

There was talk of a "wheat bonanza" more splendiferous than any gold strike, of farmers about to blossom out in striped silk shirts, then the No. 1 status symbol, and take their families to church on Sundays in Henry Ford's flivvers. Land values were shooting up, and predictions were made that the Great War would last a decade, with a continuing demand for all the wheat the northern plains could produce. Hill's homesteaders eagerly complied with the Great Northern's request for testimonials to the goodness of their new lives.

Three Dawson County settlers wrote glowingly of their prospects. H. W. Lebeck, formerly a grocery clerk in Iowa, informed the Great Northern that "with the prospects of the railroad building through this section" his land was now worth $100 an acre. Ola L. Grice enthused in his letter to the Great Northern's St. Paul headquarters that he had started farming with $500 but wouldn't take $5,000 for his homestead, what with "the railroad coming so close to me." William C. Moores, another Dawson County farmer, wrote that only 88 acres of his place was being farmed, but "I consider my place worth $8,000; land is increasing in value with the prospects of the new railroad." All those inflated hopes were based, not on what their land could produce, but on the report that the Great Northern would build a line through Dawson County—that is, on real estate speculation rather than the facts of farm life. The railroad, however, never built that spur. A Montana historian who traced the fortunes of those letter writers learned many years later that the Lebeck family had vanished, that the Grices went back to the Ozarks penniless, and the Moores family abandoned their farm and moved to California, the absolutely final Promised Land on the continent.

Jim Hill brought his "mob" out to the prairies, but the prospering fields and culture-conscious towns he envisioned as part of a new civilization never materialized. It was all done in a rush, at a pace dictated by Hill's own impatient personality and the go-getting spirit of his advertising and promotional executives. Hill was old and ailing, and he wanted to see his dream fulfilled before death came for him in his St. Paul mansion.

There were no solidly built farmhouses or tree-shaded towns with libraries and lyceums of popular culture. Everything was jerry-built, ugly, and utilitarian. Culture was represented by the local nickelodeon. From the grain elevators, which were the real symbol of what Montana had come to mean, and from the dusty little railroad towns, there radiated an endless succession of isolated and forlorn farms, a crazy quilt of small holdings separated by an occasional stockman's spread.

Hill's mob stayed a mob even after it had been transported to the prairies which Hill, through the prismatic vision of the romantic enthusiast, saw as magically providing the good life for thousands who had failed elsewhere. They had brought with them the simple determination to survive and prosper, individually, and what they built during their brief years on the northern plains testified to the drabness of their ambitions. Joseph Kinsey Howard observed:

> The log cabin, tent and tepee of the open range was displaced by the hideous "shack town" of the honyocker [a term usually reserved for the European immigrants, but which could be applied to all the new settlers]: a one-street, one-side-of-the-street "business section," stores with dirty showcases and third-rate goods with unfamiliar brands, soda fountains with charged water, a firetrap movie theater. By day the angry sun blazed down upon the treeless, dusty street; by night the town lay cold and dead and insignificant under the great sky while howling coyotes circled it and sometimes slunk into its alleys to fight the dogs nosing its garbage. . . . Most of these towns grew out of a largely speculative movement. Their founders and some of their customers were in the state primarily to "clean up" and get out.

Perhaps the greatest reward for all the constructive things Jim Hall did in building a network of railroads across the Northwestern states was that he mercifully died, in 1916, before he could realize that his splendid vision would soon be transformed into a nightmare.

Nature, outraged by what had been done to the virgin prairies, brought about that hideous transformation. It took less than a decade from the beginning of Hill's campaign to populate Montana. Deep plowing, advocated by Hill's dryland farming "ex-

331

perts," caused erosion. The wind which never stops blowing over Montana and the Dakotas, scorching out of the south in the summer, frigidly from the Arctic Circle in the winter, whirled away the topsoil which had lost its anchorage.

A single line of statistics encompassed a tragedy that involved thousands of lives. From 1900 to 1916 the plowed-up grasslands of Montana had yielded more than 25 bushels to the acre, but in 1919 the yield fell to 2.4 bushels per acre.

The disasters of the summer of 1919 began in June, which was the driest month in the state's recorded history. June was the month depended on for crop-growing rains, but even the usually verdant and adequately watered Gallatin Valley received less than a tenth of an inch of rainfall. And that almost rainless June had followed two previous summers in which the rainfall was far below normal.

That summer saw the whole northern plains turn brittle with the relentless heat, and the earth was covered with dust as fine as talcum powder. Hot winds whisked the friable topsoil in sun-blotting clouds off to the Canadian provinces. A sort of heat-stricken delirium seemed to take possession of the land. Men working on a dam being built on one of the Yellowstone's tributaries found scorpions thriving in the gravel of the river bottom; the prairie was becoming a desert. At some points it was possible to wade across the Missouri River.

Almost daily thunderheads, great masses of black clouds that looked capable of ending the drought in a few hours, formed and roiled on the horizon and then passed overhead without loosing a raindrop.

All that summer there was a succession of grass and forest fires, hundreds of them at a time, until the fire fighters simply gave up. The great open ranges were so dry or fire-blackened that hay had to be imported from the Midwestern states, and one of the larger cattle ranchers found that his spread of 25,000 acres couldn't provide enough grazing for his herds. While the state commissioner of agriculture complained that the newspapers were exaggerating the effects of the drought, the governor called a special session of the legislature, which produced more hand wringing and recrimination than emergency legislation. About all the federal government was doing to relieve the distress was to grant loans for seed, which had about as much chance of sprouting as the fish had of surviving in the threadlike rivers.

Just during that midsummer period when Montana had become one enormous blasted heath a party of Eastern industrialists arrived on an inspection tour. They shook their heads over what looked like a statewide disaster area.

"All Montana needs," one of their hosts in Great Falls murmured, "is rain."

"Yes," replied a Michigan factory owner, "and that's all hell needs."

In the county named for the late James J. Hill, where he had announced his plan to fill up the prairies just seven years earlier, 3,000 of the homesteaders who had answered his call were reported to be on the verge of starvation; the luckier ones had been living for weeks on a diet of potatoes and eggs.

Various agricultural experts held a symposium in Havre, Hill County, after making a tour of the surrounding countryside but all they produced, after days of learned discourse, was a statement that Montana agriculture was fundamentally sound and the current troubles were due "solely to unusual climatic conditions."

All over Hill County bedraggled and desperate farmers held meetings to urge that some form of governmental help be given them. Early in August District Judge W. B. Rhoades of Havre went down to Great Falls to publicize their plight. For several years, he recalled, Montanans had been urged to contribute to the Red Cross and other agencies collecting funds for the relief of European war victims. Wasn't it time some of that money went to stricken Americans even if they hadn't been shelled or bombarded? he demanded.

He told a reporter from the Great Falls *Leader* of a meeting he had attended at Chester in Hill County a few nights earlier:

> The general expression on the faces of these people was tragic. Several gentlemen undertook to talk about organizing farm bureaus, government irrigation and road work. Many an inhabitant of that region will be an expert harpist before the Milk River reclamation project is complete. That audience was not interested in such subjects—they wanted to know what they were going to have for breakfast!

333

The Red Cross, however, replied that the Montana drought was not a calamity by its definition and that it would be unable to help. It changed its mind later under intense public pressure.

By early autumn thousands of the homesteaders were abandoning their burned-out farms and moving either to various Western cities, where charitable organizations had to provide for their care, or back to where they came from or on to a hoped-for haven in California and the wetter states of the Pacific coast. They had been laboratory animals in an experiment designed to confound the dictum of John Wesley Powell, which he had expressed forty years earlier to prospective dryland settlers, "You're going to need, each year, a little more water than you're going to get."

As Joseph Kinsey Howard surveyed that disaster of 1919, which was followed the next year by gale-force dusters tearing away newly planted seed and soil and causing drifts of dust six feet high in places, Jim Hill's "mob" left Montana in a condition from which it has never fully recovered. Sixty thousand people left the state in the several years following the drought of 1919; a prefiguration of the dust bowl disaster of the thirties when the Okies and other refugees trekked in jalopies to California. Behind them they left a crippled farm economy. Howard noted in 1943:

> Not all of the land they plowed has regained its natural grass cover. The range in the eastern two thirds of Montana, except for scattered sections, is rated "50 to 75 percent depleted." Wind erosion is "severe" in a dozen counties, "moderate to severe" in two dozen. The derelict privy, the boarded-up schoolhouse, the dust-drifted, weed-grown road, and the rotting, rusted fence were left to tell the story. . . .

Today things aren't quite that depressing on the northern Montana plain, but the tidal marks left by Jim Hill's mob of sixty years ago are still visible in abandoned cabins, rotting fence posts, and forgotten hamlets along unused branches of the railroads.

The memory of that disaster has not been erased and makes Montanans severely skeptical of all "big thinking," visionary talk and large-scale projects. Recently that ingrained skepticism was evidenced in the cool welcome given Chet Huntley, who had just retired as a television broadcaster and returned to his native state with plans to build a recreational project called the Big Sky in the Montana Rockies. Huntley, the son of one of Jim Hill's railroaders, found himself suspected for "fronting for eastern capitalists," who are still held accountable for all sorts of misfortunes in the Populist West, and was forced to barnstorm the state to explain at public meetings that he wasn't about to bring down another ecological disaster. "We can't build a fence around Montana," he pleaded. "We're a depressed area. Eighty percent of our college graduates are leaving, and this year they're cutting back university money. There are no jobs and we're not going to get heavy industry. Tourism is our best hope."

But Montanans, remembering other salvationists, most particularly Jim Hill and the last fling of the railroad empire builders, remain skeptical. It will take the passage of another generation or two to make them believe anything good can come from the outside.

14.

The Coming of Amtrak

> The only thing tougher than that steak is the heart
> of a Southern Pacific ticket agent.
> —STAN FREBERG on the subject of a diner's menu

THE fun-and-games aspect of railroad operation vanished a long time ago. Railroading, once the glamor boy of American industries, when a locomotive might race into Dodge City with arrows piercing its funnels and possibly one or two trainmen, has become the drabbest. Once the lordliest, it is now given to pleading for subsidies, tax breaks, public understanding.

On the passenger side of the business, the railroads have become part of a public corporation with a title apparently fabricated from a Meccano set: Amtrak. It is a computerized project, a cannibalization designed to preserve the principal links in passenger service, a device almost as rickety as an old Katy-line bridge over an Oklahoma gulch. Never again will the Wabash Cannonball, the Missouri Pacific Eagle, the Sunshine Special, or the North Coast Limited whistle through the night and awaken in listening boys the desire to run away from home.

The riproaring saga of the promotion, construction, and competition of the Western railroads is ending, apparently, with a dying fall. Ghostly laughter may be heard from the graves of the old Populists: Railroad net income in 1971 amounted to only 2.7 percent of revenues. What the shades of the Noble Knights of

Labor would have to say about the railroad union members receiving their largest wage increase in history just when road after road is tottering toward bankruptcy is unimaginable. The Interstate Commerce Commission reported early in 1972 that five of the country's sixty-nine major lines are bankrupt and seventeen are approaching that stage.

What started out as a jolly tale of piracy has turned into a financial Grand Guignol. Undoubtedly the financial condition of the railroads is traceable to the methods with which they began operating a century and more ago; they could never have overcome the overcapitalization and other forms of self-aggrandizement undertaken by their founders. And for more than half a century the railroad industry has been a chronic invalid, unpitied, at least until recently, by the large section of the populace, which felt it had been victimized.

The Hepburn Act and other legislation which put bite into the enforcement powers of the Interstate Commerce Commission took much of the excess profit out of railroading and eliminated many of the inequities. The railroads were so shaken by outside interference in their operations that a crisis—and with it the first threat of nationalization—arose during World War I, when the railroads proved unable to cope with the transportation needs of the war emergency. Partly, perhaps, it was because the self-confidence of the operators had been so shaken by the ICC's refusal to grant them rate increases at a time when there was a severe shortage of freight cars and by Congressional action which forced the eight-hour day with increased pay for overtime.

The industry simply proved incapable of keeping the freight moving toward the Atlantic ports; shortly before America entered the war, there were 145,000 empty cars on the sidings at Eastern terminals. Just after the United States declared war, the Railway War Board was formed by railroad executives with the high purpose, as they stated it, to "be of the greatest service to our country." The board, however, could only "advise" the participating railroads to operate more efficiently and patriotically. Six months after war was declared, there was complete chaos in the transportation system, a coal famine in the Eastern states, a "shortage" of 158,000 freight cars reported while nearly 200,000 were standing empty in various marshaling yards. The railroad

338

system had broken down in its first major test. Yet one of the main reasons the railroads had been subsidized was to serve as the principal conduit of military supplies and troop movements.

With a most becoming impatience President Woodrow Wilson on the day after Christmas, 1917, took possession of the railroads on behalf of the public interest and appointed Secretary of the Treasury William G. McAdoo as director general of the railroads. In effect, this was temporary nationalization. For more than two years the U.S. government ran the railroads. There would always be controversy over just how well it performed; for one thing Czar McAdoo raised wages by 50 percent during his tenure. It was an emergency measure; the main thing was to break the transportation logjam and keep the armies in Europe supplied. Patriots though they proclaimed themselves, the railroad presidents experienced great difficulty in adjusting themselves to the idea of operating in the national interest. A railroad historian observes:

> One trouble was that too many railroad magnates could not shake off their old autocratic habits. These lordly fellows had now to take orders about the operation of their own trains over their own roads, and often from men who had been their bitterest competitors or, even worse, from Democratic politicians. Not only did they stand exposed as incompetent to manage their own business properly in a time of national emergency, but they found themselves barred from sharing in the juicy war profits that were enriching all the industrialists and financiers with whom they commonly consorted.

Confronted by the railroad presidents' intransigence, which sometimes amounted to various forms of subtle sabotage, McAdoo was forced to dismiss the companies as his agents in operating each road and instead appoint a responsbile officer reporting to a regional director—one, in other words, who could be held accountable. After that the nationalized system worked a lot better.

The moment the railroads were allowed to reclaim their property—not without misgivings in Congress, the ICC, and elsewhere—they began presenting the government with grossly inflated claims for damage they asserted had been done to their rolling stock, tracks, equipment, etc. during the period of government control. Among the Western railroads, the Santa Fe demanded almost $98,000,000, the Chicago, Milwaukee & St. Paul $26,000,000. As an indication of how rapacious the railroad magnates had become during their two years of brooding over their displacement by Washington bureaucrats, only 5 percent of their total claims were reimbursed.

During the 1920's, with the Republicans back in charge of the government and inclined as always to look kindly upon the railroads, the magnates recovered much of their self-esteem. Freight rates and passenger fares were raised, and the wages of railroad employees were reduced with the consent of the Railway Labor Board. During the depression of the thirties, their fortunes declined with the rest of American industry, all-time net profits of $1.25 billion in 1929 plummeting to $326,000,000 in 1932. Thirty-eight Class A railroads tumbled into bankruptcy or receivership. World War II revived the whole industry as it profited mightily from moving troops and supplies for a two-ocean conflict.

Everyone knows what happened after those booming World War II years when railroad presidents openly proclaimed that their net profits would burst through the $2 billion ceiling, given a prolonged war and other benefits. Within a few years the airlines were grabbing much of their passenger business, and the rapid growth of the trucking industry cut deeply into their freight revenues. Partly those losses were the railroads' own fault. They had begun lopping passenger trains off their schedules as far back as 1920. The energetic and imaginative but doomed Robert R. Young, the last man to try on the mantle of the old-style swash-buckling railroad magnate, tried to reverse the process. His life ended with suicide. A general decision was made by the industry to kill off passenger service—people were a lot more trouble to transport than uncomplaining freight—and survive on the more lucrative freight business.

Not surprisingly, considering its long record of intense self-interest, the Southern Pacific among the Western railroads led the way in shucking off the passenger business. In the summer of 1956 president Donald J. Russell of the Southern Pacific told a San Francisco newspaper that long-distance travel by rail would soon be a thing of the past for Americans. A decade later Mr. Russell's prediction was proving accurate, with fewer than 900 intercity passenger trains in service against about 20,000 in 1929. Americans began wondering aloud why their little cousins, the Canadians, could travel from coast to coast quickly and conveniently by rail while in the United States passenger trains were becoming pigpens. President Johnson in 1965 tried to upgrade passenger service with one of the many splendidly titled programs sprouted by his administration. It was called the High-Speed Ground Transportation Act. Who remembers it? What happened to the $90,000,000 the bill authorized for new passenger equipment and research into ways of improving passenger service? Whatever happened to that Johnsonian projection, the train that was supposed to hurtle from Boston to Washington?

Soon afterward, apparently as a public-relations gesture, the railroad industry pledged itself to "cooperate with the Administration by making every reasonable effort to place its intercity passenger service on a paying basis." Its actions, however, spoke louder than any publicity handout. Trains continued to be discontinued almost weekly through the remainder of the Johnson administration.

The Southern Pacific's campaign to do in the Lark, the one justly celebrated overnight train between Los Angeles and San Francisco, was just one example of the railroad's tactics. For some time the railroad had been paying for advertisements in which the railroad passenger was referred to as "The Vanishing American" and the virtues of air travel were cited. When that didn't discourage enough of its unwanted customers, the Southern Pacific reduced the level of service on the Lark to that of its cattle cars. The meal served in its dining cars called for the talents of a short-order cook: bacon and eggs, ham and cheese sandwich, hamburger or sirloin steak sandwich (the latter with a list price of $3.25). And that was the dinner menu. "The only thing tougher than that steak," wrote a Los Angeles humorist, "is the heart of a Southern Pacific ticket agent." By way of explanation for that assault on public sensibility, the Southern Pacific commissioned a study titled "The Future of Rail Passenger Traffic in the West" from the Stanford Research Institute. No doubt the SP executives were pleased with the institute's findings that it was ridiculous for any Western railroad to stay in the passenger business.

Then came the patchwork device called Amtrak; the perhaps inevitable legacy of the Goulds, Huntingtons, Sages, Harrimans, and all the rest. Americans now can ride comfortably and quickly on a railroad train only by crossing the border into Canada or going over to Europe, where the Eurail system demonstrates that travel by rail is not necessarily as outdated as the oxcart. In this country they are at the mercy of a Congress-created National Railroad Passenger Corporation, which under the Amtrak system reduced the number of intercity passenger trains from 360 to 184. "The hitch is," as one commentator has observed, "Amtrak's trains run by the grace of the same railroads that, in a fit of mass pique, deliberately sent passenger service down the tubes decades ago."

The railroads, despite their abdication of responsibility for hauling passengers, are opposed to complete nationalization. After all, there's still money to be made in the freight traffic if it is efficiently managed. Furthermore, their executives point out, it would cost the government between $28 billion and $60 billion to acquire their property at a "fair market price," whatever that might mean. In addition, they say, the government would have to spend another $36 billion in the next ten years for modernization.

No, they argue, let the railroads do it, with, of course, government asssistance. (They were, after all, our first welfare recipients.) So in 1971, with the approval of the American Railroad Association, the Hartke-Adams Bill was introduced in Congress. This provides for a $5 billion fund to provide loans or loan guarantees for the railroads to upgrade their freight service. Railroads would be enabled to abandon service that is losing them money by notifying the ICC forty-five days in advance. Each state would be required to use at least 5 percent of its federal highway allocation to improve grade crossings (a generally ignored statistic being that 1,500 deaths and 3,700 injuries occur annually at the 180,000 unguarded grade crossings in the United States). For the railroads, of course, this would be the nicest bit of legislation since the salad days of the Crédit Mobilier.

For support of that or any other measures, except those in

342

which the public would clearly stand to gain (through safeguarding the environment, for instance, rail service being so much less obnoxious than other forms of transportation), the railroad industry can hardly count on a nation grateful for past benefactions.

What the railroads did to the West alone entitles them to suspicion of their motives in whatever they undertake. The nightmare they created by populating the Western states so rapidly and haphazardly and the way they profited from it are not something from which all Americans have awakened.

Some of the railroads will not let them. The Southern Pacific, for instance, has been laboring mightily to obliterate the old octopus image, yet in California, where the greatest wealth derives from agricultural lands, the SP is the largest private landowner. Its holdings comprise an area the size of Maine; its properties range from an alpine wilderness in the north between Yreka and Redding to vast tracts on the southern deserts. It is the largest private owner of timberland. During 1971 its income from all those holdings amounted to $11,000,000. The Southern Pacific no longer sells; it leases.

Of the 17,000,000 acres the railroad received in land grants in five states, it still holds 3,800,000 acres, of which 2,042,651 are in California. The political and economic power generated by those holdings have recently attracted the attention of Ralph Nader, who contends that the Southern Pacific holds the land illegally. The federal grants, after all, weren't made on the premise that the railroads would keep them in perpetuity but would break them up into small holdings and dispose of them as quickly as possible. The idea was to help thousands of homesteaders, not a few lordly land companies.

Instead, the Southern Pacific plays the role of landlord and, as a recent Los Angeles newspaper survey indicated, "still benefits from large government subsidies similar to the land grants and direct cash payments it received in the 1800's for building rail lines to open up the west."

The political clout still wielded by the Southern Pacific, despite the fact that the state's two Senators are ultraliberal Democrats, is highly visible in the Westlands Water District on the west side of the bountiful San Joaquin Valley. This region in Fresno and

Kings counties, comprising 600,000 acres, is the richest tract of agricultural land in the United States. Southern Pacific owns much of that land, which soon will be receiving more federal irrigation than any other water district in the country.

A project costing the federal government $679,000,000 but benefiting the Westlands Water District almost exclusively, through the Los Banos Dam and a 102-mile canal, was pushed through Congress. When it is fully operative, it will increase farm income in the district from $80,000,000 to an estimated $225,000,000 annually.

Southern Pacific's largest tenant in the district is Giffen, Inc., which leases 30,000 acres from the railroad's land company. Russel Giffen, the president of the company, who lives in what has been described as "baronial splendor" in a mansion on the Kings River, is the largest cotton grower in the United States. He was also the second-largest recipient in crop subsidies in the country, taking in $4,100,000 from the federal government in 1970; the top recipient that year was the J. G. Boswell Company with $4,400,000, and that combine is also located in the Westlands Water District.

Southern Pacific's interests are represented on the Westlands Water District Board to a striking degree. Giffens, its largest lessee, is president of the board. Three other members lease land from the railroad. Another is the father of a lessee, and still another is an employee of the Southern Pacific

The advantages of obtaining water from a federal irrigation project are obvious. Users in the Westlands district will have to pay only $12 to $14 an acre-foot, while those just outside the district receiving state water pay about $30. There is a legal catch, however, to receiving the cheaper federal water: A 1902 law states that no landowner can obtain federal water for more than 160 acres. The law, of course, was designed to benefit the small holder. As with most laws, there is a loophole. Larger landowners can receive federal water if they sign contracts with the reclamation bureau agreeing to sell all but 160 acres of their holdings within ten years. That gives the Southern Pacific lessees a full decade of high profits assured through a project built with the taxpayers' money.

Fashionable liberals and hard-rock conservatives alike seem to find a cozy bedfellowship in serving the Southern Pacific'a continuing barony in the state. Senators John Tunney and Alan Cranston deployed on its behalf in 1971 when the Nixon administration froze the funds for the water distribution system, and at the same time Governor Ronald Reagan signed a bill which was for the sole benefit of the Westlands Water District.

In addition to its agricultural lands, the Southern Pacific's domain includes the largest private timber holdings in the state, most of the forested tracts being located near the Oregon border and on both sides of the Donner Pass. Of the 750,000 acres the railroad owns between Redding and Yreka, 450,000 are covered with commercial-grade timber.

Obviously the Southern Pacific still clings to an inordinate amount of power in California, even if it could not summon up the corporate strength to serve a decent meal on the Lark.

All through the American heartland, across the 1,000-mile prairie between North Dakota and Texas, the lights are going out in small towns and farmhouses once established with the high hopes fostered by the railroad promoters. Mechanization, of course, has been steadily killing off the small farms and reducing the total farm population from 15,000,000 to 10,000,000 in the last decade. But those same communities might have proved viable if their establishment had been governed by the teachings of John Wesley Powell, if they had been kept within the bounds dictated by the land's ability to sustain a modest population equally sharing the resources instead of bending to the self-serving clamor of the railroads that there was tillable land and bountiful lives for all.

The endless wheatlands of the northern tier of states, once part of James J. Hill's "inland empire," are being deserted by thousands of people annually, leaving nothing behind but empty farmhouses and ghostly hamlets where the whistle of the Great Northern is no longer heard. The fathers and grandfathers of the survivors were convinced by the railroad propagandists that they could prosper on any old quarter section of land; they learned that even a half section of good land wasn't quite enough for a marginal existence.

The 1970 census tells the story statistically, but without the thousands of personal defeats and tragedies they encompass. Five farm states in the upper Middle West showed declines in population in 316 of their 417 counties. Two of the three states which showed a loss in net population during the 1960–1970 decade were North and South Dakota. Thousands of towns and villages, mostly between the Mississippi and the Rockies, the area which the railroads populated almost overnight with their come-all-ye's, have become so depleted of their human resources that, as one contemporary report puts it, they "no longer function as economic units." For the young people left in those dying communities there is no opportunity; for the aged there are no doctors. Only the really successful can survive in the farms along the old Middle Border. In Nebraska, 67 counties of its 93 counties reported decreasing populations in the 1970 census, yet in 91 of the state's counties there were steady increases in real per capita income. It is significant that the size of a Nebraska farm has increased during the past fifteen years from 474 to 659 acres, or more than a section, and much more than even Powell thought necessary for dryland farming.

One little town on the northern plains, which like so many others sprang into existence when the Northern Pacific and the Burlington were extended through the wheatlands, is fairly typical of those deserted villages Oliver Goldsmith foresaw (though not in youthful America).

Vienna, South Dakota, boasted four grain elevators, a stockyard, a lumberyard, a flour mill, two hotels, a theater, a newspaper, three saloons, and a blacksmith shop before World War I. Each hotel operated a hack which went down to the depot and met the trains.

The modest glory that was Vienna is long gone with most of the population, which dropped from 191 in 1960 to 103 in the spring of 1971. There is only one elevator left, operated by the Vienna Grain Company, which ships out the wheat, barley, and oats raised by the remaining farmers in the bleak countryside. The two-story brick schoolhouse built in 1914 when optimism ran high over the wartime boom in the wheat market is now boarded up and used by a farmer as winter storage for his bees. There are still two small groceries in Vienna, but the village's weekend shopping is done in the supermarkets of the nearest trading

346

centers. Many of the houses on Main Street, once as busy as Sinclair Lewis' Gopher Prairie, are either boarded up and abandoned or have burned down. Even the shade trees planted by the town's founders to arch gracefully over Main Street are dying.

Unlike Goldsmith's village, Vienna never saw any accumulation of wealth or, for that matter, any decay in its people. They were driven out by the steady seepage of the opportunity to make a living. The area was settled back in the early 1880's, less than a half dozen years after the Battle of the Little Bighorn, when the Plains Indians were forced onto reservations. Most of the country around Vienna was a patchwork quilt of quarter-section homesteads. When the railroad came, there was a promise of prosperity, but it was fulfilled only during the widely separated boom periods, usually associated with a war in Europe or famine elsewhere.

On farm after farm around Vienna which has been tilled for three generations the people are selling their household goods and moving to the cities. In 1880 an immigrant named Hans Jorgensen took up a quarter section near Vienna. His grandson, Elwood Jorgensen, is one of the many farmers in the vicinity who have been forced to abandon their holdings. He managed to expand his acreage to 320 acres, a half section, and farm it alone with modern equipment. Three times, however, his harvests were wiped out late in the summer by prolonged hailstorms, and over the years the price of wheat fell from $2.50 a bushel to $1.57, flax from $8.30 to $2.44, rye from $3.40 to 93 cents. Buying new equipment kept him in constant debt, and in the last few years his net income never rose above $1,200. For all the hardships, Jorgensen recently abandoned his farm and found that, after auctioning all his equipment and other possessions and paying what he owed the banks, he had just $506 left with which to start a new life.

That was the net profit from the crushing labor of three generations on the harsh and lonely Dakota plains.

There might be comfort in the thought that Americans have learned something from the savaging of the West, but that would be an illusion. The old land-settling techniques of the rush, the stampede, the race for staking claims, so attuned to the competitive elements in the American character, are still favored, though their picturesque aspects have largely disappeared.

Just as this is written there are prospects of another land rush, this time in the state of Alaska. Eighty million acres of Alaskan wilderness have proved an overwhelming temptation for the forces of exploitation which usually, through sheer erosion of the public's will, get their own way in such matters. An area twelve times the size Maryland is up for grabs despite the protests of those concerned about the environment—which in Alaska, with its tundra and treeless barrens, is as delicately balanced and ecologically fragile as the grasslands we turned into a dust bowl. Those who care about preserving that balance want the 80,000,000 acres kept as federal land. How long they will be able to hold back the private interests, oil, mining, and others, which yearn to invade the virgin land is questionable. Perhaps as long as ecology is a modish intellectual concern.

Elsewhere, and similarly, the wide-open spaces still remaining are being exploited with the same savage enthusiasm as obtained during the last century. We have not advanced far in spirit from that noon hour on April 22, 1889, when some 50,000 settlers scrambled, elbowed, and stampeded their way into Indian Territory.

Circumstances, of course, have changed somewhat. Today's land rushes are not generally sponsored by railroads or centered on homesteading, nor are their participants gaunt pioneer types or European peasants just off the boat. The object of the new stampedes is vacation and retirement property. Yet the techniques with which the modern land rush is motivated and encouraged are strikingly similar to the blandishments of the railroad promoters and land boomers of almost a century ago. A recent account of this growingly frenetic activity observes that "property that is often much less desirable than the Oklahoma Territory is being peddled as shamelessly as snake oil." Huge tracts of wilderness, much of it on the southwestern deserts, are being bought up by development companies and sold in subdivisions. "The selling effort typically includes idyllic newspaper and magazine ads, mass telephoning, softening-up cocktail parties and dinners for prospective customers, paid transportation to the site. . . ." Even as their nineteenth-century counterparts.

348

In New Mexico there are 100 companies reportedly controlling more than 1,000,000 acres, with enough land on their hands to triple the state's population from about 1,000,000 to 3,000,000. Such projects in California now occupy an area larger than the state of Rhode Island. In Colorado the State Land Board estimates that land developers control about 2,000,000 acres. Apparently there is still an unappeased land hunger in Americans, a hangover from their peasant ancestry. One of the larger California developers has sold 40,000 plots of its land, but only 600 have houses built on them. Americans continue to experience the urge to have a place where they can "get away from it all," a transmutation of the pioneering instinct which motivated their forebears.

We also failed to learn a lesson about granting enormous power and privilege to certain industries. The railroads expanded on beneficial legislation, subsidies from the treasury, and grants from the public domain and became monsters preying on the public interest. Since then a complaisant electorate has watched with varying degrees of dismay the growth of what is pejoratively known as the military-industrial complex. The aircraft industry and the airlines have cozily occupied the same privileged position once accorded the railroads.

Nor have we prevented a virtual monopoly from being established over the equally crucial communications industry, the "media," the television networks. In this case, again, circumstances have shifted, but the effects are much the same. The airwaves are as much a part of the public domain as the lands which were distributed to the railroads a century ago, yet they are monopolized by corporations exercising the same sort of political and journalistic influence. In many cities both the newspapers and the television and radio broadcasting facilities are owned by the same company. The manner in which former President Lyndon B. Johnson obtained the television franchise in Austin, Texas, while a U.S. Senator and apparently kept out any competing interests is especially instructive. Television franchises are obtained in much the same fashion as railroad corporations wangled their rights-of-way. The FCC, judging by the way the television industry is allowed to operate, is just about as much a toothless tiger as the ICC was before the Populist Revolt.

Now, ironically, the discomfiting shoe is on the other foot. Once the defenders of what reformers called the oligarchy, of the railroads and other privileged interests, the Republicans now find themselves complaining they are being victimized by the new elite. Conservative Republicans, especially, have agreed with Vice President Spiro Agnew and others that an "oligopoly"—now a more fashionable term than oligarchy—controls the airwaves and the media using them. A conservative commentator notes that railroads, public utilities, and the manufacturing industries account for less of the gross national product each year and the "Knowledge and Communications industries are in the ascendant; their politics are liberal and usually Democratic, just as yesteryear's industrial robber barons were conservative and usually Republican. The television networks were the linchpins of, and propagandists for, these liberal   interests." The Republicans, he added, are trying to break up "unfair" concentrations of power. "Even the geography of Populism is repeating itself. Liberal and network strength is concentrated in the Northeast, especially in the Washington-New York-Boston axis. Support for the media hostility of the Nixon Administration is greatest in the South, the Rocky Mountains, the Plains, the Southwest, the Border and the Archie Bunker-Spiro Agnew neighborhoods of the industrial north. We live in a communications-based society, and the role of the broadcast media is a question of more than constitutional significance. . ."

So it appears that we have learned little or nothing from the rail-borne conquest of the West. Each new comfort provided by an industrial society, whether it was a dusty green-plush seat in a Santa Fe daycoach or a color television set, has brought the threat of constricting our lives in one way or another through the privileges acquired by that convenience. Those purveyors of our comforts and pleasures, however, should take heed of history, which has not really been abolished in favor of nowness. They risk that backlash of the outraged spirit—call it Populism—which has always been more of a popular mood than a political movement. They can become as obsolete as the remembered echo of the Wabash Cannonball whistling through the Indiana cornfields.

Notes on Sources

The complete listing of most of the sources indicated below under their authors' surnames may be found in the Bibliography, which follows.

1. THE TEMPLATE OF CORRUPTION

The now-obscure John I. Blair's activities are traceable in Iowa Documents, Reports of State Officers, 1878; the New York *Tribune*, August 27, 1899; Executive Documents, 40th Congress, 2d Session, 1867–1868, Nos. 181 to 252.

Governor Larrabee is quoted by Myers, *History of the Great American Fortunes*, p. 512.

For Russell Sage's career, there is his sole biography, Paul Sarnoff's *Russell Sage: The Money King*.

Legislative bribery in Wisconsin was disclosed in the report of the Select Committee, appointed to investigate the disposition of the 1856 land grant, which was published in 1858.

Sage's profiteering methods were revealed in his letters, deposited later in the Joseph P. Dodge Collection of the Wisconsin Historical Society in Madison. They showed how he supplied, at great profit to himself, all the equipment for the La Crosse & Milwaukee.

Sage's maneuvers in Minnesota were recounted in the report of Governor W. A. Gorman, *Minnesota Council Journal*, 1856.

Ignatius Donnelly's early career is explored by Holbrook, *Dreamers of the American Dream*, pp. 154–58, and Dudley S. Brainard, "Nininger, a Boom Town," *Minnesota History* (June, 1932).

Dr. Frank H. Dixon quotation from his *State Railroad Control*, p. 24.

The Minnesota massacres of 1862 are described in Evan Jones' *The Minnesota: Forgotten River*, *passim*, and O'Connor, *The German-Americans*, pp. 192–98.

2. The Union Pacific Arrows West

The Union Pacific stockholders' first meeting is described by Griswold, *A Work of Giants*, pp. 55–56.

President Lincoln's support of the Union Pacific scheme is cited by Perkins, *Trails, Rails and War*, pp. 57, 64.

The role of George Francis Train in promoting the Union Pacific is carefully traced by Thornton, *The Nine Lives of Citizen Train*, *passim*.

Peter Dey's letter of resignation as chief engineer for the Union Pacific is quoted by Perkins, *op. cit.*, p. 135.

General Dodge on the selection of the Union Pacific route, his memoir, *How We Built the Union Pacific*, p. 28.

How the UP work force was organized is related by Griswold, pp. 164–66, and Holbrook, *The Story of the American Railroads*, p. 169.

The description of North Platte by H. M. Stanley is from his *My Early Travels and Adventures in America and Asia*, p. 112.

E. C. Lockwood's recollections of the rigors of working on the railroad were published in the *Union Pacific Magazine* (February, 1931).

William Henry Jackson described the force of a Platte storm in his diary, now in the possession of the New York Public Library's Manuscript Division.

Lockwood's description of Spotted Tail's visit, *op. cit.*

General Sherman's report on difficulties with the Indians, House Executive Document No. 23, 39th Congress, 2d Session.

Jack Casement's letter to his wife on the spring disasters may be found in the Casement Letters collection at the North Oklahoma Junior College's library.

Dodge's report to General Sherman is quoted by Perkins, *op. cit.*, pp. 208–9.

Oakes Ames' complaint to General Dodge about Durant is quoted by Griswold, *op. cit.*, p. 217.

General Dodge's despairing letter to Sidney Dillon may be found in the Dodge Letterbooks, now in the possession of the Council Bluffs Public Library.

Dodge to Ames on pushing ahead to Salt Lake, *ibid.*

H. M. Stanley's description of hellish nights in Julesburg, *My Early Travels*, p. 112.

Dodge's showdown with Durant is described by Perkins, *op. cit.*, pp. 218–20.

Dodge's blustering letter to Samuel S. Montague, *ibid.*, p. 228.

3. CRAZY JUDAH'S DREAM

Theodore Judah's career is delineated by Oscar Lewis, *The Big Four*, pp. 3–48.

Collis P. Huntington on his pay-as-you-go policy, quoted by Quiett, *They Built the West*, p. 77.

Central Pacific's outing for the legislature, Sacramento *Union*, March 21, 1864.

Central Pacific's recruitment of child labor, Lewis, *op. cit.*, pp. 68–69; Charles Edward Russell's *Stories of the Great Railroads*, pp. 120–25.

Importation of Chinese laborers, Lewis, p. 72; Russell, p. 125.

The Reverend Mr. Gibson's protest against mistreatment of Chinese immigrants is quoted by Griswold, p. 119.

Observer quoted on the perils of building over the Sierras in Russell, p. 125.

Albert D. Richardson's description of Chinese "army" laboring over the Sierra passes from his *Beyond the Mississippi*, pp. 90–91.

Actual construction costs on the Central Pacific are cited by Lewis, p. 86.

The foothill newspaper which complained about CP freight rates was the Grass Valley *National* (undated), which may be found in the files of the Sacramento Public Library.

Description of guerrilla warfare between UP and CP work gangs in Lewis, p. 92.

Glenn C. Quiett's analysis of railroads' financial maneuvers, *They Built the West*, p. 81.

For a conservative account of how much was mulcted by the Crédit Mobilier insiders, see Robert W. Fogel's *The Union Pacific Railroad: A Case in Premature Enterprise.*

Meeting of the Crédit Mobilier stockholders in January, 1868, is detailed in the House of Representatives Report No. 77, 42nd Congress, 3d Session, pp. 45–46, 91–93.

Charles Francis Adams' attack on the Crédit Mobilier, "The Pacific Railroad Ring," was published in the *North American Review* (January, 1869).

4. A Frenzy of Expectation

Jay Cooke's disastrous experience with the Northern Pacific is described by Smalley, *History of the Northern Pacific, passim.*

Historian quoted on Cooke's promotional campaigns, *ibid.*, p. 102.

Progress of the Burlington Road is described by Overton, *Burlington West*, pp. 26–27.

Representative Knott's satiric essay on railroading is quoted by Holbrook, *op. cit.*, pp. 150–52.

Californian's description of railroads' extortionate methods is quoted by Quiett, *op. cit.*, p. 83.

William A. Bell's observations on the process of town building were included in his *New Tracks in North America*, pp. 118–20.

Albert Richardson confessed to his own participation in "land grabbing" in *Beyond the Mississippi*, pp. 177–78.

Atchison, Kansas; success in making itself a transportation center is related by George L. Anderson, "Atchison and the Central Branch Country," *Kansas Historical Society Quarterly* (Spring, 1862).

The Atchison *Daily Champion* editorial was published on May 16, 1867.

Colonel George's plaintive query on Montana's difficulties was published by the Helena *Herald*, January 2, 1873.

The background of Montana's troubles in obtaining rail service is conveyed by Robert G. Athearn, "Railroad to a Faroff Montana," *Montana* (Autumn, 1968), and Merrill D. Beal's *Intermountain Railroads, passim.*

Editorial on the "iron key" published by the Helena *Independent*, July 17, 1875.

Butte's claims for rail service were pressed in a Butte *Weekly Miner* editorial, February 17, 1880.

Dillon's correspondence may be found in the Office of the President file, March–September, 1882, Union Pacific Archives.

The handbill on the "new town of Balderdash" was quoted by Quiett, *op. cit.*, p. 280.

5. ALONG THE SODHOUSE FRONTIER

Quotation from Walter Prescott Webb on the technology's role in settling the west is from his masterwork, *The Great Plains*, p. 280.

Department of Agriculture warning to prospective settlers was included in the *Report of the Department of Agriculture, 1871*, p. 497.

Warnings on the trickiness of the Western climate were cited by Robert D. Ward, *The Climates of the United States*, pp. 337, 405.

Peter Bryant's letters were published by the *Kansas Historical Quarterly* (Autumn, 1961). Bryant survived his graphically related pioneering experiences to become a leading citizen of northeastern Kansas.

Matt Hawkinson's story is related in Walter Havighurst's chapter "The Sodbusters" in *This Is the West*, edited by Robert West Howard.

The story of Greeley, Colorado's colonization is told by Boyd, *Greeley and the Union Colony, passim*, and Quiett, pp. 115–41.

Nathan Meeker's description of Sheridan, Wyoming, was published by the New York *Tribune*, November 14, 1869.

The disgusted Greeley colonist's letter was published by the Milwaukee *Sentinel*, June 28, 1870.

Meeker on educating the Indians, quoted by Quiett, pp. 139–40.

Hamlin Garland's poems were published in *Prairie Songs*, Cambridge, 1903. Likewise "The Farmer's Wife."

His description of the plight of prairie girls was included in *The Rose of Dutcher's Coolly* (New York, 1899), pp. 70–71.

6. GOLD FROM THE RUSSIAN STEPPES

Jay Gould's testimony before the Pacific Railway Commission in April, 1887, is quoted in O'Connor, *Gould's Millions*, p. 117.

Arthur Wellington's observations on locating the Western railroads were quoted by Holbrook, *op. cit.*, p. 192.

Walter Prescott Webb on the economic prospects of those railroads, *The Great Plains*, pp. 274–75.

The violently anti-Gould editorial was published by the New York *World* on September 1, 1873.

Gould's maneuvers against the Union Pacific and Kansas Pacific were surveyed in O'Connor, *op. cit.*, pp. 103–17.

Gould's profits on the UP-KP merger were cited in the *Pacific Railway Commission Report*, Vol. I.

The establishment of the Yeovil Colony was related by Holbrook, *op. cit.*, pp. 155–56.

The extravagant claims made by railroad pamphleteers are examined by Hicks, *The Populist Revolt*, pp. 6–10; Overton, *Burlington West*, pp. 368–69.

The success of the Santa Fe is outlined by Waters, *Steel Rails to Santa Fe, passim.*

Fred Harvey's success as purveyor to Santa Fe passengers is related by Holbrook, *op. cit.*, pp. 214–16; Marshall, *Santa Fe, The Railroad That Built an Empire, passim.*

Russian background of the German Mennonites is recorded by Elmer Clark in *The Small Sects in America, passim.*

C. B. Schmidt's mission to Russia is covered by Holbrook, *op. cit.*, p. 208; Laut, *The Romance of the Rails*, Vol. II, pp. 407–9; Clark, *op. cit.*, pp. 232–33.

The Claas Epps schism among the Mennonites was related by Smith, *The Mennonites*, Chapter 7.

Carl J. Ernst's hijacking of Mennonite and other immigrants was confessed in his article "The Railroad as a Creator of Wealth," *Nebraska History* (January, 1924).

Mennonites' reception in the United States, Holbrook, *op. cit.*, pp. 208–9.

Travail of the Hutterian Brethren, Clark, *op. cit.*, p. 234.

Mennonites' importation of hardier wheat seeds, Laut, *op. cit.*, Vol. II, p. 409.

7. THE INVASION OF THE INDIAN TERRITORY

The early history of the Missouri, Kansas & Texas is sketched in lively fashion in V. V. Masterson's *The Katy Railroad* and *The Opening of the Great Southwest*, produced by anonymous hands and published by the Katy in 1945.

The most authoritative works on the history of Indian Territory were Grant Foreman's *Advancing the Frontier, Indian Removal,* and *The Five Civilized Tribes.* Foreman was an Oklahoma lawyer whose books were based on personal knowledge and sources unavailable to anyone else.

Description of hellish conditions in Denisen was quoted by Holbrook, *op. cit.*, pp. 217–18.

Other citations of violence left in the wake of Katy construction may be found in *The Opening of the Great Southwest, passim.*

The Kansas City *Times* published its charges against a corrupt "Indian ring" on April 29, 1879.

A description of David Payne's career may be found in his biography, Rister's *Land Hunger*, pp. 25, 41–50.

Boudinot's article discussing the "unassigned lands" was published by the Chicago *Times*, February 15, 1879.

Murdock's opposition to the occupation of the Indian Territory was expressed in the Wichita *Eagle*, February 23, 1879.

Payne's organization of the Oklahoma Colony, Rister, *op. cit.*, pp. 50–53.

Payne's fascination as described by the daughter of a Boomer was quoted by Alice Marriott in her chapter, "The Ladies," *This Was the West*, *op. cit.*, p. 106.

The Boomers' attempts to evade the cavalry, *ibid.*, pp. 106–7.

The story of the Oklahoma "rush" of 1889 is told by Rister, *passim*; Nye, *Carbine and Lance*, pp. 391–92, 393–94.

Gould's takeover of the Katy is recorded by Masterson, *op. cit.*, pp. 223–24, 239–40.

The Katy's "monster train wreck" was covered by the Dallas *Morning News*, September 16, 1896.

8. RAILROAD WAR IN THE ROCKIES

Thomas A. Scott's struggles to build the Texas & Pacific were related by Hubert H. Bancroft, *Chronicles of the Builders, passim*, and Russell, *op. cit., passim*.

Huntington's summation of Scott's character was quoted by Quiett, *op. cit.*, p. 239.

The Huntington-Colton letters were published by the New York *Sun*, December 29 and 30, 1883.

Leland Stanford's speech on the Southern Pacific's "destiny" was reported by the San Francisco *Chronicle*, May 19, 1875.

Gould's tale of how he took the Texas & Pacific off Scott's hands, Don C. Seitz's *Joseph Pulitzer: His Life and Letters*, p. 114.

Gould's maneuvers against Huntington, O'Connor, *op. cit.*, pp. 176–78.

General Palmer's achievements as builder of Kansas Pacific as viewed by contemporary journalist, quoted by Quiett, *op. cit.*, pp. 49–50.

Palmer's organization of the Denver & Rio Grande was described by Bell, *op. cit., passim*, and Peabody, *William Jackson Palmer, Pathfinder and Builder, passim*.

Description of construction through Animas Canyon, Quiett, *op. cit.*, p. 53.

The struggle between the Denver & Rio Grande and the Santa Fe was described in definitive detail by Peabody, *op. cit.*, and Bradley, *Story of the Santa Fe, passim.*

The strife between Palmer and Strong was detailed by the Denver *Republican*, June 2, 1879.

Account of the Pueblo roundhouse siege and events surrounding it, O'Connor, *Bat Masterson*, pp. 102–4.

How Conductor Watlington averted a train wreck is told by Holbrook, *op. cit.*, p. 213.

General Palmer's recollection of Sheridan, Wyoming, quoted by Peabody, *op. cit.*, p. 24.

Colorado National Guard attack on Ludlow reported by the New York *Times*, April 22–25, 1914.

9. A VISION OF WHAT MIGHT HAVE BEEN

Western historian quoted on slaughter of the buffalo, Wellman, *The Indian Wars of the West*, p. 104.

The Cheyenne attacks on the Union Pacific are related by Brown, *Bury My Heart at Wounded Knee*, p. 139.

Sitting Bull's speech at the Northern Pacific completion ceremony was quoted by Kate E. Glaspell, "Incidents in the Life of a Pioneer," *North Dakota Historical Quarterly*, Vol. VIII (1941), pp. 187–88.

John Wesley Powell's background and career are ably recited by his biographers: Stegner, *Beyond the Hundredth Meridian*; Darrah, *Powell of the Colorado*, and Terrell, *The Man Who Rediscovered America.*

Quotations from Powell on treatment of the Indians are from *Report of the Special Committee*, December 18, 1873, pp. 65–66.

The Washington journalist who satirized Powell's accomplishments was Donn Piatt in the Washington *Gazette*, December 19, 1875. His defender was the *Illustrated Washington Chronicle*, January 2, 1876.

Powell's speech before the National Academy of Sciences was reported in the New York *Tribune*, April 28, 1877.

Stegner's observation on his challenge to popular myths, *Beyond the Hundredth Meridian*, p. 212.

Powell's argument on interdependence was part of a speech before the Anthropological Society of Washington, as reported by the Washington *Gazette*, May 12, 1885.

The Congressional attack on Powell's report is from the *Congressional Record*, 45th Congress, 3d Session, Parts 2 and 3.

Powell's plea for understanding the Indians was from *Report on the Methods of Surveying the Public Domain*, pp. 15–16.

His definition of Indian civilization is quoted by Terrell, *op. cit.*, p. 222.

The disastrous winter of 1886 on the Great Plains is described by Sandoz, *The Cattlemen*, pp. 258–71.

Nebraska historian quoted, *ibid.*, p. 265.

Bernard DeVoto's comment on Powell's work was part of his introduction to Stegner's biography of Powell, p. XXII.

10. CALIFORNIA'S OCTOPUS (I)

Denis Kearney's speech to his following is quoted by Lewis, *The Big Four*, p. 118.

The Southern Pacific's method of exercising its monopoly was described by Daggett, *Chapters in the History of the Southern Pacific*; also Russell, *op. cit.*, pp. 212–25.

Ambrose Bierce's comment on Sacramento, *The Wasp*, April 9, 1881.

Historian quoted on Southern Pacific freight-rate structure, Lewis, *op. cit.*, p. 365.

Southern Pacific's squeeze on the Shasta gold miners was related *ibid.*, pp. 366–67.

Stewart Holbrook quote from *The Story of the American Railroads*, p. 377.

Description of the battle of Mussel Slough from the San Francisco *Examiner*, May 11–15, 1880; Lewis, *op. cit.*, pp. 385–98; Daggett, *op. cit.*, *passim*; Russell, *op. cit.*, pp. 216–24.

Major McQuiddy's message to U.S. marshal, quoted by Russell, *op. cit.*, p. 218.

Frank Norris' use of the Mussel Slough incident was related by Walker, *Frank Norris: A Biography, passim.*

The train robbery near Pixley was reported in the San Francisco *Examiner*, February 24, 1889.

The backgrounds of Evans and Sontag were sketched by Oscar Lewis, *Bay Window Bohemia*, pp. 146–52.

Petey Bigelow's interview with Evans was published by the San Francisco *Examiner*, October 7, 1892.

The scenario of the play *Evans and Sontag* was supplied by the *Examiner*, September 20, 1893.

11. CALIFORNIA'S OCTOPUS (II)

David D. Colton's background was explored by Lewis, *The Big Four*, pp. 285–91.

Colton's death and its mysterious circumstances was reported in the San Francisco *Examiner*, October 8, 1878.

The comment on the Colton verdict is from Lewis, *op. cit.*, p. 319.

The Southern Pacific's long battle with John L. Davie is related in his memoir, *My Own Story, passim*, and the files of the San Francisco *Examiner*, from December, 1894, to August, 1895.

The railroad's maneuvers against the Funding Bill were recorded by Dagget, *passim*; Swanberg, *Citizen Hearst*, p. 92; O'Connor, *Ambrose Bierce: A Biography*, pp. 227–28.

Bierce's remarks before a Washington press conference, O'Connor, *Bierce*, pp. 229–30.

Bierce's comment on Huntington's testimony, *ibid.*, p. 232.

Huntington's offer of a bribe to Bierce was reported by the *Examiner*, February 22, 1896.

Huntington's charges that he "subsidized" Hearst were recorded by the New York *Herald*, January 9, 1897; the San Francisco *Call*, October 22, 1898; Swanberg, *op. cit.*, pp. 95–96.

Representative Johnson's speech attacking Hearst's morals was included in the *Congressional Record*, 54th Congress, 2d Session, Vol. 29, Part I, pp. 592–93.

Representative Maguire's defense of Hearst, *ibid.*, p. 620.

Charles Edward Russell's praise for Bierce was published in *Hampton's Magazine* (September, 1910).

Bierce's epitaph for Huntington, O'Connor, *Bierce*, p. 227.

The observations of Thomas Storke, Charles Van Devander, the San Francisco *Call* and the Fresno *Republican* on the Southern Pacific's political influence are from Hill, *Dancing Bear*, pp. 32–33.

Southern Pacific's takeover of the 1906 Republican state convention is described, *ibid.*, pp. 38–39.

R. L. Duffus' recollection of the railroad commission hearings is from his *The Tower of Jewels*, pp. 74–75.

12. A BRANDISHING OF PITCHFORKS

Gould's testimony before Pacific Railway Commission, O'Connor, *Gould's Millions*, pp. 108–9, 117.

His trouble with the Knights of Labor, *ibid.*, pp. 193–96.

William A. Peffer's analysis of the Western farmer's problems is from his *The Farmer's Side*, pp. 72–73.

Survey of the land speculation frenzy in the eighties, Hicks, *op. cit.*, pp. 25–28; Shannon, *The Farmer's Last Frontier, passim*.

The Wichita *Eagle* published its exultation over the land rush January 14, 1887; the *Nebraska State Journal* its comments, March 2, 1887.

Regional historian describing drought of 1887, H. W. Foght, *History of the Loup River Region.*

Railroad earnings in 1883 were cited by Hudson, *The Railways and the Republic*, pp. 267, 282.

The revisionist historian quoted the Western railroads as the benefactors of the prairie farmer, Theodore Saloutos, "The Agricultural Problem and Nineteenth Century Industrialism," *Agricultural History* (July, 1948).

Shannon quote on the farmer's marketing problems from his *The Farmer's Last Frontier*, pp. 300–1.

Sidney Dillon's claim the farmers were ungrateful, quoted by Hicks, *op. cit.*, p. 62.

Minnesota railroad commissioner's protest on railroad freight policies, *Annual Report of the Railroad Commissioner of Minnesota*, 1883, p. 17.

Minnesota shippers' tracing of wheat shipment was related by Hicks, *op. cit.*, pp. 77–78.

Charge of "price-fixing plutocracy" was made by the *Farmers' Alliance Bulletin*, February 28, 1891.

William Allen White's recollections of the Populist ferment were included in his *The Autobiography of William Allen White*, pp. 177–78, 184–85, 215.

The Farmers' Alliance attack on railroad passes was published in its bulletin of November 9, 1890.

Backward-looking tendency of the Populists was remarked upon by Hofstadter, *The Age of Reform*, p. 62.

The farmer-editor writing on the railroad and mortgage "crops" was quoted by Hicks, *op. cit.*, pp. 83–84.

William Allen White's sketch of Mary Ellen Lease was included in his *Autobiography*, p. 218.

Lease quotations are from Elizabeth Barr's chapter, "The Populist Uprising," in *A Standard History of Kansas*, edited by William E. Connelley, Vol. II, p. 1115.

White's remarks about Simpson are quoted from his *Autobiography*, pp. 217–18.

His judgment of the quality of the Populist leadership, *ibid.*, p. 219.

The Farmers' Alliance "warning to plutocrats" was published in its bulletin of March 28, 1891.

Hofstadter's analysis of 1892 election results, *The Age of Reform*, p. 98.

Associated Press reporter's comments on racism at the 1896 Populist convention were quoted, *ibid.*, p. 80.

Mary Ellen Lease's recap of the Populists' accomplishments was published by the Kansas City *Star*, March 29, 1931.

13. "ALL MONTANA NEEDS IS RAIN"
Biographical details on Harriman, Hill, and George Gould may be located in Pyle's *The Life of James J. Hill, passim*; Moody, *The Railroad Builders, passim*; O'Connor, *Gould's Millions*, pp. 235–37; George H. Cushing, "Hill and Harriman," *American Magazine* (September, 1909); Kennan, *E. H. Harriman, passim*.

Judge Ben Lindsey's article on judicial corruption in Colorado was titled "The Beast and the Jungle," *Everybody's Magazine* (February, 1910).

The judgment on George Gould was pronounced by Burton J. Hendrick, "The End of the Gould Dynasty," *McClure's Magazine* (March, 1912).

Harriman's maneuvers against the Chicago & Alton were outlined in the Interstate Commerce Commission's 1907 Report No. 943, p. 337.

ICC's criticism of Harriman, *ibid.*, p. 321.

James J. Hill described as shoveling snow with a track gang, quoted by Holbrook, *op. cit.*, p. 179.

ICC Commissioner Prouty on the powerlessness of his agency, quoted by Lyon, *To Hell in a Day Coach*, pp. 127–28.

Hill's takeover of the St. Paul & Pacific was described by Russell, *op. cit.*, pp. 19–30.

Hill as dictator of the Inland Empire, *ibid.*, pp. 30–31.

Frederick Weyerhaeuser's profitable association with Hill was described by Myers, *op. cit.*, pp. 689–91.

Hill's views on the utilization of the northern plains, his *Highways of Progress, passim*.

An eloquent and moving account of Hill's overstocking the Montana plains with homesteaders is contained in Joseph Kinsey Howard's classic of regional history, *Montana, High, Wide and Handsome*, pp. 167–209.

Judge Burke's praise of James J. Hill is quoted by Holbrook, *op. cit.*, pp. 186–87.

Hill's advertising department's methods are explored in Shannon, *op. cit.*, pp. 42–43.

Artist Charles Russell on the influx of settlers, quoted by Howard, *op. cit.*, p. 176.

Howard traced the destinies of several of "Hill's mob" who wrote testimonial letters to the railroad, *ibid.*, pp. 187–88, 192.

Judge Rhoades' plea on behalf of the drought-stricken farmers was carried by the Great Falls *Leader*, August 2, 1919.

362

The exodus from Montana after the drought is described by Howard, *op. cit.*, p. 208.

14. THE COMING OF AMTRAK

The ICC's 1971 report was abstracted by *Time*, February 7, 1972.

A survey of the present condition of American railroads was provided by Harvey Ardman, "The Terrible Condition of America's Freight Railroads," *American Legion Magazine* (December 20, 1971).

Railroad historian quoted on railroad presidents' failure to adjust to federal control during World War I, Lyon, *op. cit.*, p. 142.

Railroads' rise and fall during twenties and thirties from Richberg, *My Hero, passim.*

The Southern Pacific's campaign to eliminate passenger service is related by Lyon, *op. cit.*, pp. 266–67.

Comment on Amtrak's operations by Jesse Ritter, *The Village Voice*, November 11, 1971. Mr. Ritter traveled some of the Western roads to determine what had happened to rail passenger service.

Newspaper survey of Southern Pacific land policies, article in the Los Angeles *Times* by Philip Fradkin, April 18, 1972.

Some aspects of the new American "land rush" are detailed in *Time*, February 28, 1972.

The conservative commentator remarking on the new type of "oligopoly," with the communications industry replacing the railroads as a recipient of governmental and political favor, Kevin Phillips, quoted by the *National Review*, March 3, 1972.

Selected Bibliography

ADAMS, CHARLES FRANCIS, JR., *Railroads: Their Origins and Problems.* New York, 1878.
BANCROFT, HUBERT H., *Chronicles of the Builders.* San Francisco, 1891.
BEAL, MERRILL D., *Intermountain Railroads.* Caldwell, Idaho, 1962.
BELL, W. A., *New Tracks in North America.* London, 1869.
BOYD, DAVID, *Greeley and the Union Colony.* Greeley, Colorado, 1890.
BRADLEY, GLENN D., *Story of the Santa Fe.* Boston, 1920.
BROWN, DEE, *Bury My Heart at Wounded Knee.* New York, 1971.
CLARK, ELMER, *The Small Sects in America.* Nashville, 1937.
CONNELLEY, WILLIAM E., editor, *A Standard History of Kansas.* Chicago, 1918. 5 vols.
DAGGETT, STUART, *Some Chapters on the Southern Pacific.* New York, 1922.
DARRAH, WILLIAM C., *Powell of the Colorado.* Princeton, 1951.
DAVIE, JOHN L., *My Own Story.* Oakland, 1931.
DODGE, GRENVILLE M., *How We Built the Union Pacific.* Washington, 1911.
DUFFUS, R. L., *The Tower of Jewels.* New York, 1960.
FOGEL, ROBERT W., *The Union Pacific Railroad: A Case in Premature Enterprise.* Baltimore, 1960.
FOREMAN, GRANT, *Advancing the Frontier.* Norman, Oklahoma, 1933.
———, *The Five Civilized Tribes.* Norman, Oklahoma, 1934.
———, *Indian Removal.* Norman, Oklahoma, 1932.
GILLETTE, EDWARD, *Locating the Iron Trails.* Boston, 1925.
GLASSCOCK, C. G., *Bandits and the Southern Pacific.* New York, 1929.
GRISWOLD, WESLEY S., *A Work of Giants.* New York, 1962.
HARRIS, FOSTER, *The Look of the Old West.* New York, 1955.
HENRY, ROBERT S., *This Fascinating Railroad Business.* Indianapolis, 1943.
HICKS, JOHN D., *The Populist Revolt.* Minneapolis, 1931.
HILL, GLADWIN, *Dancing Bear.* Cleveland, 1968.

365

IRON WHEELS AND BROKEN MEN

HILL, JAMES J., *Highways of Progress.* New York, 1910.
HOFSTADTER, RICHARD, *The Age of Reform.* New York, 1955.
HOLBROOK, STEWART H., *Dreamers of the American Dream.* New York, 1957.
——, *The Story of the American Railroads.* New York, 1947.
HOWARD, JOSEPH KINSEY, *Montana, High, Wide and Handsome.* New Haven, 1943.
HOWARD, ROBERT WEST, *The Great Iron Trail.* New York, 1962.
——, ed., *This Was the West.* New York, 1957.
HUDSON, JAMES F., *The Railways of the Republic.* New York, 1889.
KENNAN, GEORGE, *E. H. Harriman.* New York, 1922.
LAUT, AGNES C., *The Romance of the Rails.* New York, 1929. 2 vols.
LEWIS, OSCAR, *The Big Four.* New York, 1938.
——, *Bay Window Bohemia.* New York, 1956.
LYON, PETER, *To Hell in a Day Coach.* Philadelphia, 1968.
McADOO, WILLIAM G., *The Crowded Years.* New York, 1931.
MARSHALL, JAMES, *Santa Fe, The Railroad That Built an Empire.* New York, 1945.
MASTERSON, V. V., *The Katy Railroad.* Norman, Oklahoma, 1962.
MOODY, JOHN, *The Railroad Builders.* New Haven, 1920.
MYERS, GUSTAVUS, *History of the Great American Fortunes.* New York, 1907.
NYE, W. S., *Carbine and Lance.* Norman, Oklahoma, 1937.
O'CONNOR, RICHARD, *Bat Masterson.* New York, 1957.
——, *Ambrose Bierce.* Boston, 1967.
——, *Gould's Millions.* New York, 1962.
OVERTON, RICHARD C., *Burlington West.* Cambridge, 1941.
PEABODY, GEORGE FOSTER, *William Jackson Palmer, Pathfinder and Builder.* Saratoga Springs, New York, 1931.
PEFFER, WILLIAM A., *The Farmer's Side.* New York, 1891.
PERKINS, J. R., *Rails and War.* Indianapolis, 1929.
POWELL, JOHN WESLEY, *Report on the Lands of the Arid Region.* Washington, 1878.
PYLE, J. G., *The Life of James J. Hill.* New York, 1936.
QUIETT, GLENN C., *They Built the West.* New York, 1934.
RICHARDSON, ALBERT, *Beyond the Mississippi.* Hartford, 1869.
RICHBERG, DONALD, *My Hero.* New York, 1954.
RIEGEL, ROBERT E., *The Story of the Western Railroads.* New York, 1926.
RISTER, CARL COKE, *Land Hunger.* Norman, Oklahoma, 1942.
ROLVAAG, O. E., *Giants in the Earth; A Saga of the Prairie.* New York, 1928.
RUSSELL, CHARLES EDWARD, *Stories of the Great Railroads.* Chicago, 1912.
SABIN, EDWIN L., *Building the Pacific Railway.* New York, 1919.
SANDOZ, MARI, *The Cattlemen.* New York, 1958.
SARNOFF, PAUL, *Russell Sage: The Money King.* New York, 1965.
SHANNON, FRED A., *The Farmer's Last Frontier.* New York, 1945.
SMALLEY, EUGENE V., *History of the Northern Pacific.* New York, 1883.
SMITH, HENRY C., *The Mennonites.* Berne, Indiana, 1920.
STEGNER, WALLACE, *Beyond the Hundredth Meridian.* Boston, 1954.
SWANBERG, W. A., *Citizen Hearst.* New York, 1961.
TERRELL, JOHN UPTON, *The Man Who Rediscovered America.* New York, 1969.
THORNTON, WILLIS, *The Nine Lives of Citizen Train.* Philadelphia, 1948.
TROTTMAN, NELSON, *History of the Union Pacific.* New York, 1923.
WALKER, FRANKLIN, *Frank Norris: A Biography.* New York, 1932.
WATERS, L. L., *Steel Rails to Santa Fe.* Lawrence, Kansas, 1950.
WEBB, WALTER PRESCOTT, *The Great Plains.* Boston, 1931.
WELLMAN, PAUL I., *The Indian Wars of the West.* New York, 1954.
WHITE, WILLIAM ALLEN, *The Autobiography of William Allen White.* New York, 1946.

Acknowledgments

The author is grateful for the assistance of two old friends, Ben White of Arcadia, California, and Dale L. Walker of El Paso, Texas. Also to Robert Woodward and Sue Wight of the Bangor Public Library, the staff of the Atheneum of Boston, the reference libraries of the Sacramento *Union* and the San Francisco *Examiner*, the Sacramento Public Library for the files of the foothill newspapers, the New York Public Library's manuscript division for William Henry Jackson's diary, the North Oklahoma Junior College for the Casement Letters, the Council Bluffs Public Library for the Dodge Letter Books, the Union Pacific archives at the Union Pacific Railroad Museum in Omaha, the staff of the splendidly complete Western History Department of the Denver Public Library, the Wisconsin State Historical Society for the use of the Joseph P. Dodge Collection, and especially the state historical societies of Kansas, Colorado, California, Nebraska, Oklahoma, and Missouri.

Index

Abilene, Kansas, 125
Absentee landlordism, 29
Adams, Charles Francis, Jr., 67, 90
Advice from an Old Yeovilian, 154
Agnew, Spiro, 350
Agriculture Department, U.S., 116
Ah Ling, 74
Aircraft industry, 349
Alameda (ferry boat), 269
Alaska, 9, 348
Alger, Horatio, 21
American Federation of Labor, 286
American Railroad Association, 342
Ames, Oakes, 57, 60, 63, 89–90, 91, 92
Amtrak, 337, 342
Animas Canyon, 196
Anti-Monopolist, The, 28
Anti-Semitism, 306–7
Argonaut, The, 238
Arkansas River, 197
Army, U.S., 32, 33, 53, 54–55, 57, 62, 134, 167, 171, 177, 178–79, 180, 213, 281
Astor, John Jacob, 19
Astoria, Oregon, 322
Atchison, Kansas, 106–7, 136
Atchison & Pike's Peak Railroad, 107

Atchison *Daily Champion,* 107
Atchison *Globe,* 137
Atchison, Topeka & Santa Fe Railroad, 106–7, 153, 154–59, 173, 189, 193, 197–205, 211, 269, 295, 310, 340
Atheneum Company, 26
Atkins, John D. C., 230
Atlantis: The Antediluvian World (Donnelly), 28

Baker, George F., 317
Bank of California, 253
Bashford, Coles, 23, 43
Bell, William A., 100, 101–2, 196
Belmont, August, 39, 168
Bend, Oregon, 321, 322
Berthoud Pass, 104
Bierce, Ambrose, 69, 235, 239, 240, 243, 259, 271–72, 276
Big Four, 69, 70, 71–72, 74, 76–77, 79, 80, 188, 191, 236, 238, 239, 259, 261, 262, 309. *See also* Crocker, Charles; Hopkins, Mark; Huntington, Collis; Stanford, Leland
Bismarck, North Dakota, 96
Bismarck, Otto von, 152

371

Black Hills, 173, 212
Blaine, James G., 92, 283
Blair, John I., 19–20, 30–31, 40
Blivens, Bill, 297
Bond issues. *See* Stock and bond issues
Boomers, 176–79
Boschke, George W., 321–22
Boswell Company, J. G., 344
Bothmer, D. von, 240
Botta, Paul Emile, 44
Boudinot, Elias C., 174–75
Bowers, Claude, 92
Bozeman Trail, 53, 212
Braden, W. B., 248
Brewer, James, 107
Bridger, Jim, 104
Brooks, James, 91
Browne, Percy, 57–58
Bryan, William Jennings, 307
Bryant, Peter, 118–19, 135
Buffalo hunters, 194–95, 211–12
Burke, Thomas, 325
Burlington Railroad, 96–97, 151, 152, 153,
    295, 317, 318, 320, 346,
Butte, Montana, 111, 112, 325

Caddo Indians, 181
Caesar's Column (Donnelly), 28–29, 300, 302,
    306
California, 112–13, 156–57, 188–89,
    235–58, 259–79, 343, 349
California Central Railroad, 192
Cameron, Robert A., 131
Canadian River, 178, 179
Canyon City, Colorado, 199
Cape Horn, 68
Capitalization of railroads. *See* Stock and
    bond issues
Carrothers, Tom, 263, 266
Cascade Mountains, 321, 325
Casement, Jack and Dan, 47–48, 49, 52,
    55–56, 62, 64, 86
Catherine, Empress, 160
Cattle ranchers, 116, 155, 173, 233
Central Pacific Railroad, 48, 63, 65, 66, 70,
    71–87, 99–100, 188, 192, 236, 237, 239,
    241, 243, 244, 260, 262, 270, 272, 276
Century Magazine, 221
Cherokee Indians, 166, 170, 175, 180
Cherokee Strip, 167, 172, 176, 180
Cheyenne, Wyoming, 58, 62, 63, 100, 104,
    105, 106, 171

Cheyenne Indians, 54, 58–61, 64, 212–15
Chicago, Illinois, 84
Chicago & Alton Railroad, 314
Chicago & Northwestern Railroad, 31
Chicago & Pacific Railroad, 22
Chicago, Burlington & Quincy Railroad.
    See Burlington Railroad
Chicago-Colorado Company, 127
Chicago, Milwaukee & St. Paul Railroad,
    22, 24, 153, 340
Chickasaw Indians, 166
Chikaskia River, 179
Child labor, 73
Chinatown, San Francisco, 237, 238
Chinese emigrant labor, 73–75, 77–79,
    81–82, 237, 238
Chinese Protective Society, 78
Chisholm Trail, 173
Choctaw Indians, 166, 175
Churchill, Winston S., 39
Cimarron, Indian Territory, 173
Cisco, California, 75
Civil War, 11, 33, 38, 44, 83, 94, 166,
    216–17
Clarel (Melville), 10
Cleveland, Grover, 283, 305, 306
Cody, William F. "Buffalo Bill," 101, 177,
    195
Colfax, Schuyler, 78, 92
Colonization, 127–34, 150, 153–54, 158–64,
    165, 175–80
Colorado, 311, 349
Colorado & Southern Railway, 311
Colorado Central Railroad, 148
Colorado Fuel & Iron Company, 208–09
Colorado National Guard, 209
Colorado River, 189, 192
Colorado Scientific Exploring Expedition,
    217
Colorado Springs, Colorado, 206
Colton, David D., 190, 191, 259–61
Colton, Mrs. David D., 261
Colton Letters, 261–62
Columbia River, 321
Comanche Indians, 171, 181
Committee on Public Lands, 219
Congressional Record, 275
Connor, Patrick E., 212
Continental Divide, 63, 196
Contract & Finance Company, 79
Cooke, Jay, 94–96, 109, 189
Cooper, James Fenimore, 150

INDEX

Cooper Institute, New York City, 130
Corning, Erastus, 39
Cosmos Club, 228
Cotton Belt Railroad, 184
Council Bluffs, Iowa, 54, 100
Council Grove, Oklahoma, 178
Covered Wagon, The (film), 141
Coxey's Army, 208, 270, 307
Cozzens House, Omaha, 44
Cranston, Alan, 345
Crédit Foncier, 43, 44, 100
Crédit Mobilier, 43–44, 49, 66, 67, 79, 89–92, 97, 104, 184, 190
Creek Indians, 166, 167, 175, 180
Cripple Creek, Colorado, 207
Crocker, Charles, 69, 70, 71, 72, 73, 74, 75, 77, 79, 81–82, 236–37, 238, 239, 250, 259, 260, 262
Crocker & Company, 79
Croix & Bayfield Railroad, 97
Crook, George, 49, 213
Crow, Walter J., 247, 248, 249, 250, 251
Crush, W. G., 185
Cruze, James, 141
Custer, George Armstrong, 162

Dakota Territory, 46, 173, 213
Dallas Morning News, 185
Dalton brothers, 172, 254
Davie, John L., 263–69
Davis, Jefferson, 194
"Day's Pleasure, A" (Garland), 139
Debs, Eugene V., 305
Democratic Party, 302, 307
Denison, George, 168, 170
Denison, Oklahoma, 170–71, 172
Denver, Colorado, 97, 104, 105–6, 195
Denver & Rio Grande Railroad, 156, 193, 195–205, 311, 313
Denver & Southern Railway, 311
Denver City Tramway, 311
Denver Pacific Railroad, 106, 130, 149
Depot lunch counters, 157
Depression of the 1930's, 340
De Remer, James R., 200–1, 203
Deschutes railroad war, 321–22
Deschutes River, 321
DeVoto, Bernard, 234
Dey, Peter, 45
Diamond City, Montana, 109
Dickens, Augustus, 152

Digger Indians, 81
Dillinger, John, 257
Dillon, John F., 24–25
Dillon, Sidney, 57, 58, 62, 64, 90, 112, 147, 184, 293
Dining cars, 158, 341
Dix, John A., 22, 39, 40
Dixon, Frank H., 30
Dodge, Grenville M., 11, 45–48, 49, 53, 54–55, 56–57, 62, 63–64, 65, 66, 85, 104, 184, 188–89
Dodge, William E., 39
Dodge City, Kansas, 125, 155, 171, 202, 203, 212
Donnelly, Ignatius, 25–29, 297, 300, 302, 304, 305, 306
Donner Pass, 345
Doyle, John J., 246
Dry Framing Congresses, 328
Dubuque & Sioux City Railroad, 30–31
Duden, Gottfried, 151
Duffus, R. L., 278–79
Duluth, Minnesota, 97, 98–99
Durant, Thomas C., 39, 40, 41, 43–45, 47, 56, 57, 63–64, 66, 85, 87, 89–90
Dust bowl, Oklahoma, 165, 178, 234
Dutch Flats, California, 68

East Line & Red River Railroad, 184
Economic Theory of the Location of Railways (Wellington), 145
El Dorado Republican, 295
Ellsworth, Kansas, 125
Emery, Sarah, 300
Emigrants, 125, 140, 144, 150–51, 152–54, 158–64
Emigrants Aid Journal, The, 26
Engineering News, 145
Equitable Life Assurance Company, 315
Ernst, Carl J., 162
Eshelman, John, 278, 279
Eurail system, 342
Evans, Chris, 252–58
Evans, Mrs. Chris, 257
Evans, Eva, 255, 257
Evans and Sontag: or, the Visalia Bandits (melodrama), 257
Evans Pass, 62
Exploration of the Colorado River of the West, The (Powell), 218–19

Farley, Jesse P., 323
Farmers' Alliances, 290, 293, 294, 296, 297, 298, 299, 304
Farmer's Side, The (Peffer), 303
Federal Communications Commission, 349
Fetterman, William J., 55
Field, Eugene, 139
Field, James G., 305
Field, Stephen J., 87
Fisher, Vardis, 140
Five Civilized Tribes, 166–67, 169, 172, 183
Five Nations, 170, 171, 175, 183
Flash Age, 92
Forbes, John Murray, 97
Forbes, R. Bennett, 97
Fort C. F. Smith, 212
Fort D. A. Russell, 62
Fort Gibson, 167, 170
Fort Hays, 101
Fort Laramie, 53, 54, 63
Fort Leavenworth, 167
Fort Phil Kearney, 53, 55, 212
Fort Reno, 178, 179
Fort Ridgley, 33, 34
Fort Sanders, 54, 64
Fort Sill, 167, 181, 182
Fort Steele, 134
Fort Supply, 167
Fort Worth, Texas, 188
Fourier, Charles, 128
Fox Indians, 181
Foy, Eddie, 202
Franco-Prussian War, 95
Freberg, Stan, 337
Free Soil Party, 155
Freight rates, 135, 150, 156, 200, 240–42, 254, 291–95, 320, 323, 340
Frémont, John Charles, 144, 219
Frenzied Finance (Lawson), 325
Fresno Republican, 278
Furness Colony, 154

Galveston, Texas, 172
Gard, George, 256–57
Garfield, James A., 230
Garland, Hamlin, 136–39
Gates, John T., 208
General Land Office, U.S., 222, 223, 327
Geographical and Geological Survey, U.S., 13, 215, 218
Geology of Eastern Portion of the Uniata Mountains, The (Powell), 219

George, A. G. P., 108
George, Henry, 10, 136, 239
German Colonization Company, 127
Giants in the Earth (Rolvaag), 139–40
Gibson, O., 78
Giffen, Inc., 344
Giffen, Russel, 344
Gifford, Robert, 73
Gillat, James M., 277
Gilpin, William, 229
Galsgow, Montana, 329
Goddard, Luther M., 312
Golden Bottle, The (Donnelly), 302
Gold mining, 9, 67, 72–73, 196, 207, 212, 241
Goldsmith, Oliver, 346
Gould, George J., 208, 309, 310–13, 314
Gould, Jay, 13, 25, 144, 146–49, 183–85, 187–88, 191, 192–93, 206, 282–86, 309, 310, 313
Grand Canyon of the Arkansas, 198, 201
Grand Canyon of the Colorado, 217
Grand Island, Nebraska, 52, 119
Grange, 28, 290
Grant, Ulysses S., 44, 64, 83, 91, 169, 171, 205, 216
Great Cryptogram, The (Donnelly), 28
Great Dutch Flat Swindle, The, 72
Great Falls Leader, 333
Great Northern Railroad, 211, 317, 319, 320, 322, 323, 324, 326
Great Plains, 116–41, 145–46
Great White Ruin, (1886), 232–33
Greeley, Colorado, 128, 130, 131, 132, 134
Greeley, Horace, 9–10, 128, 129, 130, 132
Greeley Colony, 128–33
Greeley Tribune, 131, 132, 134
Green River, 64
Greenfield, Massachusetts, 87
Grice, Ola L., 330
Grinnell, Moses E., 39

Hall, Red, 171
Harriman, Edward H., 208, 276, 278, 309, 310–22
Harris, James, 249, 250
Harrison, Benjamin, 305
Harte, Bret, 85–86
Hartke-Adams Bill (1971), 342
Hartt, M. D., 247, 248, 249, 250, 251
Harvey, Fred, 157–58
Harvey Girls, 158

Hastings, Minnesota, 27
Hauser, Samuel T., 109, 111
Havre, Montana, 325, 327, 333
Hawkinson, Matt and Mary, 119-24, 135
Hawkinson, Tom, 123-24
Hayes, Rutherford B., 176, 221, 222, 261
Haymaker, Edward, 249, 250
Hays City, Kansas, 101, 125
Hearst, William Randolph, 243, 273, 274-75
Hedde, Frederick, 152
Helena, Montana, 109-10, 111, 112
Helena *Independent*, 108, 111
Hell on Wheels, 49-50, 61, 63, 81
Hempstead, Long Island, 314
Hepburn Act, 338
Herrin, William F., 227
Hewitt, Abram S., 230
High-Speed Ground Transportation Act (1965), 341
Hill, James J., 293, 309, 316-31, 333, 335, 345
Hills, L. L., 57
Hoar, George, 37, 38
Hofstadter, Richard, 299, 305
Hogg, James S., 184
Holladay, Ben, 39
Holliday, Cyrus Kurtz, 155
Holliday, Doc, 202
Holton, Kansas, 118
Homestead Act, 116, 223, 327
Hopkins, Mark, 69, 70, 72, 79, 236, 259
Horton, Albert, 107
Howard, Joseph Kinsey, 331, 334
Howe, Ed, 137
Hunt, Alexander Cameron, 204
Huntington, Collis P., 69, 70, 71, 72, 76, 79, 80, 81, 188, 189-92, 193, 240, 244, 245, 252 n., 259, 260, 261, 262, 270-75, 282, 317
Huntley, Chet, 335
Hutterian Brethren, 163
Hyde, James Hazen, 315

Indian Bureau, U.S., 32
Indian Department, U.S., 218
Indians, 12, 13, 14, 20, 31-35, 46, 49, 52-55, 56-61, 62, 64, 66, 74, 81, 107, 110, 133-34, 141, 150, 154, 161, 166-67, 169, 170, 172, 173, 175-76, 180-81, 182-83, 211-15, 217-18, 231-32, 281, 347
Indian Territory, 165-86, 348

Ingalls, J. J., 107
Insect plagues, 125-26, 132, 155, 161, 163
Interior Department, U.S., 218
Interstate Commerce Act, 135
Interstate Commerce Commission, 307, 309, 315, 319-20, 338, 339, 342, 349
Iowa, 225
Iron Heel, The (London), 28
Iron Horse, The (film), 141
Irons, Martin, 285
Irrigation systems, 132, 134, 245

Jackson, Minnesota, 32
Jackson, William Henry, 50-51
James gang, 172
Janney, Eli, 243
Jerome, Leonard W., 39
Johnson, Grove L., 269-70, 274-75, 278
Johnson, Hiram, 278
Johnson, Lyndon B., 341, 349
Jones, Horace P., 182
Jones, Mother, 209
Jorgensen, Hans and Elwood, 347
Judah, Theodore, 67-71, 87
Julesburg, Colorado, 61

Kansas, 118, 288, 289, 298, 306
Kansas & Arkansas Valley Railway, 180
Kansas & Neosho Valley Railroad, 168, 169-70
Kansas City *Times*, 173
Kansas Farmer, 303
Kansas Pacific Railroad, 100, 101, 102, 105, 135, 144, 148, 149, 194-95, 196, 211, 283
Kansas Relief Association, 124
Kearney, Denis, 237-39
Kearney, Nebraska, 126
Kelly, Daniel, 249
Kentucky Emigration Society, 127-28
Kickapoo Indians, 107
Kidder, Peabody & Company, 156
King, Clarence, 230
Kiowa Indians, 181
Kittson, Norman, 323
Kleine Gemeinde, 160
Kneutson, Iver, 249, 250
Knights of Labor, 284-85, 286, 290, 298
Knott, James Proctor, 97-99
Knowland, Joseph R., 277-78
Knowland, William F., 278
Kootenai River, 325

Kuhn, Loeb & Company, 313, 314, 317, 318

Labor, immigrant, 8, 48–49, 50–52, 62, 73–75, 77–79, 81–82, 237, 284–86
La Crosse & Milwaukee Railroad, 23
La Follette, Robert, 305
Lake Overholser, 179
Land boom (1880–90), 288–90, 295
Land companies, 18
Land grants, 8, 18, 23, 24, 30, 99, 106, 128, 130, 153, 155, 167, 189, 193, 196, 245, 324, 343
Land speculation, 290
Larrabee, William, 19–20
Lawson, Thomas, 325
Lawton, Oklahoma, 182
Leadville, Colorado, 197, 201, 205
Lease, Mary Ellen, 300–2, 306, 307
Leatherstocking Tales (Cooper), 150–51
Leavenworth, Lawrence & Fort Gibson Railroad, 168
Lebeck, H. W., 330
Lee, Robert E., 83
Legislation favoring railroads, 22, 32, 80, 105, 167, 169, 261, 269–97, 342
Lewis, Meriwether, 117
Lewis, Oscar, 71
Lewis, Sinclair, 136, 347
Lincoln, Abraham, 17, 37, 39–40, 100
Lindsey, Ben B., 311–12
Little Bighorn, Battle of the, 13, 110, 212, 214, 347
Little Crow, Chief, 33–34
"Little Old Sod Shanty, The," 119
Lockwood, E. C., 50
London, Jack, 8, 28, 263, 282
Lone Tree Pass, Wyoming, 47
Long, Stephen H., 115–16, 122
Los Angeles Times, 243
Ludlow tent colony, 208, 209

Maguire, James C., 275
Main-Travelled Roads (Garland), 137–38
Manipulation and mergers, 146–49
Mann, Horace, Jr., 33
Marsh, O. C., 228
Martin, John A., 107
Masterson, William Barclay "Bat," 202–3
McAdoo, William G., 339
McClure's Magazine, 313

McComb, Henry S., 89–90, 91
McGregor, Archibald, 249, 250
McQuiddy, Thomas J., 247–48, 249–50
Medford, Wisconsin, 154
Medicine Bow Mountains, 62
Meeker, Nathan Cook, 128–34, 135
Melville, Herman, 10
Memphis & El Paso Railroad, 143, 144
Mennonites, 159–64
Merritt, Wesley, 134
Michigan Central Railroad, 97
Michigan Southern Railroad, 39
Millenberger, Theodore, 186
Miller, Joaquin, 37–38, 239
Milwaukee & Fond du Lac Railroad, 22
Milwaukee & Green Bay Railroad, 22
Milwaukee & Mississippi Railroad, 21, 22
Milwaukee & Northern Railroad, 22
Milwaukee & St. Paul Railroad, 23
Milwaukee & Watertown Railroad, 22
Minnesota, 24, 25, 32
Minnesota & Milwaukee Railroad, 23
Minnesota & Pacific Railroad, 24
Minnesota River, 34
Mission of the North American People (Gilpin), 229
Mississippi & Missouri Railroad, 39
Missouri, Kansas & Texas Railway (Katy), 168–72, 174, 175, 180, 183–85, 211, 298
Missouri Pacific Railroad, 149, 184, 185, 211, 283, 311, 313
Montague, Samuel S., 65, 71
Montana Territory, 9, 13, 53, 108–11, 325–35
Montana: Homesteads in Three Years (Shaw), 329
Montana, National Park & Utah Railroad, 109
Montreal agreement, 323
Moores, William C., 330
More Free Homesteads: Another Big Land Opening (Shaw), 329
Morgan, J. Pierpont, 168, 309, 316, 318–19
Mormons, 65
Morton, Levi P., 92, 168, 301
Mountain Base Investment Fund, 206
Murdock, Marshall M., 174–75
Murdock, Thomas Benton, 295, 296
Murietta, Joaquin, 252
Muskogee, Oklahoma, 170, 171, 183
Mussel Slough incident, 245–52
My Own Story (Davie), 264, 266

Nader, Ralph, 343
National Academy of Sciences, 221, 228
Nationalization of railroads, 339, 342
National Land Company, 128
National People's Party, 29, 303–5
National Railroad Passenger Corporation, 342
Nebraska State Journal, 289
Nebraska Territory, 118, 119–24, 288, 289, 299, 346
Needles, California, 156
Newbold, J. G., 31
Newlands Reclamation Act (1902), 230
New Mexico, 349
New Mexico Supreme Court, 192
New Ulm, Minnesota, 32, 34
New York Central Railroad, 21
New York *Herald*, 61
New York Stock Exchange, 314
New York *Sun*, 91, 261
New York *Times*, 209
New York *Tribune*, 78–79, 128, 129
New York *World*, 283, 284
Nickerson, Joseph and Thomas, 156
Nininger City, Minnesota, 26–28
Nitroglycerin, 76, 80
Norris, Frank, 252
Northern Pacific Railroad, 95–96, 109, 112, 153, 154, 211, 212, 214, 215, 293, 318–19, 320, 324, 328, 346
Northern Securities Company, 319
North Platte, Nebraska, 55
Nye, W. S., 182

Oakland, California, 242, 262–69
Oakland Waterfront War, 264–69
Octopus, The (Norris), 252
Ogden, Utah, 65, 82, 108
Oglala Sioux Indians, 213
Oklahoma Colony, 176–79
Oklahoma Territory, 165–86, 348
Oklahoma War Chief, 179–80
Older, Fremont, 276
Omaha, Nebraska, 100, 304
Omaha *World-Herald*, 304
Ontonagon & Brule River Railroad, 22
Oregon Short Line, 316
Oregon Trunk Line, 321–22
Orwell, George, 28
Osawakee, Kansas, 103
Oshkosh & Pacific Railroad, 18–19
Overland Express, 235, 243

Overland Monthly, 85, 235–36
Overton, Nebraska, 56
Oyster Bed Act, 263

Pacific Mail Steamship Line, 77, 147
Pacific Railroad Acts (1862 and 1864), 38, 44, 68, 70, 77, 80
Pacific Railroad Commission, 30, 149, 261, 272, 282–83
Pacific Railroad Convention (1859), 68
Palmer, William J., 193–210
Panic of 1857, 27; of 1873, 94, 96, 97, 104, 109, 237, 241; of 1893, 309; of 1907, 313
Pardee, George, 277
Parsons, Levi, 168–70, 171
Parsons, Oklahoma, 171, 172
Passenger service, 340, 341, 342
Patterson, Thomas M., 229, 312
Payne, David L., 173–74, 175–80
Peabody, Governor, 311, 312
Peck, George R., 296–97
Peffer, William A., 287–88, 303
Pennsylvania Fiscal Agency, 43
Pennsylvania Railroad, 188
Pereire, Emile and Isaac, 43
Pioneer experience, 115–41
Piute Indians, 81
Plum Creek, Nebraska, 53, 59, 60
Ponca City, Oklahoma, 179
Poole, A. W., 247, 248, 249
Pope, John, 46
Populist Manifesto, 304
Populist movement, 11–12, 29, 124, 135, 136, 290–91, 298–308, 309, 350
Populist Revolt, 290–91, 307
Portland, Oregon, 321
Prairie fires, 125, 141
Prairie Songs (Garland), 138
Problem of Civilization Solved, The (Lease), 301
Promontory Point, Utah, 82, 83–87
Promotional literature, railroad, 19, 41, 115–18, 124, 125, 151–54, 161, 246, 281, 327, 328–29
Protestantism, 135
Prouty, Charles A., 319
Powder River Expedition, 212
Powderly, Terence V., 285, 286
Powell, John Wesley, 13, 215–34, 326, 328, 334, 345
Pueblo, Colorado, 195, 196, 197, 198, 203, 311
Pullman cars, 157

Quapew Indian reservation, 169
Quiett, Glenn Chesney, 88

Racine, Janesville & Mississippi Railroad, 22
Railroad Act (1886), 180
Railroad wars, 187–210, 310, 321–22
Railway Labor Board, 340
Railway War Board, 338
Rate wars, 156
Raton Pass, 197, 198
Rawlins, John A., 58
Regan, Ronald, 345
Red Cloud, Chief, 55, 212
Red Cross, 334
Red Desert, 64
Red River, 170
Redwood Indian Agency, 33
Report on the Lands of the Arid Region of the United States (Powell), 215, 223, 228–29, 234
Republican Party, 135, 144, 302, 306, 307, 340, 350
Rhoades, W. B., 333
Richardson, Albert, 78–79, 103, 104
Robinson, Albert A., 198, 199
Rockefeller, John D., Jr., 208
Rockefeller, John D., Sr., 168
Rockefeller, William, 317
Rock Falls, Oklahoma, 179, 180
Rock Island Railroad, 39, 173
Rocky Mountain News, 105, 312
Rodgers, George, 153
Rogers, H. H., 317
Rolvaag, O. E., 139–40
Rome, Kansas, 101
Rosalie (ferry boat), 268, 269
Roosevelt, Theodore, 315, 319
Ross, Chief John, 166
Royal Geographical Society, 100
Royal Gorge, 197, 198, 199, 200–1, 205
Ruef, Abe, 277, 278
Russell, Charles Edward, 275–76, 324, 328
Russell, Donald J., 340–41

Sacramento, California, 69, 71
Sacramento Union, 72, 79
Sacred Heart Creek massacre, 33
Sage, Russell, 19–20, 21–30, 32, 33, 39, 147, 183, 184
Sage Foundation, 19

St. Louis & San Francisco (Frisco) Railroad, 172
St. Louis Western Colony, 127
St. Paul & Pacific Railroad, 24, 322–23
St. Paul, Minneapolis & Manitoba Railroad, 323
St. Paul, Minnesota, 322
Salina, Kansas, 102
Salt Lake City, Utah, 61, 64, 65, 108, 206
San Diego, California, 188, 189
San Francisco, California, 72, 77, 235, 236, 237, 241, 322
San Francisco Bulletin, 274, 276, 278
San Francisco Call, 274, 277
San Francisco Chronicle, 260
San Francisco Examiner, 243, 257, 260, 265, 270, 271, 272, 273, 274
San Francisco News-Letter, 85
San Joaquin Valley, California, 245–52, 343–45
San Pedro, California, 242
Santa Barbara News-Press, 277
Santa Fe-Rio Grande war, 198–205
Santa Fe Railroad. See Atchison, Topeka & Santa Fe Railroad
Santa Rosa, California, 261
Schiff, Mortimer, 318
Schmidt, C. B., 158–62
Schurz, Carl, 222, 223, 226, 228
Schwandt, Mary, 33–34
Scott, Thomas A., 39, 188–92
Sears, T. C., 174
Second Cavalry, U.S., 57
Securities, railroad. See Stock and bond issues
Sedalia, Kansas, 172
Seminole Indians, 166, 175, 180
Separatism, 175
Settlers, 8, 14, 18–19, 20, 25, 32, 35, 66, 103, 115–41, 150–51, 153–54, 158–64, 178, 181, 234, 245–46, 281–82, 323, 326–28, 348
Settlers' Rights League, 246, 247, 248, 249
Seven Financial Conspiracies Which Have Enslaved the American People (Emery), 300
Seventh Cavalry, U.S., 173, 212
Shannon, Fred A., 292–93
Shaw, Thomas, 328–29
Shawnee-Potawatomi Indians, 181
Sheppard, George, 153
Sheridan, Wyoming, 206

Sherman, William T., 37, 48–49, 53–55, 56, 64
Sherman, Wyoming, 81
Shoshone Indians, 81
Sierra Nevada, 67, 68, 72, 74, 76, 78, 244
Silver mining, 197, 207–8
Simons, Menno, 159
Simpson, "Sockless Jerry," 291, 303
Sioux City & Pacific Railroad, 30
Sioux Indians, 12, 32–34, 52–55, 56, 213, 214
Sioux War (1862), 20
Sitting Bull, Chief, 211, 214–15
Sleeping Rabbit, Chief, 213–14
Sloan, Samuel, 39
Smalley, Eugene V., 94
Smith, Donald, 323
Smith, Milton H., 17
Smith, Will, 255
Snake Indians, 81
Société Générale de Crédit Mobilier, 43
Sod house frontiersmen, 115–24
Sontag, George, 255
Sontag, John, 252–58
Southern-Central Pacific Railroad, 157
Southern Pacific Railroad, 156, 188, 191, 192, 193, 211, 236, 239, 241–58, 259, 260, 261–79, 306, 310, 311, 315, 317, 340, 341–42, 343–45
Soviet Russia, 8, 164, 207
Spencer County, Indiana, 119
Spirit Lake (Iowa) massacre (1857), 20, 32
Spokane, Portland & Seattle Railroad, 321
Spotted Tail, Chief, 52–53
Standing Rock Indian Agency, 214
Stanford, Leland, 69, 70, 71, 72, 73, 75, 79, 84, 191, 236, 244, 259, 260, 262
Stanford Research Institute, 341
Stanford University, 270
Stanley, Henry M., 50, 61
Star of Empire magazine, 128, 130, 132
Steinbeck, John, 165
Stephens, George, 323
Stevens, John F., 321
Stevens, Thaddeus, 37
Stillman, James, 314, 317
Stock and bond issues, 18, 23, 76, 95, 96, 111, 143–50, 183, 184, 189, 191, 315
Stockwell, A. B., 147
Storke, Thomas, 277
Story of a country Town, The (Howe), 137

Strikes, railroad, 284–86
Strobridge, James H., 74, 76
Strong, Enoch, 123
Strong, William B., 193–210
Subsidies, railroad, 18, 24, 30, 72, 86, 99, 106, 109, 189, 196, 337
Suez Canal, 287
Summit Tunnel, Sierra Nevada, 75, 76
Supreme Court, U.S., 200, 210, 247, 265, 319
Sutro, Adolph, 306
Swanson (Swedish chemist), 76

Tabananica, Chief, 182
Tales of the Fish Patrol (London), 263
Tax exemptions, 24
Taylor, Moses, 39
Taylor Grazing Act (1934), 230
Teapot Dome scandal, 92
Tebo & Neosho Railway, 298
Telegraph, 213, 214
Television industry, 349
Teller, Henry M., 312
Tennessee Valley Authority, 230
Tennyson, Alfred Lord, 96
Tenth Cavalry, U.S., 171
Terry, David Smith, 247
Tertiary History of the Grand Canyon (Powell), 215–16
Texas & Pacific Railroad, 188, 189, 191, 192, 193, 211, 285, 286
Thompson, William, 59–60
Thoreau, Henry, 33
Tilden, Samuel J., 22–23, 24, 39, 40
Tillman, Ben, 302
Timber holdings, 345
Tobin, Pat, 170
Toilers of the Hills (Fisher), 140
Topeka, Kansas, 157, 161, 162
Touzalin, A. E., 158, 159
Town lots speculation, 97, 100–5
Tragic Era, The (Bowers), 92
Train, George Francis, 41–45, 100, 105
Train robberies, 253–57
Train wrecks, 60–61, 64–65, 185–86, 214, 243, 244, 286
Transportation costs, 135
Troy & Schenectady Railroad, 21
Tunney, John, 345
Turner, Frederick Jackson, 10
Twain, Mark, 235

Unassigned lands, 174–78
Union Colony, 130–34
Union Pacific Railroad, 11, 14, 19, 25, 37–66, 76–77, 80, 82, 84–85, 86, 89, 100, 102, 104, 107, 108, 119, 130, 135, 143, 147–48, 149, 151, 153, 154, 184, 206, 211, 212, 213, 276, 283, 293, 295, 310, 311, 314, 315
Union Pacific Railway Company, 38–39
United Mine Workers, 208
Upthegrove, Daniel, 184
Usher, John P., 40
Utah, 225
Utah & Northern Railroad, 109, 110, 111, 112
Utah Central Railroad, 108, 192
Ute Indians, 133–34, 217

Valley of the Moon, The (London), 282
Vanderbilt, Cornelius, 19, 70
Van Devander, Charles, 277
Verne, Jules, 41
Vienna, South Dakota, 346–47
Villard, Henry, 148

Wabash Railroad, 310, 313
Waggoner, Baily, 107
Wallace, George, 12, 290
Ward, Robert D., 117
War Department, U.S., 218
Warren, Gouverneur K., 10, 115
Washburne, Elihu B., 44
Wasp, The, 240
Watie, Stand, 166, 174
Watlington, Charles, 204
Watson, Tom, 302
Weaver, James B., 305
Webb, John Joshua, 202
Webb, Walter Prescott, 116, 145–46
Weed, Thurlow, 39

Weibrec, Robert F., 203
Weller, Lemuel "Calamity," 297
Wellington, Arthur Mellen, 145
Wellington, Kansas, 180
Wells Fargo agents, 254, 255
Western Federation of Miners, 207
Western Pacific Railroad, 313
Westinghouse, George, 243
Westlands Water District, San Joaquin Valley, 343–45
Weyerhaeuser, Frederick, 324
White, William Allen, 295–96, 297–98, 300–1, 303, 306
White River Indian Agency, 133–34
Wichita, Kansas, 176
Wichita *Eagle*, 174, 289
Wichita Indians, 181
Wichita Mountains, 167
Williamson, J. A., 222
Willow Creek, Nebraska, 120–24
Wilson, Henry, 80, 92
Wilson, Woodrow, 339
Wisconsin, 25
Wisconsin Central Railroad, 154
Women's suffrage issue, 307
Workingmen's Party, 237, 239, 240
World War I, 163, 338
World War II, 340
Wounded Knee, Battle of (1890), 12, 213, 281
Wright, Robert, 202
Wyandotte, Kansas, 103
Wyoming Territory, 54, 105

Yellow Bear, Chief, 183
Yeovil Colony, 153–54
Young, Brigham, 61, 65
Young, Robert R., 340
Younger gang, 172
Yung (San Francisco undertaker), 236–37